"I CAN'T FACE HER," HE WHISPERED.

Deborah sat beside him, "I know what a big shock this is for you."

Ryan's housekeeper, Eileen, stood in front of them, hands on her rounded hips. "The best way is to go into the conservatory, meet your daughter and granddaughter, and get it over and done with. I think it's a damned good thing she's come here."

"How can you be so insensitive?" Deborah demanded. "Can't you see how upset he is?"

"Upset? Hasn't he been avoiding his daughter all these years and her nearing forty years of age? Is it any wonder he's upset?"

Ryan lifted his head to glare at her. "Thanks, Eileen. You know how to kick a man where it hurts. It was Anne who avoided me all these years. She was the one who didn't want me."

"She's here now, isn't she? If it was always Anne who didn't want you, not the other way around, then why is she here?"

Sisters
At Heart

by

Susan Bowden

A SIGNET BOOK

SIGNET
Published by the Penguin Group
Penguin Putnam Inc., 375 Hudson Street,
New York, New York 10014, U.S.A.
Penguin Books Ltd, 27 Wrights Lane,
London W8 5TZ, England
Penguin Books Australia Ltd, Ringwood,
Victoria, Australia
Penguin Books Canada Ltd, 10 Alcorn Avenue,
Toronto, Ontario, Canada M4V 3B2
Penguin Books (N.Z.) Ltd, 182–190 Wairau Road,
Auckland 10, New Zealand

Penguin Books Ltd, Registered Offices:
Harmondsworth, Middlesex, England

First published by Signet, an imprint of Dutton Signet,
a member of Penguin Putnam Inc.

First Printing, October, 1997
10 9 8 7 6 5 4 3 2 1

PUBLISHER'S NOTE
This is a work of fiction. Names, characters, places, and incidents either
are the product of the author's imagination or are used fictitiously, and
any resemblance to actual persons, living or dead, events, or locales is
entirely coincidental.

BOOKS ARE AVAILABLE AT QUANTITY DISCOUNTS WHEN USED TO
PROMOTE PRODUCTS OR SERVICES. FOR MORE INFORMATION PLEASE
WRITE TO PREMIUM MARKETING DIVISION, PENGUIN PUTNAM INC.,
375 HUDSON STREET, NEW YORK, NEW YORK 10014.

For my dear friend and fellow author,
Margaret Buffie, with love and gratitude
for her constant support, especially
with this particular book.

For there is no friend like a sister
In calm or stormy weather. . . .

—*Christina Rossetti*

Prologue

1965

The snow began falling around five o'clock in the evening. It fell softly at first, so that no one in the basement family room noticed, but after a while it turned vicious, the wind hurling little pellets of ice against the small windows high in the walls of insulated concrete covered with wood fiberboard.

"Daddy, it's snowing," Anne said, tugging at the hem of her father's suit jacket. He ignored her. She tugged harder. "Daddy! It's snowing. See, on the window."

Now Debbie, her four-year-old sister, took up the chant. "It's snowing, Daddy. It's snowing."

Ryan turned on them both. "Okay, okay," he shouted, his eyes all red and angry. The two little girls shrank from him. He looked so different, dressed in those dark clothes and black shiny shoes. And he'd barely spoken to them for days. Debbie's bottom lip quivered and her eyes filled with tears.

Anne took her hand. "It's okay," she whispered. "Daddy's sad, that's all."

Ryan Barry swallowed the lump that had formed in his throat. He turned and knelt down to gather his daughters close against him, thinking as he did so that these two warm little bodies were all that was left of Janine. She was lying inside the cheapest coffin McBrayne Funeral Directors could provide,

deep in the earth, with the snow falling on the freshly
turned ground above her.

"Daddy, don't squeeze so tight. You're hurting
me," Anne cried, pulling away from him.

He let them go and stood up, turning his face
away from the friends and neighbors gathered in
the room.

The room became so silent you could almost hear
Will O'Brien chugging down his sixth can of Labatt's
Blue. Ryan was suddenly furious. He could have
taken Janine out for a fancy dinner in the ritziest
restaurant in Winnipeg for what this miserable little
gathering had cost him. If only she could come back
to him now he'd grab her and say, "I'm taking you
to the Velvet Glove for dinner, just like I always
said I would."

Someone coughed. Someone else was crying,
probably his Aunty Pat. She always cried. Christen-
ings, funerals, weddings . . . you could always rely
on Aunty Pat to turn on the tears. I wish everyone
would go away, he thought wearily.

"I think it's time we were going," Mary Jaworski
said. "Looks as if that snow's going to settle. I
didn't wear my boots."

Someone else from the other side of the room
spoke. "Yeah, roads could be treacherous, with that
ice."

Immediately, people began to leave, as if they'd
been waiting for someone else to make the first
move. They left so fast, muttering platitudes to Ryan
and the family as they went, that he was reminded of
greyhounds springing from the starting gate at the
dog races he'd been to at Windsor last spring.

In a short while, they'd gone—even Father Haley—

leaving only Ryan's parents, Janine's sister, Beth, and himself and the kids.

"What now?" he asked.

"Now, we clean up this mess." Beth was already gathering up dirty glasses and plates with her strong, stubby-fingered hands. Her eyes were swollen and red, but she sounded as curt as always.

"That's not what I meant," Ryan said. "What's going to happen to me and the kids?"

His mother frowned at him, casting a sideways glance at the two little girls who sat, dressed in their Sunday best, on the convertible sofa where their Aunty Beth had slept last night. "We'll talk about that later," she said.

"If you're good and sit quietly," Beth said to the children, "we'll see what's on TV, okay?" She turned on the nine-inch television Ryan had bought Janine for her birthday. She and the girls used to watch together when she was ironing in the basement.

"There you go," Beth said. "*Bewitched.* Sit down and I'll bring you some cake."

Ryan shuddered as the sound of tinkling music and canned laughter filled the room. He went behind the bar to pour himself another rye and ginger. "Want another beer, Dad?" he asked his father, who was perched on a bar stool, his shoulders hunched against the wall.

"I think he's had enough," his mother said.

"Come on, Mom. Another beer's not going to hurt him."

His mother opened her mouth and then shut it again. A miracle, Ryan thought. But her heavy sigh was eloquent enough. Ignoring it, he poured a Blue into his father's favorite beer mug with the moose-head on it.

Ryan liked standing behind his bar. He'd built it himself, lining the two shelves with his collection of beer cans. He'd collected the Canadian and American ones himself. The cans from other countries had been given to him by friends, souvenirs from their holidays. "Bring me back a beer can," he'd say when they'd headed off to Britain or Germany or Mexico. Fred had brought him a couple of great ones from Hamburg. And last year his parents had brought some from Ireland, when they'd managed to take that trip home to Dublin they'd been planning for years.

"One day," Ryan often used to say to Janine, "I'll be rich and famous and we'll travel all over the world, me and you. I can collect my own cans then."

The desire to get away, to be free had been with him for as long as he could remember. And when he'd met Janine he'd included her in his dreams of seeing the world, but then Janine had got pregnant.

Now it was too late. They'd never go anywhere together.

"The kids are settled now." His mother thrust her face, framed by the tight curls of her newly permed hair, between him and his thoughts. "I think it's time we talked."

But Ryan didn't want to talk anymore. The rye was helping him to feel cut off from the day's events. What he wanted more than anything was to be by himself.

"Come on, Jack," his mother said to his dad, "let's go upstairs."

Before Ryan had time to protest, he found himself hustled up the basement stairs, still holding his half-empty glass. Beth followed them, bearing a tray loaded with glasses and dishes.

"Want some more coffee?" she asked as she took the tray into the kitchen.

"We'll have it later," Ellen Barry said, leading the way into the living room.

Ryan sank into the old blue corduroy chair with the threadbare arms and stared down at the glass in his hand.

Beth stood in the doorway. "Mind if I join you?" She didn't wait for an answer but sat in the basket chair.

Ellen shrugged. "If you want, but I can't see—"

"Janine was my sister," Beth said. "Annie and Debbie are my nieces."

Pursing her mouth, Ellen turned to Ryan. "So . . . what are you planning to do?" she demanded.

She was like a bulldog, thought Ryan, never letting go.

"For the love of God," his father protested, "could you not give the lad time to think? His wife's only been laid in her grave a few hours."

"I know that, but hasn't he had plenty of time while Janine was sick to think things out? He must have made some plans, surely."

Ryan swirled the melting ice in his glass and said nothing.

"He'll have to give up that band of his for one thing, won't he?" his mother said. "He can't go buggering off now and leaving the kids alone."

Ryan lifted his head. "The group's the only thing I'm good at. We're just on the edge of making the big time."

"For the love of Jesus, haven't you been saying that ever since you were a pimply teenager? You're a dreamer, Ryan Barry. You always have been. Sitting in your room for hours at a time, scribbling away, strumming on your guitar . . . Face it, son, you and that folk group of yours are no Peter, Paul and Mary. You're going nowhere."

Heat surged into Ryan's face. "I'll bloody show you, if you'll only give me the chance. We've got bookings in Regina and Halifax this winter. And one in Fargo. Plus chances of a lot more in the spring."

"But it doesn't bring in regular money, does it?" Beth always gave it to you straight, without the niceties. Ryan had never liked Janine's sister much. She wasn't pretty like Janine and she was much tougher. Of course, she'd had to be tough, considering their dad had up and left them all with nothing but that ramshackle garden center when they were still at school. Ryan would never do that to his kids.

"Not regular money, no," he admitted to Beth. "Not yet, anyway. But it won't take long. We're booked to do a record next month. I tell you, there's a lot more chance of me making it big with the group than I'll ever have at some joe-job."

"What about the mortgage payments?"

"What about the kids?" asked his mother.

His father said nothing, but gave Ryan a quick sympathetic glance over his beer mug. Ryan knew that the last thing his dad wanted was to be roped into this discussion about his future.

He hesitated for a moment. "It just so happens I have got a plan, but I'd need your help."

"What is it?" Suspicion made his mother's voice even sharper than usual.

"If you'd take the girls for a short time, I'd make sure we got extra bookings so I could work with the group full time."

"How the heck could I manage the kids plus working at Kmart?"

"You're only there mornings, so I could look after little Deb then, couldn't I?" Jack Barry said, to everyone's surprise.

No one was more surprised than Ryan. Although it was true that his father was free—he'd been on disability pension from the nickel mine up north for two years now—it had never occurred to him that the old man could look after the kids.

"Won't Anne be at school all day?" his father asked.

His wife gave him a blistering look. "And what about school holidays? You haven't given a thought to that, have you?" She turned to Ryan, setting her hands sideways on her broad thighs. "I'm not getting any younger, you know. And your dad's not fit."

Ryan's stomach twisted with guilt, which was exactly what his mother wanted, of course. He was tempted to tell her to stick it, but he swallowed and said, "I know that."

She heaved a deep sigh. "But if your dad's willing to help out we might be able to take little Deb. Mind you, she's getting to be a bit of a handful. She's so darn cute and pretty, just like her mother was, that everyone spoils her."

Mom had done a big share of the spoiling herself. Poor Annie hadn't got much of a look-in after Debbie was born. Ryan suspected that the only reason his mother had accepted Janine into the family was because she was so pretty. Janine was okay, but Mom never failed to tell him he'd married beneath himself when it came to Janine's family. "One kid only," his mother was saying. "There's no way we could manage two."

"I'll look after Anne." They all turned to look at

Beth. Her red-rimmed eyes blinked rapidly. "Annie and me have always got along well."

"Thanks, Beth," Ryan said, "but I can't split the girls. They'll need each other now. Anne's been like a little mother to Debbie ever since Janine got sick."

Beth shrugged. "Suit yourself. I can't manage both, not with the garden center to run."

Ryan felt as if his fragile support system was starting to crumble. "Oh, God," he said, running his hands through his thick dark hair, "what am I going to do? I can't stand the thought of them being split up." He looked from one to the other of them, hoping that they'd help him out, but no one said anything. "But if I can't tour full time I'll never be able to make it big. That's the only way I can give the girls everything Janine and me planned for them."

Still, no one spoke.

He turned again to his mother, who was stuffing peanuts from a Planter's tin into her mouth. "Are you sure you couldn't manage both of them, Mom?"

"There's no way," she mumbled.

Ryan felt as if he'd come up against a wall with no door in it. "I suppose it wouldn't be for long," he muttered. "Once the record's released and I get regular bookings I'll be able to pay a full-time housekeeper and make a decent home for them."

"Right, son. A four-bedroom house in Tuxedo Heights, I suppose." His mother's voice was heavy with sarcasm.

Ryan set his glass down on the coffee table he and Janine had bought at a reject furniture warehouse on Main Street. He stood up, the floor feeling unsteady beneath his feet. "Mom and Dad, Beth . . ." His voice cracked. He drew in a shaky breath and cleared his throat. "Thanks for your support. I don't want to separate the girls, but I know that it won't be for long. I swear I'm going to make this thing work, but I know I can't do it without your help. So . . . thanks."

This was only the second speech he'd made in the entire twenty-five years of his life. The first had been at his wedding. "I have to get some fresh air," he muttered. "We'll make all the plans tomorrow, okay?" Grabbing his plaid jacket from the hall closet, he dashed outside.

The wind had died down, the snow falling gently and steadily now, thick white flakes covering the path down to the sidewalk, coating the fir trees he'd planted four years ago. Ryan lit a cigarette and took a long drag on it. He leaned back against the door, staring at the red tip glowing in the darkness.

Getting away from here was the only way he could provide for the girls. If he stuck around, doing his part-time work driving a delivery truck for the Bay, he'd never be able to make it. The group, his poetry that he drew from his Celtic roots and molded into songs . . . they were the only things he was good at. He knew that his songs were the best part of him. The part that was trapped deep inside him struggling to be free. Besides, he told himself again, if he went away it would only be temporary. He'd come back and make a good home for his daughters once he'd made enough money to provide all the things he and Janine had wanted for them: pretty clothes, piano lessons, a good education. Even university, if that's what they wanted.

"I'll do my best for them, Jan, I promise you," he whispered. "But I have to get away from Winnipeg to do it."

He was so used to arguing with her on the subject that he waited for her response, but this time she was silent, the only sound the scraping of a snow shovel on concrete from the Jaworskis' place. As he strained to hear something that would tell him he was doing the right thing, the whiskey sang in his ears.

"Janine's dead, you idiot," he told himself. He'd never again see her earnest expression, the sweet face framed by her long, dark hair, nor feel the softness of her breasts against his bare chest. He'd never again hear that loud laugh of hers that made everyone smile. They'd fought a lot, but, by God, they'd loved a lot, too. How in hell was he going to manage without her?

Tears welled in his eyes, frosting his face. "God, Jan, why did you have to leave me?"

The inside door opened. He jerked away from the storm door. "You okay, son?" his father asked. "Your mother was worried about you."

"I'm okay. I just needed time to think. Tell them not to worry. I'll be in in a minute."

"That's fine. You take your time, now." Ryan felt his father's hand squeeze his shoulder and then the door closed again.

Apart from going to a hockey game or having a beer together, they'd never been much for talking. It was his mother who'd ruled the roost. He'd always had strong women about him, telling him what to do. First his mother, then Janine. And now there was Beth as well.

He'd been able to take it from Janine. Janine had loved him. They'd been a team. A team with big plans for the future for the kids and themselves. But the thought of having the other women constantly telling him what to do about his life and his kids, criticizing everything he did, gave him knots in his stomach. Was he never to get control of his own life?

Suddenly the thought of getting away from it all—the pressure, the boredom, the day-to-day responsibility for the family—flooded him with excitement. Since he'd married Janine seven years ago, when she got pregnant with Annie, he'd felt trapped. But he hadn't minded that so much when he had Janine to share his life with. Now the thought of being able to tour all over North America—perhaps even Ireland and Europe—without having to worry if the family was okay gave him such a sense of relief that his head whirled with the swirling snowflakes.

He must have drunk more than he thought. He shouldn't be feeling this way. It wasn't right.

Tomorrow he'd be stone-cold sober and he'd have to face reality and the future. Maybe one day he'd even write a song about this. Something with snow and sadness in it. But for now all he wanted to do was lie down on the bed that still smelled faintly of Janine's favorite perfume, and escape from it all.

Soon, he'd be going on the road again. For the first time ever he'd be able to go with a clear conscience, knowing that he was doing it to make sure his two little girls got the best things life could offer.

"I'll make sure they're happy, sweetheart," he told Janine. "You've got my solemn promise on that."

Chapter 1

Anne Dysan hoisted up three flats of mixed zinnias and put them out on the trestle tables. Then she got Bill to help her set up the tables at the side of the shed for the impatiens, so that they could stay in the shade.

Spring had come late this year, with heavy frosts lasting into the middle of May. They hadn't been able to set up their outdoor stands until almost the end of the month. That meant a loss of at least two weeks' sales. Then it had rained for several days. She'd even heard people saying that it wasn't worth putting in flowers now, with June here and the weather still so miserable. At this rate they'd be running at a loss this year, but she wouldn't think about that now.

Thank heavens the sun was shining today and it was much warmer. A sunny June day for her daughter's graduation from university.

"Thanks, Bill," she said. She glanced at her watch, grimacing when she saw the dirt ingrained in her nails. "I'd better get going. It's going to take me forever to get clean for this afternoon."

"What time you leaving home?" Bill asked, grunting as he bent to lift the flats of impatiens onto the table.

"Two o'clock. We have to be there by two-thirty. And I have to help Beth and Sandy get dressed, never mind myself."

"You go. I can finish these." Slowly, he bent down again to get another box from the cart. At this rate he wouldn't be finished until Monday, Anne thought, and then felt guilty. Bill must be nearing eighty now. He'd been working for them since she was younger than Sandy. Now Sandy was graduating from university and he was still with them, much slower, but still willing. And no one could coax plants along like Bill could. "Bill Green-thumb," Aunt Beth called him.

"Go on, now," he said. "And don't forget to bring Sandy here after it's over, like you promised, so's I can see her all dressed up."

"I won't. Oh, by the way, someone brought a bag of old newspapers in for wrapping plants. I'll go and stack them under the counter now before I forget."

Anne carried the heavy plastic bag into the main shed and dragged the newspapers out. She was about to put them under the counter when a small heading in the Entertainment section caught her eye.

EX-WINNIPEG FOLK SINGER BUYS STATELY HOME

Heart pumping, she glanced at the date. The newspaper was almost a year old. She hurriedly tore out the small column and took it out back, where the saplings stood in tubs, to read it.

Ryan Barry, lead singer of Avoca, the famous folk group of the sixties and early seventies, has acquired a country house in England. "I've always wanted to buy myself a stately home," he said in a

recent interview in PEOPLE *magazine. "I'm cele-*
brating the reissue of Avoca's recordings on CD by
fulfilling that dream." Barry, now fifty-seven, was a
folk singer in local bars in Winnipeg before he went
on to fame and fortune in Europe.

"You ready?"

Startled by her aunt's voice, Anne crumpled the
clipping and stuffed it into her jeans' pocket.

Beth was still clad in her rubber apron and boots.
Her face was smeared with dirt. "Time we were
going." She untied the apron as she spoke.

"Okay. Are you sure Bill can manage on his own?"

"Sure, he can," Beth said. "And he's not on his
own. Mary's at the till."

"Maybe we should have closed down today."

"Are you kidding? This is the first dry day we've
had for more than a week."

"You're right. Well, as long as you think Bill
can—"

"Bill can do it. Let's move it." Taking Anne's arm
in a tight grip, Beth marched her back inside the
wooden building, into the little room that was part
potting shed and part washhouse, with wooden
shelves, a large steel sink covered with scratches,
and an old toilet in the corner.

As Beth kicked off her boots and changed into
runners, Anne scrubbed the worst of the dirt from
her hands and wrists. The rest would have to wait
until she got home.

She dried her hands on the piece of old towel
hanging over the edge of the sink and then glanced
at her watch again. "Five past eleven. Sandy will go
crazy. I told her I'd be home before eleven."

"Quit worrying, will you? She told me she and

Maria were going to Jo's place to dress. Then they'll all come back home, so we can see her before she leaves."

Anne stared at her aunt. "She didn't tell me that. She said yesterday that they were going to dress at our place."

"She wants to dress with her friends," Beth said. "Who cares where they do it?"

"I wanted to help her get dressed." Anne was immediately aware that she sounded like a whiny kid.

"Anyway, what're you complaining about? This gives you more time to spend on yourself." Beth pushed past Anne, pulling on the green nylon rain jacket she'd had since time immemorial.

Anne slid her hand into her pocket. The clipping was still there. She should have thrown it away, instead of letting it cast a shadow over this special day. She followed Beth to their old Ford pickup parked on the stretch of gravel at the front of the two sheds. To the left of the parking space were the mounds of crushed rock and topsoil—some of which had washed away in this week's rain, despite the plastic covering.

They stopped at the 7-Eleven for bread and milk and then went directly home. As she drove, Anne said very little. Her mind was preoccupied with the news item about her father.

"What's wrong with you?" Beth demanded.

"Nothing." Anne gave her a rueful grin. "Just wishing Sandy had told me she wouldn't be dressing at home. Sounds stupid, I know, but I'm disappointed."

"It is stupid. Good grief, woman, she's twenty-one years old. She doesn't need her mother to help her dress."

Anne should have known Beth wouldn't understand. Her aunt had never been particularly sensitive to emotions. And she certainly couldn't tell Beth that she suspected Sandy's real reason for not wanting to bring her friends to their house to dress was that she was ashamed of her home.

And who could blame her? Anne thought a few minutes later, when she'd taken the road just past Munroe Lumber and turned into the driveway of their two-bedroom bungalow. It was neat and freshly painted, all right, but once you got inside the house things weren't so good.

At least the front yard was nicely landscaped. Anne made sure of that. "Will you leave that yard alone?" Beth kept saying to her. "It's fine as it is." She didn't understand Anne's frustration at not having more garden space to experiment with.

As she followed Beth into the house, carrying in the bag of milk and bread, Anne was seeing it through the eyes of one of Sandy's friends. The entrance was so cramped people had to line up behind one another to take off their boots in winter. The front living room was very small, the bright needlework cushions Anne had made not quite hiding the shabbiness of the old sofa and chairs. Sandy's bedroom in the basement had just a thin partition between it and the gas furnace.

Anne had to admit that their house was nothing like the houses Sandy's two best friends lived in, with their brick fireplaces and double garages and fancy bedrooms. The girls even had their own VCRs. But then both Jo Bradshaw's parents were lawyers and Maria's father was an orthodontist, and everyone knew how much money they made.

Anne thought of her own father . . . and felt the clipping burning a hole in her pocket. She drew it out and was about to throw it in the garbage can when Beth came back into the kitchen.

"What you got there?"

"Garbage." Anne stuffed it back in her pocket. She put the carton of milk into the fridge and slammed the door.

"What's wrong with you?" Beth asked.

"Don't ask."

"Okay, I won't."

Anne filled the kettle and switched it on. "I'm going to make some coffee before I have a bath. How about you?"

"Sure."

Anne slid her hand into her pocket again. She hesitated for a moment, then pulled out the clipping, smoothing it before she held it out to Beth. "It's about Ryan."

Beth read it aloud, snorting over the "stately home" bit. "Where'd you get this?"

"In one of the old newspapers Marge Simmons gave us. I just happened to see it. I wish to God I hadn't." Bitterness tinged Anne's voice. "Especially today, of all days."

"Forget it. He's not worth worrying your head about."

As she quickly made peanut butter sandwiches for both of them, Anne wished she could tell Beth about the yearning that continually gnawed at her. But now there was something even more pressing than her constant longing to see her father and sister Debbie again.

She sat down at the kitchen table and cut her sandwich into small bite-size pieces. "Here's Sandy getting her Bachelor of Music and we're wondering how we can afford to send her to New York to go on with her studies. And he's fulfilling his dreams by buying a stately home in England." Heat rushed into her face as she thought of the injustice of it all. "It makes my blood boil when I think of how much money he must have and—" She broke off, not wanting to upset Beth.

Beth grunted. "Quit beating up on yourself. He gave up all claim of being your father when I adopted you."

But he *was* her father. No amount of legal documents could take that away. The father who hadn't wanted her. The father who'd chosen her younger sister—the "pretty one"—to take with him to live in England.

"He must have known Sandy was graduating. His father must have told him, surely."

"I doubt that Jack is in touch with him much. If you were expecting to hear from Ryan about Sandy's graduation you're a dreamer, just like he was."

Anne swallowed hard. "I know. But because it was his granddaughter, I sort of hoped . . . I thought he might at least send her a note or a card. I wasn't looking for a gift or money, or anything like that."

"You're his daughter, for Pete's sake, and he's never sent you a note or a nickel. He doesn't even know Sandy, so why should he send her anything?" Beth picked up her packet of Rothmans. She drew out a cigarette and lit it, puffing smoke all over Anne.

Anne quickly finished her last piece of sandwich. She wished she could escape from this cramped house and the smell of smoke that permeated it, and the soil that they could never completely wash from their clothes and skin, and the constant worry over money. Then she remembered how much Beth had done for her. Given her a home when her mother had died, then taken her and Sandy in again, when Scott had been killed fifteen years ago.

She blinked and rubbed the back of her hand across her eyes. Her emotions seemed to be uncomfortably close to the surface today.

"Now don't you go turning on the waterworks or I'll kick you outa here," Beth warned. "Ryan's not worth wasting your tears on."

Anne blew her nose. "Sorry. I was thinking about Scott, not my father. I wish he could be here today. I can just imagine him saying, 'Who'd have thought our little girl would become a classical guitarist.' He would have been so proud, wouldn't he?"

This time Beth was more understanding. "He sure would." Then she spoiled it by adding, "But Scott's not here, is he? I keep telling you, men are like a handful of sand. They keep running out on you."

"Scott didn't exactly run out on me, did he? He got killed."

"Yeah, I always said that motorbike of his would kill him, young fool! Men are good for one thing only. And, if you ask me, even that's no great shakes."

Anne couldn't help smiling. Beth had never tried to hide her contempt of all men.

Beth brought her back to the present. "Quit dreaming, girl," she said, stubbing out her cigarette. "Else your daughter'll arrive with her friends and you'll still be sitting here in your work duds."

Anne drank down her coffee and stood up. "You're right. I'll go have a quick shower, then you'll have plenty of time for yours."

"I thought you were going to have a nice relaxing bubble bath?"

"I'd rather use the time to make sure my hair's okay."

"You mean you'd rather use it to make me look presentable." Beth grinned at her. "But you'll never be able to do that, you know." She ran her hands through her cropped hair, making it stand on end. "I'm a lost cause."

Impulsively, Anne bent down to hug her. "You're never that."

Beth pushed her away. "Aw, quit that nonsense."

"I don't know how I'd have managed without you."

"You'd have managed just fine."

"I only wish you'd had some help."

Beth shoved her chair away from the table. "We're not back to Ryan again, are we?"

"All those years you struggled and he never helped you in any way. He was off buying stately homes—"

"Now, Annie, let's be fair. He sent me checks when he could, in those first four years after Janine died."

"But nothing since then."

"Once I adopted you, he had no more legal obligation to support you." Beth grabbed the newspaper clipping and threw it in the garbage. "Pretend you never saw the damned thing. This is your daughter's special day. Just think about her and what a clever kid she is."

"That's what I have been thinking about. It's kept me awake all night thinking about it. How can I help her go and study with Antonio Marcello at Juilliard, Beth?"

"She's going there, and that's that. We'll manage. There's scholarships and student loans."

"They won't cover all her expenses. Sandy said she'd probably be there at least two, maybe three years."

Beth shrugged. "We'll find a way. Sandy'll have to learn to spend a lot less. You spoil that kid, you know."

"She's the only child I've got."

"But she's not a child any longer. I was caring for my mother and Janine long before her age."

Beth rarely mentioned her sister's name. "I know that, Aunt Beth," Anne said gently. "You've always worked hard. I wish you could retire and get some well-earned rest."

Beth slammed the door of the cupboard under the sink. "Retire? I'd rather die."

Anne gathered up the dishes and put them into the basin of soapy water in the sink. That was the trouble. To Beth the garden center was her life. To Anne it was a millstone round her neck. She'd given up on the idea of selling the center a long time ago, when Beth told her that she wasn't about to sell the place her grandfather had started as a roadside stall when he'd first come out from England.

"You have to admit, Sandy has worked hard giving lessons most of the time she's been at university. God knows how she's managed to do so well with her studies."

"She still spends too much on clothes and disks and all that stuff," Beth grumbled.

Anne sucked in her breath between her teeth, determined not to start a fight over money—or the lack of it—today. If only she could get more landscaping work, but the people who paid well went to the big names in the city. She just got the piddling stuff. "Maybe I should start taking in some extra work at home now that I've done that computer course—"

"For Pete's sake, you work like a horse as it is. You want to kill yourself?"

"No, I just want my daughter to get the chance I—" Too late, Anne realized where she was going.

"The chance you never had, right?"

Anne closed her eyes for a moment, furious at herself. "I never meant that. You did everything you could, and more. If I hadn't married Scott and got pregnant right away I would have finished university. It was my choice to get married, remember?"

"Yeah, yeah." Beth marched to the sink, almost pushing her out of the way to sluice water into the coffee mugs.

Anne stared out the window, watching as two blue jays landed on the bird feeder, scaring the smaller birds away. "Maybe I should call him."

"Who?"

Anne gave her a reluctant smile. "Ryan."

"For Pete's sake, girl! Why would you want to call him?"

"You never know. He might be willing to help." As soon as she'd said it, Anne knew that wasn't the only reason. But how could she tell Beth that not a day passed without her thinking about her father and sister? As she grew older, time seemed to be speeding up at an alarming rate. There were too many things in her life left unresolved.

Her heart pounded at the thought of dialing Ryan's number—her grandfather would be able to give it to her—and hearing his voice at the other end. Then she shivered. Although she couldn't remember much about the last time she'd seen her father, she knew instinctively that it hadn't been a happy occasion.

Beth paused her vigorous floor-sweeping, leaning on the broom. "You haven't spoken to the man in almost thirty years. Why bother now?"

Anne wished she'd never mentioned him. "Let's drop the subject, okay?"

But now Beth was on a roll. "Here we were, thinking he'd sunk into obscurity now that folk music's out of fashion, next thing you know we read he's buying some stately home in England. He must've made more out of his records than we thought."

"You can still buy Avoca's recordings. I saw two of their CDs in HMV last week." Anne didn't mention the fact that she'd bought both of them, but hadn't been able to play them as she was never in the house alone.

"He's probably coining it in and we never knew. Jack Barry kept that quiet from us."

"Maybe he doesn't know, either."

"Well, we know Ryan sends his dad money, or he wouldn't be staying in that nice seniors' block."

Anne leaned her elbows on the countertop and gazed out the window. The blue jays flew off with a raucous screech. Immediately two nuthatches zoomed in on the bird feeder and began pecking at the seed she'd put out that morning.

"Forget about Ryan," Beth said. "He's hurt you enough."

"He can't hurt me anymore," Anne said quietly. "I'm not concerned with him." She turned to face Beth. "It's Sandy I'm thinking about. She's what matters to me. She's so talented, Beth. She could be the new Liona Boyd or Norbert Kraft. Everyone says she's going to go far."

"I know that. She got that scholarship, didn't she?"

"She did. But it's not enough to cover even the first year, never mind two more. Sandy says they told her it would cost more than ten thousand a year. Where on earth can we get that sort of money?"

Beth heaved a sigh as she wiped her hands on the dish towel. "We'll get it from somewhere. God will provide. Now, forget about Ryan and go and get showered and dressed."

Anne summoned up a smile. "Yes, ma'am." She went down the hall to the bathroom.

"Take your time," Beth yelled, but Anne ignored her. She wanted to be ready when Sandy walked in that door.

Forty minutes later she was standing by the living-room window, dressed in the new lemon cotton suit she'd found in a sale at Eaton's, but Sandy hadn't come home. She was about to pick up the phone to call her at Jo's when she heard excited laughter as Sandy and her two friends came up the path. She went to the front door and opened it.

To her surprise, although Jo and Maria were dressed in their dresses and gowns, Sandy was still in jeans and a T-shirt. "What's wrong? Has something happened to your dress?"

"Hi, Mom." Sandy came inside and gave her a hug. "You look gorgeous."

"Thanks. Why aren't you dressed?"

Sandy's cheeks turned pink. "I decided I wanted to dress here," she said. "So, Jo drove me over. Kevin and Peter are going to drive us to the university. Okay?"

Anne nodded, not trusting herself to speak for a moment. Then she swallowed and said, "That's just fine with me. But we'd better get a move on. It's getting late. Oh, damn."

"What?" Sandy demanded.

"Aunt Beth just got out of the shower. I'm not sure there's enough hot water for you."

"I had my shower and did my makeup at Jo's. Stop panicking, Mom. 'Bye," Sandy said to her friends. "See you in about half an hour, okay?"

"You both look lovely," Anne said, realizing she was a little late in saying so. "Sorry, I'm in a bit of a panic today."

"You're not as bad as my mother," Jo said. "She was driving me so crazy I shut her out of my room and locked the door on her. She was *not* happy. 'Bye, Mrs. Dysan, see you later."

Sandy closed the front door. "Okay, we'd better get started." She suddenly turned in the narrow hallway to hug her mother again. "In case I forget later, thanks for everything, Mom. I know life hasn't been easy for you, but . . . you're the best."

Anne pressed her daughter against her heart, savoring the feel of her healthy young body, the fragrance of her freshly washed hair. Sandy rarely allowed her to get this close nowadays. She knew she would remember this moment for the rest of her life. "Thank you, dearest," she whispered. "I couldn't have asked for a more wonderful daughter than you. You deserve the very best."

They hugged even more tightly for a second and then broke apart, looking at each other with the slightly embarrassed expression of those who loved each other, but rarely expressed it so openly.

"I just wish—" Anne began.

"Stop worrying about the money for Juilliard. It will all work out," Sandy said, with all the optimism of youth. "I got all the information about scholarships and loans yesterday. We'll look at it tomorrow. Come on." She started off down the hall. "I've got to get dressed."

As Anne followed her down the basement stairs, she knew that nothing must stand in the way of her daughter's future. They'd all been saving like mad since Sandy started her undergraduate studies, but then they'd been quite certain that she'd go into teaching when she got her degree. They'd never envisaged her having to go to New York for further studies and then embarking on the precarious life of a professional musician.

The question hovered in the back of Anne's mind for the entire ceremony, while she sat listening in the crowded hall to the speeches with their message that these bright young people held the future of the world in their capable hands. Toward the end of the university president's speech about the importance of education in that future, she noticed a shaft of sunlight shining through one of the stained-glass windows high in the wall. It shone directly on her daughter's dark head as she sat near the front with her friends from the music faculty.

She wasn't sure if it was a sign or not, but it was at that very moment that Anne decided to put her pride in her pocket and write to the father she hadn't seen since she was eleven years old.

Chapter 2

As soon as Anne had mailed the letter to Ryan two days after Sandy's graduation, she wished she could get it back. She was tempted to ask the woman at the post office to fish it out of the receiving box for her. She stood beside the mailbox in the counter, thinking of excuses she could give . . . she'd forgotten to include a check or she hadn't put her phone number in the letter. But she realized how foolish that would make her look in front of the line of people waiting to be served. Besides, wasn't it post office policy that once a letter was mailed it couldn't be reclaimed?

Her face burning, she turned away and walked out, wishing she hadn't been so impulsive.

Thank God she hadn't mentioned anything about it to Beth or Sandy. That way, when her father didn't reply no one else would ever know she'd written the damned thing. How *could* she have let herself down this way! She felt as if she'd groveled to him. After almost thirty years of silence, she had to be the one to break it with a begging letter.

All day, while she was digging out plants in the hot, plastic-covered greenhouse or watering the young trees that stood in pots outside on the fast-drying ground, Anne simmered. No doubt Ryan would read her letter, curse—or laugh—and throw it in the garbage.

She looked up from her digging to see a young robin watching her from the top of the fence, waiting for her to go away so that it could hunt for worms in the wet earth.

Anne couldn't help smiling. *Lighten up,* she told herself. If her plea for money worked, it was worth a little groveling. If it didn't, she hadn't lost anything, had she?

Preferring not to think about that, she put the hose away and left the yard to the robin.

She was having dinner with Marco tonight. Not in his restaurant but at his home.

"Don't you want a break from food and cooking on your one night off?" she'd said, when he suggested she come over for a meal.

"I don't like eating in other people's restaurants," he told her. "Besides, with the kids it's too expensive to eat out."

Marco was a single parent with two kids, a hybrid dog, and a restaurant to run. His wife had run, too. Run away with an American, a computer salesman from Minnesota she'd met when she'd visited her sister down there. She told Marco he could keep everything, kids, restaurant, and dog. She was tired of being a slave.

Marco had been appalled. How could any woman, especially an Italian woman, abandon her precious children that way? His family, who'd migrated from Salerno many years ago, told him he was better off without her, and pitched in to help.

Anne had met him the previous summer when he'd come to the garden center looking for geraniums to plant in the window boxes of his restaurant

SISTERS AT HEART   37

on Corydon Avenue. When she'd seen him standing
among the rows of plants, looking lost, she was
struck at first by his dark Latin good looks. Then
he'd spoken to her, his lingering Italian accent con-
juring up sunshine and mandolins.

Although Marco looked great and could cook like
an angel he was useless with plants. When he'd
returned to the garden center to complain that the
geraniums had died, Anne suggested that she'd
better plant them for him this time.

That was how it had all begun exactly one year
ago. And during the ensuing year Marco had asked
her to move in with him at least a dozen times and
she'd said no every time. Marco didn't give up
easily.

"What's wrong with me?" he asked her once. "Do
I smell or something?"

"You smell gorgeous. Tomato sauce mixed with
garlic and cologne. I love it. I just don't want to
move in with you, Marco."

Her friends thought she was crazy. "He's a wonderful father," Carol Schmidt, her closest friend
since childhood, told her. "He looks like a Roman
god. He's got a great body. What's the matter with
you?"

Anne didn't know, that was the trouble. All she
knew was that she didn't want to commit herself entirely to any man, not even a good one like Marco.
Even when they made love, she never surrendered
completely. One little part of her remained aloof,
private, making her feel unloved at a time when she
should be feeling most loved. And that made her
so miserable that she often refused to go to bed with
him, even at those times when she needed him
desperately.

As Marco preferred to work by himself in the kitchen, when Anne arrived that evening she was banished to the living room with the children. Roberto was nine, Floria six. Both were remarkably outgoing, basking in the unconditional love they received from their father and his family. Often Anne wondered how the children felt about their mother. Neither ever mentioned her.

"Dad bought us electronic Battleship. Come and see." Roberto dragged on her hand, leading her downstairs to the basement rec room. For more than half an hour she was caught up in the intricacies of Battleship, which she remembered playing years ago with Sandy in its original old-fashioned version, until Marco called them up to set the table.

Although the rest of the house was quite small and usually fairly untidy, the kitchen was large and well organized. They ate at the rectangular pine table that was set with colored straw mats and bright yellow napkins. In the center stood the wooden salt-and-pepper set that Marco's uncle had carved.

"You're very quiet tonight," Marco said softly to Anne as he handed her a bowl of fusili in a pesto sauce. "You okay?"

She stared down at the food, wondering how she could eat it. "I'll tell you later."

"I beat her at Battleship, that's why she's mad," Roberto shouted.

Anne smiled. "I'm not mad. I just feel like being quiet, that's all."

"I hate being quiet," Roberto said. "Mrs. Denton's always telling me to be quiet."

"Okay, Roberto," Marco said. "Mrs. Denton's right. Enough talking. Eat." He glanced at Anne over his glass of Bardolino.

For once he didn't complain when she didn't eat everything on her plate. Nor did he say anything when she refused a helping of the *tiramisù*.

"Daddy made it specially for you 'cause it's your favorite," Floria said, her mouth turning down at the corners in a look of reproach.

"I'm sorry. I'm not that hungry tonight."

Marco pushed back his chair. "Okay, kids, clear the table and stack the dishwasher. Anne and I are going to have our coffee in the living room and we don't want to be disturbed, okay?"

"Dad!" Floria protested. "You promised we could watch the Cinderella video tonight."

"You can. When you've done the dishes." He poured coffee from the espresso machine into the small black cups and motioned to Anne to go ahead of him into the living room.

"You're so good with them," she said, sinking with a sigh into a chair.

Marco shrugged. "They're the best, but they need to be kept in line." He handed her a cup of coffee and then sat down, stretching out his long legs, staring at his polished loafers. Good shoes were one of Marco's few extravagances. "Okay, what's going on?"

"Nothing. Why do you ask?"

"Ah, Anna. Don't bullshit me." He lifted his chin at her. "Come on. Give."

She stared down at the foam-flecked espresso. "I wrote to my father today," she said.

"Your father? But I thought you didn't even know where he was."

"I didn't, but I found out. I phoned his father and asked him for the correct address."

"Why'd you do that? He's a deadbeat. He abandoned you. You don't need him."

Yes, I do, she felt like saying. *I've always needed him, but he wasn't there. He was thousands of miles away, in England with my sister.*

"Of course I don't need him, but I decided to write and ask him for a loan for Sandy."

"I thought you said he hadn't much money left."

Anne shrugged. "I guess I thought he hadn't. Now I know different. His records are being reissued. He's probably doing well from that. Anyway, today I wrote and asked him for a loan."

"You didn't need to write to him. I told you I'd find a way to help you."

"I don't want your help. Besides, everything you have is tied up in the restaurant. And you have to think of the kids and your parents, as well."

"We'd find a way."

"I told you before, I wouldn't dream of taking money from you. I thought you wanted to get back to Italy to see your grandparents, too."

Marco raised his shoulders in a typically European expression of indifference. "It's Mamma who wants to go. For me, it's not important. I can go back there later. Cheaper to bring them here."

"Don't you want to go back?"

"Not much. I was a kid of Roberto's age when I came over here. Canada's my home now." A flame burned in his dark eyes. "No. You know what I want to do with my money. Expand the restaurant and then maybe start another one downtown to catch all the business trade from the offices there."

"But wouldn't you like to have a holiday in Italy? Or perhaps somewhere else?"

"Vacations are a waste of money. You spend all that money and you've got nothing to show for it except a few pictures."

He'd said this several times before. It was something that Anne couldn't understand, this lack of interest in visiting the country of his birth or traveling elsewhere in the world. "That's something you and I can't agree on."

"It's not the only thing."

"I'd love to travel," Anne said quickly, trying to avoid any sort of confrontation. "I've lived in Winnipeg all my life. The only places outside Canada I've been to are Minneapolis and Grand Forks. Even in Canada I've only been to Toronto for a few days."

"I took you to that horse ranch in Brandon last September, remember?" Marco grinned at her.

She had to laugh. "You did. And we had a great time. That was the first time in my life I'd been on a horse." Her smile faded. "I know it's hard for you to understand. You know exactly where you're going. But me? Sometimes, I feel as if there's so much happening in the world and I've always been on the sidelines, watching."

He came to sit beside her on the sofa and took her in his arms. Here, with her head on his chest and the comforting strength of his arms about her, she felt safe and loved. Why, in heaven's name, wasn't it enough for her?

"I've got something to tell you," he said. "That's why I wanted you to come over." Anne could feel the tension in his body.

She shifted away from him. "What?"

"My wife, she's asked me for a divorce and I've decided to go along with it."

Anne stared at him. "Oh, Marco. I thought you didn't want a divorce."

"Now I do." He took her in his arms again. "Now I want to marry you. Marry me, Anna," he whispered in her ear, "and you'll be so happy you'll never want to go anywhere again. We can build the Rinaldi empire together."

Maybe that was what she was afraid of. She drew away from him, seeking for the right words. "Marco I—I don't know what to say."

The fire in his eyes died away. "I thought that was what you wanted. That was why you wouldn't move in with me. You wanted to be married first."

"No, of course not. I knew you were reluctant to get a divorce. That had nothing to do with it." She hesitated. "I'm just not sure I want to get married again, that's all."

"I thought you loved me." It was the plaintive cry of a man who just didn't understand.

"I do love you. I really do. It's just that—" Impossible to put all those unspoken yearnings into words. Like spirits in a dream they called to her, a world unexplored, shattered loves to be mended, wishes unfulfilled . . .

"Then why won't you marry me? Is it the kids?"

"Of course not," she cried. "They're great. I love your kids."

"And they love you." He ran his hands through the dark springy coils of his hair that insisted on curling however short he had it cut. "I don't understand you at all."

She put her hand on his arm, the dark hairs soft beneath her fingers. "I don't understand myself," she said with a heavy sigh. "I'm so sorry, Marco." When he didn't reply she said, "Do you want us to break up?"

"No." He glared at her. "I'm gonna keep on asking until you say yes."

Breathing fast, she stood up. "I wish you wouldn't."

He jumped up and took her face between his large hands to kiss her. She tried to resist, but it was impossible. He kissed her with such passion, yet such gentleness, that she just had to slide her arms around his neck and open her mouth to his.

"My brother's away," he whispered. "We can use his apartment."

She drew away, reluctant to leave the warmth of his body. "We can't leave the children alone."

"My mother will come over. Oh, shit! She's baby-sitting my sister's kids tonight." For the first time Marco let his anger show. His dark eyes were almost black. "We wouldn't have this trouble if we were married. We could sleep in the same bed together all the time."

"Yes, I know." Anne brushed her fingers down his olive-skinned cheek. "Just give me a little more time to think about it. Please."

"What is it you're waiting for?" he demanded, his voice rising.

"I don't know. That's the trouble."

"Don't tell me you enjoy living in that dump of a house."

"You're talking about my home," Anne said, furious with him. "Besides, Beth couldn't manage without me."

"She'd manage fine. She's a tough old bird. And you'd only be ten minutes' drive away from her, for God's sake."

"You'd want me to give up the garden center and work with you."

"That place is a loser and you know it. Tear it down and sell the land."

Anne gave him a faint smile. "I wish. But Beth won't hear of it."

"You have your life to live. Hers is almost over."

She didn't tell him that she was beginning to feel that way herself, too. She imagined Beth and her ten years from now, still slogging away. Two women, one aging, the other old, life passing them by. Anne shivered. "Beth has done so much for me. I can't let her down."

Marco groaned with exasperation. "*Dio!* You make me crazy."

"I really am sorry. Give me a little more time," Anne asked. "I will give you a proper answer. But you must promise not to ask again until I do. To be honest, my mind's all tied up with the worry over finding enough money for Sandy. I tried the bank, but we've already got the second mortgage on the house to cover the center's losses from the last two years."

"Everything will all work out, you wait and see." He poured her an Amaretto and handed it to her with a little flourish. "*Salute!* Maybe you were right to ask your papa for help. That's what papas are for. Maybe he'll send you a big check, eh?"

Sometimes Marco's eternal optimism could be really infuriating. Her mouth twisting into a wry smile, she held up her glass, as if she were giving a toast. "And maybe pigs will fly."

Chapter 3

Ever since Avoca's first big hit Ryan Barry had wanted to buy himself a special home, something that would say he had really arrived, that he would never again have to live in seedy little houses or basement rooms where the dust from the sidewalk filtered in through the barred windows. But he'd wanted it to be *his* choice, not someone else's.

For years he'd lived in houses other people had chosen for him—mainly his second and third wife and, after them, Angie, who'd been with him for nine years. When Angie left him a couple of years ago for a rising pop star seven years her junior he decided that it was time he ran his own life. It was then that he began a serious search for his dream house.

But everything he saw wasn't quite right. Too austere or too fussy. Too formal or too rural. He wasn't into white-and-gold baroque, although that was what Fiona, his second wife, had liked. No, Ryan wanted a fun house, a place to relax in and have a good laugh. Somewhere to gather his friends around him on weekends.

A year ago he'd found the perfect place in Buckinghamshire, with easy access to London. Hammerton Towers was a Victorian mansion built in

Gothic style, with a grand central hall and spacious grounds. Replete with turrets and spires, stone gargoyles and arched windows it would make a perfect setting for a horror movie. The media had described it as a stately home, but it was more funky than stately and, besides, had only six bedrooms.

Conrad, his business manager, had warned him that it was far too expensive, but Ryan had been careful with his money and made good investments when he was doing well. Although few people would even recognize him on the street now, Avoca's recordings had been reissued on CD and money was coming in steadily from the Celtic recording company he'd put money into in Dublin years ago, at a time when everyone was saying there was no future in Irish music.

So, for once, Ryan ignored Conrad and bought Hammerton Towers, pouring a great deal of money into renovating it, adding a swimming pool and a tennis court.

Now everything was complete, so that no one who stayed there could complain that there was nothing to do. Not a weekend went by that the place wasn't filled with old friends or new acquaintances. Sometimes it seemed more like a small resort hotel than a home. But that was okay with him. As long as people came, that was all he cared about.

It was in his study at Hammerton Towers that he received Anne's letter on a Saturday morning, a week after she'd sent it. Eileen—his general factotum, as he often described her—brought it in with the rest of the mail while he was drinking his early-morning coffee. He was the first one up, it seemed. He usually was. Even when he'd toured with Avoca, playing late at night, he'd been an early riser. It was probably his prairie upbringing. Things had always started earlier in the midwest. Up with the sun and all that . . .

When Eileen came in he was glad of the interruption. Thinking about Canada made him feel jittery and depressed. He leaned back in his swivel chair, hands behind his head. "Morning, love."

"Morning. Post for you." Eileen spoke in a soft Irish brogue that reminded him more of his father than his dead mother. She put the letters down on the desk and then gave him a strange look, like some sort of warning, before she left the room.

When Ryan saw the maple-leaf stamps and the sender's name and address on the envelope he knew why. He felt a jab of excitement, followed immediately by the familiar lurch of guilt. All those *shoulds* and *if onlys* gripped him in the stomach.

He picked up the envelope and gazed at it, longing to open it but at the same time dreading what was inside. The letter was an interloper, forcing itself into his comfortable, secure life, reminding him of the past, with its bitter memories of loss and death.

He leaned his head back against the leather cushion and closed his eyes.

Anne was thirty-nine now, a middle-aged woman. God, that made him feel ancient. Of course he was ancient, wasn't he? He'd be sixty in a couple of years. He preferred to think of Anne as a little girl of four or five, frozen in time in those far-off days, as if she, too, had died. He'd grown used to the feeling that Debbie was his only daughter.

It hadn't always been that way, of course. Annie had been his sweetheart when she was a kid. Janine used to laugh and say she ought to be jealous when he waltzed Annie around the tiny living room of the duplex they'd lived in when she was a baby.

That was before Debbie had been born. Before Janine died.

Before Beth had taken Annie from him.

He'd gone back to Winnipeg a few times after Janine's death, but then his Winnipeg group had split up. Good thing, really. Apart from himself, they weren't that good. He joined an Irish Celtic group based in Dublin and renamed it Avoca. Gradually, as his music became known, they'd taken off. They were a hit in Ireland first and then in Britain, with two records on the pop charts in 1968. Despite the advent of the Beatles, there were still enough people interested in folk for them to continue with their success. By that time he'd married Fiona Sutton and London had become his base.

Fiona was a wealthy stockbroker's daughter who delighted in shocking her parents by slumming it with musicians. Something in addition to sex had attracted them to each other. Perhaps the fact that neither of them was part of the usual music scene. He came from midwest Canada, she from genteel Surrey.

Fiona had given him a little refinement and a lot of grief. But that came after he'd decided to make a home for his daughters.

He'd returned to Winnipeg after a triumphant year touring in Europe and the States to find that no one there seemed to care much about his success.

"When are you going to get yourself a real job?" his mother had demanded only a few minutes after he'd arrived.

No amount of explanation or bragging impressed her. The only thing that did get through to her was the check for $10,000 he gave her and his dad. Poor Dad. He seemed in awe of his son's sudden fame, the soft leather jacket and Italian shoes. Ryan's success had widened the gap between them.

He'd asked first Debbie and then Anne to come and live with him and Fiona in England. Within minutes of his asking, eight year-old Debbie started listing what she was going to take with her. Ryan was surprised at how easy it was. The only one who seemed sad about Debbie leaving was his father, and even he didn't say much.

But when he drove to the other side of the city to see Annie, she clung to her aunt, her brown eyes round and scared, looking at him with suspicion, as if he were a total stranger, instead of the daddy she'd once adored.

However much he'd tried to forget it, the scene was imprinted in his memory. He accused Beth of turning Annie against him. Beth telling him how just sending checks didn't make a father.

"Let's leave it to Anne to decide," he'd said, smiling at his daughter, trying to shut Beth out.

Anne hadn't returned the smile.

"I'd like you to come and live with me in England," he'd told her. "You'd have a new mommy and lots of toys ... and pets, if you want them. Wouldn't you like a pony of your own to ride?"

Her face very pale, Anne had stood there not saying a word.

"Answer your dad," her aunt said.

Anne grasped the edge of her aunt's sweater, as if she were a kid of two, not eleven. "I want to stay here with you," she whispered, turning her face from Ryan.

"Your sister Debbie's coming with me," he told

her. "You don't want your little sister getting everything and you staying here with nothing, do you?"

Beth had given him a dirty look at that, but she bit
her lips together and said nothing to influence Anne.

"How about it?" Ryan coaxed. "Your own room.
A puppy? Wouldn't you like your own puppy."

"I don't like dogs," the white-faced child said. "I
like cats."

"Then you can have a kitten. A cute little kitten,
all white and fluffy."

She'd started to cry, tears creeping down her
cheeks. As he thought of it now, sitting at his large
desk, Ryan leaned his hands on clenched fists, expe-
riencing again the desperation he'd felt then.

"I don't want to live with you," Anne had said. "I
want to live with my Aunty Beth."

He knew then that he'd lost her, that his promise
to Janine to look after both their children had been
broken. It was that thought, more than anything else,
that had brought the surge of anger he'd regretted
ever since.

"Then go to hell, live with your bloody Aunty
Beth!" he'd shouted as he walked right out of that
miserable little bungalow. "Who needs you?" he'd
added as he crashed the door to behind him. "It's
your loss, not mine."

He'd never seen Anne again. All the arrangements,
the papers for the adoption had been looked after by
his lawyer. He'd taken Debbie to England and never
returned to Winnipeg, not even for his mother's
funeral. He'd used the fact that he was on tour in Italy
as an excuse that time, but the truth was he couldn't
face seeing Anne again. Just the thought of her evoked
such strong feelings of loss and sadness—and guilt—
that it was better to forget about her.

His fingers curled around the letter. Anne had never written to him before. What had happened to make her seek him out? Perhaps she was sick . . . or wanting to visit him. How could he meet her after all these years? They'd be like total strangers. Worse than strangers.

He swallowed hard, trying to relax the tightness in his throat. Better not to think about it now. He'd put the letter away, read it later, when he felt more able to deal with it, whatever it was. He'd wait until Deborah came down and open it then.

Chapter 4

Ryan strolled through the small Gothic conservatory filled with palms and exotic flowering plants. His favorite red hibiscus had seven blossoms on it this morning. Glorious! He went out onto the flagstoned terrace. This was his morning ritual. Even on the mornings when he was driving up to London, he never missed it. It gave him intense pleasure to gaze out over the garden and smooth green lawn, contrasting the view with memories of homes he'd lived in before he'd become successful. He wished his mother could have seen this place, just so he could show her what he'd done with his life. But she'd died years ago, long before he'd bought this house. He'd asked his father to come over for a visit, but he'd evaded the invitation by saying he wasn't well enough to travel.

Today, however, his pleasure in his home and garden was overshadowed by Anne's letter. He wished Debbie would come down so that he could tell her about it. He glanced at his wrist for the time, then remembered that he had left his watch in the bedroom. Whenever possible, he like to avoid wearing a watch during weekends.

Deborah had driven from London with Graham Neville the previous evening. Ryan hoped that she'd stay in this relationship. As far as he was concerned, Graham was a keeper. He came from an upper-crust family, but that didn't stop him from being a highly successful businessman with pots of money.

Just what Debbie needed. She had expensive tastes.

The iron door of the conservatory creaked open and Deborah came out onto the terrace. "Morning, Daddy." Her blond hair was pulled back from her face by a black ribbon, and she was dressed in a cropped top and brief shorts that showed off her long golden legs. "I thought I'd find you out here, surveying the estate."

"Morning, love. Where's Graham?"

"He went home at the crack of dawn." She flung herself down in a deck chair. "I swear that bloody house of his is becoming an obsession. I wish you'd never suggested he buy it."

"He was looking for a house near London. Somerford Hall was going for a song, so—"

"No wonder. The place is falling down."

"So would you be if you were four hundred years old and hadn't been looked after properly. I thought it was a match made in heaven."

"What was?" Deborah demanded, her blue eyes icing over.

He grinned down at her. "It's okay, darlin'. I wasn't talking about you. I meant Graham and Somerford. I don't like to see a lovely old place like that going to rack and ruin. Graham's got enough money to fix it up and enough taste to do it right."

Deborah released a long sigh. "All I know is that he's going to drive me crazy. 'What colors do you think I should put in this room, Deborah? Oh, my God, look at this paneling! Isn't it marvelous?' "

She imitated Graham's enthusiasm for his new house so well that Ryan had to laugh. "It sounds as if you're jealous of Somerford."

Deborah smiled ruefully. "I am a bit. It seems to be taking up all his spare time. I'm afraid I just can't get all excited about an old ruin with a wilderness of a garden."

"I thought you'd get a kick out of having a beautiful old house to play with."

"It isn't my house."

"It could be, if you played your cards right. After all, Graham is available."

"Stop matchmaking. What's the matter? Feeling the need to be a grandfather in your old age?"

Ryan sat down on the wooden bench formed from gnarled wood and stared moodily out across the lawn.

"What's wrong?"

"I had a letter from your sister this morning."

Deborah stared at him. "From Anne?"

"She's the only sister you've got," Ryan said caustically.

"Why was she writing to you?"

"I don't know yet. I haven't opened the letter."

Deborah gazed at him and then looked away, suddenly agitated. Why should a letter from her sister affect her this way when she didn't even know her?

"Weird, isn't it?" she said, trying to sound casual. "That part of my life is a total blank."

Ryan fiddled with the tassel on his chestnut-brown loafers. He was always restless, could never keep still. "I thought you might remember Anne. You used to meet when you were still in Winnipeg with my parents, didn't you?" His words came slowly as if it pained him to say them. Deborah couldn't recall the last time they'd spoken about Anne—or Canada.

"I suppose so, but I don't remember her at all." That wasn't quite true. There were occasional images in her mind, flashes of remembrance—the warmth of an arm around her, a face pressed against hers—but they were so fleeting she wasn't even sure if the face she saw was her sister's.

She held out one hand to examine her nails. She'd had them done yesterday. She liked the shorter style with the russet polish. It looked classy. "Everyone will be down for breakfast soon. Why don't you read the letter while it's still quiet?"

"I don't want to read it."

He sounded so like a little boy that Deborah had to smile. "I know you don't. Of course, you could throw it away. Pretend you never received it."

For a moment Ryan seemed tempted, then he sighed. "No. Eileen knows. She brought it in this morning. I guess I'd better get it." He went back into the house.

The sun had gone behind a cloud. Deborah shivered. The letter seemed to have cast a blight on the day for both of them. Her father rarely spoke of his early life in Canada. When she was sixteen, she'd had to drag the story of her mother's death from him. When he'd finished telling her, looking as if he felt physically sick, he begged her not to ask him about Janine again, that he couldn't bear talking about her.

That day, Deborah had put her own feelings about her mother away, mentally wrapping them up and sealing them like a parcel never again to be opened.

Now, out of the blue, this letter from Anne,

resurrecting all those uncomfortable feelings for both her and her father.

"Just my luck," she murmured to herself. She'd wanted to get Ryan in a good mood this weekend, so she could ask him for more financial help with expanding her new company Travel Exotica. Her other travel business was doing very well, but she was sure there was a market there for an even more upscale company. She smiled as she thought of her new ad campaign in the society glossies: *The travel company for those who don't have to ask the cost.* But expansion meant she needed more money.

Her smile faded. This letter, whatever it was about, could put Ryan in one of his strange, distant moods for days.

He came back, the letter in his hand. "Read it." He held it out to Deborah.

She shook her head. "It's addressed to you. Perhaps it's a wedding invitation. Isn't her daughter in her twenties now?"

His boyish face lit up. "That could be it."

But it wasn't. There were two pages. Ryan read them, his face growing tighter as he read. It was hard to tell whether he was angry or just upset. "Money," he said succinctly, when he'd finished reading the letter. He thrust the pages at Deborah and walked away from her, down the steps, without saying a word.

"Daddy?" she called after him, but he didn't reply. She read the letter.

Dear Ryan,
It has been almost twenty-eight years since I last saw you. I shall be forty in September. During those years I have never asked you for anything, even

*when my husband was killed. With Aunt Beth's help
we pulled through okay. But I can't pretend it has
been easy.*

*Now, for the first time in my life, I am asking you
for help.*

Here it comes, Deborah thought. She glanced up
to see Ryan standing by the pool, staring into the
water. She'd always thought her father looked
amazingly young for his fifty-eight years, still lean,
with his thick dark hair only lightly flecked with
gray. But now, all at once, the dejected hunch of his
shoulders made him appear much older.

She went on reading Anne's letter, eager to finish it.

*As I said, I've never asked before, and I wouldn't
be doing it now if it weren't for my daughter.*

*Sandy is a bright, lovely girl. She just graduated
from university with her Bachelor of Music. She is
an extremely talented classical guitarist. She has
been offered a place at Juilliard to study with
Antonio Marcello. That means she must live away
from home, in New York. Of course, she can apply
for student loans and she expects to get some sort of
scholarship, but even then it is going to be very difficult for her—and for us—to manage financially.
We have been told that it could cost more than
twelve thousand dollars a year. Just recently I read
that you bought a stately home in England last
year, so I gather things are going well for you.*

*So I'm asking for your help. I want it to be a
business arrangement, please. Something I could
repay over several years. Beth and I are partners in
the old Carter family garden center. We don't make
much out of it, but we manage okay. I don't need
money for myself, just for Sandy.*

If you are willing, I should like to discuss this with you further. My phone number's at the top.

The letter was signed *Yours sincerely, Anne Dysan.* Deborah was struck by the cold formality of it. Although she and Ryan had their ups and downs, she found it hard to imagine what it must feel like to have to write such a letter to one's own father.

Stuffing it into the pocket of her shorts, she walked slowly down the steps to her father. When she reached him, she saw that his cheeks were damp. Although he must know she was there he didn't turn around, but stood staring into the pool at the exotic fish swimming just below the surface of the water.

Deborah put her arm through his. "Daddy?" she said tentatively.

Ryan drew away from her. "We didn't have to worry. It was just about money. I should have known."

"Yes." She felt a tangle of emotions: fear—and anger that this letter could cause her father such obvious distress. It was so unlike him. Why couldn't Anne have left things as they were?

She stood, her arms hanging by her sides, waiting for him to say something, but he kept his head turned from her. She felt as if the space between them was a mile wide.

"Why don't we go and sit down?" Deborah tried to guide him back to the terrace, but he resisted her.

"I'm fine," he muttered. "It was just a shock hearing from her after such a long time. I thought—" He waved a hand in the air, unable to put his thoughts into words.

"Let's go into the summer house. No one will see us there."

At first he resisted her, but then he allowed her to lead him through the copse of hazel trees to the secluded summer house. It had once been a simple structure made of birch logs, but was now glassed in and outfitted with a bar and Asian furnishings, including a large Oriental couch with brightly colored cushions that looked as if it might have come from a harem.

She made him sit down and poured him a drink. Although he rarely drank nowadays, Deborah decided that this was the time for his old favorite, rye and ginger.

Ryan took the glass from her without a word.

She went to the sink, tore off a couple of sheets of paper towel, and handed them to him. He looked at them as if he didn't know what they were for. Then he mopped his face and blew his nose.

"Better?" she asked, sitting beside him. Ryan nodded. "I hate to see you so upset. She had no right to send you such a letter."

He took a gulp of the drink. "She had every right. She's my daughter, isn't she?"

"Of course she is, but—"

He looked at her as if he wasn't really seeing her. "I feel like a shit."

"Why? Just because the daughter you gave up for adoption years ago writes to you for money doesn't make you a shit. You thought she was doing fine, didn't you?"

"I knew she couldn't be, but I didn't want to think about it. I knew what that ratty garden center was like when I was there, didn't I?"

"But it could have changed by now. After all, we're talking about almost thirty years since you were last there."

"I knew it wasn't doing well," he muttered.

"How? This is the first time Anne's written to us."

Ryan's cheeks reddened. "Dad wrote and told me. I thought to myself, she didn't want me when I came back for her, so let *her* write if she wants anything. My father wrote to me just after her husband was killed." He took another drink from his glass. "I never even contacted her then. I just sent a wreath from us both. It cost me a hundred quid. Sent a bloody wreath, that's all I did." He crashed the glass down on the marble-topped table.

"Come on, Dad, snap out of this," Deborah said. "Get that drink down and go wash your face. If anyone saw you now they'd wonder what on earth happened to you."

But nothing could get his mind off the letter. "What am I going to do about Anne?"

Deborah hesitated. "I suppose you're going to have to send her some money to help her daughter. That way you won't feel guilty anymore."

He gave her a ghost of a smile. "If only it was that easy."

"You could set up some sort of trust for her daughter, couldn't you?"

"No, if I do this I want her to have it all right away, not in installments." He gazed down at the glass in his hand, as if mesmerized by the golden liquid. "I promised Janine I'd look after both of you properly. I broke my promise."

Deborah didn't like where this was going. "Not really. You told me Anne preferred to stay with Beth. That wasn't your fault, was it? It was her choice."

"She was only eleven." His left hand clenched and unclenched in a way that scared Deborah. She had never seen him like this before. "I thought she might be asking if she could come for a visit," he whispered, obviously thinking about the letter again.

"Well, she wasn't. It was just about money."

"Does that disappoint you, Deb? Would you have liked to see your sister again?"

His question took her by surprise. Years ago, when she still thought of her mother at night, she might have said yes, but since that time when she'd hidden all that part of her life away, along with all the miserable memories of her life with her stepmother, she preferred to live each day as it came. "It's been too long," she said crisply. "We'd be like strangers."

"Worse," Ryan said. They exchanged smiles, understanding each other perfectly. "But since it's money she's after, not our company, we don't have to worry about all that, do we?"

"You can just set up some sort of low-interest loan through your lawyer and that will be it."

"Seems a bit cold, doesn't it?"

"Not at all. I think it's very generous of you. After all, she has no claim on you, does she? Your sister-in-law adopted her."

"No legal claim, no."

"I'm sure she'll be very happy if you send her a nice letter saying you'll be happy to arrange a long-term loan for her daughter's education."

"Not a loan. A gift. An outright gift."

"Are you sure, Daddy? We're talking quite a lot of money here. You've only recently finished spending a huge amount rewiring and modernizing this monstrosity." She waved a hand in the direction of the house, not even trying to hide her dislike of Hammerton Towers and what it had cost him. Now, it appeared, there was about to be another drain on his money.

He gave her one of his sharp, penetrating looks. "I like this place. It suits me fine. And I'd like to remind you, Lady Deborah, that it was my hard work that earned the money that paid for it *and* for your business, so if you don't like it you can lump it." He stood up, swaying a little as if he'd had several drinks rather than just the one rye. "I'm going to send her one check for the entire amount she needs for her daughter."

"You don't even know how much she wants. She forgot to mention that." Deborah couldn't keep the sharpness from her voice.

"Oh, that's easy to find out. I'll speak to Conrad after breakfast and get him to arrange it. One fat check and there'll be no need for any further communication between us."

Deborah frowned. "Is it wise to send it all at once? After all, they don't sound that well off. Maybe it would be better—"

"I'll do it my way. One payment. Get it all over and done with."

"I suppose you're right. I just wondered if someone who's that hard up—"

"You make her sound like some sort of hillbilly. I'd like to remind you that you came from the same background."

"I'd rather not think about that, if you don't mind," Deborah said in her best private-school accent.

Now Ryan was angry. "How do you know what she's like? Don't forget your sister went to university, which is more than you did."

"Didn't your father tell you she got pregnant and

had to give it up after one year? Besides, she was only taking horticulture." Deborah made it sound like a degree in manure spreading.

"However long she was there, I'm sure Annie would be a good manager with money," he said, giving her a cold look. "She was always the sensible one."

His words were like a slap across the face.

As he ran down the steps of the summer house and crossed the lawn, Deborah felt, for the first time in many years, totally shut out of his life.

Chapter 5

Three weeks had passed since Sandy's graduation, but she was still giving private lessons to a few of the guitar students she'd been teaching at university. She had also been engaged by the Music Conservatory for both private lessons and a few master classes.

Today was a Friday and the whole afternoon stretched ahead of her, blissfully free of work, other than her own two hours of practicing.

To her relief, when she came home she found the house empty. She could put her CD of the Rodrigo Spanish Dances on full blast without being yelled at.

She set her guitar case on the hall floor, put on the CD, and went into the kitchen to get herself a drink. It was more than eighty degrees outside, the sun blazing down in a brilliant blue sky. The house was like an oven. Last night it had been so hot that her mother and Aunt Beth had had to sleep down in the basement with her.

She'd vowed long ago that when she did her first paying concert she would spend her fee on putting air-conditioning into this crummy place. She had done several concerts this past year, but the money had gone straight into the bank for New York.

Sandy knew that she should have been far more

concerned about saving money in the past, but what was the point? Throughout her life her mother had worried so much about everything, especially money, that Sandy had always felt she could leave the worrying to her.

But since February, when she and Brian Dudeck had broken up, everything had changed. It was as if a layer of protective skin had been peeled away. Nothing in life was certain anymore. Love didn't last forever. Money didn't come from nowhere.

As soon as she'd heard she was going to New York she began to save nearly everything she earned. No more new clothes. At least, not now. She'd definitely need some new things for Juilliard. She didn't want to arrive in the Big Apple looking like a prairie hick. But, apart from that, she was going to save like mad. Fortunately, she had only one more concert and it was summertime, so she could get away with her flowery cotton. She couldn't have worn that old green velvet skirt one more time.

She gulped down a Diet Coke, savoring the cold sweetness as it ran down her throat. It was so hot her clothes were sticking to her.

There was a note from her mother attached to the fridge by a magnet shaped like a Venetian gondola. Her mother's friend, Carol, had brought it back from Venice for her. The note read: *Salad in the fridge. Be sure to phone me at work as soon as you come in. Great news!*

Sandy smiled to herself and rolled her eyes. "Yeah, yeah. Later," she said aloud. For now, she just wanted to enjoy being in the house on her own.

When she'd finished the salad she went downstairs to her room to change into a fresh T-shirt, and then sat at her desk, poring over the information Juilliard had sent her.

It was time for her to take over her own life. As far as she was concerned, being accepted by Juilliard was the best thing ever to have happened to her. Just thinking about it made her feel like leaping all over the place. On the other hand, her mother—although she was bursting with pride and excitement—was worried sick about the cost.

The back door slammed shut. "Sandy?" her mother's voice called down. "Are you home?"

Stupid question, considering Sandy's rusty old Rabbit was parked out back. Sighing, Sandy shoved the papers away in her desk drawer. Perversely, she didn't answer her mother.

Footsteps down the stairs. A knock on her door. Her mother always knocked. Sandy had no idea why, considering she couldn't very well tell her to get lost, could she? Even if she often felt like doing so. Sometimes, she preferred Aunt Beth's way. She just barged in without any warning. At least that way Sandy could complain about it.

"Come on in, Mom," she called out when her mother knocked again.

Her mother came in. "I could hear the stereo all the way down the back lane." The music was pounding away above them.

"Sorry about that. It's the new thing I'm learning. This is the last bit. Want me to go up and turn it off?"

"No, that's fine." Her mother closed the door behind her and then leaned against it, smiling. Not just smiling, but obviously bursting with her news.

Sandy had to smile, too, seeing her so happy. Mom hadn't had much to be happy about in her life.

Yet she had never been a miserable person. She'd always managed to find contentment in small things: her garden, and playing Mozart on their old upright piano, and Sandy's successes. "What's this big news? Sorry I didn't call you. I was going to once I'd had lunch."

In response, her mother held out the letter she'd been holding behind her back. Sandy took it and drew the typed page from the envelope. A bank draft fluttered to the floor. She bent to pick it up. The draft was made out to Anne Dysan and was for $15,000.

Sandy's eyes widened. "Wow! Fifteen thousand bucks!"

She glanced at the signature at the end of the letter. "Who's this Conrad Hatcher?"

"Read the letter."

The letter heading was *Barry Enterprises*. Sandy scanned the eight or so typed lines.

> *I have been instructed by your father, Ryan Barry, to send you this bank order. It is to be used for your daughter's further education. Mr. Barry asks that no acknowledgment be made of this one-time gift and that there be no further correspondence between you and himself.*

The letter was signed *Conrad Hatcher, Personal Manager to Ryan Barry and CEO Barry Enterprises.*

Sandy looked up from the letter. Her mother's smile faded when she saw her expression. "That's the coldest letter I've ever read," Sandy said. "I feel like tearing the check up and flushing it down the toilet."

Anne darted forward. "Don't you dare." She grabbed the letter and bank draft from Sandy. "It may be a cold letter, but the check's good."

"How can you possibly use it? Haven't you any pride?"

Two spots of color flared on her mother's tanned cheeks. "Not when it comes to you, Sandy. That money is going to come in very useful."

"I know that, but when you think about it he could probably have afforded a lot more, couldn't he? Why make the gesture and be so mean about it?"

"That's not very grateful."

"How can I be grateful when he sends you such a rotten letter? It takes all the pleasure out of getting the money."

Her mother came forward and slumped into the rattan chair by Sandy's bed. "You're right." She stared down at the check. "It bothered me, too. But I was so happy to get the money, I didn't want to think about the letter."

"Don't acknowledge it and never write again," Sandy quoted. "In other words, get out of my life forever. What sort of father is that?"

Anne twisted her plain gold wedding band around her finger. "I've never been in his life, have I? At least, not since my mother died." She'd hoped to be able to hide her feelings from Sandy. After all, this was a time for celebration. The only reason she'd written to Ryan was for financial help, wasn't it? But Sandy's reaction revived the chilling disappointment and feeling of rejection she'd experienced when she'd first read the letter. Somehow, despite his absence from her life for so many years it just didn't fit with the few memories she had of her father.

Sandy's voice came to her, as if through a thick fog. "You'd think he'd have grabbed this opportunity to suggest we all meet. It must make you feel awful that he—" Sandy struggled to find the right

words, words that wouldn't hurt her mother more
"—he isn't interested in seeing us? The money's
great, but . . ."

Anne closed her eyes for a moment, drawing in a
deep breath, determined not to let her own disappointment swamp her. "Yes, it does make me feel sad. For
you as well as me. But if he'd been interested in
seeing us he'd have done so years ago, wouldn't he?"

"He must be really weird. I can't believe he never
comes back here to see you or his own dad."

Anne busied herself with refolding the letter and
putting it away in the envelope with the bank draft.
"How do we know he doesn't see his father?"

"Surely Granddad Barry would have told you?"

"We rarely mention Ryan. Besides, I haven't seen
Granddad since Christmas."

In a way, wasn't she almost as bad as her father?
She should go and see her grandfather more often.
Or at least call him. But the last time she'd visited
him the specter of Ryan had hung so heavily between
them that the hour had seemed more like a day.
When she'd looked at her watch for the tenth time, it
was her grandfather who'd said, "Time you were
going, eh?"

"Why weren't you and he closer?" Sandy asked.

"You mean Granddad Barry? I guess because
they took my sister Debbie, and Beth took me. My
grandmother and Aunt Beth never got along. So we
tended to stay separate."

"That is truly weird. I can't imagine having a
sister living in the same city and never seeing her."

"We did see each other. Birthdays, Christmas . . .
times like that." Anne had usually gone to Debbie's
home. In fact Debbie had visited her so rarely that
she could hardly remember those visits. What she

could recall quite vividly was the time her grandmother had spanked both of them for trampling Plas-
ticine into the carpet. Even now, more than thirty
years later, she could conjure up her grandmother's
angry red face, the blows that hit her everywhere, on
her face, her back, her ears . . . until her grandfather
had stopped it, his usually soft voice rising almost to
a falsetto he'd been so furious.

"Mom? Mom!"

"Sorry. I was miles away. Thinking of how I
should visit Granddad Barry more often."

"I don't blame you for not going. That seniors'
home is really depressing."

"It's one of the best in the city, Sandy. Ryan obviously pays for it."

"Oh, I know it's a good place. But seeing all those
old people, propped up in their chairs—" Sandy
shivered visibly. "I hate going there."

Anne sighed. "I guess we all have our reasons for
not wanting to visit people."

"Perhaps your father thought you didn't want to
see him. Had you thought of that? After all, you
didn't write to him, either, did you?"

"As a matter of fact, I did," Anne admitted.
"When I was about fourteen. I asked Grandma Barry
if she'd send my letter on to him, as I didn't have his
address in England."

"What happened?"

"Nothing. He never replied. I decided then it was
better not to think about him anymore."

"Did you think about him lots before then?"

Anne gave her a pained smiled. "Oh, yes. I used to
run to the mailbox every day and think, maybe there's
a letter from Daddy today. But there never was."

"Geez, Mom, that's awful. I never realized." Sandy sprang up and came to hug her.

Blinking, Anne returned the hug. "Thanks, darling. Just remember there's far worse things. Like fathers abusing their children. Mine never did that."

"Not physically, maybe, but emotionally."

"Now, don't go all psychological on me. I'm sure Ryan was a very loving father when my mother was alive. After all, don't they say the first years are the most important?"

Sandy sat down on the edge of her bed. "He sounds like a jerk to me."

"Well, don't you worry any more about it. Besides, now we've got enough money for your first year at Juilliard. More than enough with your concert money."

"Money isn't everything. Anyway, I'm still going to have to get loans for the rest of the time, so I might as well get used to the idea of relying on my own money."

"That's my girl. But this money will give you a great start." Anne frowned, trying to push away the disturbing feeling the letter had given her. "I wish you could write and thank him for it."

"Why can't I?"

"His business manager says he doesn't want to be thanked. You read the letter."

"So what? That needn't stop me." A slow smile spread across Sandy's face. "I've just had a great idea."

"What?" Anne didn't like that look of mischief, which reminded her of a preface to some of Sandy's more adventurous exploits as a kid.

Sandy flipped back her long dark hair. "We're

agreed that we now have more than enough money to cover this year in New York."

"Yes," Anne said slowly. "So?"

"You know I want to go there early and get settled in before I start classes."

Anne sighed. "I wish I could come with you for a couple of days. See where you'll be staying, but—"

"Well, now you can." Sandy's eyes glowed. "Why don't we go to New York together and then travel on to England? Get some sort of cheap shuttle flight or something. Then I could thank my grandfather for the money in person."

Anne stared at her. "We couldn't afford it."

"Why not? We'd arranged the bank loan for this year anyway. Now we'll have plenty left over to take a trip to New York *and* England."

"Ryan said he didn't want us to communicate with him," Anne reminded her.

"That's too bad. He's my grandfather. I'd like to meet him."

"I'd like that, too. But it seems he doesn't want to meet us."

"That's garbage! It's also very selfish of him. After all, it's not just him, it's your sister as well you haven't seen for all these years. All I've got in my life are you and Aunt Beth. I've a right to go and see my closest relatives, haven't I?" Sandy leaned forward. "I don't think you've thought about that side of it, have you? That this is my grandfather and aunt, as well as your father and sister."

Anne looked down at the letter and saw that the hand holding it was trembling. "Yes, Sandy, I have thought about that. I've often thought about it."

"I'm sorry, Mom. I didn't mean to sound bitchy. I just think it's time you saw your father and sister again, that's all. And I'd really like to come along. How about it?"

Anne thought of the letter again. Could her father possibly have changed that much? "I'd like to do it," she admitted. "But how could I leave Aunt Beth alone? This is our busiest time at the center."

"Ask her. See what she says."

Anne had to smile. "She'll say we're crazy, that's what she'll say."

"Do it for me, Mom, if not for yourself. I'm going to be working like mad without a break for the next year or so. Then, later, I'll be on the road with concerts. This is our one chance to have a holiday together."

"Oh, Sandy, you never change, do you? You seem to think that this money will last forever. We can't afford holidays. If we go, it's because I really want to see my father and sister again."

"And I can meet my grandfather at last," Sandy said. "It's something I've wanted to do for years."

Anne glanced away from her daughter's excited face. "What happens if he refuses to see us?"

"Of course he won't."

Raising her eyebrows, Anne held up the letter.

"Even if he did," Sandy said impatiently, "you'd like to see your sister, wouldn't you?"

"Yes, I would. Of course, we'd be like strangers, but I'd love to see Debbie again."

Sandy bounced on the bed, grinning with excitement. "Let's do it, Mom. Say yes before you think of all the reasons not to do it."

"I am thinking of them. Spending that precious money, leaving Beth, barging in on people who don't want to see us . . ."

"Seeing your sister again after, what, thirty years?"

"Twenty-eight." Anne hesitated, her heart pounding so hard she felt it was going to jump through her earth-stained T-shirt. "I'll discuss it with Marco."

"Okay, but knowing him, he'll say don't waste the money."

"He'd be right." Anne looked down at her sun-browned hands, the stubborn earth in her nails. "I'm a mess. I don't have any decent clothes for England." She gave a wry smile. "I'd need one of those magazine makeovers."

She was like two people arguing with each other, putting up excuses, when in her heart she knew that she *must* go to England, *must* find out why her father had cut himself off from her for all these years.

Most of all, she wanted to know why, when she had at last made a move toward reconciliation, he had sent her such a cold, impersonal letter.

"We're going to put ten thousand bucks away in the bank immediately," Sandy was saying. "Then we'll buy two return tickets to England via New York and buy you some new clothes. You've got a great figure, Mom. All you need is a good haircut and color to highlight it and you can mix with the best."

Sandy was just the way Anne remembered herself being when she was in love with Scott and going to university. Life seemed to hold nothing but excitement and possibilities. Somehow, over the years that had drained away from her. Now, some of Sandy's excitement was rubbing off on her.

"You're a crazy kid, you know that."

"Sure I am." Sandy waited for more.

"I'll speak to Beth about it tonight."

Sandy jumped off the bed and yelled "Yes!" raising both arms in the air in a gesture of victory.

Chapter 6

That night, when she was helping Marco set up the tables in his restaurant, Anne told him about her plans. Although he was understanding about it he thought she was doing the wrong thing.

"I see why you want to do it, but I think you're gonna get hurt, that's all." He set four wineglasses on the crisp white tablecloth with a little more force than was necessary.

"I must do this. I need to see my sister again."

"And your father?"

"And my father." She gave him a wry smile. "Even if he hasn't been much of a father to me."

Sighing, Marco shook his head. "After I see that letter I wonder how you can be bothered with him."

"It's hard for you to understand. You have all your family around you—"

"No wife," he said pointedly. He turned away and went to the bar, to tidy the bottles on the shelves.

Anne followed him. "I mean your parents and your siblings. They're all here. You take them for granted. You take their love for granted. Try to see my side, Marco. For me there's just a big hole where my family should be. I keep trying to fill that hole with friends and work, but—" She paused, embarrassed at spewing this stuff out to him.

He stopped wiping a bottle of Sambuca and came to her. "You've got Sandy and your aunt Beth. She's a tough nut, but she loves you. No doubt about that. And you've got me." He hugged her close against his chest, his hands smelling of licorice. "I love you. I want to marry you. Isn't that enough?"

Her face must have given him her answer, for he released her and stepped back, his mouth tight. "Okay. Go see your father. How long you going to be away?"

"Just a couple of weeks, that's all. I can't leave Beth any longer than that."

"How's she going to manage by herself?"

"I haven't told Beth yet, but I did speak to Bill. He said his grandson could come in. He's on vacation and can do with the extra money." She tilted up her chin. "So I'm not totally abandoning her."

"Will you have an answer for me when you come back?"

"Answer?" Suddenly realizing what he meant, Anne bit her bottom lip to stem her anger. "You promised you wouldn't ask again."

"I might get tired of asking." It was a warning.

"I do love you, Marco, but I hate being pressured. I've told you that before."

"I'm not interested in a part-time lover. I want a wife who lives with me, someone to be a good mother to my kids."

"I promise I'll give it lots of thought while I'm away. I'll give you an answer when I get back."

"Okay. That's a deal."

The following evening, Anne told Beth about going to England with Sandy. Beth thought she was crazy and told her so. "If you think Ryan's going to welcome you coming in on him without any warning, you're riding for a fall."

"If I warn him, he'll make sure he's not there."

"For Pete's sake, why'd you want to visit somebody who doesn't want to see you?"

"Because one of us has to make the move before it's too late. Sandy has convinced me that I've nothing to lose. And she's right."

"Nothing but a big chunk of that money he sent. Throwing it away on airfares to England!"

"You're right, but as it's really Sandy's money and she wants to see her grandfather and aunt that's what we're going to do."

Beth's lips pursed together, emphasizing the vertical lines etched in the skin around her mouth.

God! How selfish it must seem, Anne suddenly thought. I should be giving Beth a couple of thousand, not spending it on a useless trip to England. She opened her mouth to say something, but then closed it again.

"It's your money," Beth said. "And your funeral. Don't say I didn't warn you."

"I'll go and get some salad stuff from the garden," Anne said, marveling at the fact that she hadn't caved in. It made her feel both guilty and yet triumphant at the same time.

It was a glorious evening. The sun was just beginning to sink behind the Siberian elm in their garden. Two mourning doves were perched on the telephone wires, issuing their throaty call that always gave Anne a feeling of tranquillity. Here, in her garden, at least, she was at peace.

The tiger lilies were almost out in the wide flower bed beside the back fence. She could see tinges of orange and yellow peeping through the green. Just a few more hot days and they'd burst out into their full gaudy array, for a while overpowering everything else in the flower bed, until the blossoms faded and dropped to the ground.

It was hard to believe that three months ago the snow had been halfway up the fence and she'd had to wade thigh-high through it to get to the bird feeder. Time seemed to be passing far more quickly now than it did when she was Sandy's age.

Anne squatted down and started pulling tenacious clumps of chickweed from the earth. She would be forty next birthday and what had she to show for it? Nothing. Oh, she'd created a few nice gardens. And she'd done volunteer work at the hospital and played the piano for the high school musicals. Music had always been an escape for her. A solace. "Janine always wanted you to take piano lessons," Beth told her when she'd given her the secondhand piano for her twelfth birthday. "So you make sure you practice and don't waste the money I've spent on it."

Years later Anne realized what a sacrifice both piano and lessons must have been for Beth. But even as a pianist she wasn't anything special. No, she hadn't really done anything in her life that was outstanding or award-winning.

Except Sandy, of course. Sandy was her creation. Hers and Scott's. She would go on to make her mark in the world, to give people pleasure with her music. Sandy was something, at least. Perhaps that was all one could expect. Perhaps that was what kept the human species going: the hope that your child would make more of an impact on the world than you had.

Perhaps that was what Ryan and Janine had hoped for all those years ago when she was born.

The back door flew open. "You dreaming out there? Where's those salad greens?"

"Just coming." Anne stood up, brushing earth and grass from her knees. Dreaming? Yes, she'd been dreaming. One thing was certain now in her mind. Whatever Beth or Marco said, nothing was going to stop her from going to England with Sandy.

Chapter 7

The planning had been even more complicated than they'd anticipated. In her enthusiasm, Sandy hadn't considered her students and her master classes at the music conservatory. Not only would she have to cancel them, but she would also lose the fees. The conservatory was not happy about the cancellations, saying that some of the people who had signed up for them might not be available later.

Sandy felt like telling them to stuff their classes, but knew she had to worry about her professional reputation as well as her fees. She told her mother rather sheepishly that she could spend no more than two weeks away, including the three days in New York.

That suited Anne fine. She was concerned that even two *days* might be too much, considering the circumstances. And when she saw the reality of what two transatlantic fares plus airport taxes and the price of a cheap hotel room in New York was going to cost them, she was appalled. She'd never spent so much money so easily in her entire life. It had taken all her strength and Sandy's persuasion to keep her from changing her mind.

Fortunately she didn't have to spend too much on clothes. She'd been able to find a couple of good

bargains in the summer sales. Although she rarely
had any cause to dress up, apart from going to
the Manitoba Opera productions with Marco three
or four times a year, she did enjoy wearing nice
clothes.

When she and Sandy reached New York, she
found a very pretty peach-and-white-striped dress
on sale at Bloomingdale's. That, together with the
other new things and the lemon cotton suit she'd
bought for Sandy's graduation, gave her a few
dressy outfits. She didn't want to look like the poor
relation arriving at the millionaire's mansion.

But, in fact—having flown into Heathrow early in
the morning, catching a train from London as soon
as they'd arrived there—that was exactly how Anne
felt when the taxi they'd hired at the railway station
drove into the curved driveway and pulled up in
front of Ryan's house.

"Isn't this exciting?" Sandy said.

After an overnight flight from New York, the
subway train packed with tourists up to London, and
another train journey to Buckinghamshire, Anne felt
more exhausted than excited. The crowds and bustle
had bewildered her, making her head spin. She'd
never seen anything like it. Compared with London,
Minneapolis—the only other large city she'd spent
time in—was like a sleepy village.

She wished now that they had stayed in a London
hotel for their first day, but at the time they'd made
their plans, their goal had been to get to Ryan's
house as quickly as possible.

She glanced up at the house and caught a fleeting
image of turrets and towers and arched windows,

more suitable for an ancient church than a house, before the taxi driver opened the door and she got out.

"Wow!" was all Sandy could say as she gazed up at the graystone house.

"Are they expecting you?" the taxi driver asked, when Sandy had rung the bell but no one answered. "Want me to wait?"

"No need, thank you." Anne sounded more positive than she felt.

"There must be someone here or the driveway gates would have been locked. Perhaps he's away. He sometimes goes to Italy in July."

"Oh." Anne glanced at Sandy, unable to hide her dismay. How could she have been so stupid? They might have wasted all that money for nothing.

Then they heard footsteps and the door was opened by a middle-aged woman with a round face and gray hair in an attractive page-boy cut.

"Sorry," the woman said. "We were out in the garden. Can I help you?" She spoke with a soft Irish brogue that reminded Anne of her grandfather.

"We're—" Sandy began, but Anne interrupted her.

"We're here to see Mr. Barry. And Deborah Barry, if she's here."

"Okay?" the taxi driver said. "I'll get your cases out, then."

"Cases?" the woman said, her voice sharpening a little. "Was Mr. Barry expecting you?"

"No, he wasn't." Anne swallowed the lump in her throat. "I'm his daughter, Anne. This is my daughter, Sandy."

"Holy mother of God!" the woman whispered. "He doesn't know you're coming, does he?" Anne shook her head. "No, of course not. He would have told me." After a moment of hesitation, she held out her hand. "I'm Eileen O'Meara, Ryan's house-keeper."

Anne took her hand, grateful for the feeling of warmth against hers. She was dead tired from the long journey. They'd had a snack on the train to London, but that was all. When she'd learned that a train to Princes Risborough was about to leave and they'd have to wait an hour for the next one, Sandy had insisted that they make a run for it.

"Where did you come from?" Eileen asked.

"We left Canada yesterday morning," Sandy said.

"We've been traveling ever since," Anne added.

"You didn't spend the night in London then?"

Anne shook her head.

"Sure you must be bone weary, the pair of you. Come on in."

She was so welcoming that Anne felt like hugging her, but still she held back. "I don't think we should come in," she said firmly. "Until we know—"

"Well, *I'm* sure you should. Put it on our account, Jim," Eileen shouted to the driver, who had already started up the engine. He smiled, tipped his cap, and drove off.

Eileen touched Anne's arm. "Your father's some-where on the grounds talking with Graham about gardens."

Your father. How strange that sounded. And who the heck was Graham?

"But Deborah's in the house. Come on in and relax. I'll get you a pot of coffee and some cake and sandwiches first. Then I'll go and fetch Ryan."

My sister's in this very house. My father's in the garden, Anne told herself as she stepped over the threshold. Her heart was beating so fast it made her feel light-headed. She felt Sandy's hand slide into hers and she squeezed it very tightly.

Eileen O'Meara led them across the flagstone floor of the hall. Despite her short stature and small feet, she walked so fast that Anne could catch only a glimpse of oak beams and the glint of steel swords and shields on the walls as they passed through the hall.

She was about to follow Eileen into a far brighter room, a welcome contrast to the gloom of the hall, when a peremptory English voice called out, "Who is it, Eileen?"

Anne turned. Halfway down the wide oak staircase stood a woman, her hand holding the carved banister. Her hair was ash-blond and she wore it coiled in an elegant French knot. She was dressed casually in a long, brightly colored wraparound skirt and a black cotton top. Even from a distance Anne could tell that the clothes were expensive.

"Can I help you?" she asked Anne.

Anne didn't reply. "That's Deborah," Eileen said quietly from behind her.

Anne walked back to the center of the hall. "I'm your sister Anne," she said. Her voice echoed back to her in the cavernous hall.

The light was too dim to see Deborah's expression, but Anne could sense her shock. After a moment, Deborah descended the stairs and halted a little way from them. "We weren't expecting you," she said in that cool English accent that was so alien to Anne— and to Debbie's own background. "Did you write? We certainly didn't get a letter."

Her attitude annoyed Anne. "No, I didn't. I came because I wanted to thank my—our father for sending money for Sandy. This is my daughter Sandy, by the way," she said, indicating Sandy, who was standing behind her.

Sandy raised her hand. "Hi, Aunt Debbie."

Sandy received a curt nod. "How strange to come such a long way without contacting us first," Deborah said. "Surely it would have been easier for you to thank him by letter or telephone."

"Yes, it would. And less expensive." Anne's temper was up. It was disappointing enough getting the cold shoulder from her sister, but giving it to Sandy, who was this woman's only niece, was too much. "Ryan's kindness made me realize that it was time I saw my father and sister again, and I wanted you to meet my daughter."

"I do wish you had written first so that we could have been ready for you. As it is—" Deborah faltered. "This will be rather a surprise for my father. It would have been so much better if you had written first," she repeated, obviously lost for words.

Anne smiled. "Would it? You probably wouldn't have replied," she said, remembering the cold letter Ryan's manager had sent. "Or you'd have said it wasn't convenient, right?"

Deborah's eyes widened with surprise at her frankness. "I have no idea. That would be up to my father. Has he been told they're here?" Deborah asked Eileen.

"Not yet. I thought I'd give them something to eat first. They've been traveling all night from Canada and haven't had a meal since they landed." Eileen's tone was quite civil, but Anne could tell that she disapproved of Deborah's welcome—or lack of it.

"I'll go and tell him." Deborah turned back to Anne. "It will be quite a shock for him."

"I expect it will."

Dark brown and blue eyes clashed as they stood facing each other in the hall. Anne hadn't expected her younger sister to be so tall. She had also not expected to be greeted with such hostility by Debbie—or Deborah, as she was now obviously called. From the first moment she had seen her on the stairs, remote and cool, all Anne's dreams of a loving younger sister rushing into her arms had been dashed. In fact, if this woman with the English accent hadn't been her sister she would have said she was thoroughly dislikeable. Arrogant, cold, and unwelcoming.

Anne felt her shoulders slump with tiredness and disappointment. Then she straightened them, lifting her chin. She hadn't come all this way to let this first meeting with her sister put her off. She smiled at Eileen, who was watching her anxiously. "You said something about coffee and sandwiches?"

"Of course." Eileen seemed delighted to have her offer accepted. "Why don't you go and find Ryan?" she suggested to Deborah, who was still standing in the center of the hall. "Or shall I go and tell him?"

"No. I'll do it. I have to make a quick telephone call first. Then I'll find him." Deborah marched past them, her skirt swirling about her legs. She went down a corridor and out of sight.

Eileen led Anne and Sandy into the conservatory. "Sit here and get some rest." She waved at the comfortably cushioned loungers and then hurried out, barely giving Anne time to thank her.

As soon as she'd asked Betty to take tea, sandwiches, and cake to the visitors in the conservatory, Eileen dashed outside, cutting through the kitchen garden, hoping to intercept Deborah before she reached Ryan.

She caught up with her in the priest's grotto. "Wait," she shouted.

Deborah spun around. "I thought you were giving the weary travelers sustenance," she said, her voice heavy with sarcasm.

Eileen could see how upset she was. "Why are you so angry? You'd think you'd be overjoyed to see your own sister and niece after all these years."

"Well, I'm not. She had no right to come here without any notice. Can you imagine how this is going to affect Ryan?"

"I surely can if you come at him in that frame of mind. I suggest you take a deep breath and calm down before you tell him. It's going to be a big enough shock for him without you acting like a wildcat."

Deborah did as she was told, drawing in a deep breath and slowly releasing it. "Isn't there some way we could get rid of them without him having to know they were here?"

"Shame on you to say such a thing about your own flesh and blood."

Deborah's cheeks flushed. "It's going to devastate him, Eileen. You know how that letter affected him. Think what this will do to him. I'm worried about his heart."

"It's his heart I'm concerned about, too. But not the way you mean it. To my mind, it's high time you and Ryan accepted that you have other family. If I'd had my way this would have happened years ago, but he was determined that his daughter didn't want him. And you encouraged him in that."

Deborah flinched at Eileen's accusation, but she didn't make any effort to deny it.

"We'll go together and tell him," Eileen said, taking her arm. "Where did he say they were going?"

"He was taking Graham and Conrad to see the new footbridge."

"Right. Let's go, then." Eileen strode off purposefully, not even checking to see if Deborah was following.

Deborah was not looking forward to this encounter. She was genuinely worried about Ryan's heart. Recently, he'd had some bouts of arrhythmia and was taking medication for it. The doctor said there was nothing serious to worry about, but a shock like this might make things worse.

They found the three men still standing by the new bridge, which, unlike the house, was a simple wooden structure, eminently suitable for such a sylvan setting.

Conrad Hatcher was the tallest of the three men. A handsome man in his fifties, Conrad had been her father's business manager for almost twenty years, taking over the management of Ryan's business affairs a few years before Avoca had stopped touring. Now he looked after all Ryan's personal affairs as well as his business investments and, because Ryan had put up the money for it, kept a professional eye on Deborah's business as well.

"Deborah darling," he said in his plummy voice, when he saw her. He looked over his sunglasses at her. "You look absolutely stunning."

"So do you, Conrad," she said lightly. It was true. Conrad had a firm, muscular body, honed by working out and regular tennis-playing.

Even since she was in her teens Conrad had a thing for her, turning on the full extent of his charm to get her into bed. She'd been flattered by the attentions of a very attractive, much older man. But even then she'd recognized the dangers of mixing her father's business with her pleasure and had always managed to keep Conrad at arm's length.

Now, with Graham observing them with that wry little smile he used when he was annoyed, she found Conrad's attentions annoying. She went to Graham and slipped her hand into his arm. "Hello, darling."

Graham's smile became warmer. "There you are," he said, sounding relieved.

She drew him aside. "Would you be a darling and take Conrad somewhere for a moment? I have to speak to Daddy alone."

Graham grimaced. "If I must. Sounds like something important."

"It is."

"Are you all right? Nothing wrong, is there?"

"It could be. I'll tell you later." She made an impatient gesture with her hand. "Could you—"

"Right." Graham walked back to Conrad. "Know anything about Heritage grants? I've been meaning to ask you about them. I'm hoping I could get something for restoring Somerford Hall."

Deborah could only marvel at the ease with which Graham steered Conrad away. She turned to her father who was still admiring his bridge. "It'll outlast all of us," he was telling Eileen. "Strange to think that it could be here when we're all dead and buried, isn't it?" He gave an involuntary shiver, then frowned at them both, sensing that something was wrong. "What's up?"

Eileen looked at Deborah, waiting for her to speak.

Deborah searched for the right way to do this. "You've got some unexpected visitors."

"From the look on both your faces, they must be from Inland Revenue," he joked.

"No." Deborah took a deep breath, knowing there was no way to soften it. "Anne's here."

Ryan frowned. "Anne who?"

"Anne, your daughter," Eileen said. "She's flown all the way from Canada with her daughter Sandy to see you."

Ryan's face blanched. "I don't believe it."

"Well, you'd better believe it, because she and Sandy are sitting there large as life in your conservatory."

Deborah glared at Eileen, annoyed at her bluntness. "I'm sorry, Daddy, but what could we do?"

Ryan collapsed onto the wooden bench by the stream. "I don't want to see her."

"We can't very well send her away, can we?"

He put his head in his hands. "I can't face her," he whispered.

Deborah sat beside him. "I know what a big shock this is for you."

Eileen stood in front of them, hands on her rounded hips. "The best way is to go into the conservatory, meet your daughter and granddaughter, and get it over and done with. I think it's a damned good thing she's come here."

"How can you be so insensitive?" Deborah demanded. "Can't you see how upset he is?"

"Upset? Hasn't he been avoiding his daughter all these years and her nearing forty years of age? Is it any wonder he's upset?"

Ryan lifted his head to glare at her. "Thanks, Eileen. You know how to kick a man where it hurts. It was Anne who avoided me all these years. She was the one who didn't want me."

"And I know a bunch of baloney when I hear it."

Deborah stood up. "That's enough, Eileen."

Eileen ignored her. "She's here now, isn't she? If it was always Anne who didn't want you, not the other way around, then why is she here?"

"She probably wants more money," Deborah said.

"Surely not?" Ryan stared at her. "If that's all she's here for, then Conrad can deal with it."

"Don't be daft." Eileen's tone was filled with scorn. "She's here to see you. She told me so. Wants you to meet your granddaughter."

Ryan stood up. "I'd do anything not to have to go through this."

"We'll be with you," Deborah said.

Eileen looked at her, but kept her mouth shut until they'd reached the terrace steps. Then she said to Ryan, "This meeting's too important for us to interfere. Why don't you go on in? We'll wait out here."

But Ryan balked at going in alone. He was visibly shaking and looked as if his knees were about to buckle beneath him. "No way. You come in with me or I don't go in."

"Of course we're coming with you," Deborah said, giving Eileen a dark look. "Think of it as a performance, Daddy. Performance nerves. You always knew what to do about those."

Eileen rolled her eyes. "For the love of God! How can you compare this to a stage show?"

"Will you shut up, the both of you?" Ryan said. His face looked as gray as the stone walls of his house, but it was also grim with determination. "Let's get this over and done with."

Chapter 8

Anne stared down at the food set out before her. A plate piled with two kinds of sandwiches: ham and cheese, and thinly sliced chicken and tomato. A few minutes ago a young woman named Betty had brought in a large Thermos jug of coffee and a ceramic pot of tea—covered with a tea cozy shaped like a cat—plus plates of sandwiches, fruit cake and cookies, and some floury scones.

Although little more than twenty minutes had passed since their arrival at Hammerton Towers, it seemed much longer than that. Sandy had plowed into the food, but after only half a sandwich Anne's appetite had disappeared. She was jangly with tiredness and jet lag, and longing, more than anything, for some sleep.

"What's keeping them?" Sandy asked, through a mouthful of scone and strawberry jam.

"He doesn't want to see us, I expect," Anne said prosaically.

"That's crazy."

"Don't say I didn't warn you."

"I know. But . . . I wasn't expecting your sister to be such a snob."

Anne hadn't expected that, either. Debbie's—Deborah's—accent and manner had been a shock.

"Well, I guess she's grown up here, with lots of money. Probably gone to upper-crust private schools." Anne was seeking for excuses, but really nothing could excuse the miserable welcome Deborah had given them.

Sandy said nothing. Even her usually uncrushable exuberance had been flattened. "Tired, sweetie?" Anne asked.

"A bit."

Disappointed, too, Anne could see. After all, this had been Sandy's idea originally. More than anything she hated to see how this chilly reception had affected her daughter.

Sandy got up and started to pace restlessly about the conservatory. From outside came the plunk of a ball being hit by a tennis racquet. One of the tropical birds in the large cage in the corner began whistling melodiously. A sweet floral scent hung in the air.

What a strange place this is, Anne thought. And what the heck am I doing here? She felt furious at herself for having allowed Sandy to talk her into coming here.

Sandy peered through the glass door and then darted back to Anne. "They're coming."

Anne put her cup and saucer down on the rattan table, and sat up straight, her apparent calm belying her racing heartbeat. *Oh, God. I wish I hadn't done this,* was her one thought. But it was too late now. The glass door swung open.

Although Anne remembered her father as being very tall, towering above her, the man who stood there was of little more than medium height. He had thinning dark-brown hair flecked with gray and was dressed casually in beige cotton chino pants and a yellow polo shirt.

He came forward, unsmiling. Another cold reception, she thought, the chill in her heart increasing. "Anne?" he said, the word ending with an upward inflection, as if he wasn't sure.

She was about to reply when she saw his eyes suddenly widen and then, quite unexpectedly, glisten with moisture, but it was Sandy, not her, he was now looking at. "You must be Sandy," he said.

Sandy nodded, overcome.

"You're the living image of Janine," he said, with a decided Irish lilt to his voice. He turned to Anne, blinking away the tears. "Did you realize that?"

Anne tried to smile. "Yes. Aunt Beth told me."

He took out a clean white handkerchief and blew his nose. "Sorry. It was a shock." He turned to Sandy. "You are so like your grandmother that for a moment I thought she'd suddenly come alive again."

"Is that bad?" Sandy asked anxiously.

"I—I'm not sure. It gave me quite a jolt." He smiled and Anne's heart made a leap of recognition. It was her father's smile she remembered, the warmth and charm of it. But the smile was directed at Sandy, not her. For the first time in her life she felt envious of her daughter.

Now her father was looking at her. "I wish you'd told us you were coming."

"I wasn't sure you . . ." Her voice trailed away, emotion and weariness getting the better of her. "I'm sorry. I'm half asleep. What I mean is that . . . after what you said in your letter, I was afraid you had some reason for not wanting us to come. So we decided to risk it. We wanted to thank you in person for the money you sent."

He waved his hand impatiently. "Don't mention

that again, okay? If that's all you came for, you've come a long way for nothing."

"That's not all I came for."

Anne met his gaze for a moment. Then he looked away to the table. "I see that you've been fed. Eileen and Deborah looking after you okay, are they?"

He sounded so formal, as if she were a casual visitor. If that was the way he wanted to play it, she would meet his formality with her own. "Yes, thank you."

"What do you think of your sister?"

Anne looked at Deborah. She was standing in a corner of the conservatory, staring out, as if she was wholly disinterested in what was going on. "She's beautiful," Anne said. "I didn't expect her to be so tall."

Deborah said nothing, her back eloquent in its unyielding straightness.

"Do you remember her at all?" Ryan asked.

"Oh, yes. Mainly little things like how Debbie hated any kind of fish, and Aunt Beth always seemed to make tuna casserole when she came to visit." Anne rattled on, embarrassment making her talk more than usual. "Do you remember the time we painted Easter eggs and spilled the paint all over Grandma Barry's carpet?" she asked Deborah, in an attempt to draw her into the conversation.

Deborah turned, her face a polite mask. "I'm afraid I don't."

Anne burbled on, trying to fill the void. "Boy, were we in trouble. 'Course I got blamed for it. I always did. It was quite a while before I got asked back again."

"My mother always was a bit heavy-handed," Ryan said. Everything went quiet then and Anne was just too tired to summon up any more conversation.

Glancing at Ryan's face, which was taut with strain, Eileen stepped into the breach. "You look as if you could do with a rest," she said to Anne.

"Have we any unoccupied rooms?" Deborah asked. Then even she must have realized how unwelcoming that sounded. "Daddy has friends down to stay at weekends," she hurriedly explained.

"We'll make room," Ryan said. "It isn't every day my daughter and granddaughter come to visit." The sudden warmth of his voice and smile helped to alleviate the pall of awkwardness that lay over them all.

"They can have my room," Deborah said. "I can go and stay with Graham."

"Please," Anne said, wishing even more that she'd never come. "I don't want to put anyone out. We didn't give you any warning."

"That's okay," Ryan said. "You're here. That's what matters."

Although the words obviously didn't come easily to him, Anne was grateful that he was trying to make a difficult situation a little easier. "I know I should have written, but ..." She sought for a reason, but nothing that sounded right would come. Besides, if she said any more she had the unnerving feeling she might break down.

As she stood in the center of the conservatory, feeling extremely vulnerable, Ryan came to her and quietly put his arms about her. He didn't hug her close or kiss her, but just stood there holding her loosely. It was exactly what she needed. No histrionic display of affection, only the feeling of warmth and protection and welcome. "Thank you, Daddy," she whispered.

She opened her eyes and, looking over Ryan's shoulder, caught Deborah's expression before she had time to turn away. Although her father might be willing to offer her some sort of welcome, her sister deeply resented her coming.

"The White Nun's room is free," Eileen said, "and the little dressing room next to it has a bed in it. We can move you into a better room tomorrow," she told Sandy, "after everyone leaves."

"White Nun's room?" Sandy said. "What's that?"

" 'Tis Ryan's whimsy to name the bedrooms after ghosts." Eileen raised her eyebrows and smiled. "The White Nun was a Christian martyr who was beheaded because she refused to sleep with the chief of a Viking clan that invaded Ireland."

"And does her ghost haunt the room?"

"No such luck," Ryan said with a laugh. "This place was sadly misrepresented to me when I bought it. I thought I'd be purchasing a wagonload of ghosts along with the Gothic spookiness of the house itself, but not one ghost have we seen."

"Is the house very old?" Sandy asked.

"Alas, no. It was built by an eccentric clothing manufacturer in the Victorian era. It's about a hundred and twenty years old."

"That's old," Sandy said.

"Not in England, it isn't," Deborah said.

"Deborah's right. My house is a big phony."

"I thought it was medieval." Sandy sounded disappointed.

"That's why I like it. It looks ancient, but it isn't, so no interfering bureaucrats or preservation do-gooders can tell me what I can or can't do with it." He glanced at Deborah. "Now if you want to see a really old place, you should get your aunt to take you to see Somerford, the lovely old Elizabethan house her friend Graham bought recently."

"Talking of Graham," Deborah said, obviously grasping at this opportunity to get away. "He and Conrad must be wondering what's going on."

"Then go and tell them," Ryan said, an edge to his voice. "Eileen and I can see your sister and Sandy settled in."

"Good." Deborah was about to leave, then she turned to Anne. "We'll talk later when you've had a sleep." She made an attempt at a smile.

"I'd like that." Anne watched her sister as she opened the door, descended the steps, and strode across the lawn.

"I must apologize for Deborah," Ryan said. "She's not normally as—" He sought for the right words, but couldn't find them.

"This isn't a normal occasion, is it?" Anne said. "It's been a shock for both of you. I'm sorry. I wasn't sure what my welcome would be."

"Well, as you can see, it's been a bit mixed." He frowned as he watched Deborah disappear into the trees.

"Let's get you to your room," Eileen said. "After a good sleep, you'll feel much better, I'm sure."

What a nice person she is, Anne thought, as Eileen led the way. The one source of sanity in this crazy situation.

The only concession to its name in the White Nun's room was the ornate Celtic cross in bronze that hung above the bed. It was filled with heavy, dark furniture, alleviated only a little by the light floral curtains that hung at the two tall windows.

"I was expecting a stone cell or something like that," Sandy said, dropping her large nylon duffel bag on the floor.

"Your grandfather has a strange sense of humor," Eileen said.

"Is that my employee belittling me again?" Ryan said, coming into the room. "Your room's on the other side of the bathroom," he told Sandy. "There's a door directly through to it." Carefully he set down her leather guitar case. "I expect you guard this with your life." He hesitated and then asked her, "Would you play for me sometime?"

"You really want me to?"

He nodded.

"I'd love to. On one condition."

"What's that?"

"That you'll play and sing for me. Mom has all your recordings, you know, so I know your songs."

He glanced at Anne. "Does she?" He looked as if he was about to say something to her, but changed his mind. "I rarely sing now," he told Sandy.

"Then we can play guitar duets together."

Eileen met Anne's gaze and they exchanged almost imperceptible smiles.

"You've got yourself a deal," Ryan said. "Though from what I've heard you're way out of my league. Classical, Juilliard . . ."

"I play all sorts of stuff, not just classical. When I first started, I wanted to do pop, not classical, so I love both. Give me a moment to get cleaned up and changed, then I'll be down, okay?"

"Aren't you going to have a rest?" Anne asked her.

"No way. I'm too wired to sleep." Sandy unzipped her bag and began to drag out her clothes.

"See you shortly, then. Come on down when you're ready." Ryan turned to Anne. "You should get some sleep, Annie. You look absolutely beat."

"I am," she said, warmed by his use of her childhood name. "As soon as this live wire here leaves I'll go straight to bed."

When her father and Eileen left the room, Anne sank onto the bed by the window. Shaky with tension and fatigue, she gazed out the window at the garden and the woods beyond, and the pale-blue sky with scattered puffy clouds, so different from the sheet of intense blue she was used to.

"So what do you think?" she asked Sandy, when she came out of the bathroom.

"I was just wondering if I could get away with not washing my hair until this evening."

"Sandy! You know what I mean. What do you think of them . . . of this place?"

"I think your father's really special and your sister's a bitch, but very glamorous, if you get my drift. A rich bitch." Sandy laughed, but Anne did not. Sandy's laughter died away. "It was a joke, Mom. Lighten up."

Anne looked down at her hands, circling the worn gold band around her finger. "I don't feel I have anything in common with either of them. They move in a completely different world to mine."

Sandy came to sit beside her on the bed. "But you knew that before, didn't you?"

"I suppose so, but as soon as I saw the house I knew it was a mistake to come here."

"Oh, Mom, you're just tired. You'll feel better after you've had some sleep."

"I expect you're right." Anne stood up. "I'll just have a bath and then I'll lie down."

"Let me have a quick shower first." Sandy was already halfway into the bathroom, stripping off her T-shirt and jeans as she went.

Someone knocked on the door. "Come in," Anne

said, hoping in a way that it was Deborah. The longer they postponed talking together, the harder it would be.

But it was Eileen who put her head around the door. "I've brought you some extra towels."

"Great. Sandy's having a shower now. Thank you."

Eileen set the pile of thick white towels on a chair, then hesitated, wanting to say something. Anne waited. "You were right to come," Eileen said at last.

Anne's head jerked up in surprise. It was as if Eileen had read her thoughts. She saw not a wish to gossip but warm kindness in the older woman's eyes. "Was I? They didn't seem that pleased to see me."

"You took them by surprise. After all, it has been a very long time since you were together."

"Too long, I think."

" 'Tis never too long for a father to be reunited with his daughter."

"Then why didn't he come to me? He knew where I was. I was still stuck in the same, boring place, working my butt off to keep our heads above water." Anne was appalled by the bitterness in her own voice. "Sorry," she murmured. "I've no right to unload on you. I guess I'm tired."

"And disappointed, no doubt. You've come a long way to be received so coolly."

"No, I'm not disappointed. To be disappointed you have to have some sort of hope. I got exactly what I expected. It's Sandy I'm sorry for."

"But Ryan has really taken to her, hasn't he?"

"Yes, I suppose he has." Anne was appalled to find herself bitter about this, too. What was wrong with her? "My aunt always said she looked like Janine."

Eileen moved to the door. "Was she dark, like you, then?"

"Yes, long dark hair."

"Where does Deborah get her blond hair and blue eyes then?"

"I've got a picture of Ryan when he was about ten. He was blond then."

"Ah, so Deborah takes after her dad and you take after your mum."

"I don't know who I take after. Debbie was always the pretty one. I'm just ordinary looking."

"No you're not." Eileen patted Anne's arm. "Give it a little time. Ryan will soon get used to the idea of having you back in his life."

"Did he ever speak about me? I mean . . ." Anne sought for the words she wanted. "Did he tell people he had another daughter?"

"I'm afraid not. I knew, of course. Apart from me, only Deborah and his wife—I mean Fiona—knew about you." Eileen's light-brown eyes were warm with sympathy.

"I thought so."

"It hurt him too much to talk about you. Easier to pretend you didn't exist."

"I'm sure." Anne's mouth twisted into a smile. "Much easier."

"Your coming back will be good for him."

"We'll see about that." Anne moved to her open suitcase and briskly began to unpack her clothes. "And what about my sister?"

Eileen looked over her glasses at Anne. "Deborah?" She drew in a breath and released it slowly. "Ah, now there, I'm sorry to say, you may have a more difficult time of it."

Before Anne could think of a response, Eileen had opened the door, slipped out, and closed it quietly behind her.

Chapter 9

Deborah had walked so fast across the lawn and through the beech coppice that she was out of breath by the time she reached Graham and Conrad. They stood at a slight distance from each other, Graham leaning on the handrail of the rustic bridge, Conrad restlessly pacing up and down the bank of the stream.

"Ah, there you are," Graham said when he saw her. "I was about to come and find you. Everything all right?"

Deborah shrugged. "I suppose so. My sister Anne and her daughter are here," she said defiantly.

"What the hell—" Conrad's voice trailed away.

"That's wonderful," Graham said.

"Is it? I'm not so sure." Deborah kicked at a clump of turf with her toe.

"You weren't expecting them, were you?" Conrad asked. "I certainly didn't hear anything about it from Ryan."

"No, of course we weren't. They just came, without any warning."

"How's Ryan taking it?"

"He's shocked, of course. I was worried about how this would affect him. But he's really taken to the girl."

"You mean his granddaughter?" Graham asked.

She stared at him as if she didn't at first comprehend what he meant, then said, finally, "Yes. His granddaughter."

"I should have thought you'd be happy to see your sister again, after all this time." Graham's watchful eyes sought hers.

Again Deborah lifted her shoulders in a shrug. "We've nothing in common. Poor woman, she must feel like a fish out of water here."

"Where is she now?" Conrad asked.

"Probably gone to bed. I said I had to find you both and let you know what was happening. Sorry about abandoning you so abruptly. It all happened so fast . . ."

"Don't mention it." Graham came down from the bridge. "This is a very special occasion. The surprise reunion of two sisters after . . . how many years?"

"Let's not talk about it." Deborah turned away.

"Can't you see this thing's upset her?" Conrad said, frowning at Graham.

"Yes, I can." Graham followed Deborah. "Wait a minute," he called after her, as she started off toward the house. She stopped and turned to wait for them. "Give us a few minutes alone, would you?" he asked Conrad briskly. It sounded more like a command than a request.

Without speaking, Conrad strode away from them, across the lawn.

Deborah turned on Graham. "That was rather rude."

"Not half as rude as you're being. Besides, I've had more than enough of Mr. Hatcher's company."

Deborah gave him one of her glacial looks. "I'd like to remind you that Conrad's not only Daddy's business manager, he's also a close personal friend."

"Great. Frankly, I don't give a damn about Conrad at the moment. It's you I'm concerned about." He grasped her elbow to stop her from taking off on him again and led her back toward the stream. "Your sister's arrival has really upset you, hasn't it?"

She drew away from him. "Not at all. It's my father I'm concerned about. The shock might have made him ill. It was extremely thoughtless of her not to let us know she was coming."

"You speak about her as if she were some stranger arriving on your doorstep. For God's sake, Deborah. This is your sister. Your only sibling."

"Look, Graham," she said, confronting him when they reached the bank of the stream. "Ours is not your average family. I know it's hard for you to understand, but when our mother died my sister and I were separated and raised apart. We're like strangers. We don't know each other."

"And you haven't the slightest desire to get to know her? Aren't you a little curious, at least, to see what she's like?"

Deborah gave a light laugh. "What an old softy you are! No, I've never felt the need to meet my sister. My father and I have managed very well together all these years. So why should we need to change now?" His expression showed that he didn't understand at all. "Don't look so shocked."

"I'm not shocked. I find it sad, that's all. I know I don't always get on that well with my brother and sister, but I'd hate like hell not to have them in my life."

"That's because you've always had them there. I haven't. Besides, Anne's just after my father's money."

"What makes you say that?"

"You didn't see the letter she wrote. Talk about cold as ice. All she wanted was the money."

"Then why is she here now?"

"To wheedle herself in so she can ask for more, I suppose." Deborah wondered where this venom was coming from, bubbling up like liquid mud from within her.

Graham stared silently at the stream, watching the clear water flowing over the brown stones. Deborah hated to see the set lines of his face. Damn Anne! Graham hadn't even met her sister yet and she was already coming between them. She slid her hand into his arm, feeling his tension beneath her fingers. "I could be wrong," she admitted.

He straightened up and smiled down at her. "That's better. Think positive. When do I get to meet her?"

"I think she's having a rest right now. Why don't you stay a little while longer? Then you can meet her when she wakes up."

Graham glanced down at his watch. "I'd arranged with Harry Watts from the village to come and help me clear some of that growth in the walled garden."

That bloody garden! Deborah didn't say the words aloud, but her face must have told him what she was thinking.

"Sorry about that," Graham said. "But I really must spend a few hours on it this weekend or it'll never get done."

"Can't you hire proper gardeners to do it?"

"They're not so easy to find nowadays."

"I thought there were thousands of people desperate for work."

He looked quite shocked. "I couldn't let a gang of

laborers work on it. I need an experienced gardener who knows his stuff."

"What kind of specialist does it need to clear acres of weeds?"

"There are all kinds of rare plants beneath those weeds. I don't want them destroyed. I want to restore the gardens to their original glory. That will take a great deal of time and patience."

Deborah was finding it hard to rein in her annoyance. "Go on back to your blasted garden. Can you manage to drag yourself away from it to have dinner with us tonight?"

"Don't be sarcastic. Of course I can. Then I can meet your sister and your niece." He grinned down at her. "Aunt Deborah. It has a nice ring to it, doesn't it?" he added, laughing.

"Oh, shut up," she said, but she couldn't help joining in his laughter. Graham's good humor was irresistible.

When Anne first awoke from her deep sleep, she wasn't quite sure where she was. She turned her head, expecting to see the familiar clock radio with its red digits, only to find a little silver-cased clock with ornate filigree hands on the dark cabinet beside the bed.

"Ten past three," she murmured, registering the time. Surely that couldn't be right. But when she checked her watch it read the same. She had slept for more than two hours.

She sprang out of bed and immediately became aware of the sounds that had probably woken her. Pulling on a sweater, she went to the window and opened it.

Below her was a terrace overlooking the garden.

Seated on stools set a little apart from each other were Sandy and Ryan, their heads and shoulders hunched over their guitars. They were playing "Mighty Shannon," one of Ryan's most popular songs.

> *Mighty Shannon, flowing free*
> *Past Limerick's shores to the open sea.*

A burst of applause from the group of people clustered nearby greeted the end of the poignant song of an emigrant's memories of the homeland he would never again see. Anne added her applause and everyone looked up.

"Hi, Mom!" Sandy called. "We thought we'd wake you up with a serenade."

"I can't think of a better way of waking me up. Thank you." The look of conspiracy that Sandy and Ryan exchanged delighted her. How could she not be thrilled to see her father and daughter together like this? "I'll be down in a few minutes," she told them and went into the bathroom.

She must have been nuts to have felt the way she did when she first arrived, she thought, as she brushed her teeth, recalling her spasm of envy at the spontaneous affection that had sprung up between Ryan and Sandy. It was scary how fatigue and nerves could affect you. Even if she and her father never came closer to each other, at least this crazy visit had achieved one of its goals.

She hesitated over what to wear, remembering how stunning Deborah had looked, but then decided that she was not here to compete with her sister and pulled on a simple pair of beige cotton slacks and an emerald T-shirt. The bright color looked good with her dark hair and eyes.

But as soon as she left the security of her room, and stood poised at the head of the wide staircase, she thought again of Deborah's casual elegance and wondered if the shirt was too bright. "Oh, who cares?" she said to herself and went down the stairs.

Following the sound of voices, she made her way across the dark hall, through a large room with wood-paneled walls and a painted ceiling, to the French windows that stood open. She hesitated for a moment, and then stepped through.

"There you are." It was Eileen who greeted her first. "Did you have a good sleep?"

"Wonderful. I feel like a new person."

"That's great to hear," Ryan said. He rose from his stool and came to stand by her side. A group of faces turned toward her. "This is my daughter Anne. My eldest daughter."

The faces became bodies, standing up, moving forward to greet her. "This is Joe Calloway and Sonya and . . ." Ryan rattled off the names of the six or so people that gathered around to shake her hand. Then she heard a name she recognized. "And my good friend and manager, Conrad Hatcher."

"Welcome to Hammerton Towers, Anne," said the tall man with the handsome face. "This is an exciting day for all of us." She felt the pressure of his large hand on hers.

"Mr. Hatcher," she said in a cool tone, remembering the icy formality of the letter he had sent with the check. "It was you who wrote—"

"I'd like to introduce you to a friend of Ryan, Rowena Bowles," he said, cutting her off.

She was greeted overeffusively by a woman whose skin was so tanned it was like leather. "Darling! We never realized that Ryan had another lovely daughter." Anne found herself enveloped in heavy perfume and then kissed. She was conscious that Rowena must have left a *moue* of orange lipstick on her cheek, but realized it would appear rude to scrub it off.

When he saw that Ryan was engaged in talking to Sandy again, Mr. Hatcher drew Anne aside. "Forgive me for interrupting you like that," he said quietly. "You may remember that Ryan particularly asked that there be no mention of the money. It causes him embarrassment to think you had to ask for it. I'm sure you understand." He gave her a warm smile. "We're all going to make sure you enjoy your visit."

His welcome was as warm as his smile, erasing the memory of the cold letter. "Thank you." Anne turned from Conrad to her father, who was watching them together. "Thanks for the lovely serenade," she said, giving him a tentative smile.

"Our pleasure." Ryan beamed across at Sandy, who was putting her guitar away in its case. "You have an extremely talented daughter there."

"I know. She must take after her grandfather." Their eyes locked in an unblinking gaze and then, embarrassed, they turned away at the same time. Anne, to look directly at Deborah.

For an instant, her sister had the look of a startled deer blinded by headlights, but she immediately recovered. "Did you sleep well?"

"Very well, thanks. I feel human again."

"Jet lag can make you feel pretty bloody."

They stood, facing each other, searching for things to say.

"Eileen said something about a friend of yours. Graham, I believe his name was."

"Graham Neville. He went home."

"Oh."

"He'll be here for dinner tonight."

"Good."

More uncomfortable silence.

"I visited Granddad Barry before I left," Anne said. "He sent you his love. He also sent you a little present. I'll go and get it."

"No rush." Deborah looked around, as if anxious to escape. "You must be hungry. I don't think you had a proper lunch, did you? Why don't I go and dig up something from the kitchen."

Eileen immediately materialized. "I can do that. You two sit and chat. You must have a lot to catch up on. What would you like?" she asked Anne.

"I wouldn't mind another of those chicken sandwiches. They were great."

"With lettuce and tomato?"

"Please."

"Would you like a beer with it?"

"Just water, thanks."

"How very spartan of you," Deborah said.

Anne didn't like the edge to her sister's voice. "I'm woozy enough today, without making it worse. What does Graham do?"

"Do?" Deborah gazed at her russet-tipped nails. "At the moment, he's spending most of his time renovating or restoring or whatever you call it the house he recently bought, Somerford Hall."

"Is it near here?"

"About five miles away."

"I seem to recall Ryan saying it was old," Anne smiled. "I mean really old."

"You mean not fake, like this place?"

"I gather you don't like this house?"

"It's a joke. A very expensive one, too. My father's poured money into it. Conrad and I told him not to buy it, but he fell in love with it as soon as he saw it."

Anne glanced at the back of her father's manager, who was talking to a young woman with a fabulous figure. His deep voice broke into laughter as he gazed down at the woman's face. "How long has he been Ryan's manager?" She found it easier to call her father by his first name when she spoke of him.

"Almost twenty years. My father was still touring with Avoca when Conrad came along. He's been Daddy's adviser and close friend ever since. Sexy devil, isn't he?"

Anne wasn't sure about that. She merely smiled and then wondered if she appeared a bit prissy for not agreeing.

"He's been trying to get me into bed ever since he first hooked up with Daddy." Deborah laughed. "Poor Conrad."

Anne didn't know what to say. She was extremely relieved when Eileen appeared with a tray of sandwiches and a bowl of fresh fruit.

"So what are you two going to do this afternoon?" Eileen asked as she put the tray in front of Anne on a wooden table.

Anne looked at Deborah, whose lips slid into an attempt at a smile. "I haven't had a chance to think about it," she said. "Your arrival was so unexpected," she added.

"I've got an idea," Sandy said, coming out in time to catch what was going on. "Why don't we go and visit this Somerford place you were talking about?"

"I don't think that's such a good idea," Anne said, seeing Deborah's expression.

"Oh. It's just that I really want to see an old house." Sandy grinned. "I mean a genuine old one. Ryan said there's so much he wants to show me and we've only got nine days."

"Nine days?" Deborah echoed. "Is that all?"

Anne couldn't tell if she was being sarcastic or not. "Sandy has to get back for the master classes she's giving," she explained, "and to get ready for New York. And I can't leave Aunt Beth any longer than that."

"You certainly spent a great deal of money to come for such a short time."

So that was what Deborah was thinking about. Money.

"It was my idea to come here," Sandy said. "And Mom said that my grandfather had sent the money for me, so I could decide what to do with it. I know it's extravagant, but it's worth it so we can all be together."

Watching Deborah's face, Anne saw her expression change as if something had suddenly occurred to her. For the first time her sister's mouth curved into a genuine smile, making her look truly beautiful. In that instant, Anne recalled how everyone had been attracted by that lovely smile, even when they were children. She also saw now, from the viewpoint of an adult, that Deborah had inherited her father's smile.

"If it means that much to you," Deborah said softly, as if she and Sandy were alone on the terrace together, "then you did the right thing." She caught Anne looking at her and the moment evaporated. "All right," she said briskly. "Why not? We'll drive over to Somerford. Usually Graham only comes down here at weekends so this would be a good day for a visit. I'll give him a ring to let him know we're coming." She went inside, leaving Anne and Sandy alone together.

Sandy picked up a ripe banana and peeled it. "I hope she didn't mind me asking."

"I think she was glad, really. She was at a loss to know what to do with us. With me, particularly."

Sandy sat on the edge of the table. "Give it time, Mom."

"At the rate we're going it'll take years. Still, I'm glad we came for your sake. You really like your grandfather?"

"I can't believe him! He's like someone my age. And he's a really good musician, too. He's going to show me how he worked out the fingering for 'Mighty Shannon.'" She flipped her long hair back from her face. "I just wish we had more time."

"Well, maybe we can get together again sometime. Meanwhile, make the best of it."

"I will. He's taking me to London on Monday."

Anne forced her face not to register her inner emotion at this news. But Sandy knew her too well. "Oh, I'm sure he means you to come as well, Mom," she said with all the insouciant cruelty of youth.

"We'll see."

Deborah returned. "No reply. Graham must be out in that damned garden of his. Let's go, anyway. Ready?"

Anne hastily swallowed down a piece of sandwich and grabbed another one. Her sister would make a good sergeant-major. "I'll just get my bag," she said.

"I suggest you change into trainers or some sort of walking shoes," Deborah said, glancing at Anne's light sandals. "Graham's garden is a jungle."

Chapter 10

Deborah hadn't exaggerated. The gardens at Somerford Hall were, indeed, like a jungle. As they drove over the unsurfaced lane that led to the house, bouncing in and out of the ruts, Anne gazed at the tangled bushes and the waist-high grass that grew close to the track. Frequently, branches scraped along the side of Deborah's Porsche. Each time this happened Deborah cursed. She was definitely not happy with her friend's new acquisition.

But although Anne was appalled at the way in which the parkland had been allowed to run wild and the gardens overgrown by weeds, something about the place caught her imagination. "It's like Sleeping Beauty," she said, smiling over her shoulder at Sandy, who sat in the back.

Deborah frowned, not understanding. But Sandy understood immediately. "Yeah. But the prince wouldn't make a dent in this stuff with his sword. He'd need a harvester to cut through it."

Now Deborah got it. "Tell Graham that. At the rate he's going he'll be as old as Methuselah before he's finished."

"Surely he's not trying to clear all this by himself, is he?" Anne asked.

"He's employing one professional gardener and a couple of helpers, that's all."

"Good luck."

"Exactly."

As they turned the last corner, the old house stood before them. Anne's breath caught in her throat. She had been expecting an ornate medieval castle, but this was a delightful two-story brick and timber house, with gables. Two and a half storys, in fact, as there were windows tucked into the inverted V of the gables, their tiny lattice-panes covered with grime.

Deborah ran up the steps and hammered on the thick oak door. "Graham!" She turned the handle and the door opened, rusty hinges creaking as it swung wide. Gray dust rose from the flagstone floor as they walked inside.

"Wow!" said Sandy.

The hall they stood in was immense and dark, the only light issuing from a beautiful old window set in a bay of ornately carved stonework.

"Graham!" Deborah called again. Her voice echoed around the vaulted roof, but no one answered.

"Do you want me to go around the back?" Anne asked.

"You can try. He could be anywhere." Deborah's casual tone needled Anne. "Come on, Sandy, let me show you this old ruin."

Anne felt effectually shut out. She turned and went outside again. Seeing a patch where the undergrowth had been stripped away from the redbrick wall she found a wooden door. She pushed it open and walked down the little pathway that led to the rear of the house.

Here, again, nature had reclaimed the garden. The fragrance of meadow flowers and briar roses wafted to her. A soft breeze swayed the wild grasses that had taken over what had probably once been a verdant lawn. She stood for several minutes marveling at the wild beauty of the place until the sound of whistling alerted her to the fact that there was someone nearby. The whistling was accompanied by a strange rhythmic swishing.

She took a few more steps along the narrow path until she came to a stretch of grass at the rear of the house. There, having cleared a large part of the lawn already, was the gardener, wielding a scythe. Anne recalled seeing her mother's uncle using a scythe on a prairie wheat field when she was a child. Nowadays, to see a scythe actually in use was pretty unusual.

It was like looking at an old woodcut. The gardener was stripped to the waist, the sunlight glinting on the golden hairs on his chest and arms, which were bronzed by the sun. He was so totally immersed in his work, the muscled arms and scythe moving rhythmically, that she was afraid to disturb him. Besides, she found herself strangely entranced by this old-fashioned rural picture, which could have been happening two hundred years ago.

When the man paused and bent down to take a brown bottle from the Thermos bag on the ground, she came forward and said, "Hi."

His head jerked up. "God, you startled me." His accent was not at all the rural English she'd expected.

"Sorry. I didn't want to interrupt you when you were working. That scythe looks pretty lethal."

He glanced at the curved blade. "It is. It needs to be."

"You've got quite a job here."

"You can say that again." He put down the beer bottle, reached for his denim shirt that hung on a spade stuck into the ground, and pulled it on. "Were you looking for me?" he asked with a rather quizzical expression on his angular face.

"I—that is, we were looking for Graham. Graham Neville. Deborah—"

"Ah, you must be Anne, Deborah's sister. She told me you were visiting from Canada." He rubbed his right hand on his jeans and held it out. "Excuse the dirt. I'm Graham."

"Oh!" Anne grinned. "I thought you were the gardener."

"That's exactly what I am. Actually, the gardener's assistant. My main gardener is working on the rose garden down there." He nodded his head in the direction of the far wall. "He feels it's safer to let me do the hard labor, in case I dig up something precious and throw it away."

"Is that likely?" Anne asked, keenly interested. "What sort of precious things could be here?"

"Somerford has never been modernized. And the family that lived here for centuries was renowned for its hermitlike qualities, so there are hundreds of old plants here. Roses and spring bulbs, all kinds of shrubs and perennials that were thought to be extinct because of modern breeding." His amber eyes glowed with excitement. "You are standing in what I hope will become a living garden museum. We even have a couple of ancient mulberry trees over there and apricot vines on the kitchen garden wall. Apricocks, Shakespeare called them."

His enthusiasm was catching. "Wow!" Anne gazed around. "I've read all about the famous English gardens, of course. Hidcote and Sissinghurst . . ."

"Have you? In far-off Canada? Well, well." He looked impressed. "Let's hope Somerford will be counted among them one day. Unfortunately, at the rate we're going I doubt even my great-grandchildren will see it finished."

She raised her eyebrows at him. "Great-grandchildren?" He looked as if he were in his early forties, his gold-brown hair only slightly flecked with silver.

"No, I'm not Dorian Gray. My son's only twenty. But that's my point. It's going to take decades to get this place sorted."

Anne looked around. "Oh, I don't know. Once you get all this cut down you'll be surprised how quickly the new growth will flourish, as long as you use the right lawn seed."

He looked even more impressed. "I'm encouraged by your optimism."

"I'd love to see the rose garden."

"Come on, I'll show it to you. Of course it's far from perfect, but it's better than this. By next year we hope to have it completely cleared of weeds, so that the light can get to the bushes and trees."

"I don't want to take you away from your work."

"I'm glad to get a break from it." He began walking across the part of the lawn that had been cleared. "You seem to be a garden lover as well . . . ?"

"It's my job. I work with plants. I'm also a land-scape gardener."

Graham halted to stare at her. "You're not," he said incredulously.

"Yes. That's why I find this all so fascinating." Anne sighed. "How I envy you. Working here would be like a dream come true for any gardener."

"It's a bloody nightmare. A never-ending war against weeds and tangled branches. Nature grown wild is a tough enemy to fight, I can tell you. How did you come to be a gardener?"

"Genes, I suppose. My mother's family owned a garden center. I took horticulture for a year and later joined my aunt in running the center."

"I didn't know that." He frowned. "Deborah never talks about her life in Canada."

"I don't suppose she does," Anne said lightly.

"One thing I do know is that your sister definitely has not inherited the garden gene. And speaking of Deborah, here she is."

Deborah and Sandy approached them from the opposite direction. "There you are," Deborah said. "Where on earth were you?"

"Scything," Graham said.

"Oh! I should have known." Deborah looked from him to Anne. "So you two have already met."

"Your sister thought I was the gardener."

"I'm not surprised." Deborah smiled at Graham and moved across Anne to kiss him, as if marking her territory. "Yuck, you're all sweaty."

"The sweat of honest toil, my darling. Easily washed off. Which I shall do as soon as I show Anne the rose garden." He swung around. "Sorry. I didn't mean to ignore you," he said to Sandy. "Hi, I'm Graham."

"Sandy."

"Hello, Sandy. You look like your mother."

"Ryan says I look even more like my grandmother."

"My mother," Deborah quickly explained to Graham.

"Whose family has a garden center, I hear. How is it that you dislike rural life, my pet, when gardening is your family's business?"

Deborah gave Anne a fleeting glance veiled by her thick eyelashes. She was not pleased. "That's probably why. I'm not into mud and rocks, thank you. I've taken Sandy over the house, by the way."

"Great. Let me show them the rose garden. Then I'll have a quick shower and change, and come back to Hammerton with you."

"The house is wonderful." Sandy said. "You'd love it, Mom."

"I'd love to see it," Anne said tentatively. "If there's time," she added, sensing Deborah's impatience.

Graham glanced at his watch. "Plenty of time. I'll give you the guided tour, then I'll clean myself up for my lady here." He winked at Deborah, who shook her head at him and then smiled.

The sexual chemistry between the two was palpable. Graham was an extremely attractive man. He and Deborah made a perfect couple, both tall and golden. Anne forced away the sudden twinge of envy she felt. After all, Marco was just as attractive as Graham Neville, in his own dark Latin way . But she doubted that anyone thought of her and Marco as a perfect couple. There was too much tension and unresolved conflict between them.

Graham led the way down the gravel path—that was more weeds than gravel—through another opening in yet another redbrick wall, and into the walled garden.

Anne released a vocal sigh of delight. Here, in the rose garden, the clearing was advanced. Although the lawn was not yet well established, there were patches of emerald giving a hint of how it would look in the future. It was the roses, however, that delighted the senses. Roses of every hue and size, from miniatures with tiny white and pink flowers to tall rose trees, shaped into balls, all covered with extravagant blossoms.

"What a gorgeous smell!" Sandy said.

Anne laughed aloud. "It's not just one smell. It's all kinds of different fragrances mixed together." Dizzy with delight, she lifted her face to Graham. "I've never smelled anything like this before. Never *seen* anything like it."

He was just as delighted with her reaction. "Come with me," he said, taking her arm. "There's a plain single-bloom rose over here, the white one tinged with pink, which has the most heavenly fragrance." He led her to a corner and held one of the roses so that she could smell it. "What do you think of that?"

The scent was powerful, sweet, and sensuous. "Amazing."

"That's a damask rose. It dates back to Elizabethan times."

"Modern roses don't have that scent."

"That's because they're bred for looks, not fragrance. All show, no substance."

Anne bent again to smell one of the single-bloom creamy-white roses, their petals tinged with the palest pink. Graham took a pair of secateurs that hung from his leather belt to cut a rose from the bush, and handed it to her. "Careful. The thorns are pretty lethal."

As Anne took it from him, she caught sight of her sister's face. Her expression sent hot blood into Anne's cheeks. Flustered, she muttered her thanks to Graham and promptly handed the rose to Sandy.

As they walked back to the house, Graham and Deborah leading the way, Anne felt Deborah's hostility emanating like laser beams from her rigid back. She knew, with a sinking heart, that in sharing in Graham's enthusiasm for his garden she'd made a bad start with her sister.

Chapter 11

For the rest of their time at Somerford, Anne kept her responses low-key, hiding the fact that she loved the house as much as she did the garden. It, too, would be a heck of a challenge to renovate, but also a great pleasure. However, instead of exclaiming over the molded-plaster ceiling in the gallery and the linenfold oak paneling in the dining hall, she smiled and said how nice everything was.

She hated the word *nice*, but she felt she should hide her wonder and excitement at the house's beauty.

So good was she at hiding her feelings that Graham halted in the long gallery, the dust motes dancing in the slanting beams of sunlight from the oriel window, and said to Deborah with a faintly ironic smile, "I have the feeling your sister's bored to tears with my old house."

Sandy flipped back her hair and frowned at her mother. "Graham's right."

Anne had to grip her bottom lip between her teeth to stop herself from saying, *No, I'm not at all bored. I really love this place.* "Sorry," she said, "It's not that I'm not interested. I'm just tired, that's all."

Her reticence obviously worked because Deborah said, quite kindly, "Traveling can do that to you.

Besides, this house is a mess. As far as I'm concerned, it's impossible to fix."

Anne saw how Graham's jaw tensed in response, but Deborah didn't seem to notice.

"We should get back to Hammerton, Graham. I promised my father we wouldn't be long. Why don't I drive Anne and Sandy back? Then you can follow on when you've showered and changed."

"Good idea." He gave Anne a rueful smile. "Sorry to have bored you on your first day in England."

Swallowing down her protestations, Anne smiled and shook her head.

"I can see you were just as impressed with the house as I am," Deborah said to her, as they drove away.

"It has potential, I'm sure," Anne said diplomatically.

"I'm sure it has, for someone who has pots of time to spend on it, but it's becoming an obsession with Graham."

"I think it's a gorgeous house," Sandy protested. "It even has a minstrel's gallery."

"Maybe you should play some Elizabethan music there," Anne said, "John Dowland or something like that, just to get the right atmosphere."

"Not a very good idea," Deborah said dryly. "The gallery floorboards are riddled with dry rot. Graham told me they'll have to be replaced."

Realizing that Deborah would put a damper on anything they said about the house, Anne changed the subject. "I take it rebuilding old houses isn't Graham's profession."

"Hardly. He owns a chain of exclusive hotels. His father started the business when he developed the ancestral home into a luxury hotel and leisure center."

"Their home?"

"Yes. A lovely old Elizabethan house and estate in the Cotswolds. It had been in the family for centuries. It became the flagship for their hotel line, but Graham's father eventually sold it. Made a mint from it."

It sounded rather ruthless to Anne, but she made no comment. "Graham said he had a son."

"That's right. Keith. He's visiting his mother in France at present."

"Oh." Anne didn't like to ask more, but Deborah gave her the information.

"Monique and Graham have been divorced for about ten years. She's an art dealer in Paris." Deborah glanced at Sandy in the rearview mirror. "Shame Keith's not here. You'd have liked him, Sandy. He's very good-looking. A bit wild, but that's just his age. His mother spoils him thoroughly."

"Has Graham's ex-wife married again?"

"Twice. Just like Ryan."

Anne hesitated, then plunged in, grasping the chance while she had it. "What were Ryan's wives like?"

Deborah swerved to avoid a rabbit that had suddenly dashed in front of the car. "Nearly had rabbit pie there. What did you say?"

"I was asking about Ryan's other wives." Now, the question sounded blatantly nosy.

Deborah shrugged. "They were all right, I suppose. I was in boarding school most of the time so I didn't get to know them that well."

"Boarding school? I hadn't realized—"

Deborah gave a little grunt. "I suppose you'd been imagining father and daughter living an idyllic life together."

"Well, not exactly, but—"

"If you only knew, you might discover that your life hadn't been that rough after all." Catching sight of Sandy's rounded eyes in the mirror, Deborah laughed. "What a load of drivel we're talking here. I'll tell you something, I wouldn't change anything in my life now. I have absolutely all I could want. A great career. A terrific man—as long as I can get him away from that damned house of his. And I've done it all through my own initiative."

Anne bit back the retort that her sister's privileged education and contacts wouldn't have hindered her, either. Not to mention her father's money.

"And I'm about to start a big new business venture," Deborah went on. "Who could ask for more?"

Anne looked out the window at the fields speeding past. Who, indeed? Here was she, struggling to keep the decrepit family business from going under, trying to help her daughter, and unable to launch her own landscaping business because of the demands of time and money. All her life she'd accepted what she was given and done the best she could with it, without envy of those who were better off than she was. She had always looked for the positive side of life, whatever happened. But now, as she sat in her sister's Porsche, listening to her bragging about her success and her wealthy lover, envy rose like bile in her throat, threatening to choke her.

She sensed Deborah glancing at her stony profile. "Sorry," Deborah said in a low voice. "That was pretty insensitive of me."

Anne was amazed. Tears pricked her eyes. "That's okay."

She was relieved to see that they were turning into the driveway of Ryan's house. She'd had too much togetherness with her sister for one day. Take it slowly, she told herself. But, as she stepped from the car, Anne was beginning to wonder why she was doing this. She didn't know if she could even come to like this person who seemed to have absolutely nothing in common with her, let alone love her like a sister. Yet, still, there were little flashes of sincerity or sympathy from Deborah, as had happened just now, which told her to keep trying.

Time alone would tell.

"There you are at last." Ryan stood on the front steps, beaming at them. "I was about to come and look for you."

"You know Graham when he gets going." Deborah went to her father and kissed him.

As she watched how easily her sister embraced her father, and how he hugged her against him, Anne felt another niggling little pang of envy. She stood there, waiting, wondering what she should do. Join them or hang back until they suggested something.

"So, what did you think of Somerford, Anne?"

"She liked the garden, but was bored with the house," Deborah said, walking to the front door.

"Who asked you?" Ryan said.

Anne laughed aloud, but stopped laughing when she saw Deborah staring at her. "Sorry, but out of nowhere I can remember Daddy—Ryan always saying that to you."

Ryan's eyes lit up. "You're right. Debbie used to—"

"Don't call me Debbie."

"Oh, very sorry, my lady. When I used to come home I'd ask Anne what she'd been up to and she'd try to tell me, but you, Debbie, would run over your sister like an express train, always wanting to tell me first about your day or your week."

"I must have been just a baby then. After all, Anne and I weren't together after I was four, were we?"

"True. But even then you liked to take center stage." Ryan turned away abruptly. "Let's go in. It looks like rain."

He was right. Spots of rain darkened the stone steps. The clouds had started to gather when they'd been looking over Graham's house, so that it had been hard to see the rooms properly, with such inadequate lighting.

When they went inside the sound of laughter and music came from across the hall.

"Come on in and have a drink," Ryan said. "I've invited a couple of neighbors over to meet you and Sandy."

Anne didn't feel like dealing with any more strangers at the moment. It was tough enough trying to get to know those members of her own family who were, in essence, also strangers.

"I'm a bit dirty," she said. "Would you mind if I went up and had a shower first?"

"I think I'll do that, too," Deborah said. "That house is absolutely filthy."

"Okay, but get a move on." Ryan smiled at Anne. "I want everyone to meet my other daughter."

Anne returned the smile, but wondered when she would get a chance to be alone with her father. It was as if Ryan kept surrounding himself with more and more people, using them as a barrier between her and himself.

Give it time, Anne told herself, yet again.

"You coming in, Sandy?" Ryan asked.

"Sure. Why not?" said gregarious Sandy. "As

long as your friends won't mind me like this. I can go and change later."

"You look fine. Come on then."

Anne and Deborah watched them go. "He really likes your daughter," Deborah said.

"I'm glad."

"She's a lovely girl."

"I think so, but then I'm biased."

"You're lucky to have her."

Anne was warmed by the sincerity in her sister's voice, but there was a tinge of something else there. Surely it couldn't be envy. She couldn't imagine this elegant woman, slender as an arum lily, wanting to risk her figure by bearing a child.

"You could still have children, if you wanted to," she said.

Deborah's laugh was filled with scorn. "You must be joking. The last thing I want is to be saddled with a baby at my age. I wouldn't mind a ready-made daughter like Sandy, though. At this age it's all fun to have a daughter. Shopping for clothes, planning their lives."

"You need money for clothes. And you don't have much say in planning their lives at this stage. You just give advice when you can, and worry about whether they're doing the right thing."

Deborah started up the stairs. "I shouldn't think Sandy's much of a worry to you."

"Oh, there have been times. Wanting to chuck in university because she thought it was a waste of time. Boyfriends . . ." Anne stopped, seeing that Deborah wasn't interested in hearing all this mundane stuff.

"She's an adult now. It's a shame Graham's son's not here, he'd give her a good time, show her around. It's time you untied her from the apron strings and let her have some fun."

Anne bridled as she followed her sister down the carpeted corridor. "She has a lot of hard work before she can find time to 'have fun' as you put it."

Deborah halted at Anne's door and turned to confront her. "We're not at all alike, you and I, are we? It's hard to believe we're even related."

Anne stood in the unlit corridor, wishing she could postpone this conversation, but she knew that she had to grasp at any chance she had of getting to know her sister better, however inconvenient the time or location. "I guess so. You're blond and tall. I'm dark and short—and not half as beautiful."

Deborah ignored the compliment. "I wasn't talking about looks. I like to grab hold of life and take chances. You prefer to sit at home and worry."

Anne's eyes narrowed. "I haven't had much chance to sit at home, as you put it. I was a single parent who had to work damned hard. No handouts for me."

Deborah stared at her, an annoying half-smile curving her lips. "Talking of handouts, why exactly are you here? I thought Daddy had sent you what you wanted. Money for your daughter's education."

Anne had to hold back the retort that fifteen thousand dollars wasn't exactly going to go that far over several years in New York. "I'm very grateful to him for it. It will be a big help."

"I should think it would be."

Anne's face flushed with anger. "I didn't come here for more money, if that's what you're thinking."

"That's exactly what I was thinking. You're obviously hard up for money and you know that Ryan's pretty well off. You probably thought you had a right to it, considering he's your father, right?"

"I've never asked him for a dime before. This was the first time."

"Yes, I know. But having asked once, it makes it easier the next time."

Anne edged past Deborah to open her bedroom door and switch on the light. "This isn't getting us anywhere," she said wearily. "I should have known you wouldn't understand."

"How can I understand when you won't tell me why you came here without any notice? Not even a phone call to let us know you were coming. You have to admit that was rather odd."

Anne turned her back on Deborah and sat down on the straight-backed chair that she preferred to the overstuffed ruby velvet loveseat. "I was afraid that if I called Ryan he'd make up an excuse not to see me. After all, he never wrote to me or even called me all those years, did he? For that matter, nor did you."

Deborah picked up a brush from the dressing table and examined the silver backing, avoiding Anne's steady gaze. "We didn't know each other, did we? It would be like writing to a stranger, only worse. It's been too long. Too much water under the bridge, as they say."

"Now there's another difference between us," Anne said in a low voice. "I've never given up thinking about my sister. I've dreamed of meeting you and my father again. Literally. When I was a kid I used to lie in bed at night, making up stories about how you and he would arrive on Christmas Day, carrying piles of presents, wrapped in shiny foil paper, all for me. Or how you would both send me a parcel for my birthday or even just a card when I became a teenager." She gave her sister a bitter smile. "Poor Aunt Beth knew that however much she tried, however special the party she arranged or birthday cake she made, it was never enough for me. It could never measure up to my dreams of spending a birthday with my father and sister."

Deborah's tanned face looked patchy as if the color was draining in spots from it. "You were bloody lucky to get cakes and parties. I spent most of my birthdays in boarding school. Even if my father did send a parcel—which most of the time he forgot to do until weeks afterward—I had to share everything with all the girls, even my worst enemies. So you can just stop wallowing in all that self-pity."

"Is that what it is?"

"That's what it sounds like to me. It's wasted on me, I can tell you. I've no time for it."

Anne got up and went to the window, determined not to turn this into a shouting match. She turned around. "I didn't come all this way to fight with you. I guess we'll have to agree to differ. You asked me why I came here. I came to get to know my sister and my father again. Before it's too late."

Deborah frowned. "What does that mean? Are you dying of an incurable disease or something?"

Anne had to laugh. "No, of course not. I just meant that if I didn't do it now, on impulse, I might never do it. It's getting close to my fortieth birthday. That's a sort of turning point, isn't it?" She sighed heavily. "It was all Sandy's idea, really. When the check arrived she said it would be great to use some of it to come and see you. At first I didn't want to do it, but she persuaded me by saying how much she wanted to meet her grandfather and aunt."

Deborah winced. "Not so much of the aunt bit, please."

"Oh, don't be stupid. People can be aunts in their teens."

"I'm not in my teens. I'm thirty-four."

"Thirty-four?" Anne grinned at her. "Who are you kidding? You're thirty-seven in August."

"Oh, God, that's all I need. A sister who blabs about my birthday to everyone. Just remember, Graham thinks I'm thirty-four."

"Okay. Suits me fine. That makes me thirty-eight instead of forty next birthday."

Their eyes met and they both broke into laughter. Deborah turned and walked briskly to the door as if she didn't want to be caught in this lighter mood with her sister. She paused, her hand on the door handle. "He won't talk about the past. In all these years he's barely mentioned our mother to me."

Anne's breath caught in her throat for a moment. Then she stood up. "Aunt Beth's the same way. She won't talk to me about Janine. I guess they both loved her so much that it hurts even to talk about her. Or it used to. Now they're sort of programmed to avoid thinking or talking about her."

"I suppose that's it." Deborah's eyes fixed on a space above Anne's head. "I know nothing about her."

"I've brought pictures with me," Anne said eagerly. "Do you want—"

"No." Panic flashed in Deborah's blue eyes. "Not yet, anyway. Let's take it slowly. It's all a bit . . ." She waved her hands in the air. ". . . a bit too much, if you know what I mean."

"Yes, I do." Anne hesitated for a moment. "Debbie?"

"Yes?"

"I'm sorry I didn't write to you. I should have done."

"I didn't write, either."

"I was the older sister. I should have written first. I was the one who used to look out for you."

Deborah gave her a faint smile. "That was a very long time ago. Shall I come and fetch you when I go down?"

"Please. I hate walking into a roomful of strangers."

"You'd better get used to it if you're staying here for a while. Ryan likes to surround himself with people."

"So I've noticed."

"Half an hour be enough time for you?"

"That's fine. Oh, what should I wear?"

"We usually dress up a bit for Saturday dinner. Ryan likes to play the lord of the haunted manor then. What have you got?" Deborah glanced at the old-fashioned wardrobe standing against the wall.

"I think I'll wear my brown cotton pantsuit," Anne said hastily, not wanting Deborah to see how few clothes she'd brought with her.

"Brown? You should be wearing dramatic colors with your dark coloring. Reds and oranges."

"It's a rather nice reddish-brown. Rust, really," Anne said. Deborah didn't seem convinced. "I've got a yellow suit," Anne ventured.

"Let's see it."

Anne showed her the lemon cotton suit. "I bought this for Sandy's graduation." Although she doubted that Deborah would approve of any of her clothes, she rejoiced in the fact that they were here, together. Wasn't this what normal sisters did, talked about clothes?

"That's not bad. But I still think you need something brighter." Deborah hesitated and then said, "Why don't you come up to London with me on Monday? Then we can do some shopping. We'll bring Sandy with us."

"I think she said that she and Ryan were going to London."

"Oh, he won't mind. What about it?"

Anne hesitated. Shopping in London was definitely not on her budget for this trip.

"My treat," Deborah said, filling the awkward silence.

"Thanks, but I couldn't—"

"I love buying clothes. Besides, it's July Sale time. Lots of big bargains. Indulge me."

Anne was torn between her desire to pursue this tenuous accord with her sister and her pride. She hadn't come all this way to play the poor sister to Deborah's Lady Bountiful. Besides, she wanted to spend time with her father, as well. "What about Ryan? What will he think if I suddenly rush off to London after I've just arrived?"

"He'll be delighted. Wait and see."

Chapter 12

When they told Ryan, his reaction was exactly as Deborah had predicted. He grinned at both his daughters. "Shopping in London? What a grand idea! And it will be my treat, so keep the bills, Lady Deborah."

Anne caught Conrad Hatcher's quick frown. As their eyes met, she felt a chill between her shoulder blades. If Deborah was worrying that her sister might be after Ryan's money, this man was certain of it. Anne supposed it was natural for a business manager to be careful of his client's assets. She wanted to assure him that she was not the money-hungry daughter he thought her to be, but, recalling the letter he'd written to her, decided that it was best left unsaid.

Conrad was smiling at Sandy now, turning the full-beam power of his magnetism on her. "How did you enjoy your visit to Somerford, Miss Dysan?"

"Please call me Sandy. We loved it. Especially the minstrels' gallery. Aunt Deborah was saying it needed new flooring, but it was still beautiful, with all that lovely wood-carving."

"Your aunt," Conrad said, with an emphasis on the word to tease Deborah, "is a killjoy. I can imagine you sitting in the gallery with your guitar in your lap, dressed in a green velvet gown, with ribbons in your hair."

Sandy laughed up at him, drawing her hand through her hair in an unconsciously flirtatious gesture. "Exactly."

"We'll have to try to persuade Mr. Neville to fix the flooring immediately just to fulfill your wish," Conrad said, continuing the flirtation.

"I don't think so," Sandy said. "We're just staying here for a week . . . well, another eight days."

"Is that all?" Conrad hid his relief well, but Anne, watching him closely, caught it before his expression changed to the appropriate disappointment. "What a shame to come all this way for only a week."

"It's far too short," Ryan agreed. "We'll have to see what we can do to persuade them to change their minds, eh, Conrad?"

"I'm sorry, but we can't," Anne said. "I promised Aunt Beth I wouldn't leave her for very long."

"Surely she'd understand," Ryan protested.

"You have to remember that we were in New York for a few days before we came here. As it is, I feel guilty for going away at our busiest time."

"Maybe we can arrange something," Ryan said. "Hire someone to help her."

He seemed to think that money could solve everything. "We've done that already. Thank you, but she needs me there," Anne said firmly. "She's not as physically able as she used to be. That makes her worry more, especially if I'm not there to calm her down."

"Then we'll have to make the best of it, won't we?" Ryan said, to Anne's relief. "There's so much to show you that I'm not sure where to begin. We

must draw up a plan of the places we should take
you to see."

Anne was about to say something, but Ryan didn't
give her the chance.

"Tuesday's free, isn't it?" he said, turning to
Eileen, who was washing glasses in the bar sink.
"We could drive to Hampton Court."

Her brown eyes twinkling at Anne, who had taken
up a dish towel to help her dry the glasses, Eileen
said, "You have that meeting with that fellow Mal-
oney about the band from Killarney you were interested in." She was obviously far more than just
Ryan's housekeeper, Anne realized.

"Cancel it. Make it Wednesday morning, instead."

Anne wanted to tell Ryan she'd come to England
to see him, not castles and palaces. But at least she'd
be spending the day with him, wouldn't she?

"There's a magnificent new garden at the palace,"
a voice said from behind them. Graham had arrived.

"Trust you to be interested in a new garden,"
Deborah said, taking his arm. She lifted her face to
be kissed. Graham willingly complied. "You can
count me out on that expedition."

"You know, I might just join you, Ryan, if you
wouldn't mind," Graham said. "I haven't seen the new
garden yet and I've been meaning to ever since it was
finished a couple of years ago." He turned to Anne.
"They've created a replica of the seventeenth-century
garden that was originally there," he explained.

"I'm sure Anne isn't interested," Deborah said.

This time Anne had to tell the truth. "I really am,"
she said apologetically. "It's just my kind of thing.
Why don't you come with us?"

"Because I have work to do, unlike the rest of
you, it seems."

The remark was intended mainly for Graham, but he gave Deborah a sunny smile. "You're a workaholic, my darling. This is July. We've both slogged away all year. I intend to take some time off this month."

"But you'll stay in London, won't you?"

"I'm not so sure about that. I think I'll set up a bed at Somerford so that I can stay overnight when I'm working there."

"It's all right for some," Deborah said, her voice light, but her eyes like bright blue marbles.

"Why don't you move in here?" Ryan suggested to Graham. "Plenty of room. Everyone's leaving tomorrow, after lunch. Except for Anne and Sandy, of course."

"I don't know about moving in, but I'd like to use your equipment, if you don't mind. The fax machine . . . that sort of thing."

"With pleasure." Ryan turned to Deborah. "Come on, love, stay here with us. How often do your sister and niece come to visit?"

"Never . . . until now," Deborah said pointedly.

"I'd really like you to stay, if you could," Anne said quietly. "We don't have that much time."

"Please," said Sandy.

"Oh, all right. But if I do take time off I'll have to go into the office for a couple of hours when we're in town on Monday."

"Are you coming to Hampton Court with us?" Graham asked.

"I'd rather not."

"Then why not stay in London Monday night and catch up with work on Tuesday before you come back here," Graham suggested.

"What about Anne and Sandy? How do they get back?"

"I'll drive you all to town Monday morning and bring them back here in the evening," Graham said. "If that's okay with everyone."

It was agreed that this was a good plan, although Deborah didn't appear quite as enthusiastic as the rest of them.

"If you change your mind about Tuesday you can come back with us," Anne said, not wanting to cause trouble between her sister and Graham.

"No, it's a good plan. We'll think of something to do on Wednesday," Deborah said.

How about just staying home and talking, maybe looking at photos, Anne felt like saying. Both her father and sister seemed determined to avoid any intimate conversation with her.

Later that evening, after they'd had a barbecue on the terrace, and everyone was feeling mellow from good food and wine, Conrad asked Sandy to play for them again. He had been attentive to her all evening, sitting next to her while they ate, his arm across the back of her chair. Smiling up at him, her face far too close to his for Anne's liking, Sandy agreed to play. This time, at Ryan's insistence, she played alone.

As Anne sat in a shadowy corner enjoying the familiar sight of her daughter bent over her guitar, her long hair falling to hide her face, she felt as if she were in a dream, not reality. Here she was, listening to her daughter playing Granados, with her father and sister beside her, as if it were an everyday occurrence.

"Penny for your thoughts," someone said in her ear, when Sandy stopped to tune her guitar. Anne turned to find Graham pulling up a chair behind her.

"Just daydreaming. Probably the effects of too little sleep and too much wine. I find it hard to believe that I'm really here."

"I should imagine it's a shock for everyone concerned. Deborah's been acting strangely all day. And Ryan's remarkably quiet. He's usually far more exuberant than this."

Anne had to smile. "I seem to have had a bad effect on them."

"Not at all. It's very much overdue."

Anne turned to him. "Do you think so? Did I do the right thing to come?" Although this man was a total stranger, she found herself eager for his opinion.

"Definitely. I know very little about your past history. It's not something Deborah wants to talk about. I have the feeling that hers was not a happy childhood."

Anne frowned. "Really?" She was tempted to say that Deborah had been the one who had been chosen to live with her father, while she had been left behind, but she left it unsaid. If Deborah wanted to perpetuate the myth of an unhappy childhood, what was the point of antagonizing her by playing the game of *Mine was worse than yours*? "I don't think either of us had the perfect childhood," she said lightly. "It's tough losing a mother when you're young."

"How old were you?"

"I was just seven. Debbie was four."

Graham smiled. "Hard to imagine her as *Debbie*."

"Sorry. I'm so used to calling her that it's hard to remember she doesn't like it."

"Why didn't you two sisters stay together? Wasn't it rather odd to separate you?"

"I don't know. I've tried to find out, but Aunt

Beth never wanted to talk about it. The only other close family member left now is my grandfather, Ryan's father. He doesn't like to talk about the past, either. I have a bunch of questions about my past and my family, but no one seems to want to answer them."

"What are you two talking about?" Deborah said from behind them. She slid her arm into Graham's.

"Your murky past," Graham teased her.

It was the wrong thing to say. Deborah's eyes narrowed at Anne. "If you must talk about me behind my back I wish to God you'd keep it in the family."

Anne felt her face flare up and was glad of the semidarkness to cover it. "Sorry."

"Blame me, not Anne," Graham said. "I was asking her questions."

"Anne knows nothing about me. If you want to ask questions, ask me, not her."

"You evade any inquiries about your past."

"That's because it's nobody's business but mine."

Graham smiled ruefully at Anne. "See what I mean?"

Deborah drew Graham away, leaving Anne alone. As she listened to Sandy's guitar, the notes of one of the Spanish dances that she often played as an encore vibrating in the soft summer air, Anne wondered how on earth she was going to get to know her sister in just nine days.

The applause for Sandy's playing died away. As everyone stood up to go inside, Anne saw Conrad take Sandy's arm and whisper in her ear. Sandy nodded and laughed, her face flushed and excited in the flickering light from the lanterns. She carefully set her guitar into its case, and then she and Conrad went into the house.

Cool it, Anne told herself. Sandy's not a kid anymore. She's twenty-one, old enough to take care of herself. But she doubted that her daughter had ever come across a slick operator like Conrad Hatcher before.

She sat for several minutes, staring out into the darkness, listening to the sounds of the night, the rustle of the wind in the trees, an owl hooting, a low rumble of distant thunder. The rainstorm they'd had earlier had moved on, but still the pungent smell of wet earth and grass was in the air. She breathed it all in, reveling in the smells and sounds of her first night in England.

Ryan opened the conservatory door and peered out. "What are you doing sitting out here all alone?"

"Enjoying the night air. Too lazy to get up and go to bed."

"So soon? It's not ten o'clock yet."

"I know, but I'd like to catch up on my sleep so that I feel fresh for tomorrow. Do you know where Sandy went?" she asked him casually.

Deborah joined them in time to hear her question. "Conrad took her to a club on the river near Marlow where they play traditional jazz."

"Oh."

"Do you disapprove?" Deborah asked, raising golden-brown eyebrows.

"No, of course not."

"She was going to tell you herself, but I said I would. I told her to go and have a good time, take the chance while she can. From the sound of it, she doesn't seem to get much time off for fun."

Anne bridled again at the tone of criticism in her sister's voice. "Classical music is a very disciplined profession. It needs a lot of dedication."

"Even more reason for her to let her hair down while she's here," Deborah said.

"Would you feel better if I followed them and joined them at the club?" Ryan asked Anne softly.

"Don't be so silly, Daddy," Deborah said scornfully. "Imagine how Sandy would feel with her grandfather standing guard over her. She struck me as being a very sensible young woman, if slightly straitlaced. All this discipline has got to her, I should think."

Ryan looked from one sister to the other, feeling like a referee between two bristling opponents. These two daughters he and Janine had created were like oil and water, unable to mix. How different would it have been, he wondered, had he brought them both to England with him, instead of leaving one behind? He swallowed hard. What was the use of dwelling on the past? Too late now to change it.

He cleared his throat. "Come on, the pair of you. Stop baiting your sister, Deborah. She's just concerned for her daughter, that's all. She'll be fine with Conrad," he told Anne. "I've known him for twenty years. He's a good man, for all his smooth ways and silver tongue. He'll look after her."

But Anne, seeing the slight crease on Deborah's forehead, and fearing her own instincts about Conrad Hatcher, was not so sure.

Chapter 13

When the sunlight seeped into Sandy's room the next morning, she groaned and turned away from the window. She lifted up one arm to shield her eyes and then let it drop across her face. Her head throbbed and she felt sore everywhere.

Her eyes widened. With her left hand she explored herself. Oh God, so it hadn't been a dream. She'd been hoping that was all it had been, but the soreness between her legs confirmed that it was all too real. She felt a sense of panic and then took a few deep breaths. It wasn't as if she'd been raped, was it? From the little she remembered she knew that she'd been a willing participant.

The club Conrad had taken her to had been really jumping when they'd arrived. Wall-to-wall people gyrating to the pulsating rhythm of authentic traditional jazz. Many of them had been Conrad's age, even older, but there were plenty of people her own age there, as well. She'd found herself swept up in the intoxicating beat of the drums and the sinuous wail of the saxophone.

Conrad had ordered champagne, "To celebrate your first visit to Britain," he'd shouted in her ear, drawing her closer. After the first couple of glasses Sandy had relaxed and stopped resisting him. He was incredibly sexy, with that smoky voice and the vivid blue eyes that seemed to tell her she was the only woman in the world.

When the room started to swing around her, she told him she'd had enough champagne. "I'm not used to drinking," she said. "I don't usually have more than a couple of drinks."

He didn't press her, but brought her some coffee, with sugar in it, which she didn't like. But she drank it down, grimacing at the sickly taste of the sugar. After that she became far more relaxed, drinking several more glasses of champagne and responding to him eagerly, pressing her body against him when they danced, not even caring that they were kissing in public. All she knew was that she felt really hot for this man who, a few hours ago, had been a total stranger to her. It was as if the combination of the sultry New Orleans jazz—and the sultry weather—mixed with the champagne and the anonymous crowd had helped her to cast off her inhibitions.

It was she who'd suggested leaving. The drive was a blur in her mind. All she remembered was sitting as close to him as possible, her body aching for him to touch her. He took her to a wood, driving along a narrow lane that was little more than a beaten pathway, leafy branches closing in above them. Then he stopped, helped her out, and spread the car rug on the ground.

The sex had been phenomenal. She remembered that, at least. Even now, as she lay in bed thinking about it, she felt hot and tingly. Conrad knew exactly how to turn her on. She had become a mass of super-sensitive nerve-endings, aching for him to touch her *here* and *here*. Brian Dudeck's inept fumblings had been nothing like it.

She had also felt incredibly happy, as if she had fallen madly in love in an instant with this experienced and sophisticated man. And when he told her that he'd take care of her, she knew that he would, that there was nothing for her to worry about. It was as if they existed on another planet from the mere mortals they'd left behind at the club.

When he brought her to a shuddering climax she released a cry of ecstasy and he laughed with her— or maybe at her—when she clamped her hand over her mouth to stifle it.

"Let it all out, sweetheart," he whispered in her ear. "No hanging back now."

They made love again and then she must have fallen asleep. When she woke up, Conrad was dressed and sitting on a log, smoking a cigarette, and she was shivering, feeling cold and very sick.

"I don't feel too good," she said in a small voice. She sat up, groaning as the towering trees dipped and swung above her.

"Time to get you home to your bed," he said abruptly, grinding the cigarette beneath his heel. He held out his hand. "Come on, up you get." He dragged her to her feet.

She stood, swaying. "I feel so sick," she whispered.

"If you're going to puke, do it now, not in my car." He left her standing there, and went to shake out the rug and put it in the trunk of the car. Then he came back, looming over her. "Ready?"

She stood there, unmoving, arms hanging by her sides. Some small conscious part of her squirmed with embarrassment at being seen like this by a stranger.

"Get a move on," he said, taking her arm and

dragging her to the car. He opened the passenger
door and bundled her in.

When the car began moving she groaned again.

He laughed. "Not used to champagne, eh? I told
you not to have those extra glasses, but you didn't
want to know."

The rest was unclear to Sandy now, as she sat up
in bed, her head in her hands. She seemed to remember stopping at the side of the road to throw up,
with Conrad lighting a cigarette and walking away.

"Open the window," he'd said, when she got into
the car again.

Everyone was in bed when they arrived back
at Hammerton Towers, but Conrad knew his way
around. He helped her upstairs and into her room,
and left her sitting on the side of her bed, staring
into space. That was all she remembered. At some
point she must have dragged herself under the bedclothes. She wondered if he had taken her clothes
off. She was certainly naked now. The thought of
him undressing her, looking at her with the lights
on, made her shiver.

She pulled the covers over her head and was just
sliding into sleep again when someone knocked on
the door. If she didn't answer perhaps whoever it
was would think she was still asleep and go away.

Another knock, but this time the door opened.
"I've brought you some breakfast." For a moment
Sandy found it hard to identify the voice and then
Eileen came to the foot of the bed. She set the tray
down on a small table and carried it to Sandy's bed-
side. "Are you all right?" she asked.

Sandy tried to smile, but even that small move-
ment hurt her head. "Not really." The smell of toast

made her feel nauseated. "I don't think I can eat anything. I'm sorry."

"A little dry toast and marmalade will help you. Come along now." Eileen plumped her pillows and began pouring coffee into a cup.

Sandy wished she would go away.

"Conrad said you'd had a drop too much champagne last night."

Sandy stiffened. What else had Conrad said?

"I told him I'd bring you up a tray. Come, try to sit up and take the coffee, at least."

How could she sit up when she didn't have anything on? Sandy clutched the sheet around her neck. "Does my mother know I'm still in bed?"

"She went off to church at half-past ten with Graham. He wanted to show her old Saint Peter's."

"Did Conrad tell her about . . . about the champagne?"

Eileen sat on the edge of the bed. "He did."

"Shit! How did she take it?"

"Not that well. But Deborah told her it would be the effects of excitement and travel as much as the drink that had knocked you out."

"Yes, yes. That's right." Sandy was happy to latch on to any excuse. "What time it is now?"

Eileen looked at her man-size watch. "Five past twelve. Your mother should be home soon. Unless they stop at the pub for a drink on the way home."

"I don't think having a drink after church is my mother's style."

" 'Tis an English tradition, my pet. And it doesn't need to be an alcoholic drink, either. You've got drink on the brain."

Sandy put her hand to her forehead. "You can say that again." She tried to smile, but even that hurt.

"That's better. We'll soon have you right as rain. Drink that coffee now. And try a small piece of toast just to get something into your stomach."

Eileen got up and was about to leave when the door opened again and Deborah put her head around it. "How are you?"

"She's not feeling so good," Eileen answered for Sandy.

Deborah came to the bed. "You look ghastly."

"Thanks," Sandy said. She could smell Deborah's perfume. It was refreshing, not heavy, like the fragrance of summer flowers.

"She doesn't want to eat anything."

"I'm not surprised. From the way you look I imagine you had one hell of a night."

Sandy swallowed hard. "I'm not used to champagne."

"I can see that." Deborah moved to the door and Eileen followed her. "We'll leave you to get some more sleep. You'll feel better soon, I promise. Try to drink some coffee or a glass of water, at least."

"My mother—"

"I'll keep her away. She and Graham have gone to church to pray for us sinners." Deborah gave Sandy a wry smile.

"Didn't you want to go?"

"Not my thing." Deborah opened the door. "Drink fluids and rest," she ordered Sandy before she and Eileen went out.

"Aunt Deborah," Sandy called before she'd closed the door. Deborah came back into the room. "Please don't blame Mr. Hatcher. It was my fault I drank so much."

Deborah stood looking down at her, her face smooth and expressionless. "Get some more sleep. Have you got any aspirin?"

"In my bag."

"Where is it?"

"I'm not sure. Maybe on the floor." Sandy bent to search and the sheet slipped from her shoulders. Blushing, she dragged it over her again.

"Here it is," Deborah said. "It was on the chair. Take a couple of aspirin and a glass of water, and sleep. Dr. Deborah's orders."

Now the tears that Sandy had been fighting came unbidden to her eyes. "Thanks, Aunt Deborah. You're great."

"So are you." Deborah bent to kiss her niece's forehead. "And don't you forget it." She turned abruptly and left the room, closing the door quietly behind her.

Eileen was waiting outside. "Is she okay?"

"I think so. She'd better be." They walked down the stairs together. When they reached the hall, Deborah turned on Eileen. "Don't tell Ryan about this."

"He already knows that she had too much to drink. He was there when Conrad told us, remember? Conrad said he couldn't stop her once she started." Eileen frowned. "Do you think there's more to it than that?"

"I doubt it. But there's no need to tell Ryan that Sandy's this bad. It would only upset him. If he asks, just tell him that she's sleeping it off."

"Okay." As Eileen walked away her face was creased with worry.

As soon as Eileen had disappeared into the kitchen Deborah marched out onto the terrace, where everyone was sitting drinking Bellini cocktails, Ryan's favorite Sunday morning drink. Conrad was engaged in telling a story about his safari holiday in Kenya in the spring. He was a great raconteur, able to conjure up a scene and keep his listeners spellbound. Normally Deborah enjoyed Conrad's stories, but now she was jumpy with impatience.

"Can I have a word?" she said, once he'd reached the punch line and everyone had roared with laughter.

He looked surprised for a moment and then smiled. "Of course."

Ryan stopped them before they could leave the terrace. "How's Sandy doing? Did you see her?"

"She's fine. Sitting up in bed, eating breakfast."

Ryan looked relieved. "Good. I was worried about her. You shouldn't have let her drink so much, Conrad. I should have thought you'd have more sense. She's just a kid."

"She's twenty-one, Ryan, but I still take full blame. As I told you earlier, I made her have some coffee after she'd had a couple of glasses of champagne, but she insisted on drinking more. I was afraid she might cause a scene if I stopped her." Conrad bit his lip. "I wish to God I'd never given her the champagne in the first place, but I thought it would please her to have a special celebratory drink her first day in Britain."

"Well, Deborah said she's okay now. She's obviously not used to drinking."

"That's what she told me when I brought her home."

Deborah slipped her hand into Conrad's arm. "And put her to bed," she whispered in his ear, as she led him away down the steps and around the house to the front driveway. There she released his arm and confronted him, her eyes darting blue flame at him. "What the bloody hell did you do to Sandy last night?"

Conrad looked totally taken aback. "I've told you. She had too much to drink, that was all."

"I don't think so. She had nothing on in bed."

"I never took you for a prude, Deb. Lots of people don't wear nightclothes. Me, for one." He grinned suggestively at her.

"I'm sure you don't. There were love bites on her neck."

"So? I'm not denying we both got turned on. She's a pretty girl and I'm—"

"A randy old goat. Did you have sex with her?"

"What a question! Do you really think I'd answer it if I had?"

"No. I'll ask you in another way. Did you rape her?"

Conrad's eyes narrowed. "Now you're being insulting. I've never raped a woman in my life." He gave her a wolfish smile, all white teeth. "They're always willing."

"Oh, spare me your bragging. I know you too well. For that reason I've managed to escape your come-ons. You're disgusting, Conrad. My niece has only just arrived and you take advantage of her naïveté within a few hours."

"Take advantage? How very Victorian of you. And very sexist. Your niece may be naive, but I can assure you she's not inexperienced sexually and she was a willing participant. Why don't you ask her?"

"I don't need to. She's suffering, and it's not just from the drink." She poked her finger into Conrad's chest. "I swear to you that if I ever find out that you forced her to have sex, you bastard, I'll make you pay for it."

"I can get several witnesses to testify that Sandy wasn't held down and champagne poured into her by force. I saw Samantha Gillies at the club. Oh, and George Frobisher-Smith was there with your friend Pamela Martin. Ask Pamela if you want confirmation."

"I will." But both she and Conrad knew that she wouldn't. What was the point of creating a fuss, drawing attention to what would have been an every-day occurrence on a Saturday night at the jazz club? God, Conrad was a canny bastard. Until now she'd laughed at his exploits and risqué stories, but now, for the very first time, he'd hit close to home and it was no longer funny.

"Sandy's resting now. I want you to go back to London right away."

"I can't. Ryan and I have business to discuss."

"Make some excuse. I don't want her to have to see you when she comes downstairs."

"Maybe she'd like to see me. Had you thought of that?" He moved closer to her, his breath warm on her cheek. "After all, Deborah darling, you've never had the pleasure of my company in bed. You're my one holdout. You prefer cold fishes with hot wallets like Graham Neville."

Deborah was tempted to kick him where it hurt, but she knew from experience with Conrad that her best defense was to keep cool. "If it wasn't for Ryan I'd blow the whistle on you, Mr. bloody Hatcher. In fact, I would have done so a long time ago, but I knew how much Ryan relied on you. I also know that you've been a damned good business manager to him, as well. Which, once I went into business, with his financial help, was good for me, too. That's why I've kept quiet. But I swear if you turn up here again before my niece goes back to Canada I'll tell Ryan not only what you've done to Sandy, but also how you pestered me to sleep with you from the time I was fifteen. I don't think even your undoubted value as his business manager would weigh with Ryan if he knew that. You'd be out on your ear in an instant."

"My dear Deborah, this is a revelation. I do believe that being an auntie has made you go all soft. I never thought I'd see the day when you'd be wielding a sword in defense of the honor of your sister's daughter."

"Don't play with me, Conrad. Keep away from here until my sister and niece have gone back to Canada or you're finished."

He gave her a mock salute. "Aye, aye, Captain," he said, smiling, but the smile did not quite melt the ice in his eyes.

Chapter 14

Deborah was standing on the front steps when Graham and Anne drove up in his new Land Rover. They were so late for lunch that Ryan had started to worry that there'd been an accident, and had sent her out front to watch for them.

Anne was laughing at something, but stopped as soon as she saw Deborah standing there. She opened the door and scrambled from the car. "I'm sorry we're so late. Graham said it was an English tradition to stop for a pub drink after church."

"My fault, entirely," Graham said. He came to kiss Deborah. "Hello, darling. Did you miss me?"

"Not really. I've been too busy."

"Is everything okay?" Anne asked anxiously.

"Fine. We've held lunch back for you. Let's hope the lamb isn't overdone. Daddy likes it pink."

Anne felt guilty. She'd been enjoying herself so much that time had rushed by. "I didn't realize there'd be a cooked lunch."

"Another English tradition," Graham said quietly in her ear. He strode into the house ahead of them. "Bring on the 'vittles.' I'm starving."

"So, how did you like the little church at Ilmer?" Deborah asked. "It's one of the smallest—and oldest—in England, you know."

"More than eight hundred years old. Hard to believe, isn't it? It was absolutely lovely. There were only eight of us there."

"That's a good turnout for the summer."

"How's Sandy?" Anne asked.

"Much better. She's still asleep."

"At two o'clock?" Anne was alarmed. "I think I'd better go and check on her."

"No." Deborah grabbed her arm. "Let her sleep it off. No need to make such a fuss. I'm sure this isn't her first hangover."

"As far as I know, it is," Anne said, trying to hide her resentment. "She may have stayed with friends sometimes when she'd had too much and didn't want to drive home, but I've never known her to sleep through the next day."

"Too much champagne can do that to you." Deborah started off across the hall.

"Deborah."

"What?"

"I want to talk to Mr. Hatcher."

"He's not here."

"Where is he?"

"He had to go back to London."

Was it Anne's imagination or was her sister avoiding looking directly at her? Anne moistened her lips. "Is there something else I should know?"

"I don't think so. My advice would be to let it go."

"Sandy's my daughter," Anne said indignantly.

"I know that. But she's embarrassed at having drunk too much. Better to leave it alone."

How dare this woman, sister or no sister, shut her out from her daughter! "How come you're such an expert on mother-daughter relationships when you don't have any children of your own?"

Deborah's mouth tightened. "Suit yourself," she said with a shrug, and turned away.

After a moment of hesitation Anne went after her. "I shouldn't have said that. I'm sorry."

Deborah regarded her coolly. Then her expression softened a little. "That's okay. I can see you're worried, but she is all right, I promise you."

There was something in Deborah's eyes that made Anne want to ask more, but she sensed that she wouldn't get anywhere if she did. Not now, at any rate. One thing she was glad of, that Conrad Hatcher had left. The man gave her the creeps.

Ryan came out into the hall. "Graham said you were out here." He looked from one to the other. "Not fighting again, I hope," he said with a little half-smile, not sure what was going on.

"We don't know each other well enough to fight," Anne said.

"But we're working on it," Deborah added, directing a wry grin at her sister.

Although the Sunday lunch was more like a banquet than a lunch—consommé, roast lamb with several vegetables, summer pudding, and sherry trifle for dessert, Anne only picked at her food. Several people tried to talk to her but she replied in monosyllables, her mind fixed on Sandy. Whether it was mother's intuition or just a dislike of the suave Mr. Hatcher, she was convinced that Deborah was keeping something from her.

As soon as people started to get up from the table, taking their coffee into the conservatory or out onto the terrace, Anne slipped out of the dining room and went upstairs to her room. She tried the communicating door to Sandy's room, but it was locked. She went out into the hall again and tried Sandy's door. It, too, was locked. She knocked on the door. No reply.

"Sandy," she called. "Sandy!" Her voice rose. "Are you okay?" She jiggled the handle and then knocked on the dark wood panel.

She heard a groan and then, to her relief, the sound of feet shuffling across the wooden floor.

"Who is it?" Sandy's voice said.

"Me. Mom."

She heard the sound of a lock clicking and the door opened a few inches. Sandy stood there, uncombed hair falling over her face, her cotton robe clutched around her. "You woke me up," Sandy said, peering at her through half-closed eyes.

"It's nearly three o'clock in the afternoon, for heaven's sake. Can I come in?"

"If you have to."

The response was so unlike Sandy that Anne was about to snap at her, but something stopped her. She stepped into the room, closing the door behind her. She looked around the room. The curtains were still shut. Anne went to open them.

"Don't," Sandy said.

"It's a lovely sunny day."

"I don't care. I don't want them open." Sandy turned away from her mother and sat on the side of her bed. "I'm not awake yet."

"Well, you should be." Anne picked up Sandy's clothes from the chair and went to the small wardrobe in the corner of the room.

"Mom, will you please leave those alone. I can look after them myself."

Ignoring her, Anne slid the cotton T-dress Sandy had worn last night onto a hanger and put it back into the wardrobe. She drew in a long breath and then released it slowly.

She went to sit beside Sandy on the bed, but Sandy turned her head away, drawing into herself, as if she wanted to hide. Sensing that she didn't want to be touched, Anne moved away, closer to the foot of the bed.

"Are you okay, sweetie?" she asked softly.

" 'Course I am. I had too much to drink, that's all. I was an idiot."

"Mr. Hatcher—"

"Keep him out of it. He didn't force the drink down my throat, if that's what you're thinking."

"He didn't exactly stop you, though, did he?"

"Yes, he did. He tried to. He brought me coffee and said I should drink that instead, but I insisted on drinking more. So don't blame him." Sandy's eyes widened. "You haven't spoken to him about it, have you?"

"No, I haven't seen him today."

"Thank God. It's embarrassing enough, me puking my guts out in front of him, without you attacking him as well."

"I wouldn't have attacked him," Anne said in a quiet voice.

"Knowing you, you would have said something to him about it."

"Yes, I probably would."

"I'm not a kid anymore. I wish you'd remember that."

"It's hard to stop being a mother after all these years." Anne moved closer to slide her hand over Sandy's, which were gripped together in her lap. "Mr. Hatcher's gone to London. I get the feeling he won't be back before we leave."

Sandy lifted her face and, for the first time, looked directly at her mother. "Are you sure?"

"Deborah told me he'd gone. I'll make sure he doesn't come back until we've left, okay?"

Sandy unhunched her shoulders and sat up a little straighter. "I don't want to see him."

"You won't have to. Is there anything else—"

"He was a jerk. Telling me not to puke in his car, when I was feeling like death."

Anne was secretly relieved. Sandy seemed to be suffering from nothing more than a bad hangover, plus embarrassment and regret that she'd made a fool of herself.

"Why don't you have a long shower? It'll make you feel much better."

"Good idea." Sandy looked down at the hands hanging between her legs and then suddenly turned to her mother and flung her arms around her. "I'm sorry I screwed things up," she whispered, her head pressed against Anne's breast.

Anne's hand went up to stroke the tangled hair. "You didn't. Not at all."

"Does Ryan know? About me, I mean."

"Deborah had to give him some explanation for you staying in bed. He understood. But he wasn't too pleased with Mr. Hatcher."

Sandy drew away again and stared straight ahead at the wall, her fingers lacing and unlacing. "I don't want to talk about him. It was my fault, not his." She turned impulsively to her mother. "I really like Aunt Deborah. She knew exactly what to say to me this morning."

"Unlike me?" As soon as she'd spoken, Anne regretted it. The question sounded petty.

"No, Mom. She's not my mother. She was different, that was all. But she seemed to care."

"I'm glad." This time, Anne meant what she said. She was glad that her sister was bonding with her daughter. She just wished Deborah would extend that bonding to *her.*

"Are you two getting any closer, do you think?" Sandy asked, slowly coming out of her shell.

"I'm not sure. It's too early yet to tell. What bothers me is that Deborah won't let me get close to her. Each time I think we're getting on better Deborah says something in that high-and-mighty tone of hers and we're back to square one again. It's like she's determined not to let me get closer to her, so she gets bitchy if I do."

"What about your father?"

"He's even worse," Anne said with a sigh. "I haven't once sat down with him, just the two of us, to talk. He's not hostile like Deborah. He just makes sure he's never alone with me, that's all."

"Poor Mom." Sandy's hand turned upward to clasp Anne's hand. "Give it time."

"We don't have much of that. And what we do have Ryan seems to be filling up with excursions. Anything to avoid being on our own together." Anne gave Sandy a rueful smile. "Here I am, supposed to be making you feel better and I'm whining away about my own troubles."

"We're here for the same reasons," Sandy reminded her. "Whatever happens, you'll never again be strangers, you and your dad and sister."

"You're right." Anne leaned over to hug her. "You're the best daughter in the world."

"Even if I'm a drunk?"

"Oh, get lost! You were dead tired from traveling and had too much champagne, that's all."

As her mother's arms tightened around her Sandy stared at the wall, wishing to God it was that simple.

Chapter 15

Anne hadn't expected London to be this hot, even in July. She was standing with Sandy outside Tower Records at Piccadilly Circus, waiting for Graham to meet them, the heat bouncing off the stone walls surrounding her. From the leaden sky came a rumble of thunder.

"Looks like rain."

"I hope so." Sandy wiped the perspiration from her forehead. "This heat is killing me."

"I know. So are my feet."

They'd walked for miles, packing in so much that it all seemed a blur in Anne's mind. A quick whirl through Harrods—where the prices had horrified Anne—a salad and wine lunch in Covent Garden—where Deborah also bought a dress of gauzy Indian cotton at Monsoon for Sandy—a taxi ride past Buckingham Palace, at Anne's insistence, and a mini-tour of the National Gallery .

Deborah had gone to her office at three o'clock, leaving them at Tower Records. Sandy had been subdued all day, dragging around London behind them, showing little enthusiasm for anything she saw, but Tower Records miraculously restored her to her normal bright self. She dashed from section to section—classical to rock to folk to New Age and back to classical—like a starving woman facing a banquet, not knowing which delectable goody to sample first.

They had both been delighted to find three of Ryan's CD reissues in the folk section. "We don't have this latest one. Let's buy it," Sandy suggested.

"Why don't you ask your grandfather for one? I'm sure he's got piles of them."

"That's a good idea. You don't think he'd mind me asking, do you?"

"I think he'd be very flattered."

Anne had bought a couple of CDs herself. Early Beatles recordings to add to her collection.

They came out of the store just before four o'clock, clutching their plastic bags. The heat hit them like a wall after the coolness of the air-conditioning. A souvenir vendor's stall stood directly outside the store. "Get yer postcards 'ere!" the man yelled, his voice frequently drowned out by the screech of brakes and honking of car horns.

Anne leaned her back against the stone wall of the store, trying to take the weight off her aching and blistered feet. People walked past in packs rather than singly, all surging ahead purposefully, heads bent, as if they knew exactly where they were going. All except those tourists who ambled along, heads buried in their maps, getting in everyone's way.

Anne exchanged smiles with Sandy. "Quite a change from Winnipeg, isn't it?"

Sandy nodded. "Talk about culture shock."

"You'd better get used to it. You'll be performing in cities like London soon."

Sandy shook her head and rolled her eyes in exasperation at Anne. It was okay for other people to talk positively about her future, but not her mother.

Graham arrived at four-fifteen, rushing up to them from the latest throng that had crossed Piccadilly at the lights. "My apologies for being late. I was held up in traffic at Hyde Park. How are your feet?"

"Feet?" Anne repeated.

"Yes, feet. Do you feel like walking down Piccadilly?"

Anne's feet were so sore she didn't feel like walking to the curbside, but she didn't want to complain.

"My feet are fine," Sandy said.

"What about your mother?"

Anne was about to say she was fine, too, but Graham was looking at her over his sunglasses with a humorous glint in his eyes. "My feet are killing me," she confessed. "I got a blister on my left heel about two hours ago. I don't think I could walk very far."

"Then we'll get a taxi. Can I help with your bags? No? Let's go, then."

Graham started off. As soon as they rounded the corner he flagged down a big black taxi, ushered them inside the roomy interior, and pulled down the small seat behind the driver, to sit opposite them.

"I thought you'd like to have a traditional English afternoon tea, rest your feet, before we drive back to Buckinghamshire."

Anne released a long, drawn-out sigh. "Sounds like heaven."

"Okay for you, too, Sandy?" Graham asked. "Or are you up for more shopping?" He cast an eye at her shopping bags. "I see you've been spending the family fortune."

Sandy gave her mother a guilty glance. "I've spent far too much."

"You did go a little crazy, but then, so did I."

Graham grimaced. "I seem to have said the wrong thing. Sorry."

"Not at all," Anne said.

"Ryan did say we were to charge stuff to him," Sandy muttered defiantly.

Anne sat up very straight. "Your grandfather has been generous enough without presenting him with a bill for CDs and posters and clothes." She saw that Graham was watching her intently. "Sorry about that," she said, embarrassed to be discussing money—or the lack of it—with him there.

"Ryan told me to—"

"Let's drop it, Sandy." Anne smiled at Graham, trying to ignore the fact that Sandy had slumped like a sulking child beside her.

The taxi drew up at the steps of a hotel. Immediately, a doorman in a uniform of black and gold darted forward to help them out. "Good afternoon, ladies, Mr. Neville." Unused to such attention, Anne dropped one of her bags on the ground and almost crashed heads with the doorman, who had bent at the same time as she had to pick it up.

What a stupid klutz, she told herself, the blood rushing into her face. She looked up to find Graham laughing. "If only we'd had a camera you'd have had the perfect souvenir," he said.

Somehow by not trying to cover up her clumsiness he made her feel much better.

The doorman chuckled, too, as he restored her bag to her. "Mind how you go now," he said to her kindly.

Smiling, Anne thanked him.

"Wow!" said Sandy, as they walked into the foyer,

their feet sinking into the crimson-and-gold carpet. "This is something else."

Three crystal chandeliers hung from the molded ceiling, bathing the foyer in soft light, rather than the harsh fluorescent lighting Anne was used to seeing in hotels. Another man in uniform approached them, offering to take their bags.

"I'll keep this one," Sandy said, holding on to her Tower Records' bag.

"Very well, madam."

Sandy made a face at Graham. "Is that okay?" she whispered.

"You do just what you want."

"I wanted to show you the CDs I bought," she explained.

Although Sandy had cultivated the natural grace for meeting the public that was necessary in her profession, she was by nature quite shy. Yet it was obvious to Anne that she was fully at ease with Graham. That was entirely due to Graham's ability to make people feel relaxed with him.

Another man, dressed in a dark suit, came to lead them across the foyer. "Good afternoon, ladies." He turned to Graham. "A pleasure to see you, Mr. Neville."

Graham shook hands with him. "How are you, Raymond?"

"Very well, sir, despite the heat."

"Not hot in here." They exchanged smiles as if they shared a secret.

"Not anymore, thanks to you. How is Sir William?"

"Trying to adjust to semiretirement. He's in Italy at present, probably driving my poor mother crazy."

"Lady Celia will survive, I think." With a dazzling smile, the man—whom Anne realized must be the hotel manager—led them into a large room decorated in blue and gold, and gave them a table by the window, overlooking the park. "May I bring you anything—a cold drink, perhaps, while you're looking at the menu?"

"I'll have some mineral water," Sandy said quickly. "With lemon and lots of ice, please."

"Sounds perfect," Graham said. Anne agreed.

"Forgive the shoptalk," Graham said, when Raymond had left them.

Anne gave a sudden drawn-out "Oh!" as the reality of the interchange between the two men sank in. "This is one of your hotels, isn't it?"

Graham nodded.

Sandy's mouth dropped open in amazement. "I don't believe it."

"Why? Isn't it good enough for me?"

"You're not—I mean, you don't seem—" Sandy floundered to a halt.

"I'm not quite up to its standard, you mean?" Graham asked, laughing. "That's probably because I wasn't born into the trade. I was press-ganged into the business by my father."

Sandy frowned, not quite sure what he meant, but Anne understood.

"It wasn't my first choice of profession," Graham explained. A shadow seemed to glide across his face, like a translucent blind drawn down.

Anne was about to ask him what he would prefer to be doing, but decided against it. "It's a beautiful hotel. You should be proud of it."

"I am. It's a particular favorite of mine, I assure you."

"What was all that about heat?" Sandy asked.

"Heat? Oh, you mean what Raymond and I were talking about. Well, much against my father's will, I had air-conditioning installed here two years ago, at great expense to the company. As you can see, London can be very hot in the summer, yet Londoners tend to excuse not having air-conditioning by insisting that it rarely gets hot enough for it here."

"Was it worth the expense?"

"It certainly was. It was extremely hot last summer, but staff efficiency increased by almost fifty percent, and the guests certainly seem to prefer it."

Anne stretched out her legs. "I agree with that. Did you say your father had retired?"

"My father will never fully retire. He does take more time off nowadays, but he finds it difficult to leave his business to others."

"He's a workaholic?"

"Yes. And expects everyone else in the family to be so, as well." Graham picked up the menu, signaling his wish to change the subject. "Now what are we going to have? I would recommend the complete tea, with sandwiches and scones and cakes, as we'll be on the road a couple of hours. We're going to hit the busiest traffic time when we leave London."

Graham was right. When he launched the car into the craziness that was Hyde Park Corner—with traffic swirling in every direction—Anne was tempted to close her eyes. Giving her an amused glance, Graham assured her that the traffic was quite normal for this time of day. When they reached the motorway, they joined endless lines of bumper-to-bumper traffic stretching both ways.

Only when it thinned out a little and they were speeding along the M40 was Anne able to relax and think about what had happened at the hotel. The ease and lack of superiority with which Graham had interacted with his staff. Yet when the conversation had turned to his father, there had been a tension in him that she hadn't seen before. She recalled what Deborah had told her about Graham's father turning the ancestral family home into a luxury resort. Having seen Graham's love of Somerford, she wondered how the loss of his home had affected Graham.

Graham glanced at her. "You're very quiet. Thinking about your first day in London?"

Anne wondered what he'd say if she told him she'd been thinking about him and his family history. Considering she'd met him only a couple of days ago, she was thinking far too much about Graham Neville.

She smiled back at him. "I was wondering how long it would take to see everything there is to see."

"In London? A lifetime. You know what Dr. Johnson said about London."

Anne didn't like to admit that she didn't know, but fortunately Graham told her.

" 'When a man is tired of London, he is tired of life,' " he quoted. "Personally, I think London's better taken in small doses. So don't feel badly if you see only a little bit at a time. Each time you return you can see a little more."

"I don't expect we'll be coming back for quite a while." Anne glanced at Sandy in the backseat. "Not until Sandy makes her English debut here."

"Oh, Mom!" Sandy heaved an exaggerated sigh. "That will be a long time from now, if ever."

"But you don't deny you'll be performing internationally one day," Graham said in a matter-of-fact tone.

"No. I know that I will be. It just takes time, that's all. Mom doesn't seem to understand that."

Dumb Mom. "I do understand. I'm just proud of you, that's all."

"With good cause," Graham said.

There he goes again, thought Anne. Saying just the right thing.

The storm had broken by the time they arrived at Hammerton Towers, the rain spilling down as they dashed from the car into the house. There, Ryan greeted them with the news that Deborah had changed her mind. As soon as she'd got her desk in order and made some phone calls she'd be driving down from London.

"And she's coming to Hampton Court with us tomorrow," he told them, when Graham had parked the car.

Anne was dismayed to feel a twinge of disappointment. She had been looking forward to enjoying this historic garden without having to endure Deborah's caustic remarks. She pushed away the discomfiting thought that she'd also wanted to share the experience with Graham, without having to share him with Deborah.

To her surprise Graham put some of her doubts into words. "Let's hope she won't be bored to tears. Deborah can be very annoying when she's bored."

When she eventually arrived later that evening, Deborah was far from bored. She swept into the dining room, apologizing for turning up late for dinner, exuding a warmth and verve that suggested she had been rejuvenated by her visit to London.

"What time are we leaving tomorrow?" she asked Ryan. "Not too early, I hope."

"We should be there by eleven at the latest. Any later than that and it will be overrun by busloads of tourists."

Deborah shuddered at the thought. "You're right. You coming with us, Eileen?" she asked, as Eileen came into the room, carrying the phone.

"To Hampton Court? Why not?" Eileen turned to Anne. "There's a call from Canada for you, Anne. Do you want to take it here or in Ryan's office?"

Anne frowned. "Is it my aunt?"

"No. It's a man."

Marco, perhaps? But Marco hated calling people. To him, the telephone was strictly for business or emergencies. "I hope everything's okay." Anne took the phone from Eileen.

"Why don't you go over to the bench in the corner there, where it's more private? Just press that little button on the phone when you want to speak."

Anne moved across the room and then said "Hello?" wondering who on earth could be calling her from Canada.

"Hello, Anne? Are you there?" The voice roared down the line as if he had to shout to make her hear.

"Bill?"

"Yeah, it's me. Thank God I got you right away. Sorry to bother you, but it's Beth. She's had an accident."

Chapter 16

In a moment, with great clarity, Anne saw all her hopes and plans erased like chalk marks from a blackboard. "What's happened?" she asked, her heart racing.

"Beth fell and broke her ankle," Bill roared.

"Oh, no. How did it happen?" Anne asked. Sandy came to stand beside her, her face anxious. "Aunt Beth broke her ankle," Anne mouthed to her.

"She stood on a pile of boxes to reach one of the shelves," Bill said. "Next thing we know she's toppled down and landed on the floor and she can't get up for the pain in her foot."

"Oh, God," was all Anne could say.

"We knew when she couldn't stand she must've broke it. Mary took her to Emergency at the hospital. She was passing out with the pain."

"Poor Aunt Beth."

"They said it was a bad fracture and she'd be in a cast for at least six weeks."

"Is she still in the hospital?"

"No, they put her foot in a cast and then sent her home."

"But there's no one there to take care of her." Anne's voice rose in panic.

"Now, hold on. She's fine. I called Marco. His

sister Carla came over to stay the night with her. It was Marco who brought Beth home."

"Thank God for that." Anne sat down on the arm of the nearest chair. "Is she still in a lot of pain?"

"Eh?"

Anne repeated the question, wishing that Marco had called her instead of Bill. The old man's hearing was particularly bad on the phone.

"She's doing okay. Doctor gave her a shot of morphine, but that didn't suit her stomach much. I said I'd call you and let you know."

"Thanks, Bill. I don't know how quickly I can make it, but I'll be home as soon as I can."

"Beth said not to tell you, but I knew you'd want to know."

"You're damned right, I do. Can you and Mary manage the center until I get home?"

"Sure we can. 'Course Beth's frettin' herself silly about it, but I jest told her we don't need her there. We can manage fine without her."

"Good." She gave a little laugh. "She won't believe that, but I know you'll manage fine, so don't worry."

"Sorry to do this to you."

"It's not your fault. I'm just glad you called me right away. As soon as I know what flight I'm getting I'll call you back. But that may not be until tomorrow. It's eight-thirty in the evening here now."

"Eh?" Bill didn't seem to be able to take that in. To him it was two-thirty in the afternoon.

"Thanks again, Bill. Give Aunt Beth my love, will you?"

"Think I should tell her I called you?"

"Yes."

"She'll be mad as hell."

"Too bad. Tell her I'll be home as soon as I can to take care of everything."

"I will. Oh, meant to tell you. Marco said to say he'll call you later, okay? He had to go back to the restaurant. So long for now." Anne winced as Bill crashed the phone down in her ear.

She stood there staring at the phone in her hand until Sandy took it from her. "How bad is she?" Sandy asked.

"She's in a lot of pain." Anne turned to face the others, who were still at the table watching her. "Aunt Beth fractured her ankle," she told them. "I have to get home as soon as I can."

"You can't be thinking of leaving," Ryan protested. "You've only just got here."

"Aunt Beth needs me."

"Surely you can arrange a private nurse for her."

"It's not just the nursing part. She'll be worried sick about the garden center. I have to get back to look after things." Anne looked blindly around her, uncertain what to do first.

"Drink this." Graham materialized before her, a glass of brandy in his hand.

"I shouldn't. I need to be able to think straight."

"Sit down and drink it." His hand was on her shoulder, gently forcing her to sit. "You'll think much better if you've relaxed."

Her father came to hover above her, his face creased with anxiety . . . and something else she couldn't quite fathom at the moment. Then he sat down beside her. "Will you tell me the situation there?"

Anne thought she already had. "Aunt Beth fell and broke—"

"No, no. I mean who's there to look after her and the garden center?"

"No one to look after Aunt Beth. Carla, the sister of a friend of mine is looking after her tonight, but Carla has a family and I'd imagine she won't be able to stay after tonight. I'll find out more when my friend calls me later."

She wouldn't wait. As soon as she was alone, she'd call Marco at the restaurant.

"And the center?"

"There's Bill Sawerchuk, the man who just called. But he's old and mainly takes care of the plants and trees. His grandson is helping him with the heavy work and there's a part-time employee who looks after the till. But someone has to do the banking and the stock-taking and the book entries and arranging deliveries."

"Can't you hire someone to do that?" Ryan asked, his voice rising with impatience.

"No, it has to be someone who knows the business."

"Maybe Aunt Beth could do some of the book work," Sandy said. "It's only her ankle she's broken. She could do it sitting in a chair."

"She's not a kid," Anne said, her tone a rebuke. "A fall like this is a big shock to the system when you're older. The last thing I want is to have her worrying about things. If I'm there with her she may still be frustrated, but she won't be worrying about the business falling apart."

Ryan's hand came out to cover hers. "I don't want you to go," he said in an undertone, as if he didn't want the others to hear. "We haven't had enough time together."

Graham and Deborah were standing near the

door, talking quietly. Now Graham came over to them. "Can I be of any help? I could drive you to the airport."

"Hold on now," Ryan said belligerently. "She hasn't definitely decided she's going yet."

"Of course I have to go." Anne turned her head away from Graham's searching gaze and back to Ryan. "I'm sorry, but I must."

"We can arrange something. All these years we've wasted. I'm not having you leave now, before—" He shook his head, lost for words.

Deborah joined them. "Anne has to go. She has no alternative."

"Oh yes, she has," Ryan said, his words staccato, like pistol shots. "You can go in her place."

"Me?" Deborah's mouth opened in exaggerated surprise. "You must be joking."

"No, I'm not joking. After all, Beth is your aunt as well as Anne's, isn't she?"

"I don't even know the woman," Deborah said, her voice rising in disbelief. "She's your sister-in-law, too, so why don't you go and help out?"

Ryan glared at her. "Don't talk nonsense."

"It's no more nonsense than suggesting I go to Canada. Next thing you'll be telling me I should help with the garden center as well." Deborah laughed and looked at them all a little wildly, as if she were surrounded by a pack of lunatics.

"And why not? Are you afraid of soiling your lily-white hands? Your sister has been doing it all her life. Why not you?"

Deborah stared at her father as if he had suddenly become a stranger. Anne jumped into the silence. "There's no need to discuss this any further," she said firmly. "I'm going home."

"Wait a minute here." Ryan stood up to confront Deborah. "I'm asking you to do this for your sister and me, Deborah. We haven't seen each other for thirty years. All that time you've had it easy, with money being lavished on you, while your sister's been scraping a living. And a fine job she's made of it, too. A daughter who's a talented musician. And Anne's given up her own profession to help her aunt, as well. Maybe it's time you paid your dues."

Deborah's face was white with shock. Graham looked from her to Ryan. "Perhaps you should sit down and discuss this—"

Ryan cut him short. "Keep out of this, Graham. It's a family discussion we're having here."

"Then I'd better leave," Graham said through tight lips. "Unless you'd like me to stay," he added in an undertone to Deborah.

"No, thanks. I'll deal with this myself." She waited until Graham had left the room and then turned on her father. "That was bloody rude. You have no right to speak to Graham that way."

"Don't you go telling me my rights. This is my house and I'll speak to anyone I like in any way I like." Ryan's face was mottled with angry red splotches.

Sandy moved closer to Anne. Eileen glanced at them and then spoke. "Now that's enough from the both of you. Can't you see how you're upsetting Sandy and her mother? It doesn't help them a bit for you to have one of your fights when they're so upset about their aunt, does it?"

One of your fights? Anne was surprised. In the three days she'd been there she'd thought that this was the perfect father-daughter relationship. "There's no need for any fights. I'm going back to Canada."

Ryan sat down again. Anne could see that his hands were trembling. "Don't you want to stay?" he asked her, very softly. "We've hardly said a word to each other since you came."

Whose fault is that? Anne wanted to say. "Of course I'd rather stay. I came all this way to see you."

"Then stay. We'll work this out, I promise you."

"But I also came to see my sister." She felt Deborah's gaze turn to her. "So what's the point? Unless we all went back to Canada together."

"Now, there's a good idea," Eileen said, beaming. "Why couldn't you do that?"

"Keep out of this," Ryan told her.

Eileen wasn't daunted. "It would solve all your problems. You'd all be together and you could all pitch in and help."

Sandy had detached herself from the group and was watching them from the window. "I'll go back and look after Aunt Beth," she announced.

They all turned to her, halting in midargument.

"I have to go back in five days, anyway, so what's the difference?"

"You have classes and a concert to do," Anne said.

"So? I can sit Aunt Beth in front of the television while I do those. We'll get her a wheelchair and she can get herself into the kitchen to heat up something in the microwave, if I leave it for her."

Deborah crossed the room to Sandy. "What a great idea," she said, putting an arm around her shoulders and hugging her. "Then your mother won't have to leave until next weekend, as planned."

Anne smiled at Sandy. "Thanks for the offer, sweetie, but I have to go back to look after the garden center."

"Sandy can do that, too," Ryan said.

Anne turned on him, anger sparking in her eyes. "No, she can't. Not only won't she have the time, she can't risk damaging her hands working with tools or lifting heavy things."

"Mom's right there, I'm afraid," Sandy said. "I have to go to Juilliard in a few weeks. I don't dare risk spraining my wrist or breaking a finger. But I can help look after Aunt Beth at home."

"There's no need to cut your visit short," Anne said.

"I don't mind." Sandy looked around at them all. "I've met everyone. I've seen London." She summoned up a smile. "I've even spent a heap of money in Tower Records. What more could I ask?"

"There's lots more we'd like to show you," Deborah said.

"I'd really like to go home." Sandy bent to pick up her Tower Records' bag and her purse from the floor, her hair falling forward to hide her face. "I've got so much to do before I leave for New York I don't know how I'm going to manage it all. But I don't want Mom to have to leave. She really needs this visit." She sent a direct appeal to Deborah. "Why don't you come with me? I'd really like it if you would."

Anne frowned at her daughter. "Sandy, you can't expect—"

"At least Sandy knows how to ask," Deborah said, glaring at Ryan. She turned back to Sandy. "Darling, I have my own business to run. Besides, Graham would tell you I don't know a spade from a trowel. I'd be worse than useless in a garden center."

"It would only be for a week, until Mom gets

home, and you wouldn't have to do the heavy work yourself. We could easily get in extra help for that. But you'd be able to do all the book work and deal with customers at the center. That sort of thing. You'd be great at it."

Anne had to stifle a giggle at the thought of her elegant sister wading through the muck in her Gucci shoes, digging out a six-pack of yellow rocket snapdragons.

"That's enough, Sandy," she said, half laughing. "Don't keep on."

"What's the matter, Deb?" Ryan asked. "Don't think you could hack it?" His words and tone of voice were like a gauntlet thrown at her feet.

Anne caught the fleeting look of bewilderment and hurt on her sister's face before it hardened into a mask.

"Oh, I'm sure I'd be able to manage extremely well." Deborah threw a defiant look at Anne. "In fact, from the sound of it, this garden center of yours needs some shaking up. Watch out, you may not recognize it by the time you get back."

Anne raised her eyebrows. "In one week?"

"Why not make it two—or even three weeks?" Ryan suggested. "That will give Anne more time to see the sights here and for us to get to know each other again, after all these years."

Seeing Deborah's expression, Anne opened her mouth to protest, but Sandy got in before she could speak. "That's a great idea. Don't worry, Mom. Aunt Deborah will have me there to help show her around." She grinned at her aunt. "We'll have a great time together."

Deborah slipped an arm around her waist. "I'll keep you to that promise." Her arm still clasping

Sandy, she faced the others in the room. "All right, I'll do it."

"I knew you would." Ryan went to kiss Deborah's cheek, but she pulled away and stood very erect, her eyes fixed on Anne.

"It's very kind of you. Thank you," Anne said, not at all sure that she meant it.

Deborah gave her an enigmatic smile. "I warn you. There's no guarantee that things will be the same when you get back to Winnipeg."

Chapter 17

As she left the room, Deborah was perilously close to shedding tears of anger. But she wasn't about to let any of them see her break down and perhaps misinterpret the reason for it.

She marched across the hall and out the front door, slamming it behind her, shivering Ryan's precious panels of stained glass. She wished they'd fallen out and shattered on the ground. It would serve her father bloody well right. He'd never before spoken to her in that way, treating her as if she were a spoiled brat who'd deliberately usurped her sister's position in the family; when, in fact, she'd had no control over the situation whatsoever. Well, she'd show him and that mealymouthed sister of hers what she could do.

She tramped down the graveled driveway, wishing she'd at least stopped to put on some walking shoes. Her new Italian leather sandals would be ruined. But who the hell cared? She was off to the backwoods of Canada, wasn't she? To work in a filthy garden center. She wouldn't need expensive clothes there, that was certain. A pair of old jeans and a torn country-and-western T-shirt would be just fine.

"I must be stark staring mad," she shouted into

the rain that was falling heavily now, soaking her full silk skirt so that it clung to her legs in clammy folds.

She could hear a car engine close behind her, but ignored it. Probably Ryan coming to apologize. Whoever it was leaned on the horn. She turned around, to find Graham's Land Rover directly behind her.

He pulled up beside her. "You're getting soaked."

"Who cares?"

"I do. Get in."

"No, I need to be alone."

"At least get into the car while I drive back to the house for a raincoat for you."

"I don't want to go near that place." But because her clothes were now drenched, she did open the door and climb into the passenger seat.

"The car rug's behind you. Wrap it around you. I'll drive you back."

"I'm not going back to the house. Not yet, anyway." Deborah reached for the rug and pulled it around her shoulders. Then she opened the glove compartment, rummaging through it. "Got any cigarettes?"

"You gave up smoking last year."

"I need one now. Damn, I could have sworn I left a packet in here."

"If you did, I would have cleared it out by now. You are upset, aren't you? Things must have worsened after I left."

"You don't know the half of it." She folded her arms beneath the rug and stared out the rain-smeared window.

"What happened?"

"I got shanghaied into taking my sister's place in Canada."

Graham glanced across at her. "You mean you caved in? I don't believe it."

"You'd better believe it. And if that's a smile on your face, you'd better get rid of it quickly, or I'll do it for you."

"Yes, ma'am." Graham drove through the open gateway and then drew up at the side of the road. "Where do you want to go? I can't offer you much home comforts at my place, I'm afraid. What about the Friar's Head? We could have a drink there."

Deborah felt the water from her skirt trickling down her legs. "I'm soaking wet. I can't go anywhere public."

"We could take a room at the Spread Eagle hotel in Thame then. You could have a hot bath and dry off."

"Could you just leave me alone for a moment, instead of forcing me into doing something I don't want to do? You're almost as bad as they are."

"Sorry. Tell me what happened."

"I've told you."

"I left just after Ryan told you that it was time for you to pay your dues."

"Thanks for reminding me."

"Sorry. At that point I would have sworn that there was no way you would cave in."

"I didn't bloody well cave in. It was Sandy's fault."

"Sandy? What did she do?"

Deborah had to smile. "She asked me nicely."

Graham leaned back his head and laughed. Deborah punched him hard on his arm.

"Ouch! That hurt."

"I told you not to laugh at me."

"I couldn't help it. How did Sandy do it?"

"She said she would go with me and we could be together in Canada. That was after Ryan said he wanted to spend more time with Anne, of course."

"That's understandable, isn't it?"

"Is it? When he hasn't even spoken her name for donkeys' years? She turns up unheralded on his door-step and suddenly she's his golden girl."

"Well, you must admit that you've been the golden girl until now. That's one hell of a long time in comparison with Anne's week here, isn't it?" He glanced at Deborah's averted profile. "I like your sister."

"So I've noticed."

"Oh, for God's sake stop playing the martyred sister act. Ryan's right. You've had it good for a bloody long time. From what I understand, your sister hasn't."

Deborah was amazed at Graham's sudden surge of anger. "Well, well. Anne certainly has a strong advocate in you, doesn't she?"

"Surely you can't begrudge your sister a week with her father after all these years. Frankly, I think helping her out is the least you can do. After all, this is your aunt, too, isn't it?"

Deborah dragged off the rug, but then decided she needed it. "Well, thanks a lot for all your sympathy and concern." She struggled to open the door, her wet hand slipping on the handle.

Graham grabbed her arm. "Don't be stupid. What are you doing?"

"I'm getting out of the car."

"And what then?"

"Don't worry," she said with biting venom. "I'm not going to murder your precious little Anne. Al-though I must say that's what I feel like doing at this moment." She scrambled out of the car, almost slipping on the muddy verge at the roadside.

Graham opened his window. "Don't be an idiot," he said in his annoyingly reasonable voice. "Get in and I'll drive you back."

"No thanks," she yelled back at him. "I want to walk."

"You're behaving like a child," he said coldly and closed his window.

She was about to start off down the road, away from the house, but decided that wasn't such a good idea when it was dark and raining hard. Turning around, she began walking back down the driveway. She heard Graham take off with a squeal of tires and felt a wave of anger and disappointment at his lack of concern. A real man would have grabbed her and forced her back into the car, wouldn't he?

The rain poured down her face as she made her way back to the house in the darkness, her feet twisting in the wet gravel. She could see ahead of her the illuminated windows of the house, the symbol of light and warmth mocking her.

It was a long time since she had felt so utterly abandoned. It reminded her of the time she was eleven when Fiona had punished her by locking her out of the house because she'd come home late. She shivered, fervently wishing that she had somewhere else to go other than this house she loathed so much.

Well, her wish would soon be granted, she thought ironically when she reached the steps. *Look out, Canada, here I come.* She shivered again. Pulling Graham's car rug more closely about her, she mounted the steps, unlocked the front door, and went inside.

Chapter 18

Deborah was awakened the next morning by the telephone ringing at her bedside. Still half asleep, she reached for it, almost knocking over a cup of tea that Eileen must have left for her earlier. It was now stone cold with a light brown scum floating on top. "Hello?"

"Good morning, darlin'."

She felt like crashing the phone down on Ryan's bright morning voice.

"Are you coming down for breakfast?"

"No, I'm not. You woke me up." She ran her hands through her hair. "What time is it?"

"Half-past seven."

"Half-past seven!" she repeated incredulously.

"If you're quick you can join us for breakfast. We'll wait for you," he added, trying to coax her.

"Don't bother. I'll eat in my room."

"Then I'll send Anne up. She wants to talk to you."

"About what?"

"About you going to Canada."

Deborah felt a coldness like a lump of ice in the pit of her stomach. "So that's still on, is it?"

"As far as we're concerned it is." Ryan's voice was sharp. "That's why we're all up so early. Except for you, of course."

"That's fine," she lied. "I was just making sure."

"We'll need to make all the arrangements this morning. That's why I woke you."

"I'll make the arrangements myself, thank you."

"Sure you will. But Anne will have to let her aunt know when you and Sandy are coming. You marched out last night leaving us all up in the air. Nothing could be arranged without you."

"Send Anne up."

Deborah slammed the phone down. She wasn't about to apologize after the way they'd treated her. And that included Graham, as well. Last night, when she'd slipped into the house and gone straight to her room, she'd expected him to phone her, but he hadn't. After waiting for a while, she'd lain in a hot bath, seething with anger, made herself a cup of tea with the kettle in her room, and gone to bed.

Even there she was unable to relax, unwanted images and vague, uneasy memories from the past—or perhaps from her imagination—invading her head. It had taken her ages to get to sleep.

A knock at the door. "Come on in," she shouted.

Anne entered, bearing a tray. "I've brought you some fresh tea and toast."

Deborah was about to reject it, but realized that might sound churlish—and childish. "Thanks. Eileen must have left me this tea earlier. I never heard her come in."

"I'll take it away." Anne looked for somewhere to set down the tray.

"Put it on the table over there." Deborah swung her legs over the side of the bed and dragged on her silk kimono. "I have to get up, anyway. I have a great deal to do," she added with a false smile. "I know you want to get everything arranged quickly."

Anne did not respond to the smile. "You were forced into this. It wasn't fair."

Deborah was surprised. She padded over to the chair by the fireplace and sat down, her bare feet tucked under her. "Everyone else thought it was fair." She leaned over to pour herself some tea, but Anne lifted up the teapot.

"I'll do it. How do you take it?"

"Just lemon, thanks."

"No wonder you're so slim." Anne handed her the cup of tea and then poured herself a cup, with milk this time. "You were pushed into it by Sandy as well as Ryan."

Deborah sipped her tea, then gave Anne a twisted little smile over the rim of her cup. "To be honest, it was Sandy's input that did it."

"I thought it might have been. She can be very manipulative when she wants to be."

"Let's call it persuasive, not manipulative. Whatever it was, it worked. I'm Canada bound, it seems. Did you phone your aunt last night?"

"Yes."

"How was she?"

"Not very good. The morphine was wearing off and she was in a lot of pain."

"I'm sorry." Deborah took a piece of toast and spread diet margarine and lime marmalade on it. "I'm also sorry that I ran out on you last night."

"That's okay. I understand."

"Do you?" Deborah raised her eyebrows.

"It wasn't just the pressure. It was the way it was done." Anne leaned forward. "I meant what I said last night. I didn't come here just to see my father. I came to get to know my sister as well. By saying what he did last night, Ryan set us up against each other. That wasn't the idea at all."

Deborah set her cup back down on the tray. "But he was right, really, wasn't he? It does appear as if I was the lucky one."

"That was just the way it turned out. Ryan chose you to come to live with him." Anne looked down at her hands. "I guess he thought I was fine with Aunt Beth."

"And weren't you?"

"Yes. She was good to me, in her way. I suppose I just felt—" Anne seemed to be looking for the right words but unable to find them. "It's hard to describe it. Lost, I suppose. Alien. As if I belonged somewhere else. I kept thinking Daddy would come and get me so that we could all be together again." Avoiding Deborah's eyes, she bent forward to adjust the teapot so that the handle was toward her.

"Sounds a lot like my time at school." Deborah didn't expand on this. Her past life was none of Anne's business. Besides, she didn't want to think about it. Ever.

Then she remembered that she was going to have to think about it. She was going back to Winnipeg, the place of her birth. The thought made her feel shivery and nauseated, as if she were starting a bout of stomach flu.

She stood up. "Okay, no more chat. Let's get this thing organized. I'm not sure I can get away today, but—"

"No way. You'd never be able to make it."

"You don't know me. Have you found out about flights?"

"Yes. Air Canada's last flight for Toronto leaves at one o'clock, which would be impossible to catch.

There is a later British Airways flight from Heathrow, which would connect with a flight to Winnipeg, but you'd wouldn't be able to make it, either. Any other flights would be too late to make the connection."

"How long is the flight from Toronto?"

"Two and a half hours. The British Airways flight leaves at three o'clock, Ryan said."

Deborah glanced at her watch. "Three? I can do that." She thought for a moment, calculating driving times. "We'd need to drive directly to Heathrow from here."

"What about clothes?"

"I have enough here with me to get by." She gave Anne an acid smile. "I don't think I'm going to need my Versace for Winnipeg, am I?" She didn't wait for an answer. "If I need anything else I can buy it when I get there. I have to contact my P A and get him to—"

"What's a P A?"

"Personal assistant."

"Like a secretary?"

Deborah smiled. "In a way, but Timothy wouldn't like to hear himself called that."

"We also have to arrange a new ticket for Sandy, as she flew in from New York. Ryan said that he'd pay—"

"Just give me her current ticket. I'll get Timothy to work it all out. He can meet us at the airport."

"What can I do to help?"

"I thought you were going to Hampton Court today."

"Are you kidding? Sandy's going nuts trying to get all her stuff packed. I must admit I was doing some packing myself." Anne grimaced. "I never thought you'd go through with this."

"I'm rather stuck with it now, aren't I?"

"Not where I'm concerned, you're not. If you can catch that plane by three, so can I. To be honest, I'm going to feel really guilty about not going back to Winnipeg myself."

"Good. You can wallow in guilt for all I care," Deborah said with a grin, "but you're staying here to bond with Daddy and I'm going to Winnipeg with Sandy. I have my pride, you know."

"I still think this isn't fair to you."

"We've been through all that," Deborah said abruptly, "so don't waste your breath."

Anne's face reddened. "Okay. So how can I help?" she asked again.

"Send Sandy up here with her plane ticket. Once I've phoned Timothy to arrange our flights and had my shower you can help me pack. What the hell do I wear in Winnipeg in the summer? Boots and a ski jacket?"

"Get lost! It's hot there now. Thirty degrees at least every day."

"What's that in fahrenheit?"

"Eighty plus. Dry heat. Lots of sunshine."

"So I wear shorts, that sort of thing. Resort wear."

Anne had a vision of her sister turning up to work at the dusty garden center in her sarong wrap-skirt and almost choked. "Why don't you show me what you've got and I'll make suggestions?"

"Good idea. I'll have a quick shower first, though."

Anne sighed. "I hope you know what you're doing. Aunt Beth's difficult enough when she's well. God knows what she'll be like now."

Deborah was already in the bathroom, turning on the shower. "Did you tell her I was coming instead of you?"

"I didn't dare. Besides, I wasn't sure you were going." Anne went to the bathroom door. "If you did go, I thought it best if you just arrived without any warning."

Deborah stood in the center of the bathroom, dressed only in her silk boxer shorts, her small breasts firm above her flat stomach. "She's going to get one hell of a surprise, isn't she?"

"You can say that again." As she imagined Aunt Beth's face when Deborah walked in, Anne burst out laughing. She just couldn't hold it back. Deborah glared at her for a moment and then her face crumpled, too, and she joined in the laughter.

It occurred to Anne as they stood there, laughing together like two idiots, how cruel it was that fate was parting her and her sister at the very time they were beginning to get to know each other.

Chapter 19

Deborah's flight to Toronto was uneventful. The usual long, boring journey across the Atlantic squashed into too little space for too long a time. She'd frequently flown to the States, but this was her first flight to Canada.

Her first visit to the country of her birth since she'd left it almost thirty years ago.

Sandy had been a good companion, eager to talk about her future . . . going to New York, her hopes for her professional career. But when Deborah touched upon the one subject that had drawn them together, Conrad Hatcher, Sandy clammed up and took out a score and her portable CD player and headphones, explaining that she had to learn a new piece of music. Deborah had the feeling that there was still unfinished business there, but she knew that she mustn't push Sandy too hard.

As they were nearing Winnipeg on the second leg of their journey, she asked Sandy if she had anyone special in her life at the moment.

Sandy glanced at her and then away. "No. I broke up with Brian a few months ago."

"Sorry to hear that."

"No need to be. We'd grown apart. Brian's big ambition was to have his own pharmacy one day. In

Winnipeg. He didn't ever want to leave. We'd been going together since grade twelve. It was time to break up. My acceptance by Juilliard was the catalyst, I guess."

"It happens. One day you'll find the right one."

"Like you have. I think Graham's great."

Deborah grimaced. "He has his moments." As Sandy listened to her music, her fingers instinctively moving over an invisible guitar, Deborah closed her eyes and began to enumerate the many men she'd had in her life. Most of them exciting to be with, good lovers. Some older, some younger than she. Some wealthy, some not. It depended what mood she'd been in at the time as to what attracted her. Lately, though, she had begun to realize that the men she was interested in preferred younger, less experienced women. Perhaps it was time to settle for something more lasting, more secure, even if that meant something less exciting.

Then she'd met Graham and discovered that it was possible to combine security and excitement. That was before he'd bought bloody Somerford. She'd thought at first that this was a short-term obsession with a new toy. That he would soon grow tired of mucking around in gardens and getting his thrills from discussing wood paneling with restoration experts. But so far there was no sign of this boring new interest of his abating. She could only hope that once the summer ended and everything stopped growing he would become his dynamic, business-oriented self again.

"We shall be landing in Winnipeg shortly. Please fasten your seat belts and return your seats to an upright position. The weather in Winnipeg is a warm twenty-seven degrees."

As the plane descended through the light cloud, Deborah gazed out the window, feeling tense and angry. She was dreading this. Why in God's name had she allowed herself to be bullied into doing it? The ground below was a patchwork of vast flat fields intersected by long straight roads. It looked deadly monotonous.

"I thought you said there were lakes and forests," she said in a complaining tone to Sandy.

"There are." Sandy leaned across her to peer out the window. "We've passed them, I guess."

"Where's the city then?" There wasn't even a sign of habitation.

"We should be seeing it soon."

Deborah gritted her teeth. Better make the best of it, she told herself. After all, it was only for two weeks. "Thank God for that," she said aloud.

"What?" Sandy asked.

"Oh, sorry. I just meant thank God we're nearly there. I'm getting stiff from sitting in planes."

"Me, too." Sandy stretched. "I'm glad Marco's meeting us. You'll like Marco."

"Good." Sandy had told her that her mother's friend owned a small family restaurant. "How nice," had been Deborah's response. The thought of meeting a middle-aged Italian-Canadian pizza parlor owner did not exactly excite her.

Now the plane was circling over a collection of suburban houses that spread out from a cluster of taller buildings, which she took to be the city center. Some city! she thought to herself. Set down on the flat prairie in the middle of nowhere. As the plane came in to land, however, she was surprised to see trees everywhere, lining the streets and along the

banks of the winding river, and in groups that suggested parks of some kind.

"I didn't expect to see trees on the prairie."

Sandy laughed. "We don't live in the middle of a
wheat field, you know."

Having cleared customs in Toronto, they were
able to go directly to the baggage area. As they
stepped off the escalator a tall, dark-haired man
came forward, moving with a fluid grace that immediately caught Deborah's eye.

"Hi, Sandy." The man gave Sandy a hug and
stood looking at Deborah with open appreciation.

She suddenly wished she had done more with her
hair and makeup before they'd landed.

"Hi, Marco," Sandy said. "Deborah, this is Marco."

Deborah found her hand clasped in a strong grip.
It was difficult to hide her surprise. Her sister's
friend was hardly the short, plump restaurant owner
she'd envisaged. He was drop-dead gorgeous. Tanned
face and arms, ink-black wavy hair that curled over
the collar of his sports shirt, not a sign of super-
fluous fat anywhere.

"Hello, Marco. It's very kind of you to meet us."

"You are Anne's sister." He pronounced her sister's
name as if it were two syllables, his accent making it
sound pretty rather than mundane. "What else would
I do?"

"You didn't bring the kids with you?" Sandy
asked.

"They're with my mother. Too noisy after you've had
a long journey, yes?" He smiled at Deborah, flashing
teeth that gleamed white against the tanned face.

"How's Aunt Beth?" Sandy asked.

"Not so good. She's in a lot of pain."

"Did you tell her I was coming instead of Anne?"

Deborah asked, as they moved to the baggage carousel.

"No. No use upsetting her before the time comes. She'll see soon enough."

Deborah caught the disapproval in his voice. "Anne wanted to come home. But it seemed a shame for her to have so little time with our father."

"She should have come. Her aunt needs her."

"I'm sure she does, but I'm perfectly capable of helping."

He raised his shoulders in a slow shrug that was typically Latin, his mouth turning down at the corners in a twisted smile. " 'Scuse me saying so, but I can't see you working at that old garden center." Again, quite openly, he looked her up and down.

Deborah's chin lifted. "I'm a working woman."

"Not with those hands, you're not. Not manual work, anyway."

He turned away to the carousel, leaving Deborah smoldering. Insolent oaf! How dare he look at her like a farmer examining the stock.

"Which bags are yours?" he asked Sandy.

Sandy had retrieved her guitar case and opened it, examining her guitar carefully for damage. "We'll need a cart. I've got a big nylon bag and Deborah brought two cases."

"Only two?" Marco glanced at Deborah, his eyes gleaming with amusement. "We won't need a cart."

"I can deal with my own bags, thank you," Deborah said, trying hard not to sound as annoyed as she felt.

But when the bags came around, Marco picked up Sandy's nylon carryall and one of Deborah's cases as if they were light shopping bags. "You can manage the other one. It has wheels," he told Deborah, and started off toward the exit, with Sandy and Deborah following behind.

"I thought you'd want to go home first, rather than coming to my place to eat," he said, when he'd stowed the bags in the back and ushered them into his minivan. "Okay?"

Deborah glanced at Sandy. "I think we should go straight—" she hesitated, unwilling to say 'home.' It wasn't her home. "Straight to your aunt's home, don't you?"

"Yes. I want to see Aunt Beth. I promised I'd call Mom as soon as possible and let her know how she is."

Deborah glanced at her watch. "It's about four in the morning British time. I don't think even your mother would welcome a call now. Leave it until we wake up tomorrow."

"I'd still like to go home directly," Sandy said.

"Okay, that's what I thought," Marco said, slightly impatient with all this discussion. "Home it is." He started up the van and drove out of the parking lot.

Deborah had wondered if she would recognize anything when she arrived in the place of her birth, but everything—from the small detached houses lining the narrow streets near the airport to the wide, eight-lane road they called Portage Avenue—was unfamiliar. Schools, churches of every possible denomination, pizza parlors, a hospital, all kinds of shopping malls . . . she saw them all, but nothing sparked any kind of memory.

In a way she was glad of it. She preferred to think of this as somewhere new, a place she'd never been before.

A place she'd never have to return to again.

There was space everywhere. Space between houses, all of which, however small, had their flower beds and square of lawn at the front. Space covered with a great expanse of verdant grass fronting schools and hospitals. Small parks at regular intervals. Trees lining the main road and shading the gardens of the larger houses.

"This is the main road through Winnipeg," Sandy said, "and also part of the highway that goes across Canada.

They moved at a steady pace, with none of the massive traffic snarls that Deborah was used to in and around London. But she also noticed how casual drivers were about signaling.

"That would make me very angry," she told Marco, when yet another car had cut across in front of him to get to the outside lane without any warning. "I'd blast him with my horn if he did that to me."

"Canadians don't," he told her succinctly. "Not western Canadians, anyway."

She felt as if she'd been reprimanded. "Why is that?"

He shrugged. "Waste of time and energy."

Sandy leaned forward. "We're nearly there. Who's with Aunt Beth at the moment?" she asked Marco.

"Carla. My sister," he added, for Deborah's benefit.

"That's very kind of her," Deborah said.

Marco gave her a quirky grin. "Kind? Maybe. I think she wants to meet Anne's sister from England, that's why."

Deborah wasn't sure whether he was being serious or not.

He turned off the main road and then took another turn that led to a narrow road lined with tiny bunga-lows, each one with wooden sidings painted a different color. Marco drew the car up before a house painted in a particularly virulent shade of mustard yellow. It also had the prettiest garden.

"Here we are," Sandy said. "Home."

Deborah tried hard to hide her dismay. "It's—it's very small, isn't it? Like a tiny cottage." She felt claustrophobic just looking at it. The entire house looked small enough to fit into one of the rooms in her father's house. "What a lovely garden!" she added hastily, catching the disappointment on Sandy's face.

"That's all Mom's work, of course. She's the great gardener of the family."

"What about your aunt?"

"Oh, she looks after the vegetable garden at the back. Mom prefers flowers and shrubs." Carrying her guitar and shoulder bag, Sandy started up the path to the front door.

Before Marco could stop her, Deborah grabbed one of her cases and rolled it up the path of concrete slabs, many of which were cracked and breaking up into small pebbles. Heart sinking, she followed Sandy through the doorway and into the tiny entrance hall that led directly into the living room. Although it was warm outside, the heat inside the house hit her like a furnace blast.

A dark-haired woman, noticeably pregnant, was hugging Sandy in the living room. She looked younger and was far shorter than Marco, but there was a distinct resemblance. She came forward to greet Deborah, hand outstretched.

"Hello, hello. Welcome," she cried.

To Deborah's dismay, Carla gathered her in her arms and hugged her. She felt herself go stiff. She hated being touched by strangers. Even friends knew better than to embrace her when they met, but Carla didn't even seem to notice her reaction.

"Hello," Deborah said. "How kind of you to take care of—"

Sandy interrupted her polite speech of thanks. "Where is she?" she asked in a whisper.

"In her bedroom," Carla replied. "She wanted to wait for you in the living room, but she was too uncomfortable to sit up. She's in a lot of pain."

"Poor Beth. Come on, Aunt Deborah. Let's go and see her."

But Deborah hung back. "I don't want to give her a shock." She turned to Carla. "Your brother said she didn't know yet that I was coming instead of Anne. Unless you've told her," she added.

Carla looked troubled. "No, I didn't think I should. Ever since last night she keeps asking what time will Anne be here."

Oh, God! Deborah shut her eyes for a fleeting moment. This wasn't going to be easy. What an idiot she'd been to let herself be pushed into this! She drew in a deep breath and let it out in a long sigh. "Well, I suppose there's no point in putting this off any longer, is there?"

She met Marco's gaze as he stood in the doorway. "Good luck," he said, setting down the bags. This time he didn't smile.

Deborah followed Sandy along the narrow passageway. At the end of it Sandy hesitated and then knocked on the partially open wood-stained door. She was greeted by a grunt. "It's me, Aunt Beth. Sandy."

"Don't stand out there, girl. Come on in."

Sandy went in first, walking to the single bed and bending over to kiss her great-aunt. "What have you been doing to yourself? Can't leave you for a minute without you getting into trouble." There was a slight wavering in the pseudo-cheerful voice that betrayed how nervous Sandy was.

The room was small, the dark cumbersome chest and bedside cabinet making it appear even smaller. The only touch of light color in the room was the lemon curtains covering the small rectangular window. The wallpaper had possibly once been white-and-green flowers, but now it was stained a mustard-brown, no doubt from the cigarette smoke that presently shrouded the room.

The old woman lay in the bed, her right foot propped up on a cushion, a cigarette gripped between nicotine-stained fingers. She glared past Sandy, her eyes trying to focus on the woman standing in her doorway.

"Where's Anne?" she demanded. "And who the hell are you?"

Chapter 20

Deborah moved closer to the bed. "I'm Deborah."

"Deborah?" Beth mimicked her English accent, grossly exaggerating it. "I don't know any Deborah."

Deborah felt like turning around and marching right out of this wretched, dingy house. "Your niece," she said crisply.

"What niece? I don't have any—" Beth's mouth fell open. "You mean Debbie? Janine's little Deb?"

"That's right," Deborah replied.

"Anne never told me she was bringing you with her." Something like a smile crept across the cracked lips. "Well, well. Little Debbie. Come into the light so's I can see you better."

Deborah did as she was told, her nose wrinkling involuntarily as she drew nearer and smelled stale tobacco.

"Quite a looker, eh?"

"I'm sorry?"

"You look like one of them Hollywood film stars. Done well for yourself, haven't you? Janine would be proud. Where's Anne?"

Deborah hesitated before she answered. "She's staying with my father a little longer. She should be home soon."

Beth tried to lever herself upright by leaning on her fist, groaning with pain as she did so. "Goddamn this foot. You mean Anne hasn't come back with you?"

"No. I'm here instead of her."

"Instead of her what?"

Deborah said a silent prayer for patience. "I'm here to look after the garden center for you."

"You're what?" Beth let out a raucous cackle of laughter. "In those clothes? I'd like to see you do it."

"I assure you I'm perfectly aware of how to dress for hard work."

"Assure away, missy. I'm not putting my garden center into those lily-white hands."

"I'm going to look after you, Aunt Beth," Sandy said, intervening in what was shaping up to be a full-fledged battle. "I'll have you feeling really comfortable before you know it."

"Well, that's a lot more likely than your Aunt Deb's idea."

Deborah folded her arms and leaned her back against the wall. "Have you a better suggestion?"

"I sure have. I'm going to call Anne this minute and tell her to get her butt over here."

Deborah smiled sweetly. "Over my dead body you will."

Beth's eyes narrowed to slits, making her look like a beat-up boxer. "And how're you going to stop me?"

"For one thing I'm going to remove your telephone. It's not good for you to be disturbed with business matters while you're trying to get well."

Beth grabbed the telephone on the bedside cabinet and set it on the bed, between her knees. "Oh, no, you don't. Miss Bossyboots."

In one swift move, Deborah went to the other side of the bed and yanked the telephone cord from the wall.

Beth let out a screech. "Put that back. Who d'you think you are, coming in here and throwing your weight around like Lady Muck?"

"I'm your niece and I'm here to help you get better by looking after your business for you."

Beth fell back, panting, onto her pillows. "Running it into the ground more like. Sandy, sweetheart, plug in your Aunty Beth's phone for her like a good girl, will you?"

Sandy glanced at Deborah, who shook her head. "Sorry, I can't. Aunt Deborah's right. The more rest you get the sooner you'll heal. You look as if you're in a lot of pain. Have you taken any painkillers tonight?"

Beth turned her head away from them. "Don't want to be drugged."

Sandy sat down on the bed.

"Don't sit on my goddamn foot," Beth screeched.

"I'm nowhere near it," Sandy said calmly, taking Beth's hand. "No one's going to drug you, but you must take something for the pain so you can sleep."

"I'll find out what she's had this evening," Deborah said and left the room.

"A feisty witch, that one," Beth said. Her hand stirred restlessly beneath Sandy's. "I wish your mother was here. Why didn't she come?"

"She really wanted to, but she'd hardly had any time with her father. He persuaded her to stay a little longer and asked Aunt Deborah to take her place."

"No one could take your mother's place," Beth whispered. Her eyes flew open. "But don't you go telling her that and swellin' her head."

"I won't."

"I just wish she'd come." Beth's eyes squeezed

shut again as she stifled a groan, her hand convulsing on Sandy's.

"Hang on," Sandy said softly. "We're going to give you something for the pain right away."

Deborah came back into the room. "Carla said she wouldn't take her pills," she told Sandy in a low voice. "She hasn't had anything since early this morning."

"That's awful."

"Carla keeps them in the kitchen so she can tell what she's had. I've got them here." Deborah held up the container of pills. "She's supposed to have two every four hours. Do you think she'll take them?"

Beth's eyes opened. "For Pete's sake, stop talking about me as if I'm already in my box."

Deborah smiled. "Sorry. I thought you were asleep. I'll leave you in Sandy's good care."

"You do that. Don't want to see your bossy face in here again."

"I'm sorry to hear that. I was hoping you'd be able to tell me all about the garden center tomorrow." Deborah shrugged as she moved to the door. "I suppose I'll just have to work things out for myself."

"Like hell you will. You come here first thing tomorrow, before you set foot in my place, you hear me?"

"I'll do that. Good night. Sleep well."

Deborah went back to the kitchen and slumped into a chair. "You look tired," Carla said.

"I am," Deborah admitted. She glanced at her watch. "It's four-thirty in the morning British time."

"How about a drink?" Marco asked. He seemed to be taking up all the space in the cramped kitchen.

"I'd love one."

"Wine? Scotch?"

"I'd prefer a gin and tonic."

He bent down to look through a corner cupboard. "Gin, but no tonic. No one here drinks the stuff."

"Okay, I'll have wine." It would probably be the worst sort of plonk.

Marco held up two bottles. "Bardolino or Lugana. That's an Italian white. I brought a couple of each, so you had some wine in the place if you wanted it."

"Thank you. I'll have Bardolino." Instinctively, Deborah ran her fingers over her mouth, wondering if she had any lipstick left on.

As Marco crossed behind her to get to the glasses, his bare arm brushed against hers.

She moved away quickly. "Sorry. I'm in your way."

"That's okay. Why don't you go sit down? Carla's heating some pasta I brought from the restaurant."

Pasta at this time? Deborah was about to decline, but then decided it sounded great. "I'd love some."

Carla took her arm and guided her into the cramped living room. "You sit down here and rest. Marco put your bags in Anne's room. Your bed's all made up."

"You didn't need to do that."

Marco came into the room, carrying a tray bearing glasses and the bottle of Bardolino. "She didn't. Anne left it fresh and tidy when she went away. The rest of the house isn't the same as Beth's room. It's always a fight for Anne to get into it to clean it."

"What about a bath for my aunt?"

"She can't get into a bath because of the cast. She did wash herself with a basin of water this morning," Carla said. "She wouldn't let me help her. But don't you worry your head about it. I've arranged for a VON nurse to come in tomorrow to do it properly."

"You've both been so kind." Deborah took a glass of wine from Marco and then sipped it. It tasted very good. "It's rather difficult for me, not knowing who to get in touch with."

"No problem," Marco said. "It's tough for you coming in here new, knowing nobody but Sandy."

"She's a good kid," Carla said. "Anne's going to miss her when she goes away."

Deborah hadn't considered Anne's side of it. All she'd thought of was that Sandy should get away as soon as possible from such a possessive mother. But now that she'd met Beth and seen Anne's home, she could see how much she was going to miss the vital company of her bright daughter. A shiver ran across her shoulders at the thought of being stuck in this house with her aunt. God, what a fate!

On the other hand, Anne did have Marco. What on earth was going on between her sister and this man? Obviously they were pretty close for him to be doing so much for Anne's family, yet they weren't actually living together. So what exactly was their relationship?

"I must be going." Carla stood up. "Marco will serve the pasta for you."

"No need," Deborah said. "I can do that for myself. You'll want to drive your sister home," she added, smiling at Marco.

"I have my own car, thanks." Carla went to hug Deborah, who steeled herself not to flinch. "Sleep well. Anything you want to know, ask Marco. And I've left my number on the fridge in case you need anything."

"You've been very kind. Thank you. I know Anne will be very grateful."

"She's done things for me plenty of times," Carla said. "That's a good sister you've got yourself."

Deborah nodded mechanically. She didn't want to

get involved with any of these people. They were complete strangers and not at all her type. Yet somehow she could feel herself being drawn in, whether she liked it or not.

When Carla left, Marco brought in two plates heaped with steaming pasta. "Sandy said she'd have hers later, when Beth falls asleep. Spaghetti with fresh tomatoes and roasted pine nuts," he announced. "Eat."

The pasta was excellent. "This is very good," Deborah said, genuinely impressed.

Marco just nodded and kept eating, expertly twirling his spaghetti around his fork in that relaxed way Italians had with their native food.

Deborah felt too tired to make conversation and yet silence between them seemed too intimate. She was keenly aware of the way Marco's dark hair shone in the light from the standard lamp as he bent to eat. From the direction of Beth's room came the soft strumming of Sandy's guitar. Marco looked up, wiped his mouth with the napkin, and smiled.

"She's playing for her aunt. That's nice."

Deborah nodded, but said nothing and continued to eat, allowing the music to flow over her. When she had finished the food, she drank more wine. The combination of tiredness, pasta, wine, and music was relaxing her almost to the point of falling asleep, yet she was also very conscious of this man who was now sitting back in his chair, watching her lazily with dark liquid eyes.

"So . . . you're gonna look after the garden center for Beth, eh?"

"That's my intention, yes." She took another sip of wine and waited for him to renew his earlier taunts at her ability to work in the center.

"Think you can do it?"

"Of course I can. I run my own business in England."

"What kind of business?"

"Mainly conferences and business travel. I'm planning to add a luxury holiday travel subsidiary to the company."

"Hmm. Sounds pretty fancy. A city business-woman." He stretched out his long legs and put his hands behind his head. "Beth's garden place will be quite a change for you."

Deborah bristled, sensing the mockery in his voice. "I'm sure it will be, but I'll manage very well, thank you." She stood up. "I hope you don't mind, but I really must get some sleep."

He glanced at his watch and got to his feet in one easy motion. "Me too. I promised my mother I'd be back by eleven."

"Your mother?"

Marco was busy gathering up the plates and cutlery onto a tray. "Yes. She's looking after the kids."

"Oh, you have children." Somehow, he didn't seem the domesticated sort. Then she remembered Sandy asking about his children at the airport.

"I have two. Roberto and Floria." Setting down the tray, he drew out a thin leather wallet from his shirt pocket to show her a photograph. "My two motherless children."

Deborah tilted her head in a question.

"My wife left me three years ago. Just walked out on us without any warning."

"Really?" Somehow Deborah couldn't believe this.

"Really." He gave her a wry smile. "She didn't like the restaurant. Too much hard work, she said."

"That's too bad." She felt uncomfortable talking about such personal matters with Marco. She hesitated, wanting to ask the obvious question but not wanting to sound that interested. Then she plunged in. "What about you and the children? Didn't she like you either?"

"Not enough, I guess," he said with a twist to his mouth.

Despite her discomfort, Deborah was curious enough to want to get to the bottom of this. After all, he was the one who'd brought the subject up. Besides, she was interested to know what kind of man her sister's friend was.

"Did you expect your wife to work in the restaurant? I mean ... did she have a choice in the matter?"

"Choice?" He frowned. "You mean, did I force her to work there? No, no, no. What she didn't like was *me* working there. Me building up a fine restaurant and a good clientele. She'd like me to be a nine-to-five office guy, but that's not me. She didn't like my dreams. And she sure didn't share them." He looked at his watch again. "I'm talking too much."

Like a whirlwind he scooped up glasses and condiments and place mats, setting them on the tray, and pushed it into the kitchen through the old-fashioned hatchway.

"I'll do the rest," Deborah said, but it was done. He was already in the kitchen rinsing off the plates and putting them in the small dishwasher.

"There's some pasta left for tomorrow," he told her. "It's in a bowl in the fridge. You can heat it in the microwave. You know how to work it?"

"I think I can find out." Deborah was starting to wonder if Marco's wife had left him because he made her feel totally inadequate. "Thank you very much. I can manage for myself now," she said firmly, taking the dish towel from his hands. "Don't forget, I've got Sandy."

"I know." He stood quite close to her in the confined kitchen, so that she breathed in the light scent of his cologne. He held out his hand to her. "Welcome to Canada, Miss—"

"Deborah."

He repeated it, sounding all the syllables. "Give me a call if you need anything, anything at all." He went to the door. "Say good night to Sandy for me. I don't want to yell and wake Beth."

"I will. Thank you for everything. You and your sister have been so kind."

"You're welcome." He started down the path, then turned back. "Forgot to tell you. The truck's filled with gas."

"Truck?"

"Yeah. The old Ford pickup. Sandy'll show you how to start it. Takes a minute to get it turned over first thing in the morning." Even in the rustling darkness she could see his teeth gleam in a grin. "Good luck."

"Thank you," Deborah said again, this time with much less warmth, and closed the door on him.

Chapter 21

Deborah awoke with the strange sensation that she was at the bottom of a well and had to force her way up through murky water for air. Trying not to panic, she fought her way to the top . . . and opened her eyes to find her arms stretched above her head and Anne's quilt covering her face. It was stifling hot in the room, the open window issuing nothing but a slight current of warm air.

She threw off the quilt and sat up. Two sounds had awakened her: a low hum as if a lightweight engine were operating right there in the room, and someone groaning. The latter, no doubt, came from Beth's room. She swung her legs over the side of the bed. As she was searching in the darkness for her dressing gown her hands encountered a large, furry creature that was decidedly alive. Letting out a muted scream, she hurriedly switched on the bedside lamp.

There, at the end of her bed, was the source of the humming sound: a very large, gray, long-haired cat blinking at her in the sudden brightness, with what looked decidedly like a smirk on its broad face.

"Someone could have warned me," she muttered to herself as she tied her kimono around her. It wasn't that she was afraid of cats, but it was rather unnerving to find some unidentified creature on one's bed in the middle of the night, especially in a strange country. After all, it might have been a skunk or something equally ghastly.

She opened her door and crept down the narrow corridor, pausing outside Beth's room. She knocked very gently on the door and opened it a crack. "Anything I can do to help?" she whispered.

To her relief Sandy was there. She came to the door. "I've just given her more pills and made her a bit more comfortable." As Sandy carefully shut the door behind her and came out, Deborah could see the dark smudges beneath her eyes.

"You look dreadfully tired. Have you had any sleep at all?"

"Not much." Sandy turned away as if she didn't want to talk. "I'm okay."

"I wouldn't mind a cup of tea before I go back to bed. How about you?"

Sandy hesitated and then shrugged. "Okay. But I'll have a SevenUP." She led the way into the kitchen and slid the door shut.

"Will we be able to hear her?" Deborah asked.

"I've given her a couple of saucepan lids she can clang together if she needs me." Sandy sank onto the chair at the tiny kitchen table, covering her face with her hands. "Geez, I'm tired."

"You must be." Instinctively, Deborah put her hand on Sandy's shoulder and then worried that she'd done the wrong thing. When Sandy lifted her face up Deborah saw that she was crying, her eyes drowned in tears.

For an instant, she was tempted to run like hell from this place. She just wasn't equipped to handle

sick or emotional people. Anne should be here, dealing with this, not her.

Feeling both annoyed and inept, Deborah put her
arm around Sandy's shoulders. Sandy's even more
disconcerting response was to turn and fling her
arms around her, pressing her face against her waist.
Deborah could feel the dampness from her niece's
tears seeping through the thin silk of her nightdress.

As Sandy sobbed against her, she stood erect,
wondering what to do. Then she gently disengaged
Sandy's arms, pulled up the other chair to sit in front
of her, and took hold of her hands. "This isn't only
about your Aunt Beth, is it?" she said softly.

Sandy shook her head, her face hidden by the fall
of dark hair.

"Can you talk to me about it?" But even as she
asked the question, Deborah knew what it was about.
Bloody Conrad. "Are you still worrying about what
happened last Saturday night?" she asked, when
Sandy didn't respond.

Sandy nodded.

"I'm sure everything's fine. It's all forgotten now.
No one need know."

Sandy's hands convulsed on Deborah's. "I'm not
sure he—he used any protection," she whispered. "I
keep trying and trying to remember, but I can't.
Everything's a blur until I sort of . . . woke up feeling really sick."

"How many drinks do you think you had?"

"Drinks?" Sandy shook her head impatiently. "How
can I remember that? Two, to start with. Then . . . a
lot more after the coffee, I think. Why?"

Deborah didn't answer her. "And you can't actually recall him using a condom?"

"All I can remember is feeling incredibly sexy,

like I was . . . I can't describe it. I've never felt like
it before. It was the most fantastic high I've ever
had. But afterwards I felt like I wanted to die."

Deborah went cold. Sandy had just described
exactly how it felt to be high on Ecstasy, the bloody
pills that had killed a couple of girls in England
recently. That bastard Conrad had drugged Sandy.
Deborah wished to hell now that she'd advised her
to tell Anne everything, instead of encouraging her
to keep quiet about it.

Let's face it, she told herself, you were protecting
your precious business assets, yours and Ryan's.
Question was, should she go on protecting Conrad?
On the other hand, what was the point of telling
Sandy now that she had been drugged and making
her feel even more lousy about it all?

"Conrad's a sophisticated man," she told Sandy.
"I'm quite sure he would use a condom. Besides,
you're on the pill, aren't you?"

"No. I stopped taking it when I broke up with
Brian. My boyfriend."

"I see. No wonder you were worrying about
protection."

"Could he—I mean Conrad—have AIDS?"

God in heaven! The poor kid was also worrying
about an even bigger peril than an unwanted pregnancy. Deborah was overwhelmed by a surge of
fierce anger at Conrad. Goddamn him! This was her
own flesh and blood he'd abused, not just some
stranger. It was a good thing he wasn't here now.
She felt like tearing his foxy face to shreds.

Deborah suddenly realized that she hadn't answered
Sandy, who was staring at her with eyes round with
fear. "Conrad's as healthy as can be," she said hastily.
"He lifts weights and runs, and plays tennis and golf

and racquetball. I'm quite sure he hasn't got AIDS."
Which was a wonder considering what a randy old
goat he was. On the other hand, she thought with a
stab of doubt, there were many men, especially men
of Conrad's kind, who got a thrill out of having un-
protected sex.

"I hope you're right."

"I'm sure he used a condom, Sandy. He certainly
wouldn't have wanted to get you pregnant. I can't
quite see Conrad as a daddy, can you?" Deborah
added, in a desperate attempt to lighten the tension,
but Sandy didn't smile.

"I wish I'd asked him," Sandy said. "But I didn't
want to see him afterwards."

"I don't blame you. If I'd thought about it, I'd
have got you to a women's clinic for morning-after
medication to prevent pregnancy, but it never occurred to me that Conrad wouldn't use protection—
or that you wouldn't be on the pill."

"Anyway, I couldn't have done that in England
without Mom knowing. And I don't want her to
know, ever!" Sandy's eyes seemed enormous as she
looked at Deborah. "Okay?"

"If you say so." That made it easier for Deborah,
but she also felt uncomfortable about not telling
Anne, as if she were deceiving her. What in God's
name would happen if Sandy *was* pregnant? "I'm
quite sure you'll be absolutely fine," she said, sounding much more confident than she felt. "When are
you due?"

"Another ten days."

"Good. Then you don't have too long to wait.
Meanwhile, it wouldn't hurt for you to see a doctor,
just to get checked over."

Sandy's eyes widened with fear. "I can't go to our family doctor."

"You don't need to. Isn't there a women's clinic in town?"

"I—I guess so."

"Then go there."

"Will you come with me, Aunt Debbie?"

Oh, God! Let me out of here, was Deborah's silent reaction. "Of course I will. We'll go in the morning. But now we both need our sleep or we'll be like zombies tomorrow."

Deborah hesitated and then put her arms around Sandy. She wasn't used to hugging people, especially women, but when Sandy responded by hugging her back and saying, "Thanks for being there for me," it gave her a feeling of warmth that was quite new to her.

Chapter 22

The doctor at the women's clinic confirmed that it was too late for morning-after antipregnancy treatment, but she recommended a heavy dose of birth-control pills and to come back in two months for an HIV test. As they drove home in the ancient Volkswagen Rabbit, Deborah could see from Sandy's ashen face and the tremor in the hands clutching the steering wheel that she had really been shaken up by the experience.

There wasn't much point in talking about it all over again. Better to hope to God that Conrad wasn't a total bastard and to encourage Sandy to get on with her life as best she could. The only thing Deborah did say was that it might be a good idea to keep on the pill permanently from now on.

"I hate taking them," Sandy said, her eyes fixed on the traffic ahead. "Who knows what damage they do to women's bodies."

"But—"

"I've got a much better idea. From now on I'm going to keep away from men." Sandy's voice shook with suppressed anger.

"That's rather drastic, isn't it?"

"I don't think so. I had a great chance ahead of me and I may have blown it. Juilliard, my professional career . . . everything! Just for a quick fuck with a man old enough to be my father."

Coming from Sandy the statement was doubly shocking.

"Hold on now. You didn't have much control over this. You were—" Deborah paused, still not sure she should tell Sandy.

"Don't tell me he forced me to drink. I did that myself." Sandy's voice was filled with self-loathing.

"I think he may have given you something else."

The traffic light had turned green, but Sandy remained immobile, staring at Deborah until a blast from the car behind her urged her to get going. "You mean he could have given me some sort of drug?"

"From what you've told me it seems very likely that he slipped something into your coffee."

"God, what a shit!" Sandy said, when this had sunk in.

"I agree."

"That would explain things, wouldn't it? The way I suddenly changed. I mean it was like . . . I wasn't me anymore."

"That's right. You weren't."

Sandy slammed on the brakes as another car slowed down in front of her. "Sorry about that."

"Do you want me to take over?" Deborah asked nervously. "I'm not sure you're in a fit state to drive."

"Sorry. I'll be fine. I just— You don't think I'll get flashbacks . . . something like that, do you? You see, I've never taken drugs before."

"Not even pot?"

"No." Sandy gave her a sheepish smile. "Sounds corny, I know, but I was too ambitious, too much wanting to succeed, to risk messing up my life.

There was plenty of the stuff around, even in high school, but I never wanted to do it."

Remembering her own fairly wild youth, Deborah grimaced. "Don't worry, one pill isn't going to affect you."

"It has affected me, though, hasn't it? I could be pregnant or, even worse, I could have AIDS."

"You'll know about the pregnancy very soon. The other possibility is highly unlikely. What you're going to have to do now is put all this behind you and get on with your life. When do you leave for New York?"

"If I'm going."

"Now, stop it, Sandy. You are going. When?"

"The third week in August."

"Good. That will give you a month to sort yourself out, get those classes and concerts done, and go on a shopping spree."

"No more shopping. I have to save every cent I get."

"This will be my treat," Deborah said.

"You can't use shopping as a cure-all," Sandy said severely.

"That sounds like your mother talking."

"Maybe so, but it's right. When you don't have money you have to find something else to console you."

"What do you use?"

"Music, both listening and playing. And frozen chocolate cake," Sandy added with a grin, her first smile since they'd entered the clinic.

"Frozen?"

"Straight from the freezer, out of the foil pan. Yummy."

"I'll have to remember that if I ever lose all my money."

"Works for me."

"Have you got any at home?"

"I think so."

"Then we'll both have some, with a cup of strong coffee to keep me awake."

Sandy turned down the road that was becoming familiar to Deborah, and pulled onto the driveway behind the little house.

They had left Beth with a neighbor, Elsie Penner. When they went in, Mrs. Penner was sitting in the living room, eating a packet of taco chips, her fat thighs straining against oversize floral cotton shorts.

"Hi there, how'd it go?" she asked.

"Fine. How's Aunt Beth?" Sandy asked.

"Won't let me do a thing for her," Mrs. Penner said. "How did you guys get on at the doctor's?" Sandy had told her that they were going to get allergy medication for Deborah. "You were gone a heck of a long time."

"I am sorry," Deborah said frostily. "The medical clinic was extremely busy."

"That's okay. I watched *Young and the Restless* and *Jenny Jones* while you were gone. So, what did they give you? My Ron takes those anti—"

"We've kept you quite long enough, Mrs. Penner. You've been very kind." Deborah took out her wallet. "How much do I owe you?"

Elsie Penner's mouth dropped open. Then it snapped shut. Her round button eyes looked at Sandy and then back at Deborah. "I don't want money for looking after Beth. She and me are old friends." She gathered up her navy sweater and the two empty chip bags, and swept regally past Deborah, stopping only to kiss Sandy's cheek as she went out. "Ask me any time you need me," she told Sandy with a definite emphasis on the *you*.

The back door slammed shut.

"Oh dear! I seem to have upset Mrs. Penner."

"You sure have. You shouldn't have offered her money."

"Sorry. I just thought—"

"She's been Beth's neighbor since before Mom and I came to live here."

"Sandy!" Beth's voice yelled from the bedroom.

"Coming right away," Sandy called back. "Why don't you put the kettle on for that coffee?" she suggested.

"I will. Tell Beth I'll come and see her as soon as I've had my coffee. She was asking me this morning when I was going to the center. I think I should go this afternoon, just to reassure her."

"Good idea," Sandy said and went to Beth.

Deborah was dreading going to the garden center. Since she'd arrived, she had been feeling like an alien on another planet. Everything in this place was strange to her. It wasn't just the different accents or the feeling of space or the vast blue sky or the intense heat that were getting to her. It was also the downright friendliness of the place. The chummy informality. *You guys?* She shuddered. She knew that her reserve was putting people's backs up, but that was the way she was and she certainly wasn't going to change for people she would never again see in her lifetime. She didn't want to be a *guy* nor to engage in conversation with the youth at the petrol (gas, she must remember) station or the woman in the bank, as Sandy did. "Hi, how're you doin'?" the teller had said.

It was all too folksy for Deborah. It was hard to believe that she had lived her first seven years in these surroundings. How on earth had she survived?

Sandy came back, carrying a tray.

"How is she?"

"Still in a lot of pain. I helped her into the wheelchair to get her to the bathroom. She won't use the bedpan."

"I can't say I blame her. Does she want to see me?"

"I told her you'd come in a minute."

It was more like half an hour by the time they'd talked and finished eating the cloyingly sweet chocolate cake that Deborah had indulged in solely to please Sandy. She was about to go to Beth when the telephone rang. As she was nearest to it, she picked up the receiver. It was Anne.

"Did you have a good flight?" There was an edge to Anne's voice. "I was getting a bit worried when I didn't hear from you."

"It's your mother," Deborah mouthed to Sandy. "Very good, thanks," she told Anne. "Sorry we didn't call you first thing this morning. We've been unpacking . . . that sort of thing."

"Are you settling in okay?"

"Fine." She couldn't very well say, "I took Sandy to see about an HIV test and birth-control pills," could she?

"How's Aunt Beth?"

"I'll pass you on to Sandy, as she's the one looking after her."

"Would you like to speak to Ryan first?" Anne was saying, but Deborah handed the phone to Sandy, as if she hadn't heard. She had no desire to speak to her father at the moment. She was too damned angry with him for having forced her into this ridiculous charade.

She ran hot water into the coffeepot, scrubbing at it furiously, and then realized that she was so angry she'd forgotten to put on rubber gloves. Hurriedly she dried her hands and started searching in the cupboard under the sink. No sign of gloves. She'd have to wait until Sandy got off the phone.

"Ryan's asking if you want to speak to Graham," Sandy told her, her hand covering the mouthpiece. "He's over there for dinner."

"I don't want to speak to anyone. Tell them I'm too busy."

Sandy's dark eyebrows lifted. "Okay." She was about to repeat the message to Ryan, but Deborah thought better of it.

"Ask my father to tell Graham I'll call him back in a few minutes. I have to go and speak to Beth first."

Sandy gave the message and again turned to Deborah. "Ryan says would you please call them later tonight or tomorrow, as they're all going out to the something Angler for dinner tonight and are leaving right away."

"The Compleat Angler," Deborah said automatically. Damn them! That was one of her favorite restaurants. Deborah felt utterly abandoned. Here she was in hick city and they were going off to dinner in one of the most elegant country hotels in England. "Fine. I'll speak to Graham sometime when I'm not busy. Tell them to have a great time tonight." She slammed the coffeepot on the draining board and marched down the hallway to Beth's room.

"Are you awake?" she asked in a low voice, tapping on the door.

"Not much chance of sleeping with all that racket going on." Deborah pushed open the door and went in. "Who's calling?" Beth demanded.

"Calling? Oh, you mean the phone. Anne. Would you like to speak to her?" She went out into the hallway again and called to Sandy. "Ask Anne if she has time to speak to Aunt Beth." Then she went back into the bedroom.

"You mean you'll allow me to speak on the phone?" Beth said. "Thank you so much, kind lady."

"Now, now, don't be sarcastic. I was just trying to get you to rest last night." Deborah knelt down on the dusty floor, looking for the phone outlet in the baseboard. "Ah, there we are." She plugged the cord in and then picked up the receiver. Sandy and Anne were still speaking. "Excuse me for interrupting," she told them, "I have the phone ready for Beth now, all right?"

She helped Beth sit up a little, plumping up the pillows behind her, handed her the phone and left the room.

Still fuming, she went into Anne's room and sat on the edge of the bed. No doubt Beth would be blasting Anne for not coming home. Serve her right. She deserved it for being so selfish. Then she remembered that it hadn't really been Anne's fault. It was Ryan who had coerced them both into this ridiculous switch. Whoever was responsible, she sincerely hoped that Beth would persuade Anne to come home immediately and that would put an end to all this nonsense. Ryan wouldn't be pleased, of course. At least, not at first, but he'd soon get used to everything returning to the way it had been, before Anne and Sandy had arrived in England.

But something told her that even if Anne did decide to come home right away, things would never again be quite the same.

Less than five minutes later, she heard the phone being crashed into its cradle. She hurried back to Beth's room.

Beth was slumped down in the bed, a picture of

angry dejection. "That's all the thanks I get for taking her into my house, giving her a home when her and her kid hadn't a cent." She tried to move and let out a drawn-out groan. "Shit, that hurts!"

"Can I help you?"

"No, you can't. I guess I'm stuck with you. Your ungrateful sister prefers to stay with her daddy."

Deborah didn't want to get involved in this, but to her surprise she found herself defending Anne. "They didn't have much time to get to know each other. It won't be long before she's home. Meanwhile, you have Sandy and me to take care of you and the business."

"I won't have any business by the time I get out of this goddamn cast."

"Of course you will. I'll take care of the garden center until Anne comes home. Your cast will be off in six weeks and then you'll be running around like you always did."

"The season will be almost over by then," Beth said gloomily. She threw back the bedclothes, uncovering the right leg in a white cast up to the knee, propped on a couple of pillows. "Geez it's hot."

"It certainly is." The room was like an airless oven. "Let's open the windows wider. Do you have a fan?"

"Somewhere. Sandy will know."

"We'll set it up in here."

"D'you want me to get pneumonia? That would solve your problem, wouldn't it?"

Deborah dredged up a smile. "I have no problems. Before I get Sandy to find that fan I'd like you to tell me what you want me to do in the garden center. Better still, if there's someone there who can tell me, it would save you having to tire yourself."

"It would take me a month to tell you all there is to do there."

"Well, we don't have a month, do we?" Deborah sat on the only seat in the room, the dressing table stool that had once been covered in a pale-blue silky fabric, but was now worn to mere threads. "How about going through your day with me? Tell me what you do from the time you arrive until you leave to come home."

With much grumbling—and impatience with any questions Deborah asked her—Beth went through her day. To Deborah's surprise, once her aunt got going she was perfectly lucid, so that her description of her workday was easy to follow.

When Beth paused for breath and a drink of water, Deborah said, "It sounds as if you have a great deal of work to do," and meant it.

"Too much for you, eh?"

"I wouldn't say that, but I will say I admire how much you do. Lots of physical hard work as well as all the books and the orders."

"Think you can handle it?"

"I don't see why not. I'm going to go to the center this afternoon."

"In that rig-out?" Beth eyed the pale-sage Irish linen pantsuit Deborah was wearing.

Deborah was determined the old battle-ax wasn't going to get the same rise out of her twice. "I'm just going to meet everyone and have a look around today. Then tomorrow I can get down to work. I shall pick up the books and bring them home with me," she added quickly, when she saw Beth ready to explode.

"Good thing. Thought you were here for a cushy vacation from the sound of it."

"If I have any questions," Deborah said, ignoring her, "you can explain things to me on the spot. Then I'll be ready for action for tomorrow. Don't worry, I'm well prepared. I brought some jeans and T-shirts with me."

Beth still looked disgruntled. "You'll need 'em. What size boot d'you take?"

"Boot?"

"Yeah. Rubber boots. Mine are eights."

Deborah had no intention of swanning around in rubber boots, but she played along. "I'll try yours on."

"If they're too big, try Anne's. Hers are smaller. You're sisters, so you should have the same size feet."

Beth's logic escaped Deborah. "Before I go, do you have a small television you could set up in here?"

"Why? I never watch TV."

"It would help to pass the time."

"Don't need it. Soon as that nurse comes to wash me this afternoon, I'm getting out of here."

"Where do you intend going?"

"Living room. This place's like one of them saunas."

Deborah had hoped to keep her in her bedroom. The thought of that voice bossing them around all day was not a happy one. "That depends on how you're feeling, doesn't it?" she said brightly.

"I'll feel just as bad in the living room as I do here, but at least I'll know what's going on."

That was what Deborah was afraid of.

Chapter 23

The sky began clouding over when Deborah and Sandy were eating their lunch of tuna sandwiches and apples in the back garden. At least Sandy was eating the sandwiches. Deborah had never tasted anything quite so revolting and said she wasn't hungry. She'd give the world for the food hall at Harrods now—or even a good Marks and Spencer's—so that she could stock up on some preprepared *edible* food.

"We'll eat Marco's pasta this evening," she was saying to Sandy, when the rain suddenly started to fall. Light spots at first and then, suddenly, a downpour. They hurriedly gathered up their plates and glasses and ran inside.

"You'd better change before you go to the center," Sandy said, eyeing the rain-spotted linen suit and medium-heeled shoes.

"I'll put on my flat shoes," was Deborah's only concession. She wanted to make sure that the employees at the center knew who was going to be boss for the next couple of weeks. Walking in dressed in jeans would only put her on their level. Time enough for that tomorrow, when they'd accepted that she was in charge.

"Okay, you're the boss," Sandy said, unaware that

she was confirming Deborah's intentions. "You'd better take the Rabbit. The pickup's pretty messy inside."

"Are you sure?"

Sandy handed her the keys from her pocket. "It's a bit temperamental." She grinned. "Not quite as smooth a ride as your Porsche."

"That's okay. Now, how do I get there?"

"Oh, of course. Tell you what. Why don't I lead you there in the pickup?"

"What about Beth?"

"Oh, she'll be okay. I'll be away half an hour at the most. I'll just go and tell her, see if she needs anything before I go."

Within minutes, everything was arranged, with Beth still shouting instructions at Deborah as she was walking out the back door, but the pounding of rain on her umbrella drowned out whatever Beth was saying.

Deborah scrambled into the Rabbit. It was grungy inside, but not sufficiently bad for her to wipe the seat before she sat down. Sandy leaned from the window of the pickup to give her directions in case they were separated, and then drove out into the back lane.

The car took three turnovers to start and when it did the engine sounded like several cans rattling together, but it did move when Deborah pressed the accelerator. She stopped to find the switch for the wipers, and then backed out, following Sandy down the lane and into Oakland Road.

It took little more than ten minutes to drive over the bridge, clear the outskirts of the city, and get out onto the main highway. Once clear of the discount stores, she found herself driving down the broad highway into what was obviously the real prairie. Through the curtain of heavy rain, she could see fields of wheat and some bright-yellow crop stretching for what seemed like miles on both sides of the road. The huge heavily clouded sky was like an immense canopy above and around her. She couldn't recall ever having seen such a vast expanse of space before.

Yet this land was part of her own past, her habitual environment for the first seven years of her life. Why didn't she remember any of it? What had made her blot it all out?

She was so engrossed in her thoughts that she almost missed the fact that Sandy had moved into the center lane and was signaling a left turn. Deborah tucked in behind her and then followed her down a rural road lined with trees. After driving a short distance, Sandy slowed down. Now Deborah could see a collection of what appeared to be flimsy greenhouses constructed of wooden lathes and plastic sheeting and two large wooden shacks.

Dear God, surely this wasn't it? She hadn't been expecting anything special—and Beth had told her that the greenhouses were roofed with plastic—but she'd thought that at least the main building would be a well-built store with, perhaps, trellises with yellow and purple clematis trailing along the walls and attractive windows filled with plants to entice passersby inside.

Instead, this looked like some sort of long storage hut with one small window. Moreover, there weren't any passersby to entice. This wasn't a busy road. The only people coming here would have to know about the garden center ahead of time.

Yes, this was it, she thought grimly, reading the sign above the doorway, CARTER'S GARDEN CENTRE, as she followed Sandy into the gravel parking lot.

To her right were small individual hills of rock
chips and sand and dark—almost black—soil, the
latter escaping from its plastic cover and running
across the lot in a stream of black mud to mingle
with the yellow. White plastic birdbaths and gaudily
painted pixies and fawns were the crowning touch.

The place was an utter disaster.

She knew as soon as she pulled in that she was in
big trouble. The yellow gravel, which had been
sparsely spread in the first place, was now barely
existent. The entire parking lot in front of the ramshackle buildings was a sea of yellow mud pitted
with waterlogged potholes. How in hell could she
make it across the lot and into the main building in
the driving rain? That yellow gunk would ruin her
shoes. But she was damned if she was going to go
back to the house to fetch Beth's rubber boots.

Sandy got out of the pickup and ran to the car.
Deborah opened the window a crack, the rain immediately blowing in and drenching her arm and lap.
"Shall I see if there are some boots inside?" Sandy
yelled.

"No, I'll manage," Deborah shouted back. "It isn't
that far."

Famous last words, she thought, but she wasn't
going to give up now. She scrambled from the car
and opened her umbrella, but it was no match for the
rain that poured down in torrents and bounced up
from the ground, nor for the wind blowing against
her. As she struggled to get to the building, she caught
sight of another woman juggling two umbrellas, one
for her head and one to fend off the windblown water
from her body.

Sandy reached the door first and held it open for
Deborah. When the door swung shut behind them

Deborah stood there, soaked through, her hair hanging in limp strands around her face.

The main entrance had led them into a large, dimly lit shed with metal shelves lined with cans and boxes of fertilizer and insecticide. Wooden tubs and plastic flowerpots were stacked on the floor, with bags of soil and peat moss. She breathed in dust and the acrid smell of weed killer. On the wooden counter beside the till was a stand of seed packets and several pots marked *Manitoba Honey.*

"Hi, Sandy," said the woman behind the counter. "So you're back home again, eh? I guess you came home to look after Beth. What a shame. Where's your mom?" Her words came out at top speed, lickety-split, with no breath between sentences.

"Hi, Mary. Mom's staying in England for another couple of weeks. This is my Aunt Debbie. She's going to help around here while I look after Aunt Beth. This is Mary Fitch."

It was not quite the introduction Deborah had envisaged. She stood there, her linen suit plastered to her body, shoes squelching, feeling like killing the next person who called her "Debbie," niece or not.

"You're Anne's sister? Well, I'll be ... how about that!" Mary leaned over the counter and held out a grimy hand. Deborah knew she had no alternative but to shake it. "Welcome to Winnipeg. You look half drowned. Isn't this weather the pits?"

"It certainly is," Deborah murmured.

"Sandy, why don't you take your aunt into the office? She can dry herself off there. Your mom's got some old clothes in there, I think. Pair of sweats and some boots. Don't want to get sick your first time here, do you?" Mary said maternally to Deborah. "This is not your regular July weather, I can tell you. It's been one miserable year, hasn't it, Sandy?"

"It sure has."

A man trundled a flat wagon loaded with bedding plants up to the counter. "Hi, Joe," Mary said, leaning over to count the plants. "You're about our only customer this afternoon. Rotten weather, eh?"

Deborah turned away as Mary started ringing up the man's purchases on the till. Sandy led her through to the next building, another shed which, from the racket the rain was making on the roof, must have been covered with corrugated iron. Here, two more customers were looking at wooden trellises.

"Need any help?" Sandy asked them brightly.

"No, we're fine at the moment. Terrible weather, isn't it?"

"It certainly is. Just holler if you need some help. Mary's in there," Sandy nodded to the other door, "and Bill should be somewhere around."

Was everyone here on a first-name basis? Deborah wondered, or was it just that everyone knew everyone else? But they couldn't surely. After all, Winnipeg was a city of half a million people. On the other hand, Carter's seemed to have so few customers, it might just be possible.

An elderly man with a stooped back lumbered in from the attached greenhouse, bearing two potted rosebushes and a scarlet geranium. His face brightened noticeably when he saw Sandy. "Hey, girl, you're back."

"Hi, Bill." Sandy kissed his muddy cheek.

Bill frowned as he set the plants on the counter. "You and your mom had to come home early 'cause of Beth, right?"

"I came home early to look after her. I brought Mom's sister with me. This is my Aunt—"

This time Deborah was determined to get it right. "Deborah Barry," she said firmly. "How do you do, Mr. . . . ?" She cocked her head, waiting for his name.

"Bill. Everyone calls me Bill," he said.

"Bill Sawerchuk," Sandy told her. "But he likes to be called Bill," she added unnecessarily. Deborah had got the point.

Bill looked her up and down. "Someone should've told you not to wear fancy duds here," he said. "You're all messed up."

Deborah felt her mouth crack into a smile. "Yes, I am, aren't I? I hadn't expected such bad weather."

"Even in fine weather, this place's not much good for fancy clothing."

Deborah was beginning to lose her patience. She turned away. "The office?" she said pointedly to Sandy. Then she turned back to Bill. "I'm planning to take over my sister's work while she's away. Perhaps we could have a meeting later today, so that all of you could tell me what exactly you do." She looked around for a suitable place to meet. "Possibly the office might be the best place."

Bill chuckled. "Not much of an office. Couldn't swing a cat by the tail in there."

"We'll manage something," Sandy said hurriedly, catching Deborah's expression. "Come on, let's find you something to wear." she took Deborah into the office and closed the door.

"I see what Bill means," Deborah said. "Not much space in here. She sat down at the table that served as a desk. It had once been painted green, but was now mainly bare wood. The cramped room also contained two plastic chairs, a battered two-drawer filing cabinet, and an ancient stove with two electric rings.

The sweatsuit that Sandy found hanging behind the door was a nondescript color of gray, patterned with dried mud stains. When Deborah put it on, the pants were three inches too short, but she had to admit it felt good to get out of her wet suit. God knows if it will ever be wearable again, she thought, as Sandy hung it up to dry. Her shoes definitely wouldn't be. She slid one foot into the clammy depth of the rubber boot Sandy had given her. It fitted her, but wasn't exactly her look.

"Those are mine," Sandy said. "I take one size larger than Mom." She stood back and surveyed her aunt. "Very nice," she said, laughing. "If only Graham could see you now. He'd say you looked ready to help him in his garden."

"Wouldn't he just! Don't you ever dare tell him about this," Deborah warned.

"Oh, I thought I'd take a picture and send it to him. Hey, just kidding," Sandy added. The laughter died as quickly as it had come. "I'd better go and check on Aunt Beth. I'll be back in an hour or so, okay?"

Deborah wondered what had suddenly changed Sandy's mood. Poor girl, she was going through a rough time. "Of course. I'll just get acquainted with the files in this cabinet, if that's all right."

"Sure. See you later."

Deborah gathered up an armful of files and had been looking through them for almost half an hour when a familiar voice rolled through the building. Strange how even when they were speaking, some Italians sounded as if they were singing.

"So, how're you doing, Bill? I need more geraniums for the window boxes. Good thing Anne's not here. She'd be mad as hell at me. I forgot to water the last ones I got from you. Damn things died on me. Oh, and my mother asked me to get her a couple more basil plants while I was here."

Damn! Deborah sought frantically for a lock on the office door, but there wasn't one. Maybe no one would mention she was here and Marco would go away without seeing her.

"Is Anne's sister here?" she heard him ask.

"She's in the office," Mary replied.

Deborah's heart sank. She hurriedly checked the round mirror hanging on the wall by a loop of green garden twine, wiped the smear of mud from her cheek, and waited for the inevitable.

He knocked on the door and opened it at the same time. "Hi," he said, looking around the door. "How's it going?"

"Very well, thank you," Deborah said crisply.

Marco's smile broadened as he surveyed her, taking in the gray sweatsuit and the boots. "Had to change, eh?" He accompanied the question with that singularly annoying Latin gesture of the swinging hand and the raised eyebrows that made her want to smack him.

"That's right," she replied calmly. "The rain was very heavy when we arrived. Fortunately Anne had left her old work clothes here." She enunciated each word very carefully, as if he were deaf. "Are they looking after you all right?"

He frowned, not quite understanding. "Oh, you mean the flowers. Sure, they are. Come and meet my kids. I needed some plants. Roberto and Floria wanted to meet you. So here we are."

"Floria?"

"My daughter. I named her after Floria Tosca.
You like opera?"

Deborah was surprised. "I love it. Where do you
get to see opera?"

"Here, in the winter. If you stayed on you could see
Traviata, Cenerentola . . . We had a great *Turandot*
here couple of years ago."

"Amateur opera, you mean."

"Amateur?" He looked astonished at her igno-
rance. "You're kidding, right? We have the best professional opera here. Not enough of it, but what we
have is good. I'm on the opera board so watch what
you say, okay?"

"Sorry. I'd better come and meet your children
before you get really cross with me."

The boy was tall and dark like his father, his hair
a slightly lighter brown and curlier, and he met her
with the same easy, open manner. Marco's daughter
was more reticent, shyly watching her with round
brown eyes, before she smiled and said, "Hi."

"When's Anne coming home?" Roberto asked.
"She said she'd bring me something from England."

Marco frowned at him. "Enough. Go find some
good basil for your nonna."

"Anne's coming home in another couple of weeks,"
Deborah told Roberto.

"I'm going to leave you with Mary and Bill now,"
Marco told the children. "You choose some flowers
for your own garden, Floria. Not too big. Nice small
ones that you can plant easily. And you get that basil
. . . and a couple of parsleys for me," he told his son.
"We'll be back in about half an hour."

He took Deborah's elbow and began moving to
the door.

She shook herself free. "Wait a minute. Where are we going?"

"Oh, sorry. I told Mary I was taking you for a decent cup of coffee."

"That's very nice, but you forgot to tell—or ask—me."

"I am so sorry." He stepped back and inclined his head in a little bow. "Will you do me the honor of accompanying me for a coffee at Salisbury House?"

"Can we come, too, Dad?" clamored the children.

"I'll take you to Dairy Queen for ice cream when I get back. You find those plants and get them all ready to take home, okay?"

Deborah looked down at herself. "I can't go into a restaurant dressed like this."

"They won't mind at Salisbury House. They take people as they come there."

"But how far is it? I have a lot of work to do." This man had a habit of rolling over you like a steamroller.

"Over the bridge and a couple of miles down Highway One."

"I'll get my umbrella."

"You won't need it. The rain's almost stopped. You've been too busy to notice."

Deborah halted at the door. "Are you sure I can go into . . . whatever it's called looking like this?" She had never in her life gone out in public dressed this way.

"They won't even notice you." He opened the door, ushered her in front of him, and then led her to his minivan. "It's a truck stop."

She stopped as she was about to get in. "A truck stop? You mean where—"

"Where truck drivers stop for food and drink, and gas. That's right."

She was about to say more, but decided against it. It would be pleasant to get out of the clammy confines of the office and she could do with a good cup of coffee. The mug of instant Mary had given her had been quite dreadful.

"Thank you," she said, and climbed into the van. It wasn't until they were bowling down the highway that she remembered she had left her bag in the office. "I left my bag behind."

"You don't need money. I'm buying today."

"There's quite a bit of money in the purse—and some travelers' checks."

"Want me to go back for it?"

"No, it's all right. Will it be safe there?"

He looked down at her, his lips quirking into a smile. "Why not call Mary when we get to the restaurant, ask her to put it away for you?"

"Good idea."

"Mary's worked at the center for fifteen years," he said after a moment of silence. He glanced across at her. "You're not too good at trusting people, are you?"

"Not when it comes to money, no."

"Not when it comes to anything, I think." He was very relaxed as he drove, one brown hand holding the wheel, the other resting on the window ledge. "Strange, that."

"Why?" she asked sharply.

"You don't look one bit like your sister, but she's the same way. Doesn't trust people until she knows them really well."

That was the second time today she'd been told

that she was like her sister. It annoyed her intensely. To her, they were totally different in every way.

"Must be something to do with the way you were raised, I guess. Losing your mother."

"That doesn't seem to have affected your children." As soon as she spoke, Deborah wished she hadn't, but Marco didn't seem offended.

"They've got me and two aunts . . . and their grand-parents to spoil them rotten. Anyway, you're wrong. I can't get Floria even to go to day camp in the summer, and she's too shy with strangers."

"That's not such a bad thing nowadays."

"I guess you're right. But they were hit hard when their mother left them. At least your mother died, she didn't just decide to go. Think how that must feel to a kid, to have your mother choose a crummy insurance salesman over you."

His hand tightened on the steering wheel. Quite instinctively Deborah reached out and touched it. "I'm sorry, Marco. That was very tactless of me." She quickly pulled her hand back and clasped it with her other one, as if it might move again of its own accord if she didn't hold it.

"No problem," he said, smiling at her with all the warmth of the sun in his eyes. "All kids got problems. But as long as they've got someone to love them they'll be okay."

Deborah was surprised to feel tears at the back of her eyes. "I can see that your children will be okay, then."

"Children are your investment in the future. You don't have any, do you?"

"Me? No." Deborah laughed. "I'd have been a rotten mother."

"No, not you. You could still have babies if you wanted."

Deborah looked at him as if he were crazy. "I don't want, thank you."

"Or you could marry someone with children. Your boyfriend, does he have children?"

"Graham has one grown-up—or almost grown-up—son."

"So you do have a boyfriend, eh?"

"Yes, I do." To Deborah's relief, they were turning off the highway into a large parking lot lined with dozens of transport trucks. She would never get used to the casual way everyone here asked such personal questions.

Marco pulled past them to park in the car parking lot beside the restaurant. Then he turned off the ignition. "What does he do, your friend?"

"Graham is the director of a chain of luxury hotels," she said in a tone designed to squash any further queries, but it went right over his head.

"And very rich, right?"

"Reasonably so."

"So he can give you all the things you want in life."

"That's the idea," she said, smiling sweetly at him.

"Hotels, eh? So you two sisters are alike."

Before she could reply Marco had slid out of his seat and was at her door to open it for her.

"Alike how?" she asked when she got out of the car.

He strode ahead of her to hold the restaurant door for her. "With you it's hotels, with Anne it's restaurants."

The comparison was laughable. "I thought you had only one restaurant."

"Now, only one," he said as he held open the

second door, "but I have big plans for the future. One day Rinaldi's will be spread across Canada, maybe in the U.S. as well."

She followed him into the restaurant. It was decorated in western style, with tables and chairs of a warm golden-brown wood.

The coffee was delicious. Marco even persuaded her to have a chocolate donut with it. It made up for the tuna sandwich she hadn't eaten for lunch.

"Tell me more about your plans for these restaurants," she said. "I must say it sounds extremely ambitious."

He grinned. "It is, but with good food—real Italian, but simple—and a training system for staff to make sure the service is always one hundred percent efficient, it can work. My big job will be to find someone to put enough capital in."

As he enlarged upon his plans to expand, Deborah was fascinated. It was a long time since she'd met a man who was literally starting from the bottom rung of the ladder, yet had the big ideas and the drive to want to get to the top. But she could also see how such ambition might have driven his less-committed wife away.

"What does Anne think of all this?" she asked, voicing the thought that had suddenly come into her mind.

He grimaced. "She's thinks I'm crazy. *Patsa!*"

"She's a little more cautious about it all, then?"

"You could say that, yes."

Their eyes locked across the table. Deborah diplomatically kept her thoughts to herself, but she knew from his expression that Marco understood exactly what she was thinking.

Chapter 24

The rain had ceased and the sun was out by the time Marco drove Deborah back to the garden center. As they pulled in, they saw Marco's children playing Frisbee with Sandy in the parking lot.

"Hi! Where did you get to?" Sandy shouted, as they got out of the van.

Deborah glanced at her watch. "We just went for a cup of coffee. Have you been back long?" She felt like an employee who'd taken too long for her tea break.

"Not very. The kids were getting restless, so we decided to play outside. Where did you go?" Sandy asked Marco this time.

"Salisbury House. I thought Deborah should get some local color."

"Great. They have the best burgers. Did you have one?"

"No, just coffee," Deborah replied.

"And a chocolate donut," Marco added.

"Oh, that's right! Tell the entire world that I had a donut." Deborah shook her head at him.

Sandy gave them a little frowning look that disturbed Deborah. Were she and Marco appearing too friendly? "I must get on with work," she said abruptly.

"Thanks for the coffee." She tossed the words at him over her shoulder and began walking to the door.

"You're welcome," Marco said.

Then she remembered that she hadn't said good-bye to the children. " 'Bye, Floria, Roberto. See you again sometime." She was inside the door, with it safely closed behind her as they were shouting good-byes to her.

When Sandy came into the office, Deborah was immersed in examining the order book. "I hadn't realized that those little trees in pots were so expensive," she said, without looking up.

Sandy perched on the edge of the table. "That was nice of Marco to take you out for a break," she said.

"Very nice, but he had to drag me out. I was just making some headway."

"Do you like him?"

Deborah turned the page and read a couple of lines. Or pretended to read them. "He's very pleasant."

"He keeps asking my mother to marry him."

Deborah lifted her head. "Does he? And?"

"She told him she can't make that decision just yet."

"What's stopping her?"

"From marrying Marco?"

"No, from deciding whether she wants to or not."

"I don't know. I don't think she really knows why, herself."

"Would you like her to marry him?"

"Yes, I would. She's been alone for too long. My dad died when I was only a baby. She's been stuck with Aunt Beth ever since."

"Surely she must have had some relationships in all that time."

"Sure she has, but nothing really serious, until

Marco came along. It's nuts. He's great looking. Got a terrific sense of humor. Reliable. Nice kids."

"Perhaps your mother doesn't want to raise someone else's children."

"She and Marco's kids get on really well. No, I don't think it's that." Settling herself more solidly on the table, Sandy swung her legs back and forth. "Know what I think?" she said, after a moment of silence.

"No, what?"

"I think she was waiting to get all this unfinished business out of the way before she could settle down with anyone."

"You mean seeing her father . . . that unfinished business?"

"Yeah. Her father . . . and you. I bet she'll be a different person when she gets back. Able to look forward to the future."

Deborah sensed there was something more to this than just a concern for her mother's future. "Are you worried about leaving her when you go to New York?"

"Ha! You mean *if* I go to New York."

"*When* you go," Deborah said firmly.

Sandy sighed. "I just wish she'd *do* something with her life, instead of just . . . carrying on the same old way, year in, year out."

"You can't be responsible for your mother's life, you know," Deborah said gently.

"I keep telling myself that, but . . . it's tough leaving her. I know how much she's going to miss me."

"And that's why you'd like her to marry Marco. That would take the pressure off you, right?"

Sandy gave her a rueful smile. "I guess so."

"Think of it this way. Maybe your moving away will force her into making a decision."

Sandy brightened visibly. "You could be right. You know, I'm going to miss you when you go home. You're so easy to talk to, not like Mom."

"I am?" Deborah was genuinely surprised. She'd never considered herself as a potential Agony Aunt. "You do surprise me."

"I just wish you weren't on the other side of the Atlantic. Who knows when we'll see each other again once you go back."

"You'll have to come and visit us when you get a break. There are lots of cheap flights from New York to London, you know."

Sandy slipped down from the table and began tidying a pile of papers. "I don't think I'll ever go back to England."

"Why on earth not? Of course you will."

"I don't really want to go back when he's there," Sandy whispered, "at Hammerton Towers, I mean."

"Do you mean Conrad? He won't be there."

Sandy turned to her, eyes widening. "You're not going to say anything ... I mean ... about me. Please don't."

"Of course not. Don't you worry about Conrad. I'll find a way to get rid of him." Deborah got up and briefly put her arm around Sandy's shoulders. Then she quickly changed the subject. "Bill was right," she said, looking around. "I don't think this office is big enough for a meeting."

"It's pretty small."

Deborah sat down again. "Sandy, be honest with me. How on earth do Beth and your mother make a living out of this place?"

"It's not usually this quiet," Sandy said defensively. "Usually in the summer we're really busy, especially on weekends. This is just a bad day because of the weather."

"That's very loyal of you, but from the look of this place I'd say they barely make ends meet. Am I right?"

Sandy chewed on her lip . . . and then nodded. "My mother's worried sick. She's been trying to get Aunt Beth to sell for years, but she won't. Aunt Beth says this place was started by her grandfather and she's not going to give up on it. 'You can do what you like with it when I die,' she keeps telling Mom, 'but I don't give in that easy.' " Sandy sighed. "Mom makes a bit extra on the landscaping side, but not enough. She's really good, you know, but she's never had the chance. People with fancy yards just don't come here."

"Are there other garden centers in Winnipeg that do well?"

"Oh, sure there are. Several. Especially Goodchild Nursery and McNab's Centre. They stay open all year round. You should see Goodchild's at Christmas. It's like a winter wonderland, with decorated trees and potted plants, and poinsettias of all sizes and colors."

"You couldn't do that here?"

"Not a hope. That needs money for proper buildings and decent insulation and for the extra staff, of course. Goodchild's has about forty people working at peak times."

"I must take a look at this Goodchild's," Deborah said thoughtfully.

"Looking won't do much good. It's more money we need."

"Money's no good without original ideas and forceful advertising."

"Well, we can't afford much of that, either." Sandy looked directly at Deborah. "Maybe you understand a bit better now why Mom wrote to your father and asked him for money to help me. I can't tell you how much she hated doing that."

"I know she did."

"You thought she was after his money, didn't you? I mean lots of it, not just the loan for me, but she wasn't. You were pretty mean to her when she arrived."

Deborah winced. The honesty of youth. "I know I was. It was a shock. Still is. We don't really know each other." She picked up a pen and began doodling on the pad of paper in front of her. "It's . . . it's worse than meeting a stranger. After all, you're not supposed to know someone new. But a sister . . . you're supposed not only to know a sister, but also to have . . . some sort of feeling for her."

"And you didn't feel that way?" Sandy's tone wasn't at all critical, but there was a trace of surprise in it.

"You want the truth?"

"Sure, why not?"

"Because you'll tell your mother, that's why."

"Not if you don't want me to."

Deborah shrugged. "What does it matter? In a couple of weeks Anne and I will change places and probably never see each other again."

"How can you say that? She's your sister. I'd give the world to have had a sister or a brother."

"But I didn't really have one, did I? I barely remember her. And Ryan never talked about her. It upset him even to hear her name mentioned. Something must have happened way back, perhaps when Beth adopted your mother, but I do know that he didn't want to talk about her, so . . . she just wasn't any part of my life."

"That's awful."

"Not really. On Ryan's part, perhaps, it was pretty reprehensible, but he wouldn't be the first father to forget about his children, would he? And you must remember that she was legally adopted. He felt he had no further legal obligation. Anyway, none of that was my responsibility. Besides, what stopped your mother getting in touch with us once she grew up?"

"Good point," Sandy conceded. She thought for a moment. "Some of it was pride, I think. Resentment that her father didn't come to her. Most of all, she was afraid of being rejected. She's had a tough life. First losing her—your—mother, then her dad and you, and then my father. She probably felt it was better just to get on and make the best of her life. She's sort of built up a tough shell, but underneath she's pretty sensitive." Sandy stared at Deborah and then started to smile.

"What?" Deborah demanded.

"It's weird, but I've suddenly realized that you and Mom are more alike than I thought. I don't think you're quite as tough as you seem, either, Aunt Debbie."

Deborah slapped her hand down on the table. "You had better believe I am."

"In business, perhaps, but not—"

"In everything. Business, personal affairs. You let your guard down, you get hurt."

"That sounds pretty cynical to me."

"Believe me, sweetheart, it's the way it is." Deborah stood up. The direction this conversation had taken was making her feel extremely uncomfortable. What the hell was she doing baring so much of herself to a twenty-one-year-old girl? She looked at her watch. "I have an idea. Why don't we have our meeting now, as there are so few customers? If we pull up some chairs in the space by the counter, we can easily keep our eye on customers if they come in."

"Sounds like a good idea."

"What are we going to do about Aunt Beth next week, when you're teaching your master classes?"

"I'm hoping I can get Elsie Penner to check in on her when we're both out at the same time." Sandy grinned. "If you promise not to offer her money again."

"I will. But we must buy her something to repay her. Right. We should be able to manage quite well, then. I can probably do much of the book work and any phone calls from home. Besides, it's only for a couple of weeks. We'll manage."

"Sure we will. And Aunt Beth should be more active by then, too." Sandy went to the door. "I'll go see how busy it is."

Mary and Bill were working in the greenhouse. Wayne said he'd come as soon as he'd finished serving a couple of customers. Once they were all assembled, each answered Deborah's questions about the day-to-day workings of the center in their own way. Bill succinctly, Mary rambling on until she was stopped. Although Wayne was only temporary he seemed to have more useful opinions than the others about what was wrong with the place.

By the end of the meeting, Deborah felt even more pessimistic about the business. The best thing would be to cut their losses and sell it, but from what Sandy had said, Beth wouldn't even contemplate such a move.

After the short meeting Bill and Sandy took her on a tour of the greenhouses, walking up and down the beaten earth paths between the rows of trestle tables that were covered with plants of every kind—annuals, perennials, herbs, vegetables—all at different stages of growth. Then they led her out to the section behind the greenhouses to see the young trees and shrubs lined up outside in pots. As she watched Bill's soil-ingrained hands touching the plants with obvious affection and listened to his slow explanations and Sandy's interjections, a tiny seed of interest began to take root in Deborah.

It was a wretched, rundown, no-hope business, but, God, she thought to herself, adrenaline shooting through her, what a challenge it would be to take this place on and make it a success!

Chapter 25

Once Deborah and Sandy left for Canada, Anne had expected the comparative emptiness of the house to throw her and her father together. Now, she thought, she could talk to Ryan about the past, ask him all those questions she was longing to ask, especially about her mother.

But she soon found that nothing had changed. In fact, probably realizing that he couldn't evade her quite so easily now, Ryan suddenly became very busy with important business matters that necessitated shutting himself away in his office. Telephone calls to Europe that just could not wait, he told Anne apologetically.

"I might as well have gone back to Canada with Sandy," Anne complained to Eileen. "I've barely seen Ryan in the last ten days."

"Didn't I tell you? If you want to talk to him about your mother it's you who'll have to bring up the subject. Ryan's not a man to talk about the past to anyone."

"I've tried, but he always finds some way of talking about something else. Last night he said he wanted to enjoy my last week with me, not to dwell on the morbid past. Then he went off again to speak to Conrad Hatcher on the phone." Anne suppressed the shiver that ran down her spine whenever she thought of Conrad's glacial eyes.

She stared gloomily into the bowl of peas she was helping Eileen shell in the kitchen garden. She could feel the warmth of the sun on her back. The little tiled courtyard by the kitchen door was a sun trap. For the past few days, the weather had been glorious, golden days with a heat haze misting the Chiltern hills. The smell of new-mown grass mingled with the sharp fragrance of the warm herbs that grew in the kitchen garden.

But despite the fine weather and the lovely English countryside, Anne wished that she had gone home with Sandy. Her main reason for being here was to get to know her father and sister before it was too late. But nothing had turned out the way she'd wanted it to. Although they'd had some time together, her sister was now in Canada and her father was constantly avoiding her.

"I said it wouldn't be easy, didn't I?" Eileen leaned forward to give her a sympathetic pat on the knee. "Ryan's not one for sharing his feelings. Unless he's talking about a horse or his music."

As Eileen turned her head away to gather up another handful of peas and put them in her lap, Anne realized with a flash of insight that this woman loved Ryan. Probably had loved him for many years, and never told anyone, least of all the man she loved. For a moment she thought of saying something to her, but then decided against it.

The thought of Eileen's quiet, unspoken love saddened her even more. If a woman who'd lived with Ryan all these years couldn't break through the barriers of his reserve, how could she, a comparative stranger—even if she was his daughter—do so?

She set the golden earthenware bowl filled to the brim with peas on the ground.

Eileen looked up. "Finished?"

"It's getting too hot for me. I'm going inside. Would you like something to drink?"

Eileen half rose from her chair. "Let me—"

"No. You do more than your share of all the work in this house as it is. I'll take these peas in with me."

Anne was about to open the kitchen door when Graham came around from the front of the house. "I rang the bell but there was no answer," he explained. He was dressed in work clothes, a pair of well-worn jeans and an old check shirt with the sleeves rolled up. Anne couldn't help thinking that Graham had the knack of making even old clothes look elegant.

Eileen stood up, peapods tumbling to the ground. "I am sorry about that. Were you hoping to see Ryan? I'm afraid he's gone up to London on business."

"That's fine. It was Anne I came to see."

Anne smiled. "More work in the rose garden?"

"You make me sound like some sort of slave driver."

"Not at all. You know how I love it."

"Actually, for a change I'm not asking you to labor in my garden. I have to drive into Princes Risborough tomorrow morning. I thought you might like to come with me. We could have lunch and then go on to see Blenheim in the afternoon."

"What's Blenheim?"

"Blenheim Palace. Home of the Marlboroughs. Where Winston Churchill was born."

"Oh, okay. Is it on Ryan's list?"

"I'm sure it is." Graham frowned. "Perhaps you'd rather wait to go there with your father."

"I might be waiting a long time."

Graham glanced at her over his sunglasses. "Do I detect a hint of sarcasm there?"

"What do you think?"

"You could ask your father to come with us?"

"That's an idea." Anne wasn't very enthusiastic. What she wanted was Ryan on his own, not with other people there.

"He'll be working with Conrad tomorrow," Eileen reminded her.

"Right. I forgot."

Eileen was gathering up bags and bowls. "He said something about bringing him back here with him."

"Oh, no," Anne said involuntarily and then reddened as she caught Graham's glance.

"Would you be a pet and open the door for me now?" Eileen asked Graham.

"Why don't you come to Blenheim with us tomorrow?" he asked Eileen as he opened the kitchen door for her. He handed her another bowl filled with peas, once she'd put everything she was carrying on the pine table inside.

"Thank you for asking, but I've seen it before. You take Anne. She'll enjoy it. 'Tis a lovely place." Eileen went to the closet and took out a broom.

"I'll sweep outside," Anne told her, trying to take the broom from her hands, but Eileen wouldn't give it up.

"Away with you. Stop wasting your afternoon. You've got precious few of them left. Take her away from here, will you, Graham? She's getting in my way." She bustled them outside again and shut the door on them.

"She seems to think it's a mortal sin for *her* to take time off," Anne said, "but she won't let me do anything to help." She met Graham's eyes. "I'm going crazy with nothing to do," she admitted. "I'm not used to it."

He gave her his slow smile. "That sounds like too good an opening not to take advantage of it. Would you like to come and help me pull weeds at Somerford?"

"I thought you'd never ask. I'll go and change into shorts."

As she was changing, Anne felt a glow of happiness that was quite out of proportion to the situation. For heaven's sake, she told herself, all he's done is ask you to work in his garden. But the truth was that she was increasingly enjoying Graham's company. She found herself confiding in him about all kinds of things: Sandy's future, her concern about the garden center . . . It had become so easy to talk to him while they worked together, either in the gardens or, sometimes, in the lovely old house itself.

And, more and more, Graham had been seeking her advice. Although she was not as knowledgeable as he was about old English flowers, he seemed to value her ideas about the development of the entire grounds of Somerford.

She found his trust in her ability as a garden designer a great boost to her morale. He was the perfect antidote to the strain that had developed between her and her father. Despite their differing backgrounds she felt very much at ease with this man, whether she was working silently beside him in his garden, or arguing passionately with him over a mug of cider and a thick ham sandwich on the merits of different fertilizers for the roses.

The realization that she was, in fact, enjoying Graham's company far too much dampened her pleasure at the thought of spending more time with him.

"You're very pensive," Graham said, as they sped along the narrow lane that led to Somerford.

She shifted her gaze from the sunlit green field bordered by a shady beechwood. "Sorry." She gave him a faint smile.

"Is it your father?" he asked as he turned into the driveway.

Although that wasn't what had been bothering her this time, she grasped at this reason for her quiet mood. "Kind of. I'm leaving in a few days and we've spent hardly any time together."

Graham drove the car around the back of the house to the old stable and switched off the engine. He turned to her, his arm resting along the back of her seat. "Why is that?"

"He's avoiding me."

"Why would he do that?"

Anne shrugged. "He knows I want to talk to him about . . . about things that are important to me."

"Such as?"

"My mother . . . Why he took Deborah and left me behind in Canada . . ."

"Heavy stuff."

"Yes." Anne stared ahead of her, at the door of the horse stall, hanging on rusty hinges at an angle. "Too heavy for him to face, I guess. But they're really important to me. If I can't talk to him about them I'll have wasted my time and Sandy's money."

"Have you spoken to Eileen about this? She's pretty wise when it comes to Ryan."

"You're right, she is. She says I must pin him down."

"Then do so. Don't let him put you off." He drew his arm away and pushed open the car door.

"Graham."

"Yes?"

"Do you think I'm being selfish?"

Graham looked at her in surprise. "About what?"

"Wanting to force my father to discuss things that obviously hurt him."

He gave her a little ironic grin. "Not selfish, exactly. Just being a typical woman."

"That's rather sexist, isn't it?"

"Is it? I didn't intend it to be. I merely meant that women like to talk about emotions, feelings . . . that sort of thing. Men usually don't." He leaned forward to take the keys from the ignition, so that his face was hidden. "Especially if they are uncomfortable feelings."

Anne thought of the few times Graham had mentioned his own father and knew that he was thinking of himself now.

She got out of the car. "Thanks."

"For what?"

"For being such a help. Giving me a shoulder to . . ." She waved a hand in the air in a gesture of embarrassment. "You know."

He nodded. "Yes, I do." He hesitated and then said, "Perhaps Eileen is right. Perhaps confrontation is the best way, however much it might hurt. Better than letting it fester inside." He turned abruptly. "Come along, my trusty horticultural companion, we have weeds to hoe and perennials to transplant before the sun goes down."

He strode ahead of her, putting an end to their conversation about Ryan.

Nothing but the garden was discussed until they took a much-needed rest in the middle of the afternoon, after deadheading roses.

"Not long now until I fly back to Canada," Anne said. She sat down on the stretch of close-cut grass in the rose garden. "Sometimes I wish time would stand still."

Graham handed her a can of lager from the insulated bag. "You're thinking about Ryan again."

Ryan . . . and other things.

"Why don't you remind him that you're leaving in a few days? Tell him it's essential that you speak to him."

She pressed the cold can against her temples. "I'm afraid he'll find some excuse—"

Graham sat down beside her. "Don't let him."

"And Conrad Hatcher's coming. If I don't do it before he arrives I'll never get the chance."

The skin on Graham's bronzed cheek tightened. "I can't say I've missed Mr. Hatcher."

Anne leaned forward to hug her knees, her bare arm brushing against his. A few days ago she would have pulled away. Now she allowed herself the pleasure of this light companionable touch of skin against skin. "You don't like him either, do you?"

"To be perfectly honest, I can't stand the man. Deborah and I have had a few arguments about him in our time, I can tell you."

Anne shivered.

"What's wrong?" Graham said, glancing down at her.

"I was just thinking about him and Sandy, and how he got her drunk." She drew in a deep breath and released it in a heavy sigh. "I suppose that's not fair. Sandy would say she was in control of herself, but . . ."

"Sandy's quite safe now, thousands of miles away from the man. Don't think about him anymore." He stretched tanned arms above his head and leaned his back against the seat of the wooden bench behind them. "It's too lovely a day to spoil it thinking of unpleasant people."

He was right. Anne smiled at him and relaxed, breathing in the mingled scents of the rose garden. To their right bloomed the lovely old *rosa mundi* roses, with their variegated pink-and-white petals, and behind them, clambering up a trellis on the brick wall, was a rambling rose covered with fat creamy-white multipetaled flowers. In the past few days, Anne had learned more about old-fashioned roses from Graham than she had ever known before.

The enclosed garden was like a sunlit room bordered by the old russet brick walls covered in climbing roses and honeysuckle. The only sounds were the hum of bees and Graham's light breathing. It was so warm they might well have been in some tropical country. She breathed in the heady fragrance even more deeply, her body relaxing, her aching muscles like molten rubber . . . until she awoke with a start, to find her head resting on Graham's shoulder and his arm comfortably around her.

She pulled away and sat up, nervously pushing her hands through her hair. "Sorry," she said, warmth rushing into her face. "I must have fallen asleep."

"Not surprised, with this heat," he said, smiling. "Nodded off myself for a few minutes. That's what comes of drinking beer in the middle of the day." He made no move to get up, but sat close to her, an unfathomable half-smile on his mouth. She could see tiny dewdrops of sweat on his upper lip. Then he was too close to see anything but shadow with light streaming from behind, and he was kissing her.

It was a light kiss at first, almost brotherly, but then it deepened and she opened her mouth to him like the petals of a rose blossoming in the sunshine, and they were locked together, mouth against mouth, lost in the warm sweetness, bare arms and necks and faces slick against each other.

Graham was the first to pull away. From under drowsy eyelids Anne could see the patches of white under the tan as the color drained from his skin. "Sorry," he said, through tight lips. "That shouldn't have happened."

"No, it shouldn't," she muttered, looking everywhere but at him. Then she hurriedly added, in case he thought she was blaming him, "It was just as much my fault."

He held out his hand and helped her to her feet. "Too much sun," he said lightly, "and lager."

But Anne knew that it was not lager that had intoxicated them.

He turned away to pack the glasses and cans into the insulated bag. Anne waited, her body now aching from more than just physical exertion. She said nothing. What was there to say?

"Enough outside work for today, I think," he said. "It's too warm." Gathering up his garden secateurs and the bag, he began walking back in the direction of the house.

"Would you mind driving me home?" Anne asked.

"Now?"

"Please."

"Happy to," Graham said.

She couldn't tell if his eagerness to be rid of her stemmed from embarrassment or relief. When she washed her hands in the deep porcelain sink in the scullery, she doused her face with cold water to cool it down. She was being attacked by all kinds of feelings, but at the moment she didn't want to analyze any of them. All she knew was that whatever had happened out there in the rose garden must never happen again.

She told Graham as much as they were driving back to Hammerton Towers. "I'm sorry about that," she said at last, after trying several different ways of starting up the conversation in her head. "You were right, the heat got to us. It won't happen again."

He glanced sideways at her, a faint smile twitching his lips. "I hope you won't misunderstand me if I say that's rather a pity."

She turned in her seat to glare at him. "It's not funny, Graham."

"Quite right, it's not." This time he didn't smile.

"My sister's been gone less than two weeks and we're . . . we're—" She halted, lost for words.

"Kissing each other."

"Exactly. I've waited more than thirty years to be reunited with my family. I can't afford to screw that up now because of a . . . a—" She swallowed hard. What the hell was wrong with her that she couldn't even deal with what was, after all, a minor incident, without feeling close to tears?

"I understand." Graham changed gear as they took the bend in the road a little too fast for Anne's comfort. "I would remind you that you'll be leaving for Canada in a few days. Your sister will come home. Everything will be exactly as it was before."

Was it just her imagination, Anne wondered, or did Graham's voice sound as bleak as she was feeling?

Chapter 26

As Ryan drove up to London that morning he felt relieved, glad to be getting away from the house. He had a lot on his mind. It was so much easier to think things out on his own. The only noise was the quiet hum of the engine. Usually he put a disk into the CD player as soon as he got into the car, but not this time.

His life was out of whack, that was for sure. He missed being able to talk about business with Deborah, particularly now, when there seemed to be some problem with figures. A major problem. Too major to work out over the phone or by fax. That was why he was going to London to see Conrad. He would soon sort it out. When Ryan had spoken to him on the phone Conrad had sounded quite casual about Ryan's concerns, assuring him that he'd probably misread some of the figures that had come in from the Dublin studio.

But still Ryan wished that he had Deborah here to talk it over with. He'd thought about calling her in Canada, but from the sound of it she had enough on her plate. He was sorry they'd parted in anger. He'd been too rough on her. Sending her off to Canada like that had been a big mistake. He was missing her. He was also missing Sandy more than he'd expected. They'd barely got to know each other and then she was gone. All he had left was Anne and her constant probing into the past.

Even Eileen had been getting at him, telling him he should sit down and talk to his daughter, give her the answers she needed before she went home again. Didn't they realize how it felt just to think about the past, never mind talk about it? It wasn't only Janine he didn't want to think about, but also the grinding poverty of those days and . . .

A horn sounded impatiently behind him. A big black BMW on his tail, impatient to overtake him. Ryan swerved into the middle lane, letting him shoot by. Bloody Grade-A personalities!

No, he wasn't going to think about all that stuff in the past, ever again. If Deborah didn't need to know about her mother, why should her sister? Surely Beth would have told her all she needed to know. After all, Janine had grown up with Beth.

Janine.

"I did my best for them, sweetheart," he whispered, his hands damp on the leather steering wheel. "You know that. Debbie had the best schools. Fine clothes. All that money could buy, she got. And now Anne has the money for her daughter. What more can I do?"

He hadn't spoken to Janine for a long time, especially aloud. Holy Saint Pat, it made him think of those first few months after she died when he spoke to her all the time, the past merging with the present until he thought he'd lose his mind. His music had saved his sanity then. Now he didn't even have that to fill his time. He hadn't written anything for almost a year now. All he had was his business ventures . . . and something was cockeyed there, too.

Not to worry. Conrad would soon sort it all out. They'd work on it for the next few days. Then Anne would be gone and he'd be free to fly over to Dublin, check up for himself that everything was okay, before Deborah came home and life returned to normal.

Anne wasn't too keen on Conrad. Ryan had caught her expression when he'd told her he was bringing Conrad back to Hammerton with him. "Sorry about that," he'd said. "I know you don't like Conrad. Can't say I blame you, after what happened with Sandy."

"Don't worry," she'd said, her mouth all stiff. "I'll keep out of your way."

"I don't want you to do that." Neither of them had mentioned the fact that she'd be leaving in a few days, but the knowledge hung between. He had come to her then, putting his arm around her shoulders, wanting to show that he cared about her feelings, but she'd drawn away from him and left the room.

No wonder he found it so hard to talk to her. She was like a hedgehog, all prickles. Sighing, he drew a glossy black packet of Players Special from his pocket and lit a cigarette. He'd have to spend some time alone with Anne before she left, he supposed. Maybe they could go somewhere interesting together. There was racing at Epsom this weekend. Or he could take her to Stratford for a show. She might enjoy that, even if he wouldn't.

"See, I am trying," he said, addressing the space between him and the windshield.

The first thing Anne heard when Ryan returned was Conrad's voice booming in the hall, as treacly as molasses. "God, I've missed this funny old place. Where's Anne? I'm looking forward to seeing her again."

Upstairs in her room she gritted her teeth, but she knew that she couldn't hide away from him forever.

Better to face him right away than to put it off. She
came out of her room and down the stairs, forcing a
smile.

"Hello, Conrad. I heard your voice."

"Anne." He came forward. For a horrible moment
she thought he was going to kiss her, but something
in her expression stopped him in his tracks and he
held out his hand to her instead. "Wonderful to see
you again." The bright blue eyes and the white teeth
flashed at her from his tanned face. He reminded her
of a cartoon wolf.

She turned to speak to her father, so that she could
avoid taking Conrad's hand. "Did you have a good
drive from London?" she asked.

"The M25 was hell, as always, but the rest was
fine." Ryan hugged her. "Thanks, Annie," he whispered in her ear, before turning back to Conrad.
"Let's all have a drink first, before we get down to
business." He led the way into the living room. "Is
Graham coming for dinner?"

"I don't know." Anne bent to tidy the hearth rug,
aware of Conrad's sharp gaze on her.

"You didn't see him today, then?" Ryan was busy
at the lovely old oak dresser that served as his
drinks' cabinet.

"Yes, I did. I helped him in the rose garden for a
while, then I came home. He didn't say anything
about coming here this evening."

"He probably will. Graham doesn't like eating
alone."

Conrad settled back against the sofa that looked
like something out of the Addams Family, with its
bright-red leather cushions and sides of gnarled
black wood. "So, you've been helping Mr. Neville
with his garden, have you?"

Anne was furious to feel the heat rushing up her neck and into her face, but her voice was cool and steady when she spoke. "Yes, I have. Designing gardens is my profession. It's been nice to work on a really old garden for a change."

He looked at her over the glass of single malt Ryan had handed him. "Oh, Somerford's really old, all right. Neville's absolutely besotted with it, to the point of neglecting his business." He gave that little laugh that annoyed Anne intensely. "Deborah thinks he's trying to re-create his family home. Very deep, our Deborah." He laughed again.

Anne turned her back on him and picked up Joanna Trollope's latest book, which she'd been reading when he'd arrived.

But it wasn't that easy to deflect Conrad Hatcher. "Hang on." He began riffling through some old *Country Life* magazines stacked in the corner by the log box. "There's a picture of Graham's ancestral home in one of these. Beautiful old house, it was. A showplace, so they say. It's in here somewhere."

"I'm not really interested," Anne said coldly.

"There we are," he said triumphantly, thrusting the open magazine in front of her. "Newcombe Hall."

Anne didn't even look at it. "Thank you," she said, and closed the magazine.

"Of course, I don't suppose it matters that much if Graham spends all his time at Somerford. He has plenty of flunkies to run things for him. But Sir William might not be too happy to learn that his son is neglecting the family business."

Anne felt her face grow stiff as she made an effort to keep her temper. "I hardly think Graham is neglecting anything. It is the summer, after all."

"My dear Anne, one doesn't stop conducting one's

business because the sun is shining. In fact, summer is high season for tourism in England. Of course, Deborah thinks Graham was gypped. Paid far too much for Somerford. She says it's falling apart. Dry rot, woodworm . . . you name it, Somerford's got it. Not her cup of tea at all. Your sister likes her home comforts. Prefers twentieth-century air-conditioning to sixteenth-century drafts."

"Good evening, everyone. I knocked but no one answered. The door was open, so I came right in."

The sound of Graham's voice made Anne jump, so that some of her white wine spilled onto the table. "Damn!"

Conrad was on his feet, bending to help her, a paper napkin in his hand.

"Thank you, I'll do it," she said icily, snatching it from him. "Hi, Graham." She wondered how much he'd overheard.

Ryan must have been wondering about that as well, for he gave Conrad a quick frown before greeting Graham with an offer of a predinner drink.

"No, thanks. I'm driving into town tonight. An early business meeting in the morning. Can't neglect business for pleasure, can I?" he said, the dark irises in his gray eyes almost black as he glanced for a moment in Conrad's direction. "I must apologize, Anne. Our visit to Blenheim will have to be postponed."

Their eyes met and glanced away from each other at the same moment. "That's okay."

"Perhaps your father could go with you."

"We'll see. Thanks for letting me know."

She sensed that Conrad was watching them both closely, trying to work out their relationship. Probably storing everything up to report it all back to Deborah when she came home. Well, there was nothing to report, Mr. Hatcher. Whatever had happened between her and Graham was over almost before it began.

"Sure you won't stay for dinner?" Ryan asked, as Graham moved back to the door. "I don't know what we're having, but I'm sure there'll be enough for you."

"I'm cooking tonight," Anne said. "I thought it was time Eileen got a break. I should go and check on it." She went to join Graham by the door. "It's nothing exciting. Just spaghetti and meatballs, but there's plenty of it if you'd like to stay."

"It sounds very tempting, but I want to make an early start. I'll say good-bye then." He held out his hand to Anne. It was a strangely final gesture that gave her a sinking feeling in the pit of her stomach.

"Sounds very formal," she said with a laugh, but her eyes were searching his.

"I'm not sure when I'll be coming down to Somerford again and I know you're leaving in a few days."

"Okay." Anne tried to smile but the muscles of her face wouldn't move. "Then I'll come out to your car with you."

Graham stood back to let her go before him, raised his hand to Conrad and Ryan, and left the room. Anne walked ahead of him to the front door and then turned. "I've a feeling I've driven you away from Somerford."

"Not here," he said abruptly, nodding his head in the direction of the living room. He took her arm as they descended the steps to his car and then released it.

"Have I?" she demanded.

"Have you what?"

"Driven you away."

"Of course not. Don't talk such rubbish."

"Then why are you leaving so suddenly? There was no talk of your going to London this afternoon.

You were full of plans for clearing the herbaceous border and thinning perennials."

"Sounds quite ridiculous, doesn't it?"

She didn't like the acid tone of his voice. "I don't think so."

"Well, it is." He sighed and then gave her that ironic, slightly crooked smile of his. "It's been an idyllic few weeks, working in my house and my garden, particularly this last week. But all good things must come to an end."

She felt her lips tremble. "Must they?"

"I'm afraid so. I have an international business to run. After all, we wouldn't want my father to think I was neglecting the business he'd entrusted to me, would we?"

"So you did hear what Conrad said. Damn that man! I can't stand him. Surely you're not going to let something that jerk said get to you."

"Of course not, but unfortunately what Mr. Hatcher said holds more than a grain of truth. My preference for slopping around in gardening clothes would be seen as a sign of weakness by not only my father, but also our competitors."

"Tell them all to go to hell," Anne said, eyes blazing.

He smiled. "Just the way you've told your aunt Beth to go to hell?" he said gently.

She stared at him for a long time. "Oh, Graham," she whispered, grasping the lapel of his dark linen jacket.

For a fleeting moment he lifted his hand to cover hers, pressing it against his chest. Then he stepped back to set a distance between them. "I hope you manage to speak to your father."

"Can I call you in London?"

"Is that a good idea, do you think?"

"Maybe not, but I'd like to feel I could if I needed to." She made an ineffectual little flutter with her hands. "Maybe just to say good-bye." She tried to smile. "To save having to do it now."

"Ryan has my London number."

"I don't want to have to ask my father for it."

"It's in the leather-bound book by the phone on the hall table."

"Okay. Thanks."

He took her hand in his, turning it palm upward, as if he were reading her fortune. "Thank you. I shall never forget this past week."

"No." She looked down at their hands. "Promise me one thing."

"What?"

"That you won't let them take Somerford away from you."

"Who's they?"

"Professional pressures. Your father." She swallowed. "Deborah."

He gave a dry little laugh. "Did anyone ever tell you that you're a dreamer, Anne Dysan?"

"I'm afraid so. Teachers at school. Aunt Beth. She kept saying that I was just like my father. I used to tell her that my father's dreams got him out of poverty and made him a musical icon."

"I thought you were angry with your father."

"I'm allowed to be angry with him. No one else is." She smiled at him, but then the smile faded. "I mean it, Graham. Keep coming back to Somerford. You need it to keep you sane . . . and human."

He folded her fingers into her palm, his hand tightening around hers. "And what about your dreams?"

She shook her head at him, slowly drawing her

hand away. "My daughter is about to become a famous guitarist."

"That's Sandy's dream, not yours."

"Oh, a mother always has dreams for her children. And I have all kinds of other dreams. The garden center will make lots of money. I'll have a great landscaping business . . . things like that."

"Is there any . . ." He hesitated, as if he didn't know quite how to put it. ". . . anybody else involved in these dreams of yours?"

"Oh, yes." Anne gave him a brilliant smile. "I hope you've not been thinking of me as a lonely, middle-aged widow."

"No. That's not the way I've been thinking of you at all."

"I have someone waiting for me back in Winnipeg. He's got a thriving restaurant and lots of ambitious plans for expansion."

"Good." Graham looked down at his watch. "I must be going." He held out his hand. "Good-bye, Anne. And good luck."

She shook his hand briskly as if he were a business acquaintance and then released it. "Thanks. Good luck to you, too."

Not wanting to prolong this anymore, she went back up the steps and watched him get into the car, smiling and waving until she was certain he could no longer see her in his mirror. Then she went inside the house and directly up to her room.

Dinner at Hammerton was going to be later than usual tonight.

Chapter 27

Deborah felt like a juggler juggling a dozen balls all at the same time. How on earth had Anne managed all these years? Mind you, she hadn't had to deal with her aunt shouting orders from a wheelchair and a daughter worrying herself sick about whether she was pregnant and/or stricken with AIDS. Sandy's period still hadn't started and Deborah had to hide her deep concern, knowing that it wouldn't help Sandy. It felt very strange to be worrying about someone other than herself.

How the hell did I land myself in this mess? she asked herself as she ran the ancient vacuum cleaner over the living-room rug after Beth had eaten her supper there. Now her aunt was lighting up one of her venomous cigarettes, puffing the smoke in Deborah's direction.

Roll on next week, Deborah thought, as she put the vacuum cleaner away in the narrow hall closet. She couldn't wait to get out of this dump. But then she felt a spasm of sadness in her chest. She was forced to admit to herself that it wouldn't be quite as easy to leave Winnipeg as she'd expected.

"You going out?" Beth asked, as Deborah took away her tray.

"Yes. I'm going to the center. I'll do the cash, wait to close up, and then I'm going to a film."

"Who's going to be here with me?"

"Sandy," Deborah shouted back to her from the kitchen, as she rinsed off the dishes and put them in the dishwasher.

"Then who are you going to the movies with?"

"Marco."

"Oh?" The word sounded like a long question mark. "With the kids?"

"No, it's not a children's film." God, it was like the Spanish Inquisition. Deborah went back into the living room. "Marco's children went to stay with his other sister, the one in Brandon, for the week. Don't worry. Sandy said she'd be back by seven. That's less than half an hour from now. I'll make sure you get to the lavatory before I leave."

"I can do it myself, thanks very much."

"Would you tell Sandy there's some chicken cacciatori in the fridge?"

"What would you do without Marco's food? You haven't cooked a thing since you came here."

"I told you before, I don't cook."

"So what would you do if Marco and his mom and sister didn't keep us fed?"

"TV dinners. Takeouts. I promise you, I wouldn't let you starve."

"Humph!" Beth glared at her over her glasses, then tried to move, wincing with pain as she did so. It seemed to Deborah that she was looking very pale and tired, and she seemed to be getting less, rather than more, active.

"Are you feeling all right?" she asked, adjusting the cushion under Beth's leg.

"Sure I am. But I'd be a darned sight better if I

could get out of this goddamned chair and do things for myself, instead of having to rely on you for everything."

"I'm sorry about that, but for the moment I'm all you've got."

Beth looked up at her, dark marks like thumb-prints on the wrinkled skin beneath her eyes. "You're not as bad as I thought you'd be."

"Why, thank you, Aunt Beth. Such praise."

"Don't let it go to your head. When are you going to see your granddad Barry?"

The question shot out of Beth like a bullet from a gun, taking Deborah by surprise. It was the second time Beth had spoken of her visiting her grand-father. Deborah fetched the television guide and put it on the table beside Beth. "I told you I would visit my grandfather before I left."

"I know you did. But you haven't got much more time, have you? It would be like you to forget all about it."

Deborah turned from her, closing her eyes for a moment. "I won't go back to England without seeing him, so you can stop nagging me about it."

"You don't want to see him, do you?"

Deborah felt like turning and shaking the old woman. She wanted to yell, "No, I don't bloody well want to see him. I don't want to be reminded of what my life was like here when I was a child, don't you understand that, you stupid woman?" But what was the point?

"She's dead now," Beth said suddenly.

"Who's dead?"

"Your grandmother. Ellen Barry."

"Yes, I know she is. What about it?"

"She can't hurt you now."

Deborah turned slowly to confront her aunt. "I don't know what you mean."

"Oh, yes, you do. I know what an old cow she was. She used to hit Ryan, too, when he was a kid."

"I don't know what you're talking about."

"Play it that way, if you want, but I could tell you were scared stiff of that woman."

Deborah's hands curled into fists, the nails digging into her palms.

Beth wasn't finished. "I told Ryan he'd better come and get you before she did you a permanent injury."

Deborah stared down at her, feeling a terrible urge to hit out at the seamed face. "My father came for me when he married again. Besides, how would you know anything about it? You had absolutely nothing to do with me when I was a child."

"He came for you because both me and his dad told him he'd better come."

"His father?"

"Yeah." Beth drew on her cigarette, the ash falling onto her lap. "I spoke to Jack when he brought you over for Anne's birthday party. Told him I knew what was going on. He said he couldn't stop it. I said he'd better, or I would get in Children's Aid or one of them services. So Jack told your father."

Deborah was trembling now. "I'm going." She turned and walked stiff-legged to the back door.

"Wait a minute. I haven't—"

Deborah crashed the door shut. When she got into the truck, she locked the door and sat there in the cabin, shaking uncontrollably. She leaned her head on the steering wheel, waves of nausea passing over her.

After a while, she sat up and started the ignition,

but as the engine chugged over she still stared out the window at the back fence, the wooden boards bare in places where the paint had peeled away. God, how she hated this place. It reeked of poverty and failure. No wonder Sandy wanted out.

She couldn't bear the thought of facing the garden center tonight. Not now. There was only one place she wanted to be, and that was with Marco. From the day she had arrived, Marco had come to represent laughter and warmth and optimism for her. Just a few minutes with him could erase all the stress of dealing with a cantankerous old woman and working in a rundown business. He seemed to have none of the self-doubt that sometimes drove her wild with Graham. In fact, Marco could even make her feel optimistic about her ideas for making the center successful.

Nothing seemed impossible to Marco.

Gripping the steering wheel resolutely she reversed into the back lane and drove out into the road, heading in the direction of Corydon Avenue.

Corydon was lined with trees that shaded the sidewalks and with small one- or two-story shops and restaurants. Marco had told her that this particular part of the long avenue, and the surrounding area, was the Italian district, and although it was multiethnic now, was famous for its plethora of Italian cafes and restaurants.

She parked across the street from Marco's restaurant, ran across the road between the traffic, and then walked in, past the few tables beneath umbrellas in the little courtyard off the sidewalk.

For a moment she observed Marco, dressed in his close-fitting black trousers and full-sleeved white shirt, relishing the pleasure of looking at him.

As if he could feel her gaze upon him, he looked up from pouring wine at a table against the far wall and then came to her, across the room. "What you doing here so early?"

Before she could reply he held up a finger to tell her to wait while he showed a family to their table. While Deborah waited for him by the cash desk she looked around, able to examine the restaurant more thoroughly without Marco standing beside her asking her what she thought of it.

It was a trifle kitsch in style, with rather crude Roman-style murals on the walls and candles in straw-covered Chianti bottles on the tables, but perhaps that was what Marco's clientele expected from an Italian restaurant. After all, this wasn't a London restaurant in Soho with fancy prices, and it certainly got the business. The place was packed, with two couples lined up waiting for a table. They were eyeing her now, ready to pounce if she got a table before they did.

Marco came back, his face glowing with the heat. "Just a few minutes more," he told those who were waiting. Then he took Deborah's arm and drew her toward the window. "What's wrong?"

"Why should anything be wrong?"

"I can tell. You've got worry lines here." He ran a thumb between his own dark eyebrows, then, to her utter surprise, bent to kiss the same place above her nose. "There, I make it all better." He grinned at her. "That's what I do to Floria and Roberto when they worry."

"Really? What does Roberto think of that?"

"He likes it. Why? You think a dad shouldn't kiss his son?"

"I didn't say that."

"Roberto's Italian. He's used to me kissing him."

"I'm sure he is." Deborah glanced over her shoulder, aware that the four people behind them were listening in with interest. "Could we go somewhere else for a moment, do you think?"

"Sorry, no. I'm too busy to get away now."

Deborah knew that he didn't mean to be rude. It was a simple statement of fact, but she felt hurt, nevertheless. She had come to him, needing him, and he hadn't time for her.

She turned to the door. "Okay. I'll be back around eight-thirty."

"Where you going?" he shouted after her as she opened the door and went out.

"I don't know."

In an instant, he was outside standing beside her on the sidewalk. "Something's happened, right?"

"No, nothing's happened. I told you that." She kept her head averted from him.

"Okay, nothing's happened. But you're feeling bad about something."

Deborah smiled, shaking her head in exasperation at herself. "You could say that. Yes."

He held up his index finger again. "Give me fifteen minutes—"

"No, Marco. I know how busy you are. I'm sorry. I'm being very stupid."

"Not at all." He took her chin in his hand, forcing her to turn her face to his. "I like you like this, not so tough."

"Oh, shut up," she said, batting his hand away, but she couldn't help smiling.

"Did you drive the car here?"

"No, Sandy has it. I brought the truck."

"Okay, wait in it for me. Then we'll go back to

the house. We can talk there. It's quiet without the kids."

"I don't want to take you—"

"You said that already." He opened the door, went inside, and shut it behind him. Through the window Deborah could see him laughing and talking to the people by the cash desk. Marco genuinely liked people, that was the secret of his success, she was sure. That, and his skill in creating good food without being too artsy about it all. No fancy cuisine for him. "Winnipeg's a good place to start up a restaurant business," he'd told her late one night in the restaurant, when they were eating veal *a limone* he had cooked himself, after everyone else had gone home. "Eating out is very important in this city, with winters sometimes lasting six months. And if you can make a go of it here, you'll do it anywhere in the world. Careful with their money, Winnipeggers. You have to fill their plates, or they think they've not got their money's worth. But give them what they want and they'll keep coming back ... and bring their friends with them."

She got into the truck and sat there, with the window rolled down, watching people stroll along the sidewalks, in couples or groups or, occasionally, alone. From another nearby restaurant came the pungent scent of espresso coffee and the taped sound of mandolins playing "Arrivederci Roma." A cliché, yet somehow fitting into the atmosphere of mellow warmth.

She had forgotten all about summertime in Winnipeg. All she recalled was struggling into boots and parkas and mittens, getting her tongue stuck on an ice-covered metal pole someone had dared her to lick, and skating on the frozen pond at Assiniboine Park.

She could remember lying in the deep, white snow making snow angels in the backyard, her long hair escaping from her woolen cap and turning to wet tendrils. Sometimes other girls' mothers put marshmallows on sticks and toasted them over the barbecue for a special winter birthday treat or dropped them into hot chocolate, so that they melted on the outside. Delicious!

She'd always hated her own birthdays. Her grandmother would buy the most gaudy invitations from the Regal catalog and then serve nothing but Kool-Aid and cheap potato chips and a chocolate cake from a mix, which usually fell apart when she took it from the pan, so that they had to paste it together with gooey icing. The party favors would be a balloon for each child. Nothing else. The year before her father had rescued her, she'd told her grandmother she was too old for parties.

Her grandmother had looked relieved, but Granddad Barry had peered at her in his shortsighted way and said, "Are you certain of that, pet? Sure, you're only seven years old."

"Let the girl be, Jack Barry," had been her grandmother's answer, before she took her away to scrub her face and brush her long blond hair until her head ached, so that she could take a photograph to send to Deborah's father.

Deborah hated that hairbrush. Large, with a wooden handle and bristles embedded in a rubber base, it had a twofold purpose. Both of them painful. But what she hated most was the fact that it was never cleaned. Until the day she washed it herself, dousing it in boiling water and soapsuds, so that the handle came away and the rubber perished.

After that, it was the slipper her grandmother used

on her bare bottom. Or one of her grandfather's belts on the backs of her legs, if she was really bad. As she often was.

Fiona, on the other hand, had been far more subtle. Escaping from Grandma Barry and living with her father and his new wife had seemed like heaven to Deborah, at first. But she soon learned that there were more ways of being cruel than the mere physical. She could do nothing right in Fiona's eyes. She called her a prairie peasant and a slut, belittling her attempts at aping her new mother's English accent—which Deborah did from sincere admiration—or ridiculing her when she used the wrong words—Canadian words—for things. Like "cookies" for biscuits or "sidewalk" for pavement.

Boarding school—which was Fiona's idea, not Ryan's—had come, after the first few days there, as a great relief to Deborah. She found that although she made very few close friends she had a knack for organization and leadership, both qualities prized and applauded by the nuns. Beneath their approval she blossomed and succeeded . . . and made a vow at the age of eleven that she would never again allow herself to be bossed around by anyone, child or adult. Nor to cry, not even in private.

Now, after almost thirty years of being in total control of her life, everything was falling apart. First her sister, appearing on Ryan's doorstep and upsetting everyone's lives and, today, Aunt Beth, resurrecting memories about her childhood that Deborah thought were buried and forgotten.

A shadow fell across the truck window. She looked up and saw Marco.

She opened the door. "You were quick."

"Give me the keys. I'll park it in my space at the back of the restaurant."

She jumped down from the pickup before he could help her. "I'm sorry about this. I feel rather stupid."

"Don't worry about it. Meet you by my car."

He said nothing to her when they got into his car, so that she wondered if he was angry with her.

"You must be wondering why—" she began, as they turned into Stafford.

"Leave it till we get home," he told her gently. He put out his hand and squeezed both of hers where they lay, clenched, in her lap.

He didn't move his hand away until they pulled up in front of his old two-story house. The house was a combination of dark green clapboard siding and white stucco, and was pleasantly shaded—as were most of the houses in River Heights—by lofty old elms that grew in profusion along the boulevards. Marco's garden, however, could only be described as a mess.

"You may be a great chef, but you are definitely not a gardener," Deborah said, looking at the wilting marigolds and shriveled-up snapdragons.

"That's what Anne keeps telling me."

The sound of Anne's name seemed to make the temperature drop twenty degrees.

He led her into the narrow hallway of the house. It was very quiet. The children had always been there before when she'd visited. She breathed in the scents of old wood and basil and garlic.

"I love this old house," she said. He was standing very close to her, so close she could hear him breathing. "How is it that one old house can smell stale and musty, and another can smell delicious."

"You smell delicious." He lifted her hair from the nape of her neck and buried his face against it.

She stood very still, willing herself not to move. "No, Marco. We mustn't."

He began to kiss her, first the back of her neck, then her ears. She closed her eyes, lifting her chin, and his mouth moved to the white column of her neck, small, infinitely tender kisses until she released a low moan from the base of her throat . . . and his lips brushed along the taut skin until it reached her open mouth.

He tasted of wine and wonderment, of sun-ripened tomatoes and volcanic heat. As she melted against him, she was aware of his hands everywhere, lighting flame in her wherever they touched. Then he was drawing her into the living room, still kissing and touching, until they reached the fireplace and tumbled to the hearth rug, Marco's arms taking the weight of her body as she went down.

This is wrong, wrong! a tiny voice called out from a dark corner of her mind, but nothing could stop the inevitability of it all as they fought zippers and buttons, feverishly dragged off each other's clothes, and Marco drew her down on top of him.

Later, much later, when she lay there pressed against him, with his hand cupped comfortably around her left breast—and his arm heavy on her right one—and the carpet was starting to prickle her naked body, Deborah realized that it was the first time in her life she had made love without drinking a considerable amount of alcohol, the first time she hadn't insisted on a condom.

She was the first to speak. "Oh, Lord," she said. She felt Marco's mouth on her back.

"Vesuvius," he said.

"I beg your pardon?"

"Mount Vesuvius. The volcano. Near Naples."

She smiled, unable to see his face. "Oh, you mean it was like that. An eruption."

"Mmm hmm."

"You're right. It was." Now his leg was feeling heavy on hers. "I hate to say it, but my leg's numb. I think I'm going to have to get up." She looked up. It was dark outside now. "What time is it?"

"Almost ten."

"We must have slept."

"Hmm, part of the time." He hugged her against him, his fingers rounding her nipple.

The phone rang and his hand stilled. Deborah tensed, feeling as if whoever it was on the phone could see them. Thank God they couldn't. "Should we answer it?"

"Leave it. I've got it on the machine."

They heard the beep, then a pause as the machine relayed its message, and then Sandy's voice. Despite the distortion, it was obvious that she was in a panic.

"Marco, I tried the restaurant but they said you'd gone already. Could you or Debbie phone me as soon as you get back from the movie? Aunt Beth's had another fall."

Chapter 28

"Oh my God." Deborah scrambled to her knees, clutching her skirt against her chest.

"—and she's in the Health Sciences, the General Hospital part," Sandy was saying. "I came home and found her—"

Marco was the first to get to the phone. "Hold on, Sandy. We're here." He handed the telephone to Deborah, and then went to the bay window to close the curtains before turning on the lights. As Deborah was speaking to Sandy, he struggled into his trousers.

"Where are you?"

"At the hospital." Sandy started to cry. "Oh, Debbie. She was on the bathroom floor when I got home. In terrible pain. And she'd been sick. And—"

Deborah went icy cold. "Okay, darling. It's all right. We'll be there very soon and you can tell us everything then." She turned to Marco, her hand over the receiver. "How soon, do you think?"

"Quick shower, dress, drive from here. Say half an hour." He was all brisk efficiency. "Find out where to meet her," he said, leaving the room.

"Where are you?" Deborah asked Sandy.

"Still in Emergency. They've got her on morphine now, so the pain's not quite so bad. Oh, Debbie.

They think she's broken her hip this time. I was late getting home. If only—"

"I know, I know." Deborah was shivering now. Then she felt the warmth of a blanket around her and Marco's hands clasping her shoulders. "We'll meet you in the waiting room as soon as possible. Around half an hour, Marco says."

"Okay. I didn't know what movie you were seeing. I'm so glad you were still at Marco's. If you hadn't been—"

"Well, we were," Deborah said firmly. "Go and have a cup of coffee. By the time you get back we'll be there with you." She put down the phone and stood there, staring at Marco. "Oh dear God, what have I done?"

"What do you mean, what have you done?"

Deborah twisted her hands. "Don't you see? This is all my fault."

"Santa Maria! How can it be your fault when you're not even there?" Marco's accent grew more noticeable in his confusion.

"I went out before Sandy got home."

"So? You've left Beth alone before. She had the wheelchair to get around the house, didn't she?"

"Yes, but—"

"I'm gonna take a shower. You want in with me?"

Deborah looked at him in amazement, then realized that he was not suggesting showering together for any other reason but speed. She shook her head. "I'll just use the washbasin." This evening was bizarre enough without showering with her sister's lover, after having had sex with him while their aunt lay in the hospital suffering from a broken hip because of her neglect.

"You can wash in the downstairs bathroom. Won't

get in each other's way, then." Deborah was grateful
for Marco's understanding.

As they gathered up their clothes from the living
room they spoke hardly a word to each other. In a
couple of minutes the place was as it was, as if what
had happened between them had never been. Looking around, Deborah felt a sense of relief tinged
with desolation and then she hurriedly left the room.

It was a scramble, but they were both ready to go
in fifteen minutes. Marco had even managed to find
time to brush his teeth. Deborah could smell the
aroma of mint as he opened the door for her. We've
both scrubbed away the scent of each other, thought
Deborah.

She wondered if it was going to be quite so easy
to remove the memories from their minds.

As they drove to the hospital Marco glanced
across at her several times, but said nothing, as if he
was intent on getting to the hospital as fast as possible. But then, as they were almost there, he said,
"So what happened between you and Beth, eh?"

"You don't think I hurt her, do you?"

"Don't be crazy."

She twisted the strap of her bag between her fingers. "I was . . . upset when I left."

"Beth upset you? She does that to Anne all the
time."

"I wish you wouldn't keep mentioning Anne. I
don't want to think about her."

"Sorry. What did Beth do to you?"

"She talked to me about my life in Winnipeg,
when I was a child."

"Bad things?"

Deborah nodded.

"You want to talk about it?"

"Not now. Now isn't the time."

"Later?"

"No." She stared straight ahead. "I want to forget about it."

"Bad things keep coming back. Was it your grandfather?"

She turned to him, frowning. "Was it what?"

"Did he . . . bother you when you were a kid?"

She had to smile. "Granddad Barry? He wouldn't hurt a fly. No, it was my grandmother. She was a witch."

"She's dead now. Can't hurt you."

"Easy for you to say."

"Did she beat you? My mamma used her pasta ladle to swat me."

"But I expect she'd hug and kiss you later."

"Sure she did. And I'd get extra almond biscotti after supper."

"That's the difference. I got the punishment without the kisses."

"You got your kisses tonight."

"Don't," she snapped, glaring at him. "How the hell can you joke about it?"

Marco sighed. "Maybe because I don't know what else to do." He drew up at the front of Emergency. "We'll talk later. You go in. I'll find you when I've parked."

The Emergency waiting room was packed with people. Children screamed with pain or frustration. An elderly man smelling of alcohol fought off a nurse who was trying to press a patch of gauze on his bleeding temple . . . Deborah shuddered, wishing she was anywhere but here. Then she saw Sandy, sitting with a tattered copy of the *National Geo-*

graphic magazine on her lap, staring into space.
"Sandy."

Sandy sprang up, the magazine falling to the
floor. She flung her arms around Deborah's neck.
"Thank God you're here."

Deborah hesitated for just a moment and then put
her arms around Sandy and held her tight. She
brushed the fall of hair from Sandy's eyes and bent
to peer into her face. "Are you all right? We made it
here as fast as we could."

"Where's Marco?"

"Parking the car. Have you heard any more?"

Sandy shook her head. "They've called in an
orthopedic surgeon, but he hasn't arrived yet. I think
someone said he's operating at some other hospital."

"I'll go and see what I can find out." Deborah
strode up to the desk. "I want to inquire about Miss
Carter."

"There's no change." The woman at the counter
didn't even look up. "We'll let you know when you
can see her."

Deborah's anger welled up. "I would like to see
your supervisor," she demanded, using her most
superior English accent. "Someone in charge."

The woman sighed. "Won't make any difference," she said wearily. "The patient is waiting to
see Dr. Bileski. I'll tell him you're here."

Marco came up behind her. "Come on. Don't
waste your time. We're going for a coffee," he told
the nurse. At the sound of his voice the nurse looked
up. He gave her a brilliant smile. "We'll be back. If
you could possibly—"

"I'll see what I can find out," she told him, returning the smile.

"Sexist witch," Deborah muttered beneath her

breath as Marco led her away. She could hear him chuckling as they rejoined Sandy.

When they heard the news after almost an hour of frustrated waiting, with Deborah alternately pacing and sitting and Sandy perched on the edge of her hard seat, biting the sides of her fingers, it wasn't good. In fact it was even worse than they'd expected.

"Apart from the broken hip, I'm concerned about Miss Carter's general health," said Dr. Bileski. He was surprisingly young, with thick black hair and eyebrows. "I would like to admit her and set up a series of tests in conjunction with an oncologist."

"What's an oncologist?" Sandy asked, looking even more scared.

Deborah answered for him. "A cancer specialist." She took Sandy's hand and squeezed it. "Do you suspect bone cancer?" she asked the doctor bluntly.

"We shall know better when we've run the tests."

"Can we see her?" Sandy asked.

"For a few minutes. Then I suggest you go home and come back tomorrow, when she has been assigned a bed."

"Tomorrow?" Deborah repeated, aghast.

"There is a shortage of beds," he said brusquely.

"What about a private room?"

"I understand there are no private rooms available at present."

"There must be," Deborah insisted. "I'm happy to pay."

"I'm sure you are," the doctor said with a sour smile, "but there are none available. Don't worry, she'll be well looked after," he added, and strode away as fast as his short legs would take him.

Seeing Sandy's white face, Deborah curbed her

annoyance at the doctor's offhand manner. "It's a good hospital," Marco assured them both. "Mamma was in here last year and they treated her well."

When they were allowed in to see her, Deborah and Sandy found Beth still lying on the stretcher, hooked up to an IV pole. Her eyes were closed and she looked very much smaller, as if she had shrunk since Deborah had last seen her.

Her eyes opened for a moment when Sandy bent to kiss her on the forehead. She tried to smile. "Clumsy . . . idiot . . ." she managed to get out.

"You're going to be fine," Sandy said brightly.

"Sure I am." The eyelids closed again as if the effort to keep them open was too much. Then, after a moment of silence, her lips formed the word "Annie."

Sandy straightened up, her eyes meeting Deborah's across Beth's narrow bed.

"Annie will be here very soon," Deborah told Beth.

Marco insisted on driving them home, telling Deborah she could get the truck some time tomorrow.

The house was filled with reminders of Beth's fall and her hasty departure with Sandy in the ambulance. The abandoned wheelchair in the hallway, a Safeway bag containing a quart of milk and a French baguette on the kitchen counter . . .

After much discussion they decided that there was little point in waking Anne in the middle of the night. Better to get some sleep themselves tonight and call Anne tomorrow.

"Do you want me to call her in the morning?" Deborah asked Sandy.

"Would you?" Sandy said eagerly. She tried to smile. "It's not going to be easy telling her."

"Just tell her about the fall and the broken hip," Marco suggested. "The rest can come later."

"We don't even know yet if there is any rest, do we?" Deborah said, avoiding looking directly at him.

"That is true."

"I think Mom would want to know," Sandy said. "You should tell her they're running tests."

"All right," Deborah said, her stomach muscles clenching at the thought of having to call her sister.

"You want me to stay here tonight?" Marco asked.

"No, of course not," Deborah said, a little too hastily. "We'll be fine," she added. "I don't know about Sandy, but I'm absolutely exhausted."

Sandy nodded. "Me, too. I'm not sure I can sleep, though." She went to hug Marco. "Thanks. You've been truly wonderful."

He hugged her close, kissing her on the top of her head. "Hang in there, *cara*. Take care of yourself, eh?" He went to the door and then turned, looking across at Deborah. "You, too."

The door opened and he was gone.

Chapter 29

Since Graham had gone to London, everything seemed flat and colorless to Anne. Even the weather reflected her mood, turning gray and dismal, the sky heavy with cloud. She'd known that her friendship with Graham couldn't last, that she'd been living in a fool's paradise ever since Deborah had left for Canada, but for a short while she'd allowed herself not to think about tomorrow. Stupid! Tomorrow always came.

What made it even worse was having to put up with Conrad at Hammerton. She'd endured two wretched evenings and an entire day with him in the house. When Saturday came, she knew that she couldn't take any more of him without blowing up. She would have to think up some way of escaping.

Friday had been bearable until midafternoon. Her father and Conrad had been shut away in Ryan's office poring over computer printouts and balance sheets all morning. But then they'd emerged for lunch, her father's forehead creased as if he was still trying to fathom something out.

For the rest of the day, he seemed a thousand miles away. Eventually, he said he was going for a walk to clear his head. "A walk by myself will do me good," he said, putting an end to Anne's idea that they might walk together through the grounds. So, as Eileen was at the village hall, immersed in preparations for the annual summer fête, Anne was left alone with Conrad.

Not long after their first meeting, Anne had decided that Conrad was like a conjurer, adapting his bag of tricks to his audience. Yesterday he had tried to dazzle her with what he obviously thought was attractive to women: the slightly risqué stories of his travels and exploits in exotic places. The little flattering smiles and touches. No doubt it usually worked. It had with poor Sandy, to whom he must have seemed wonderfully urbane and sophisticated, but it was all totally lost on Anne. She had thought him cold and ruthless on their first meeting. Nothing since then had given her cause to change her mind. Besides, she had already been exposed to what she believed to be the epitome of true English charm. Conrad's brand left her cold. Indeed, it merely convinced her that he was a pathological womanizer, a Don Juan who couldn't bear to meet a woman and not add her to his list of conquests.

"As this is my last weekend in England," she announced as they were drinking coffee just before noon on Saturday, "I'd like to do something special this afternoon."

Ryan looked stricken. "I've been sadly neglecting you, love. Tell you what, Conrad and I will set aside our work until Monday and we'll go out. How about the seaside? We could get to the Sussex coast in a couple of hours."

"No, I'm not going to interfere with your work," Anne said hurriedly, wishing she'd kept her mouth shut. That was all she needed, to be confined in a car with Conrad for several hours.

Conrad leaned back in his chair, one arm draped down its side, the sun glinting on the heavy gold ring on his right hand. "We could go to Brighton for the day tomorrow. You'd love the pavilion. I was sorry that we didn't have time to take Sandy to the coast while she was here."

Anne was amazed at his nerve. To speak about Sandy in such a nonchalant way after what he'd done. All her anger boiled up, spewing over like lava. "I'd prefer it if you didn't mention Sandy."

His eyebrows rose in surprise. "Why on earth not?"

"Because your short association with her was a disaster. She wasn't even here twenty-four hours before you got her drunk."

"Hold on there," he protested. "We've been through this before. Your daughter's not a child. How could I stop her drinking if she wanted to?" He gave her an unpleasant smile. "I know it's hard, but you're just going to have to accept that your daughter's a woman now, no longer in your control. A very lovely young woman."

"You've said enough, Conrad," Ryan said. Anne was surprised by the stone-hard quality of her father's voice. "Keep my granddaughter out of the conversation, okay?"

"Whatever you say, boss." Conrad tipped his chair back, one long leg stretched out, his arm swinging back and forth. He glanced at Anne from underneath his heavy lids and gave her a lazy smile. "My apologies, Anne. I didn't mean to upset you."

"Okay." She gathered up their coffee cups and took them out to the kitchen, slamming them down on the pine-topped table. "If I don't get out of this house today," she announced to Eileen, "I swear I'm going to kill that man."

Eileen was bustling around, putting cakes and trays of cookies into boxes for the fête. "Which one? Your father or Conrad?"

"Both." Anne grinned. "No, Conrad."

"Him? Oh, he's harmless."

"Don't you believe it."

"Sure it's all blarney with him. Can't bear to see a woman who's not taken by his charm."

Anne put the cups and saucers into the dishwasher. "He's got all the charm of a cobra."

"It's too bad Ryan had to bring him down on your last weekend."

"You can say that again, but it's quite typical, isn't it?"

"Well, at least he hasn't any other guests coming."

"I wish he had. It might diffuse Conrad a bit if someone else was here. Anyway, what difference does it make? Even if they don't spend the time working, anything we do will have to be with Conrad."

"I'm not so sure about that."

"What can we do? Lock him in the cellar?"

"Let me see what I can come up with."

"You must be joking. You've got the fête all afternoon. Are you quite sure you wouldn't like me to help?"

"Not on your last weekend. It'll be a madhouse." Eileen cut two large fruit cakes topped with green and red cherries into slices—handing a big chunk to Anne—and covered them with plastic wrap. "If you're not going anywhere, why not get Ryan to bring you along to see what a genuine English summer fête is like?"

"I will."

"Meanwhile, I'm going to think of something to

get rid of Conrad for a while, so's you can spend the time alone with your dad."

Impulsively, Anne reached out to hug Eileen. "You're a good friend, Eileen, but you can't solve this problem. It's between me and Ryan alone."

"I know that. It's the getting rid of Conrad I'm working on. But make sure when I get him out of this place that you take advantage of it and talk to your dad, before 'tis too late, all right?"

"I'll try."

Anne went back into the living room, to find Conrad and her father talking in low voices by the window. It looked as if Conrad was trying to persuade Ryan to do something he didn't want to do. They stopped talking as soon as they saw she was there. Ignoring them, she was cleaning Ryan's ashtray when Eileen flounced into the room, looking flustered and quite unlike her usually calm self.

"That's all I need," she announced.

"What's wrong?" Anne asked, as if on cue. Only when Eileen turned to her and gave her a little wink did she get it.

"The car's got a puncture and I'm already half an hour late, as it is. I've got all the cakes and things for the baking table as well as food for the tea. There's no time to change the tire. Conrad, would you be a pet and drive me to the hall?" Eileen didn't wait for him to reply. "We'll have to unload everything from my car and put it in yours. Come along, then. I'm late," she said, as Conrad hesitated.

He shrugged. "Don't go anywhere without me," he said to Anne and Ryan with a bemused smile, and followed a still-grumbling Eileen from the room. "I'll be back as soon as possible."

The dining room fell silent. Ryan smiled across

the room at Anne. "She's quite the character, isn't she?"

"She certainly is," Anne replied, delighted to see Conrad being outmanipulated. "I hope you know how lucky you are to have her."

"Oh, I do, I do. She's a wonderful woman. I'd be lost without her." Ryan turned to look out the window, as if stalling for time to think up something else to say to his daughter. Standing there, a lock of hair falling forward on his forehead, he reminded Anne of pictures she'd seen of Irish poets such as Yeats and Fitzgerald. She'd never thought of her father as a poet before, but she supposed that was what he was, really, for he had written all the words as well as the music for his songs. Somehow the realization made him seem different; more the sensitive creator than a popular and successful singer.

He turned back. "So, what shall we do today?"

"I want to spend some time with you."

"Well, of course. That's what we'd planned, isn't it?"

"Alone."

He glanced across the room like a cornered animal, desperate to find an escape.

"It won't take long, I promise you. Please, Ryan. All I'm asking for is a little piece of your time to ask you a few questions. How about now?"

"It's not really a good time, Annie. I've got a load on my mind at the moment. Conrad was just telling me that the manager of my Dublin business might be cooking the books."

Anne was tempted to say that he might check into what Conrad was doing with the books.

"It won't take long, I promise."

He brushed a nervous hand across his forehead. "I don't want to talk about my wife."

"But she wasn't just your wife. She was my mother, too."

"Didn't Beth tell you about her? After all, she knew her far longer than I did."

"That's what you keep telling me, but Beth has only told me about Janine as her sister. I want to know about her as my mother. Surely you can understand that? It's like I—I lost the first seven years of my life. I don't remember any of it. I must have blotted it all out in some way."

He gazed out the window, which had leaded panes to make it look ancient. "I'm the same. I don't remember much at all."

"Then why don't we share our memories with each other?" She came to him, touching his arm. "Please, Daddy. I'm going back to Canada in just a few days."

He shook her hand from his arm. "What I'd like to know is why you suddenly want this from me, when you've lived quite happily without it for more than thirty years?"

"I wish I knew why. But I do know that I'd been wanting to get in touch with you for a long time."

"Then why didn't you?"

"Pride, I suppose. I wanted you to come to me. After all, a dad is supposed to keep in touch with his kids whatever happens, isn't he? Do you know how much it hurt not to get even a card from you for my birthday? I'd watch for that mailman and say to myself, 'This time, please God. Just a card. Doesn't need to be a present. Just a card with *Love from Daddy* written on it!"

"Holy Mother!" he said beneath his breath. Then he turned from the window and faced her. "Why are you telling me all this? Is it meant to make me feel guilty?"

"No. Not at all. I just want to understand why."

"Why what?" he demanded, exasperated. "I thought you wanted to know about your mother. Make up your mind."

Tears gathered at the back of Anne's eyes. "I do. I want to know all about her. I want to find out exactly what happened when my mother died." Her voice rose. "Why you left us. Why you split me and my sister up between the two families. Why you went away to Europe. Most of all, I want to know why you chose Debbie to live with you, and not me." Her voice had risen. Now it broke and she sank into a chair, turning her face from him.

She heard his feet in his favorite leather moccasins cross the parquet floor to her. Then she felt his hands on her shoulders, squeezing them from behind.

"Sorry," she whispered. "I didn't mean to yell."

"That's okay." He pulled up a chair, setting it in front of her, and sat down. "First of all, I have to tell you that it hurts like hell to talk about all this. All that stuff about opening old wounds has nothing on this."

"I'm sorry." She looked up at him through damp lashes. "I really am. But I must know."

"I can see that. I thought you were just being . . . I don't know, just wanting to know. As if you were gathering information for a family biography, something like that."

She shook her head, marveling at his utter lack of understanding. "You must be joking. This is a huge, raw chunk of my life we're talking about here."

"Okay, okay. I said I was beginning to understand."

"You make it sound as if everything happened only to you, not to Debbie and me at all."

"Then why isn't Debbie bombarding me with questions all the time?"

"Maybe she's tried and nothing worked, so she just gave up and hid all the pain away."

"You sound like a shrink."

"Oh, I've been to one of those, too. At least, a counselor."

"What did he tell you?"

"She. Said I needed to grieve for the loss of both my parents and my sister, as if they had all died, not just my mother. Said it must be tough for me to understand why a father would abandon me like that. That it wasn't because I had done anything wrong."

"Holy Mother!" Ryan sprang to his feet and paced to the window and back. "I suppose you didn't happen to mention to your counselor that you chose to stay in Canada?"

"What? What do you mean?"

Now Ryan was mad at her. "Your very convenient memory seems to have wiped that bit out."

Anne stared at him.

"I came to Canada to ask you to come and live with Fiona and me in England."

"You asked Debbie."

"I asked both of you. You don't really think I'd ask one of you and not the other, do you? Why would I do that?"

Anne shook her head. "I don't know," she said in a low voice. "I didn't know. I thought maybe you preferred Debbie because she was prettier or younger, or something like that."

"Is that what Beth told you?"

"No, of course not. She used to say that she hadn't any children so she wanted to adopt me and you said that was okay."

"I asked you to come to England with me. You said you didn't want to live with me, you wanted to stay with your aunt Beth."

Their eyes met. "I don't remember it at all."

"Do you believe me?"

"Were you mad at me for saying it?"

The skin over his cheekbones flushed dark red. "I was disappointed as hell. Before she died, I promised Janine I'd care for you both and I'd worked like a dog, touring, so that I could carry out that promise. Then, when I'd made enough money to look after you properly, you said no to me."

"So you were mad at me."

"Yes. I yelled at you."

She closed her eyes, the images that had lain just beyond her reach since her childhood suddenly coming into focus. "You told me to go to hell."

"I'm ashamed to say I did. Beth was furious with me for that."

"Did you ever think I was just scared? That maybe I didn't know you that well because you'd been away so much? Beth and her home was all I knew, really. Maybe if you'd been around a bit more I wouldn't have reacted the way I did," she added.

He said nothing, but stood staring out the window, while Anne considered what might have been had she agreed to coming to England with him.

Ryan sat down again. "I should have called you, written to you," he said. "But I thought you didn't want me to." He looked away from her. "You cried when I asked you to come with me. My little Annie. You cried as if you were scared of me."

Anne put out her hand to touch his. He didn't move. "I used the money for Sandy as an excuse, really, to get in touch with you," she told him.

His hand turned and clasped hers. "I'm glad you did. It's probably not enough. I want you to—"

"It's a terrific help. Fifteen thousand more than we had before."

He frowned. "Fifteen thousand?" he repeated, with an emphasis on the amount.

"Yes, we appreciate it so much."

"Fifteen, not fifty?"

"Yes," said Anne, wondering what he was getting at.

Ryan stood up, looking extremely agitated. "I told Conrad to send you fifty thousand dollars, not fifteen."

Chapter 30

"When I said fifty, he must have heard it as fifteen."
Ryan stared at her, shaking his head. "You must
have thought me a miserable bastard to be sending
only fifteen thousand. That wouldn't have lasted
poor Sandy a year in New York."

"We were thrilled," Anne protested.

"Thank God you told me. Otherwise I'd never
have known."

Anne suddenly felt very cold, recalling Conrad's
covering letter. "Did you ask Conrad to write a letter
telling me there must be no further contact between us?"

"What are you talking about?"

"That you didn't want me to make any acknowledgment of the bank order?"

He looked completely puzzled. "To be honest, I
was surprised you didn't call me or at least send a
note, but—"

"According to Conrad, you didn't want me to.
That's why I came here without telling you ahead of
time. The letter said you wanted no acknowledgment or further contact between us."

"Well, he definitely got that one wrong. I suppose
he's so used to doing everything for me he thought
that was what I wanted." Ryan seemed to be trying

to convince himself, but wasn't quite succeeding.
"As soon as he gets back we'll ask him."

"He'll have some plausible explanation ready,
I'm sure."

"Now, Annie, that's not very nice. I know you
don't like Conrad, but—"

"It isn't just that I don't like him, I don't trust
him. Oh, I know he's been a terrific manager over
the years to you—"

"He's made me a wealthy man."

"No, Daddy, *you* are the one who's done that,
through your talent and hard work."

"But Conrad has built up my investments, advised
me on every aspect of my music business. I was like
a babe in the woods when he took me on. But for
Conrad, I wouldn't have had the fifty thousand to
send you for Sandy's education."

"Or fifteen," she said with a ghost of a smile.

"Right," he acknowledged. "Let's settle this now,
before Conrad comes in." He led the way into his
office. "The old checkbooks should be in this
drawer." He turned the key in the bottom drawer of
the black filing cabinet and pulled it out, squatting
down in front of it. "Can you remember what the
date on the check was?"

"It wasn't an actual check. It was a bank draft for
Canadian dollars."

"Of course it was. So there won't be a check stub
for it."

"But I think it was dated about ten days before I
received it, which was the twenty-eighth of June."

"How can you remember the exact date?"

"It was one of the most important days of my life,
that's why."

He blinked rapidly and then shut the drawer. "It

will be a withdrawal then, not a check." He stood up, levering himself up by holding on to the desk, a small concession to his age. "I'll ask Conrad to show me the entry when he comes in."

Anne said nothing, but her expression obviously spoke for her.

"Oh okay, doubting Thomas. We'll look it up ourselves."

But when he looked for his personal accounting record book, it wasn't there. Nor were his bank statements for the current year. "Conrad must have them in his briefcase. I know he's been working on them all week."

Conrad opened the front door at that very moment, as if he'd been waiting for his cue. "I have returned from the boundless pleasures of the English summer fête, God help me," he announced theatrically. "Anybody home?"

"We're in the office," Ryan called out. "You're just the man we needed."

As Conrad crossed the hall, Anne's heart was pounding hard.

"What's going on?" Conrad asked, taking in the pile of papers and accounting books on the desk.

"I was looking for this year's bank statements."

"What for?"

Ryan gave him a sharp glance. "Because I want them, that's why."

"They're in my briefcase. It's right there. You should have helped yourself," Conrad said, all open-faced honesty.

"I tried. It's locked."

"Oh, so it is. Sorry. What is it you want to know? Knowing you, my friend, it would be easier for me to look something up for you than to do it yourself.

Your father's genius was always for music not figures," he explained to Anne, with a smile. She did
not return the smile.

Nor was Ryan amused. "You made a bloody
serious mistake, Conrad."

"Did I? How?"

"You sent Anne a bank order for fifteen thousand
dollars, not fifty as I asked."

Conrad was all bewilderment. "But you told me fifteen, Ryan. It was definitely fifteen. We discussed it."

"I said fifty. There's a hell of a difference
between fifteen and fifty."

"Quantitively, perhaps. But not in sound. I obviously misheard you. I am truly sorry to—"

"How the hell did you think Sandy would have
managed several years in New York City on fifteen
thousand?"

"My dear Ryan, it wasn't my business to question
your gift to your granddaughter. After all, it was the
first and only time you had sent her anything, so I
had nothing else to measure it by. By many people's
standards, fifteen thousand would have been most
generous."

"Is that what you thought? That fifteen was
enough, so you'd just send that amount and ignore
my wishes?"

"I think I'll go and make some coffee," Anne
said, feeling extremely uncomfortable.

"No, I want you here," Ryan said. He turned back
to Conrad. "And what was all that stuff about not
wanting an acknowledgment?"

Conrad's face was incredulous. "I think Anne's
right. She should go and make some coffee if you're
going to take that tack."

"What do you mean?" Ryan was belligerent.

"You surely haven't forgotten our discussion about what form the letter should take." Conrad glanced at Anne. "I don't think it's fair or kind to Anne to go over it while she's here."

"Remind me," was all Ryan said, but he looked less sure of himself now.

Conrad shrugged. "Have you seen the letter I wrote to Anne?"

Ryan shook his head.

Conrad turned to Anne. "Your father told me to make it as businesslike as possible, because that is what you wanted. I'm sorry to have to tell you this, but he intimated to me that he did not want to start up a correspondence with you. So naturally I couched the letter in those terms."

"I'm surprised you would send a letter of that sort without my seeing it," Ryan said.

"It was a business letter." Conrad was like a man reaching the end of his patience. "That's what you'd said you wanted me to send." He turned in appeal to Anne. "I'm sorry if you were upset by the letter, but I was only carrying out your father's instructions."

Anne hesitated, her mind in a turmoil. Was it possible that her father was using Conrad as a cover for his own actions? Suddenly she didn't know which of them to believe.

"It doesn't matter," she said wearily. "None of it matters. I'm going to make some coffee."

"Annie," her father protested, but she ignored him and went to the kitchen.

Ryan stood looking at the doorway, then he turned to Conrad. "Something's going on here. I'm not sure what it is, but I don't like it."

"For God's sake, Ryan, face it," Conrad said in a low voice. "Your daughter has upset you. I'm not surprised. She's a difficult woman. Look how she keeps on at me about Sandy, when—"

"I told you before not to mention Sandy, okay?"

Conrad held up his hands. "Fine, fine." He sat down at the desk, crossing his long legs. "Look. You and I have got along for more than twenty years. We've worked as a team. Then Deborah became part of that team. She has a hell of a good business head on her shoulders, that girl. Then along comes your other daughter and doesn't like the cozy nest we have here because she's not included, so she makes trouble for everyone. To the point that you send Deborah off to Canada to look after an aunt she doesn't even know. Think about it! Wasn't that crazy? All that was Anne's doing. Face it, old man. Anne wanted Deborah out of here so she could get her share of the pie. Now, having got rid of Deborah, she's after her sister's boyfriend."

"You mean Graham?"

"Sure, I mean Graham. Didn't you notice her making nicey with him? He's a wealthy man. A great catch."

"They're both interested in gardening. That's all."

"I'm sure they are." There was no mistaking Conrad's meaning. He hurried on. "And now that she's got rid of Deborah and is wheedling herself in with you, she wants to get rid of me. So what does she do? She complains about me, using first the episode with Sandy and then the check to turn you against me."

"Show me the entry." Ryan held out his hand.

"What entry?"

"The entry for the fifteen thousand dollars."

"Weren't you listening to me?"

"I listened okay. I heard you talking a load of

horse shit and for the very first time I began to think I shouldn't be trusting you."

Conrad sighed. "I told you Anne was getting to you. She's been here only a couple of weeks and she has you suspicious about someone who's been with you twenty years. That hurts, Ryan. I can't pretend it doesn't."

"Show me the entry."

Conrad shifted in his chair. "I have no recollection of the date."

"It was around the eighteenth of June."

"Are you sure?"

"Absolutely."

"Then that should be easy to find." Conrad bent to open his briefcase and brought out a sheaf of bank statements. Before he had time to look through them Ryan had taken them from him.

"Here we are. What would fifteen thousand be? How many Canadian dollars to the pound?"

"Just over two dollars. Around two twenty. Give them to me," Conrad said impatiently. "I can find it."

"Here we are. There's only one entry for that date." Ryan was silent for a moment, staring down at the amount. "A withdrawal for twenty-three thousand pounds." Keeping his finger on the entry he stared across the desk at Conrad. "That would buy a hell of a lot more than fifteen thousand Canadian dollars. You'd better start explaining fast."

Conrad leaned back in the swivel chair and smiled. "That was a withdrawal for the month. Not just for the bank order for Canada. There were bills to be paid and—"

"Since when did I pay my bills with cash?"

Conrad gave a little laugh. "You really are out of touch. What about your credit card bills? Hold on and I'll get my records out for that date. We'll have it all sorted in no time. I must tell you though that I do resent this line you're taking with me. Your daughter has you well and truly spooked, doesn't she?"

Ryan was about to reply when the telephone rang. He picked it up. "Hello," he barked into it.

"Daddy?" It was Deborah's voice.

"Can I ring you back, love? I'm in the middle of something important."

"Sorry, you can't. Is Anne there? I need to speak to her. I must warn you, it's bad news about her aunt, so be there for her, all right?"

Ryan looked down at the telephone in his hand and then across at Conrad, who was watching him like a blue-eyed hawk. "Okay," Ryan said. He drew in a long breath and released it slowly. "I'll get her."

Not wanting to leave Conrad on his own in the office he went to the door and shouted for Anne. "It's Deborah for you," he told her when she came, handing her the phone.

"Deborah?" She looked at him, her eyes registering his concern.

Placing his hand on the side of her face, he stroked it gently. "We'll be in the kitchen," he said.

He motioned to Conrad to leave Anne alone in the office, but when Conrad picked up his briefcase to take with him, Ryan said, "Leave it there," and held the door open until Conrad had joined him.

Chapter 31

A broken hip and tests for bone cancer! Anne looked down at the telephone in her hand, unable to believe what Deborah was telling her.

"How could she have broken her hip? You told me she was managing very well," she added, her tone an accusation.

After a moment of silence Deborah said, "She fell getting from the wheelchair to the toilet. Apparently she forgot to put the brakes on."

Anne sat in silence.

"I am so sorry," Deborah said.

"What gets me is that I'm not there with her," Anne said, swallowing hard.

"I know. But she's getting the best care possible."

Anne scrabbled for a tissue in the pocket of her jeans. "I'll be there as soon as I can get things arranged."

"Get Ryan to do it. Or Conrad, if he's there. He's good at organizing stuff."

He sure is! thought Anne.

"Let me know as soon as you can what flight you'll be on and we'll pick you up."

"Marco can pick me up," Anne said. "You and Sandy must be going crazy with so much to do. Oh poor Sandy, how's she managing?"

There was a moment of hesitation, then Deborah said, "Quite well, in the circumstances."

"Thank God for that."

"She's at the hospital at the moment. She said she'd speak to you later."

"Good." Another silence. "I won't keep you, then," Anne said. "I have to arrange my flight. Give Aunt Beth my love, would you? Tell her I'll be there very soon."

"I will."

"Deborah."

"Yes?"

"Does she know? About the possibility of cancer, I mean?"

"We've not actually told her yet, but she knows it's more than just a broken hip."

"Yes, I suppose she would, with all those tests." Anne paused, looking for the right words. "Thanks for being there with her."

"She'd much rather have you."

"She'll soon have both of us. But I'm sure you'll want to get home again once I've arrived."

Again, an awkward stretch of silence. This conversation seemed to be filled with them. "Not necessarily. It depends on what you want."

Anne hesitated, not knowing how Deborah would react. "You want me to be honest?"

"Of course."

"I'd really like you to stay, if you could manage it. Just for a few days, until I'm settled into everything again. That way I can ease in, if you know what I mean."

"That's fine." There was a taut quality to Deborah's voice that made Anne not sure that her sister was being quite honest with her. But how could she tell? This was a unique situation for both of them. One sister asking for the other's support.

"Thanks."

"How are things going back home?" Deborah asked.

"Here? Fine." For a moment Anne was tempted to tell Deborah what was going on, but she decided it was far too complicated to go into now. Anyway, it was Ryan's business, not hers.

"Good. I'll let you go," Deborah said abruptly. "Let me know when you're arriving."

"I will."

When she had said good-bye, Anne set the telephone down on the desk and stared at it, feeling utterly numb. She sat for a very long time, gazing into space. She knew she should be jumping into action, arranging her flight, packing . . . but everything seemed to have shut down.

She looked up and saw Ryan standing in the doorway. "Aunt Beth has broken her hip and she may have bone cancer," she told him.

He stared at her, frowning, and then came to her, arms outstretched, and she went to him, to be clasped against his chest, breathing in the smell of clean shirt and shaving lotion. "Poor Beth," he said. "She doesn't deserve that."

That was right. That was exactly right. Beth didn't deserve it. She was a good woman. She'd worked hard all her life. Taken on her sister and then her sister's child. Anne found herself weeping silently and she couldn't stop. There was bitterness in her weeping, for she knew now that she would never be able to repay her aunt in the way she'd wished. But there was also comfort in the knowledge that she was being held in her father's arms, with her father's hand stroking her hair and her father's voice soothing her.

After a while, she pulled away from him and blew her nose. "I have to fly back to Canada."

"I know you do. I'll come with you."

She looked into his eyes and saw his courage, knowing how he dreaded going back. "What about Conrad? Is everything okay?"

"No, but I'll deal with Conrad when I get back."

"You can't leave it, Daddy. It's too important."

"It's just money."

"It's your life. You've worked hard for it. Did you find the entry for the bank draft?"

"Yes, I found it." He didn't need to say any more. It was all there, in his eyes.

"I am so sorry."

"Thank you for that. Oh, Conrad blustered a bit, but then he as good as admitted he'd fiddled the books. It's tough. You have a friend for a great part of your life and then you find out that there's a chance he's been screwing you all this time."

"Where is he now?"

"Sitting in the kitchen, drinking a bottle of my best Glenfiddich."

"It's more than he deserves."

Ryan shrugged and gave her a sad little smile.

"Is it a lot of money?" Anne asked.

"I don't know. It could be. It'll take a while to find out exactly how much. I worry less about my investments than I do about Deborah's business."

"You should go to the police."

"Of course I should." He looked over her head, across the room. "But I won't."

"No, I didn't think you would, somehow. You aren't planning to give him another chance, are you?"

"Not on your life. I may be a gormless eejit, as my mother used to call me, but I'm not that gormless."

"If you let him go he may do it to someone else."

"I'm sure he will. I don't think he can help it. But I'll not put a friend behind bars for the sake of money."

"So . . . ?"

"I engage a discreet financial firm to track everything down, regain control of my affairs, see what's left, and start all over again. From what I understand—and he's being remarkably frank—the Celtic recording company in Dublin is still strong enough to keep going, and that's the one my heart is in, as well as my money."

"What about this house?"

A shadow crossed his face. "I think it'll have to go. And I'm really worried about Deborah's company."

"I have a suggestion."

"What is it?"

"Tell Graham. Ask his advice."

He brightened visibly. "Now that is a good idea, Annie. And he'll also be discreet, as he's involved in the family, so to speak."

Involved in the family. It was a good way of describing it.

"So you see, it's all settled," was Ryan's conclusion. "I can come with you to Canada."

"No. You have too much to arrange here. If you leave now you could lose absolutely everything. Conrad can't be trusted, Daddy. You must realize that now. He could just empty your accounts and disappear. You must not trust him, however frank he seems to be at the moment."

"Maybe you're right."

"I am. Much as I'd love to have you come with

me, you must get everything out of his clutches immediately."

"Before I do anything else, I think I'll take your advice and phone Graham."

Anne wished she could do the same. She'd give the world to pour everything out to the man who had become far more than a friend in such a very short time. "Good idea. And I have to see about my flight."

"Get Timothy to do that for you."

"Timothy? Oh yes, Deborah's personal assistant. But it's Saturday."

"So? He gets paid well. I'll call him. It won't take a minute to arrange. Might as well use him while we can, eh?" he said in an attempt at humor.

It took rather more than a minute, but within half an hour Anne's flight to Winnipeg via Toronto had been confirmed. She would arrive tomorrow evening.

"I wish I could have gone today," she told Ryan.

"I know, but there was no way. Don't worry, love. Once I've got everything sorted out we'll go out somewhere special for dinner."

The last thing she felt like was eating. "Is he still in the kitchen?"

Ryan nodded.

"Can't we get rid of him?"

"Graham said to keep him here if he's in a co-operative mood. Safer that way."

"You mean we have to put up with him in the house?"

"At least until Graham arrives."

"Graham's coming here?" Anne asked, trying to hide her panic.

"Yes. Said he'd be here as soon as he could make it. There's a good friend for you."

"He certainly is." What an interesting day it was going to be, with her trying to dodge both Conrad and Graham. It wasn't going to take her that long to pack. What the hell was she going to do with herself? Then she thought of Eileen and the village fête. "I think I'll go and help Eileen at the fête."

"I thought she'd said no to that."

"She did. That was before all this happened. It will help to pass the time," she said in explanation. "And you'll be all caught up with business."

"True. God alive," he groaned, "I'd forgotten about Eileen. What is she going to say about all this?"

"Do you want me to tell her?"

He brightened. "Would you? No need to go into any details yet."

"I don't know any details."

He looked stricken. "What if I can't even afford to keep Eileen on? How in God's name would I manage without her?"

"Surely it won't be as bad as that."

"I don't know." He slumped into a chair and put his head in his hands. "That's the trouble. I haven't a clue how bad it is."

She touched his shoulder. "There's no point in worrying yourself sick until you do know. Eileen's not going to run out on you." She could have added that Eileen would stick around if she didn't get paid a cent, but decided that where Eileen was concerned it didn't hurt to let him suffer a little. "I'm off to the village. Can I take the Rover?"

"I thought it had a puncture."

"Oh, that's right." She reddened, as he looked directly at her. "I'd forgotten."

"Sure you did." he said, smiling. "Is it really punctured?"

She broke into laughter. "To be honest, I don't know."

"That Eileen! Wait till she hears what's happened. She won't believe it, will she? I wish I could be there with you to see her face when you tell her."

"You can't leave here," she said, still convinced that Conrad would get the best of her father if he got the chance.

"Don't worry. I'm not going anywhere. Take the Rover, if it's okay."

It was just her luck that, when she quietly turned the handle of the door and stepped gingerly into the hall, Conrad came out of the kitchen. Or perhaps it wasn't luck at all. Perhaps he had been waiting for her to come out.

"There you are," he said in a too-loud voice. "Ryan's little Annie. My nemesis." He stood there, slightly swaying back and forth.

Anne said nothing.

"Did you know you were my nemesis? Or perhaps you don't know what the word means."

"I'm well aware of its meaning," she said coldly.

"You are the goddess of retribution." He had a little trouble saying the word.

"Am I? If I am it's a shame I didn't come a little sooner, isn't it?"

He laughed. "Damned right. Could have spoiled my fun. Least you didn't spoil my fun with the divine Sandy. What a mundane name for such a lovely creature. Sandy. Most unimaginative."

She took a step closer to him, eyes narrowed. "Don't you talk about my daughter that way. Ryan warned you not to talk about her."

"Ask your lovely daughter if we didn't have fun together."

Anne's mind flew back to that afternoon when she'd come in from church to find Sandy still in bed. *It was my fault, not his.* "If you've hurt her in any way, I swear I'll—"

"What will you do?" he said, his eyes mocking her.

"I'll make you pay for it."

"You already have, my dear."

For a moment she felt a primeval urge to leap on him and scratch those glacial eyes out, but then Ryan came into the hall and, before he could say anything, Conrad had gone back into the kitchen and it was over, leaving Anne trembling.

Ryan put his arm around her. "I am sorry. I thought he was safely tucked away in the kitchen with his bottle."

"He said something about Sandy," she said, wiping damp palms on her jeans.

"Ah, don't worry about him. He's had too much to drink and he's trying to get at you. I'll deal with him. You go and change into a pretty dress and go off to the fête and forget all about Conrad."

That was easier said than done, she thought later, as she drove down the lane, shadows of the windblown trees on the car. There was something in Conrad's mockery that had rung with truth. But there was nothing she could do about it at this moment.

The bright stalls and bucolic merriment of the crowd gathered in the field by the village hall were all a bit much to take in her current rather shell-shocked state. The weather had cleared, the sun was shining and a light wind had blown most of the cloud away. It looked as if the entire population of the village had turned out, except for a few deserters, like Ryan, engaged in the more demanding dramas of life.

Eileen was in charge of the baked goods stall, reigning over plastic-wrapped Madeira cakes and gingerbread loaves and bags of rock cakes and macaroons ... She waved exuberantly when she saw Anne approaching. "Thought you weren't going to come," she shouted above the noise of the crowd.

Anne waited until she had reached the table before replying. "Can you take a few minutes off?"

Eileen's smile changed to a look of concern. "What's happened? Is it Ryan?"

"Ryan's okay," Anne assured her. "Could we go somewhere a bit quieter? Then I can tell you all about it."

Eileen nodded. "Jim," she called to a man who was passing by, carrying a box of paperbacks to the nearby books' table. "Could you give me a minute?"

"Be with you in a sec," he told her. He set the box by the table and came back to her. "What can I do for you?" He was red-faced and almost as round as a ball, with his green-and-white belt the ball's circumference.

"This is Ryan's daughter," Eileen told him. "Something's come up. Could you take over for a while? I could do with a break and a bite to eat, anyway."

"Certainly, certainly," he said in a hearty tone. When he sat down on the plastic chair Eileen had vacated, Anne was afraid it might break beneath his weight, but its legs just settled a couple of inches deeper into the damp ground.

"Let's go to the tea tent and get a cup of tea and a plate of sandwiches," Eileen suggested. As they walked across the field, her gaze darted every now and then to Anne's face, but she didn't ask any questions until they were settled in a quiet corner behind the tent.

"What's happened?" Eileen demanded, her mouth full of salmon-and-tomato sandwich.

"Two things. Neither of them good."

Eileen's hand went to her heart. "Oh my God."

Anne told her about Beth first.

"Oh, you poor darling." Eileen set down her food and took both of Anne's hands in hers.

"I have to fly home tomorrow."

"Of course you do."

"Ryan offered to come with me."

"He did?" Eileen was ecstatic. "That's a miracle. Normally he can't bear even to talk about Canada, never mind—"

"But he can't come with me," Anne said, cutting Eileen off midflow.

"Why not?"

"Because of the other thing that's happened."

"What?"

"He thinks that Conrad has been systematically embezzling him."

"Oh, oh, oh!" The series of little cries culminated in "Oh my God!" accompanied by several pats over her heart. "Jesus, Mary, and Joseph," Eileen whispered. "How did he find this out?"

Anne shook her head. "It's crazy, really. It was all because of me."

"How?"

Anne told her about the bank order. "If only Conrad hadn't changed the amount, or even if he'd sent the fifteen thousand, but not taken out enough for fifty thousand dollars from the bank, he might have managed to get away with it—at least for a lot longer."

Eileen looked very pale. " 'Tis the greed gets to

them every time. But Conrad? I can't believe it. How bad is it?"

"Ryan doesn't even know that himself yet. He's told Graham about it."

"Good. I'm glad. Was that your idea?"

Anne nodded, not wanting to speak about Graham at this point. Bad enough that they'd have to meet again before she left England for good. Knowing Eileen was waiting for her to speak she said, "He's coming down from London."

"That's great. And Ryan? How's he taking it?"

"Amazingly well. I don't think he's really taken it all in yet." She smiled at Eileen, wanting to lessen the shock for her. "He's worried about how he can cope without you."

Immediately she realized she had said the wrong thing.

Eileen's head shot up. "Why should he have to cope without me?" she demanded.

"In case things are so bad he couldn't pay you."

Tears sprang to Eileen's eyes. "Oh, that poor man. Does he think I'd worry about something like money at a time like this? Doesn't he know I'd never desert him, whatever happened. Doesn't he know—" She broke off, her face and neck bright red with embarrassment.

Anne clasped her hand. "I didn't mean to upset you."

Eileen sought in the pocket of her floral skirt for a tissue. "You didn't. I suppose it's good to hear he'd miss me, anyway," she said with a shaky smile.

"That's true."

"Where's Conrad now?"

"In the kitchen, getting drunk on Ryan's best

Scotch. Apparently Graham said to keep him there if possible, to avoid him taking off."

"And getting his hands on more money."

"Exactly."

"You were right about him, weren't you? You said he was no good. I just said he was all blarney, but you said he was as charming as a snake. I wish I'd listened to you."

"Don't worry about it. It wouldn't have made any difference, as he's probably been milking Ryan for a very long time. He's very clever. You wouldn't notice anything because you've all been so close for such a long time. Graham didn't trust him. He said he and Deborah had arguments over him."

The thought of Graham pinched at her again. If only she could avoid spending time with him this evening. "It's a really bad time for me to have to leave. I should be here for my father, but I must go."

"Of course you must. Ryan will understand. When do you leave?"

"The plane goes from Heathrow around eleven tomorrow morning. I'll have to leave here terribly early. Unless . . ." She was trying to work it out as she spoke. "Unless I went to London today. I could stay at an airport hotel." Which would mean she wouldn't have to spend the evening with Graham. "Do you think Ryan would mind? He'll be involved with Conrad and Graham for most of the time, I'm sure. And he does have you."

"He has that," Eileen said with feeling.

"I hate good-byes. This one's going to be particularly tough."

"Sure, you'll be together again in no time, the two of you."

"Then that's what I'll do. I'll go back and pack

and leave as soon as possible." She knew that Eileen must be surprised at her almost indecent haste.

"Won't you wait until Graham gets here?"

"No. No need. He'll be all caught up with Ryan. Besides, we've already said our good-byes."

Nothing more was said about Graham, but before Eileen picked up her cup of tea and downed it in one gulp, Anne caught her glance of sympathy.

Chapter 32

It had been difficult at first for Anne to convince Ryan that she should catch the four o'clock train to London, but his preoccupation with Conrad made it easier than it might otherwise have been.

There were tears in his eyes when he said goodbye to her on the steps of Hammerton Towers. "This is a miserable send-off, I must say."

"I would have been going in a few days, anyway," she reminded him.

"It won't be for long, I promise you. We'll get together very soon."

"I know that," she told him quietly, and meant it. Strangely, this business with Conrad had finally drawn them closer. "And you'll soon have Deborah home."

He grimaced. "Not sure I'm looking forward to that. She's going to be fighting mad about Conrad. Depends how much is gone, of course. But it'll be hard living with her."

"Oh, I think you're underestimating her."

"Am I? Knowing Deborah, she's bound to put all the blame for it on me."

Anne had to smile. "Don't worry. I'll explain everything to her. Then she can call you and find out all the details."

"When I can find them out myself. I wish it weren't Saturday, with the business world shut down." He glanced at his watch. "You'd better be going, love, or you'll miss that train. Are you sure you don't mind that I'm not driving you to the station?"

"No, it's far more important that you keep your eye on Conrad. Mind you, I don't think he's going to be much use to you after all he's had to drink."

"We'll catch him when he's most vulnerable, trying to sober up."

Knowing that Graham could arrive any minute, Anne was anxious to get away. The thought of seeing him again was tempting, but she knew it would only cause more pain.

As Eileen drove her down the avenue lined with trees, she looked back to give her father a last wave, the house like a Gothic backdrop behind him. Then they turned a corner and he was gone.

The impersonal airport hotel gave Anne a place and time to think and to prepare herself for what was to come. There were no demands on her, other than her telephone call to her father to let him know she had safely arrived in London. From now on, until she arrived in Winnipeg, she was completely alone, and glad to be so.

To her surprise she slept on the plane. Emotional exhaustion, she supposed.

The first person Anne saw when she came down the escalator at Winnipeg Airport was Marco. She felt a lurch of guilt, and wished she could turn around and get right back on the plane again.

Then she was at the foot of the escalator, being kissed on the cheek by Marco and hugged by Sandy, and swept along to the baggage carousel.

"Where's Deborah?" she asked, when they'd exchanged the usual questions about the flight and the weather.

"She's at the hospital. She felt that three of us meeting you would be a bit overwhelming."

"Oh." Anne knew that it was foolish to feel disappointed. What did she expect, instant sisterly love?

"We weren't sure if you'd feel like going straight to see Aunt Beth or want to go home first," Sandy said.

"I think I'd like to go to the hospital right away, but I'm dying for a cup of something. What do you think?" Anne turned to Marco, who was being unusually quiet for him, she suddenly realized.

"Why don't we stop at a Robin's Donuts on the way and get a drink and something to eat, if you're hungry?" he suggested.

"Good idea." Anything to postpone going to the hospital, she thought with another pang of guilt.

When they did reach the hospital and took the elevator to the fifth floor, the old familiar fears swept over her. The squeak of rubber soles on linoleum, the constant messages on the PA system, the smells of disinfectant mingling with institution food . . . all these brought back memories she preferred to forget. Perhaps it was natural to feel this way. After all, two of the people closest to her had died in this very hospital, both of them taken before their time.

Deborah was standing in the corridor, outside Beth's room. She was casually dressed, her blond hair tied up in a knot, but even in jeans and an oversize T-shirt she had that air of elegance that made people turn to look at her as they passed.

She pushed herself away from the wall she'd been leaning against and came to greet Anne. For a few seconds there was an awkwardness between them, then Anne hugged Deborah, and felt good about doing it.

"Flight okay?" Deborah asked.

"Fine." Anne nodded to the door. "How is she?"

Deborah shrugged. "Not much change. They're taking blood again for more tests."

Marco hung on the periphery and then said, "We can't all go in. I'll go to the visitors' lounge."

"I'll join you," Deborah said.

"No, let me," Sandy said, a sharpness in her voice that surprised Anne. She glanced at her daughter and noticed now how pale she was.

"Have you been dieting again?" she asked.

"Mother!" Sandy responded. "For heaven's sake."

"You just look thinner, that's all."

"Well, you certainly don't."

Anne groaned. "Don't I know it."

"Come on, Marco." Sandy walked away, leaving the two sisters alone together.

Anne frowned as she watched the two of them walk down the corridor to the elevator. "Is she okay?" she asked Deborah.

"She's worried about Beth. And Juilliard . . ."

Anne felt a twinge of resentment. It seemed so strange to have someone else tell her what her daughter was worried about. Then she realized that Deborah had let her last words hang in the air, as if there were something else. "Is there anything else bothering her?"

"I should have thought that was enough." Deborah glanced down the corridor. Then she turned back and said in a rather breathless voice, "This isn't fair to you. There is something else, but Sandy must tell

you about it herself. I can't betray a confidence, but
I think it's time you knew about it."

Something resembling a fog drifted across Anne's
eyes and then cleared. "It's to do with Conrad, isn't
it?" she said, her heart hammering.

"How did you know?"

"Because that bastard talked about her as if . . ."
The words stuck in Anne's throat.

Deborah was about to respond when the nurse
came out of the room and nodded to them to go in.

Anne grasped Deborah's arm. "I've got a lot to
tell you," she said in a low voice, "but it will have to
wait until we get home."

Beth was lying in the narrow bed, propped up by
three pillows, her arm attached to an IV. The first
thing Anne noticed was how clean she looked. Even
when she came out of the shower Beth always
looked as if the earth had sunk into her pores. Now
she had a white, pasty look, which emphasized her
bony nose and grizzled eyebrows.

"Hi there, Aunt Beth." Anne bent to kiss her
cheek. It felt leathery and smelled of soap.

Her aunt's eyes flew open and, for a moment,
blazed, before dimming to an indeterminate grayish
blue. "So you got here. 'Bout time."

Deborah dragged a chair over and put a hand on
Anne's shoulders to sit her down in it. Anne glanced
up and smiled before she lowered herself onto the blue
vinyl seat. "Yes, I'm here at last. Did you miss me?"

"Sure as hell did. Miss Smarty-pants here's been
pushin' me around, givin' orders like you wouldn't
believe."

Deborah grinned, but said nothing.

With a jolt like a tiny electric shock, Anne realized that these two disparate relatives of hers had

somehow hit it off. It was so entirely unexpected that she didn't know what to say. "Well, as long as she's been looking after you, that's what matters," she said, rather lamely.

"Don't know about that, but she's sure been stirrin' things up at work. You'll barely recognize the place."

"A slight exaggeration," Deborah said.

"And without a by-your-leave as well. I comes in there last week for the first time and I thought she'd brung me to another store it were so different."

"Come on," Deborah said, "you agreed it looked better."

"I did nothin' of the sort. You had no right to make changes without my permission."

Anne didn't know whether to laugh or cry. Here she'd been thinking that Beth and the garden center would have missed her badly. Instead, she found her sister had taken charge in no uncertain terms and, despite her protestations, it was obvious that her aunt approved.

"Them fancy ideas of yours will make me bankrupt in a week," Beth was saying.

"I can't wait to see this transformation," Anne said diplomatically, trying not to let resentment creep into her voice.

"You will. I've been telling Deb here something. Now you're back, I want you to hear it, too."

"It can wait until tomorrow," Deborah said.

"No, it can't." Beth turned to Anne again. "I don't want none of that chemo stuff, okay? I've had a good life, so . . ." She began to cough and then fell back on her pillows, breathing heavily. "Get . . . tired . . ." she gasped.

Anne pressed her hand. "Of course you do. We're not going to stay. You know I'm home now."

Beth nodded. To Anne's dismay, her aunt's eyes suddenly filled and tears began running slowly down her cheeks onto her neck. Behind Anne, Deborah slipped out of the room.

Anne took a tissue and gently pressed it to Beth's face. "We're all here for you," she whispered. "You're not alone."

"Not sad," Beth said. "Happy."

"That's good." Anne waited for Beth to elaborate.

Beth's grip tightened on hers. "Janine would have been so happy to see her girls together again."

Anne couldn't speak. For several minutes they sat, hand in hand, and then, when Beth's breathing had quietened and become more rhythmical, Anne slid her hand away and left the room.

Chapter 33

Deborah was waiting outside in the corridor for her. "She's sleeping," Anne said. She suddenly felt incredibly tired. "Boy, I'm beat."

"You look tired." It was said without any sense of criticism. "Time to go home, I think. You go and wait by the front door. I'll fetch Marco and Sandy and meet you there."

Deborah certainly was bossy, Anne thought, but tonight bossy wasn't so bad. She didn't feel like making any decisions. Nor did she want to discuss any heavy-duty stuff. But she knew that some of it would have to be discussed before she got to bed.

Two cars rolled up at the front entrance, Marco's van and the Rabbit. Marco got out, leaving the engine running.

"You mind if I let you three girls go home?" he asked. "I have to go back to the restaurant."

"That's fine," Anne said. "We can talk tomorrow."

In fact, she was rather relieved. It gave her one less problem to think about. But she also wondered why Marco was so cool with her. It was hard to remember that this was the man who'd proposed to her several times before she went to England. "Everything okay with the kids?" she asked.

"They're fine. Ready to go back to school. They're in Brandon this week, visiting their cousins."

"Oh, I was hoping to see them."

"Next week. But come over tomorrow, I'll make dinner for all of you."

For all of you? Something strange was going on here.

As Sandy drove them home Beth was the only topic of conversation. Anne had the impression that any other subject had the potential of a land mine ready to explode.

When they got home, Anne cringed inwardly at the sight of the cramped little house, partly because she was thinking of how it must seem to Deborah, but mainly because she had grown used to the space and comforts at Hammerton.

A hibiscus plant with four bright-red blossoms stood on the coffee table with a card that Sandy had made. It said *Welcome Home* and was signed by both Sandy and Deborah.

"Thanks. Thanks a million," Anne said. She looked down at the card again. "I just wish it was a happier homecoming."

"Debbie bought the plant."

"It's beautiful. Thanks, Deb—" Anne hesitated and then laughed. "Sorry, I'm not sure which to call you."

Deborah waved a hand at her. "Oh, don't worry. I've given up trying. Nearly everyone here calls me Debbie."

"You don't mind?"

"Not here, I don't. I'll become Deborah again when I get back to England." She turned abruptly and went into the kitchen. "Coffee or a drink?" she shouted.

"Something cold."

"A beer?"

"That's fine."

To Anne's surprise, her sister came into the room carrying a couple of beers and poured them into glasses for the two of them. She'd never seen Deborah drink beer before. Sandy, who was drinking a glass of Coke, sat down on the edge of the footstool, her face gaunt and white.

"You look as if you've been stuck indoors since you came home," Anne told her.

"I have. I've been studying new pieces and teaching, and sorting out all my stuff ready for going away."

She glanced past Anne to Deborah and then hunched forward, turning her face from them.

"What's going on?" Anne asked. "What's happened to you?"

Sandy looked up, startled by the sudden questions. "Me? Nothing. Why do you ask?"

"You have to tell your mother, Sandy." Deborah said. "You can't leave her in the dark."

Sandy's eyes grew huge in her face. "Did you tell her?" she shouted at Deborah. "How could you tell her? You promised me you wouldn't."

"No, I did not tell her. She guessed that something was wrong with you." She gave Anne a faint smile. "I suppose you call that mother's intuition."

"You can say that again. Okay, sweetheart. What's going on? It's to do with Conrad, right?"

Sandy looked at Deborah again with suspicion. "How do you know that?" she asked her mother.

"Because you were acting weirdly from that first day in England, but I just thought it was because you got drunk."

Sandy glared at her. Then she looked down at her

lap, picking at her nail. "I think I'm pregnant," she whispered. She said it so softly that Anne could barely hear her. "I'm a week overdue."

Pregnant! The word stunned Anne for a moment, then she got up. "Oh, my poor darling!" She went to Sandy to hold her, but Sandy pushed her away. "Conrad, of course. You knew about this?" she asked Deborah.

"I knew that Conrad had had sex with her that night," Deborah said baldly.

Anne was bewildered. "How could you, Sandy? You didn't even know the man." She suddenly felt as if she'd been doused with ice water. "Don't tell me he raped you."

Bending over, wrapping her arms around her knees, Sandy started to cry.

"Hold on there," Deborah said. "I must tell you that, from what Sandy told me, it sounds very much as if Conrad gave her a pill of some sort. Ecstasy, probably."

"He drugged her?" Anne couldn't believe her ears. She looked wildly from Deborah to Sandy. "Why the hell wasn't I told about this? I just happen to be her mother, but that didn't matter, I suppose. You just waded in and took over."

Deborah sat there, head erect. "I wanted you to be told. Sandy thought that if her period started there was no need for you to know. She begged me to keep quiet about it. I was wrong to agree to that."

"You can say that again." The enormity of the situation—the effect of this trauma on Sandy's entire future and this further evidence of Conrad's depravity—hit Anne so hard that her knees buckled and she had to sink into the nearest chair. "That bastard, that absolute bastard," she whispered. "How could you let him get away with it?" she asked her sister. "He should have been charged."

"With what?" Sandy demanded. "I did it willingly. He didn't force me."

Anne shuddered, recalling the hypnotic charm of the man, which had no doubt been attractive to a young, fairly inexperienced woman. Despite her fury at Deborah, she could recognize the dilemma in which she'd been placed. "Does Ryan know?"

"God, no. He'd strangle Conrad if he knew."

"You didn't think he should know? He had a right to know?"

"Wait a minute, Mother," Sandy said. "This is my life you're talking about. You have no right to dictate to me who is told about my private affairs. That's my right, not yours."

"There are repercussions with a situation like this that—"

"I'm only concerned about how they affect me, I'm afraid."

"I can understand that. Have you had a pregnancy test?"

Sandy didn't answer. Anne looked at Deborah.

"She won't have one."

"I'm still hoping," Sandy explained. "If the test is positive I've lost all the hope, haven't I?"

It had a ring of rather warped logic to it.

"I think the not knowing is harder to bear than anything," Anne told her. "At least once you know you'll be able to deal with the situation."

"I don't believe in abortion," Sandy said flatly. "You know that. A baby would be the end of Juilliard."

"But not the absolute end of the world," Anne said. "You would still have your music and—"

Susan Bowden

"Please, Mom. I don't need your platitudes at the moment, if you don't mind." Sandy got up. "I'm going to bed. Welcome home," she added ironically.

"Wait a minute. There's something you should know."

Sandy paused in the doorway. "About what?"

"About Conrad."

"I don't even want to hear his name, thanks. It makes me feel like throwing up." Sandy left the room.

Anne stared at the space where she had been, aware that her daughter had been thrust into mature adulthood by one ruthless act. She felt responsible. She should have stopped Sandy from going off with Conrad. She felt angry at Deborah for having kept this from her. She wished she had never gone to England. If she hadn't been so hell-bent on seeing her father and sister again this would never have happened.

"I am so sorry," Deborah said. She made a little move, as if she was about to get up and come to Anne, but then sat down again.

"So am I." Anne felt utterly exhausted. She sat, head down, hands dangling between her legs, limp as a rag doll. There wasn't even enough energy in her to get mad at Deborah.

"More beer?" Deborah asked.

"I've got enough, thanks."

"What's this about Conrad?"

"I'm not sure if I can tell you after what I've heard. What Sandy said about him is how I feel, too. Just the sound of his name makes me feel like throwing up."

"Is it bad?"

"It's bad, all right."

Deborah's gaze locked with hers. "Tell me."

Anne told her all she knew, which, as she said, wasn't that much. "Ryan's going crazy because he can't find out exactly what's happened, but he knows it's pretty bad."

Deborah looked utterly shattered. "I never thought— It's hard to believe. Is he sure?"

"Oh, yes. Conrad's admitted to it. The last I saw of them Ryan was plying Conrad with Scotch to keep him from running away and doing any more damage. Graham was on his way from London."

"Graham?"

"Yes." Anne felt a rush of feeling just talking about him. "I thought he'd be a good person to confide in, so Ryan called him."

"You were right. And he can keep his mouth shut, too."

"That's what I thought. I hated leaving Ryan at such a time, but he seemed to understand."

"Oh, God. Poor Daddy. Is he all right?"

"He was when I left, but then he'd only just found out."

"What an idiot Conrad is. He might have got away with it if he hadn't changed your bank draft."

"Exactly. He got greedy."

"Did Ryan say anything about my company?"

Anne had hoped she wouldn't ask that. She didn't know what to say. "He wasn't sure about anything."

"But it doesn't look good, right?"

" 'Fraid not. I'm so sorry." Anne gave her a wry little smile. "Conrad called me his nemesis, but I think he's been ours." She stood up. "I don't think I can stay awake any longer."

Deborah said nothing, but remained upright in the chair, looking slightly dazed.

"Are you okay?" Anne asked her.

"Rather numb, I must admit." Deborah looked up at her and then slowly got to her feet. "I'm sorry you had to be the one to bring the bad tidings."

"You seem to have had the same problem yourself."

"I'm sorry now that I didn't tell you about Sandy."

"She trusted you."

They stood awkwardly, each waiting for the other to make a move. When they did, it was in unison, their arms wrapping about each other and holding on tightly, cheek pressed to cheek.

Chapter 34

Anne awoke with a start to a loud scream followed by a rapping on her door. At one and the same time she shot up in bed, saw by her digital clock that it was ten minutes to five, and found Sandy in her room, yelling and prancing about like a four-year-old.

"I've started. I've started. Yeah, yeah, yeah! I've started."

For a moment, drugged with sleep, Anne couldn't understand what was going on. Then she came awake with a crash. "You haven't," she said, crazy laughter starting in the pit of her stomach and bubbling up.

"I have." Sandy was laughing and crying at the same time. She hugged her mother so tightly Anne could barely breathe.

Then Deborah was in the room, to see what all the noise was about. "She's got her period," Anne told her.

"Oh, my God," Deborah said and then it was her turn to be hugged and kissed. Anne had never seen Sandy quite so happy.

Nobody could sleep again after that. Anne made pancakes and Sandy cooked up bacon and eggs, and they had a feast to celebrate this momentous occasion.

"How could that have happened?" Sandy wondered.

"I guess you've been so stressed out, worrying about it—"

"Not wanting to talk about it," interposed Deborah, "bottling it up inside you—"

Everyone laughed at that.

"—and telling your mother was, in a sense, a relief for you," Deborah concluded.

Anne gave her a look of gratitude. "Whatever caused it," she said softly, "I just thank God it happened."

"So do I," Sandy agreed, pouring a liberal helping of maple syrup on her pancakes. "I'd really forced myself to stop thinking about Juilliard."

"Well, sweetie, you'd better start thinking about it again because you'll be leaving here in, what, about ten days?" Anne's heart twisted at the thought of losing her, but she kept smiling. Better by far this than her not being able to go and realize her dreams.

Sandy suddenly went all quiet. "We aren't quite out of the woods yet," she said glancing at Deborah and then back down at her plate. "There's still the second test."

"What test?" Anne asked.

"HIV."

"What?" Anne screeched. Then it sank in. "Oh my God."

She felt as if she'd been hit with a sledgehammer.

"She has to wait two months before the first test," Deborah said. "Then she must have another one in six months to be absolutely sure."

"I still can't believe you two kept this from me . . ." Anne said distractedly. "Conrad could be HIV positive, couldn't he? Given his lifestyle."

"Actually, knowing Conrad," Deborah said, "I

don't think so. He's far too careful of his body to risk anything like that. As I told Sandy, he's an absolute fanatic about his health and about keeping fit. Tennis and racquetball, working out with weights . . . all that sort of thing."

Anne turned to Sandy. "You can't remember if he used—"

"That's the problem. I don't remember a thing."

"She was drugged, Anne," Deborah reminded her.

"I don't suppose there's any use asking Conrad."

Deborah gave a yip of cynical laughter, but then stopped to think. "Wait a minute, though. Do you intend to tell Daddy about what Conrad did to Sandy?"

"I think he should know, but it's up to Sandy."

"I don't want anyone else to know," Sandy protested.

"If we were to tell Ryan we might well have a murder on our hands," Deborah said. "But, seriously, Ryan might be able to force Conrad to submit to HIV testing. If he was clear, Sandy wouldn't have to worry anymore." She looked at Sandy. "Might be worth it to have it off your mind."

"I think Ryan should know," Anne said slowly. "I think it might influence him to prosecute Conrad."

"No!" shouted Sandy. "I can't believe you two! Do you really think I want to go into court and talk about this?"

"I didn't mean prosecute Conrad for what he did to you, sweetie," Anne quickly assured her, "although I wish he could be prosecuted for it without involving you. No, I mean for the embezzlement."

"What embezzlement? What are you talking about?"

"Oh, I forgot you didn't know about that." Anne felt able to tell Sandy now.

"Oh, poor Ryan! What a jerk Conrad is," Sandy said, her mouth curling in disgust, when Anne had finished telling her. "I can't believe I fell for his line."

"Obviously, you weren't the only one," Anne said. "I think he should be put away, to stop him preying on other people, but your grandfather doesn't agree."

"He might," Deborah said, "if he knew what Conrad did to Sandy." She and Anne turned to look at Sandy.

"Boy, you two." Sandy shook her head. "Talk about ganging up on me."

"Why don't we call Ryan and see what's happening?" Deborah suggested.

"You do it," Anne said, gathering up the dishes. "You must be worried sick about your company." She also didn't want to risk having Conrad answer the phone. Or Graham.

"You're right. I'll take the phone into my room and then call you when I've finished speaking to him, all right?"

"Fine."

As Deborah sat on the edge of the bed, ready to punch in her father's number, she was surprised to find that she was far less disappointed about losing the successful company she'd built up all by herself than she'd expected. Somehow, she realized now, the excitement had diminished since it had become successful. Even the almost phobic fear of poverty that had always been the whip that drove her on seemed to have become less powerful.

Ryan answered the phone. As they spoke about

Anne and Beth, Deborah sensed Ryan's anxiety beneath the conversation, so she plunged right in.

"Is Conrad still there?"

"Yes. Anne told you, of course."

"Yes. How bad is it, Daddy?"

"We've still a lot of figures to confirm, but it could be worse."

"You mean we're not quite bankrupt."

"Certainly not. He's taken a great deal of money from us systematically over the years, but because he's had to be careful not to arouse suspicion he's not been too greedy, thank God."

"You were always more than generous with him. It wasn't his money to take," Deborah said flatly. "That's fraud. In other words, he's a thief and should be prosecuted for it."

"You're right, of course, but he also made a lot of money for me by investing it well and—"

"Oh, Daddy, you're such an easy mark!"

"He won't be the first manager or agent to steal from a client who trusted him," Ryan said, his voice filled with resentment. "There have been many famous cases of that happening."

"I know. I'm sorry, I shouldn't have said that. I just can't believe you don't want to prosecute him." Part of it was vanity, she was sure, the desire not to have one's gullibility made public. "Does my company have to go?" she asked lightly.

Ryan hesitated. She could hear his heavy breathing down the phone. "That . . . or the Dublin recording studio."

"Well, you're not getting rid of that. It's what keeps your interest in the music business going. And you've found and developed some damned fine acts there."

"I hoped you might say that. Graham thinks you

could sell your company at a profit and use what you make to start up something new. And Conrad said I should sell Hammerton and move into a smaller place, somewhere that takes less upkeep."

"Conrad?" Deborah couldn't keep the tone of incredulity from her voice. "I can't believe you're still taking advice from Conrad."

"He's been most cooperative. Given us facts and figures that save all sorts of detective work."

"Well, isn't that nice of him. I must say, though, that I do agree with him about Hammerton."

"You always hated it, didn't you?"

"It's phony, that's why."

"It was Hammerton and all the improvements that broke the bank, Conrad said. Without that, he would have just kept taking a percentage and nothing would have showed up."

"You certainly seem to be very cozy with Conrad, I must say, considering he's a crook. What does Graham think of all this?"

"Why not ask him yourself? He's right here, working with the accountant we've brought in."

Before Deborah could stop him, he put down the phone. The last thing she felt like was speaking to Graham. He represented all the problems that awaited her back home, things she would have to deal with, now that her life had changed.

But Graham seemed as reluctant as she was to talk. He was totally businesslike, in the way he used to be before he bought Somerford. It made him sound rather cold and distant, which suited her very well.

"I have reservations about a prosecution," he said in response to her question. "It might prove to be bad publicity for both Ryan and you. Investors might see you both as a bad risk, as people lacking in good judgment."

"Is that a personal or just a general criticism, might I ask?"

"You asked for my opinion, I gave it."

Deborah sighed. "Sorry. You never did like Conrad, did you? And you did warn me about him."

"Yes, I did, but it was hard for you and Ryan. You were both too close to him to see him for what he was."

"So you're saying we should avoid a prosecution?"

"That would be my advice. Particularly as he is cooperating fully, which could save many months of work. It appears," Graham said dryly, "that Mr. Hatcher was as methodical in his personal book-keeping as he was in his professional capacity."

"Shouldn't people know about him? He could do this to someone else if it isn't publicized."

"Oh, there are ways of spreading the news with-out actually charging him. I should imagine it will be all over the city on Monday morning."

"That's good." Deborah hesitated and then said, "I'd like to speak to him. Is he available?"

"Who?"

"Conrad."

"Now, Deborah—"

"Put him on, please. Then I'd like to speak to my father again."

"I'll put Ryan on now."

"Graham," she shouted down the line, "don't be such a royal pain. Put Conrad on!"

"What's all this about speaking to Conrad?" Ryan's voice asked.

"I just want to ask him one question about my

company. Surely I have a right to do that, considering he's embezzled *my* money."

"Okay, okay, I'll get him, but first tell me. Is Annie really okay?"

"She's fine. Really, Daddy."

"Look after her, won't you? As soon as this all blows over, we'll all get together again."

"Are you planning a trip to Winnipeg, Daddy?" Deborah asked sarcastically.

"You never know," was his surprising answer. "You never know. I'll get Conrad for you now."

Deborah was still wondering about what Ryan had said when Conrad's voice boomed down the earpiece. "Hello, there, darling. How is wintry Canada?"

"Very hot, thank you."

"You do surprise me."

"Let's cut the nonsense, Conrad. I want to ask you one question."

"Ask on. I take it that it's about your company."

"Well, you're wrong. I'll say only one thing about what you've done to us. You're a bastard, Conrad. I'll ask you one question and, don't forget, your future may depend upon your answer, so make sure it's the truth, for a change."

"You intrigue me. Ask away."

"Have you been tested for HIV?"

A long pause ensued. "I'd be very interested to know how that's any of your business."

"Well, I shall tell you. My niece has gone through one hell of a time since you assaulted her—"

"Now, hang on. She was a willing participant—"

"She was drugged, Conrad. And that's the main problem. Because everything's a blur, she doesn't remember if you used a condom or not. For the past few weeks she's been through hell, worrying that she might be pregnant—"

"God forbid." To Deborah's relief, Conrad sounded quite genuine in his exclamation. That must be a good sign.

"—or that you might be HIV positive and have passed it on to her."

"You jest, surely."

"No, I don't. You know the trouble with people like you, Conrad," Deborah said, her voice rising, "is that you walk through life taking whatever you want without a clue what carnage you create."

"I used a condom and I am *not* HIV positive."

"Telling me isn't good enough. I want proof. Genuine proof from a bona fide medical practitioner. Then I can show it to Sandy, so that she can get on with her life, which has been on hold ever since you fucked with her in more ways than one."

Nothing but silence at the other end.

"And if you don't do this right away," Deborah continued, "I will tell Ryan what you did to his granddaughter. Then we shall see if he is quite so magnanimous about keeping you out of prison."

"That sounds like blackmail to me."

"Aww," Deborah groaned. "Poor little Conrad."

"You'll have your proof, damn you."

As Conrad slammed the phone down in her ear, Deborah got just as much pleasure out of knowing that she had at last rattled him as she did out of achieving her goal.

Chapter 35

When Anne had asked about the garden center, Deborah had told her not to worry about it for the next few days. She would look after it until Anne felt able to get back to work.

In fact, Deborah was glad to have something to do. She was desperately missing Marco. Since that time at his house, they had exchanged only stilted conversation and—as there was always someone else present—had to avoid looking at each other. The fact that he was so near, yet she was unable even to call him to tell him about the collapse of her business or the problem with Conrad, distressed Deborah. She needed his optimism, his encouragement and, most especially, his arms.

She certainly didn't expect to see much of Anne, who had more than enough on her mind, between Beth's illness and Sandy's imminent departure. But it seemed she had underestimated her sister, for that afternoon, when Deborah was working in the little office she had created at the garden center, Anne suddenly walked in.

Deborah didn't even know she was there until she sensed that someone was standing behind her, looked up, and saw her sister.

"My God, you gave me a shock. I didn't hear you come in."

Anne looked around, at the new shelving, and the newly painted filing cabinet and the neat rug on the floor. "I can't believe this is the same place. You've worked wonders. And in such a short time, as well."

Deborah pushed back the accounts book she'd been working on. "I hope you don't mind the few changes I've made."

"Mind? You must be joking. This is fantastic. And Mary was showing me the new checkout counter. How did you pay for all these changes?"

"I used my own money. I haven't taken anything from Carter's, I can assure you."

Anne laughed. "I wasn't accusing you of raiding the till. But we can't have you using your own money, especially not now." She looked around the office again. "It all looks so wonderful that I'd pay anything for it. Why didn't I do this a long time ago? It would have been so much nicer to work in."

"Probably because Beth would have told you it didn't need doing."

Anne grinned. "How did you know?"

"I have been living with her for a couple of weeks," Deborah said caustically. "The only reason I managed to get this little bit done was because she wasn't here to stop it." She jumped up from the new desk. "I have so many ideas for this place, Anne, you wouldn't believe it," she said, bursting to share them with her sister.

Anne stood staring at her, a strange expression on her face.

"What?" Deborah asked. "What's wrong?"

"You." Anne shook her head. "I just can't believe you're the same person I met in England."

"What on earth do you mean?"

"Look at you. Dressed in shorts and a dusty T-shirt, getting all excited about this mucky old garden center. It's unbelievable."

"I don't do things by halves." Deborah reached down to the little fridge, also new. "Want a cold drink?"

"Do I ever? It's like an oven outside."

Deborah pushed the chair over. "Sit. How's Beth?"

Anne slumped into the chair. "Much the same. When did she get to be so frail? I just didn't notice it happening. She always seemed just the same to me, except she'd slowed down quite a bit, now that I think about it. The doctor doesn't know when she'll be able to come home. Depends on the hip."

"Has she changed her mind about the chemotherapy?"

Anne shook her head. "No, she said she doesn't want any treatment. That she's lived her life and she'll go when she has to go."

"I think I'd be the same way." Deborah handed her a Coke. "You look tired. Why did you come here? You should have gone home for a rest."

"Yes, big sister."

"I'm naturally bossy."

"I've noticed."

They exchanged smiles.

"I wanted to see how you are," Anne said, after taking a drink and letting the coolness wash down her throat. "Between Sandy and Beth, your concerns seem to have been shoved aside." She peered up into her sister's face. "Are you okay?"

"Me? Yes, why shouldn't I be?"

"Because you've had a major setback in your professional life, that's why."

Deborah sat on a corner swinging. "You know you're an

"Why?"

"Anne, the earth mother. You see capacity for understanding and sympath, the scope of mere mortals like me."

"Was that meant as a compliment?"

Deborah laughed. "As a matter of fact, yes, it was. You've just had a long flight, you have so much on your plate with your daughter and your aunt, yet you're thinking of me, as well."

"You're my sister. The only one I've got. I care about you. I care about what happens to you."

Deborah stared at her, as if she couldn't quite believe what she was hearing. Then she shook her head. "I was a bitch to you."

"But that's what being sisters is about. That's what family is about, Debbie. If a friend is a bitch to you, you say 'Who needs her?' and dump her. If a sister is bitchy, she's still your sister, whatever happens, so you try to work it out, or you wait until things change between you. Because you're sisters for life. It's not a hot or cold thing that you can turn on or off at will."

"How is it you know so much more than I do about sisters?"

"I don't know." Anne thought for a moment. "Maybe," she said slowly, "because of Beth and our mother. Beth may have been a difficult person, but, boy, was she a good sister to Janine. And she loved her so much. Wait a minute, there's a file in the cabinet that had a picture of them, taken outside this place."

Before Deborah could stop her, Anne had pulled out the top drawer of the cabinet and was rooting

...nd inside it. "Wow, you've even tidied up the filing system. Here we are. Beth and Janine." She held out the old black-and-white picture to Deborah.

Deborah took it and saw two girls. One older and stout, dressed in an old sweater and a pair of men's trousers, the other dark and pretty with large eyes and a heart-shaped face, in a tartan skirt and white blouse. The contrast between them was marked, but the camera had caught the pride with which the elder girl looked down at her little sister and the firm clasp of her hand.

Deborah saw the picture through a mist. "I don't think I've ever seen a picture of my—our mother before."

"You take after her," Anne said.

"Me? Rubbish! She's as dark as I am blond."

"Your coloring is different, but you have the same shaped face."

"Why didn't you want to go to England with Ryan?" Deborah asked.

Anne frowned, not understanding.

"When you were a child, I mean," Deborah explained.

"Strangely enough we talked about that, Ryan and I, when you phoned to tell me about Beth. I asked him why he'd taken you to England, and not me. You see, I didn't know he'd even asked me to come with him, but he told me he had, and that I'd been afraid of him, and cried."

"Do you mean you thought he'd only asked me to go with him, and not you at all?"

"Yes." Their eyes met, and then glanced away, as if they'd been stung.

"Strange how you get the wrong idea about something, isn't it?" Anne said. "But he had never been there to set me straight, so I'd grown up thinking he'd chosen just you to go with him."

"If that's what you thought, you must have felt very hurt by it."

"I did," Anne whispered. "I thought he preferred you because you were so pretty. That's the reason Grandma Barry chose you, you know. I can remember that quite clearly."

Deborah's eyes blazed with a cold light. "Wasn't I the lucky one! I suppose you thought you got the short end of the stick by being left with your aunt Beth."

"I've never thought of it that way, but I know I never quite understood why we had to be parted."

"Lucky little me." Deborah leaned back, her gaze on the wall above Anne's head. "Grandma Barry was a sadistic witch. She'd tie my hair up in ribbons so tight that my scalp hurt all night. She kept me perpetually terrified. I swear that if it hadn't been for Granddad Barry, I might have been badly injured. She had a wicked temper."

Tears came to Anne's eyes. "Oh, God." She put out a hand to her, but Deborah ignored it.

"When my father came and took me away I couldn't leave there fast enough. Poor Granddad Barry, he must have thought I was an ungrateful wretch, but to me he was part of it all. I couldn't think of him as being separate from her. My father came like a white knight on his charger to carry me away. It was all I'd dreamed about and longed for."

"Me, too," whispered Anne. "But when he came I didn't recognize him as my knight and I rejected him."

"Well, I certainly did better than you there. I got

carried off to England and to my charmed life with Ryan's wife, Fiona."

Deborah's tone chilled Anne like a north wind in November.

"Fiona didn't believe in physical punishment. She believed in psychological warfare. She didn't like my looks, or my Canadian accent, or my manners, and proceeded to make sure I knew what a disaster I was."

"Oh, Debbie, I never knew."

"Of course you didn't. You weren't there to know. You never were. You were happy with Aunt Beth who loved you, living in my mother's house, with my mother's pictures around you. My father told me, you know. He said, 'Anne doesn't want to live with you and me, Debbie. She wants to live with her Aunt Beth.'"

Tears slid down Anne's face. "It's not true," she whispered. "It wasn't true. I was only a child. I didn't know what I wanted to do."

They were both standing now, staring at each other.

"I hadn't realized until now how much I missed you," Deborah said, her voice tight and high. "How much I wanted to be with you. When I lived here, every time you went home with Aunt Beth, I wanted to beg you to take me with you."

"I wanted that, too. I've always wanted to be with you. That's why I came to England." Anne took Deborah's tense face between her hands. "I never, never stopped loving you. Even when I was too young to realize it, you were always here"—she pressed a palm to her breast—"in my heart."

"Is it too late to be real sisters, do you think?" Deborah asked. "I mean like the ones who've grown up together."

"Maybe we'll be even better than that. We haven't had all the sibling rivalry normal sisters have in childhood. We'll just have to make up for lost time, that's all."

They smiled at each other in the cramped little office, but each hid from the other the one, supreme danger to their fragile new relationship.

Chapter 36

When Anne went home she felt wrung out emotionally and physically. Although it was only mid-afternoon, she had had more than enough for the day. She was glad to find the house empty, a note on the fridge from Sandy to say she was spending the day with her friends, Jo and Maria.

"The three of them probably won't be together again for ages," Anne murmured to herself, "if ever." It seemed pessimistic, but that was the way life went.

She checked the answering machine. No messages. That was strange. She'd expected to hear from Marco. After all, he'd said last night that he would have everyone over for dinner.

It was hard to believe that this was the same man who'd told her when she'd left for England that he wanted a definite answer from her about getting married. He'd hardly spoken to her when they'd met last night or later on at the hospital. Of course, they hadn't had much of a chance to talk, but . . .

Anne poured herself an iced tea and slumped into a chair in the living room. It was almost as if Marco had sensed the specter of Graham hanging between them. That was nonsense, of course, but he had been unusually quiet.

She picked up the portable telephone and started to press out Marco's number. Then she stopped. Why was she so keen to speak to him, when she didn't even know what she was going to say? She set the phone down again, and held the cool glass against her burning cheeks.

Marco was a good man in so many ways. A family man, a successful businessman—even if she did think his business plans were far too ambitious—great sense of humor, sexy . . . She set the glass down on the table with a sharp rap and began pacing the room, tidying a pile of newspapers and smoothing out Beth's afghan on the sofa.

Surely she wasn't going to let a brief interlude of what had amounted to nothing more than shared interests and a few kisses interfere in her future here in Winnipeg? Graham belonged to her sister, that was enough for Anne. What she really wanted to know was where her future with Marco was going. Or if it was going anywhere.

This time she didn't hesitate, but dialed the number. She wasn't sure if she felt relief or dismay when Marco answered on the third ring.

"Marco, it's Anne."

A slight pause, then, "Sorry I didn't call. How's Beth?"

"She's resting. I was with her all morning. I just got back home. If I come over would you be able to take some time off?"

"I've got a wedding reception this Saturday. Desserts to prepare. But sure . . . sure. Come on over."

It was the most halfhearted invitation Anne had ever heard from him. "I wouldn't want to trouble you."

"No trouble," he said, seemingly oblivious to the

ice in her voice. "Tell you what, better I come over to your place when I've finished this *strufoli* I'm making. Around five okay?"

"Sure."

"How you doing?" he asked. "Not a very good homecoming, eh?"

"You can say that again."

"You on your own?"

"Yes. Sandy's out with friends and Deborah's at the center."

"Good. You can have a sleep maybe."

"Sounds like a good idea. See you around five."

"Sure."

They might have been two casual acquaintances, Anne thought, as she carefully put the phone down. No one overhearing their conversation would have thought them to be lovers. What was going on?

She had a short rest and then got up and showered, changing into a colorful cotton skirt and top to make herself feel better. But nothing could remove the pall of apprehension that hung over her.

Marco brought food with him: a vegetable lasagna and a small version of his famous orange *sformato*. "Had some left over," he said, handing it to her. "Be careful. It's very fragile."

Somewhat like me at the moment, thought Anne.

When he'd put everything away in the fridge for her, he busied himself in the kitchen, insisting on making the coffee.

He still hadn't kissed her.

She went to him and put her arms around his waist. His entire body tensed. She could feel it. His muscles, his spine . . . all resisting her. She released him.

"What's wrong, Marco?"

"Wrong? Nothing," he said, his back still to her.

"Then I'd like a kiss, please."

His laugh was just a little too hearty. "Watch the kettle," he warned. "It's hot." He turned and kissed her. It was the kiss of a friend, not a lover.

Anne felt a sense of panic. She couldn't have Graham. Now, it seemed, she'd lost Marco. She saw very clearly an empty road ahead of her, devoid of her daughter, her aunt, and her lover.

"Would you please tell me what's wrong? I know there's something," she insisted, when they sat down in the living room.

"You're crazy, imagining things," Marco said, his dark eyes avoiding hers.

At that moment, they heard the back door open and Deborah's voice. "Hallo! I'm in for just a minute. I forgot to take the—"

She paused in the doorway, a tide of red rushing into her face when she saw Marco.

Marco had half risen from his seat when he'd heard Deborah's voice. Now he was looking directly at her.

It must have all happened in a flash, but to Anne it was as if time had been suspended so that she saw it all in infinite detail: the look of burning recognition, the tremor of a smile on Deborah's lips, the invisible lightning bolt that shot across the room, uniting them.

"—the tape measure," Deborah concluded, turning away. "I need it to measure for the new shelves. Hi, Marco."

"Hi." He sat down again, breathing fast.

Deborah and *Marco*? Marco and *Deborah*?

Boy, she sure didn't waste any time, was Anne's first thought.

She stood up. "What's going on?"

"I told you," Deborah said. "I came for the—"

"Yes, we know. The tape measure. You know damned well that's not what I'm talking about. What's going on between you two?"

They'd deny it, of course, pretend nothing had happened. What infuriated Anne was that all she and Deborah had accomplished in their new relationship as sisters was now turned to ashes. "How could you do this to me?" she asked Deborah. "To *you* and *me*?"

Deborah stared at her for several seconds, without blinking. "I don't know. It—it just crept up on us."

Anne was surprised by her instant admission. "What did you do? Say to yourself there's Anne's lover, wouldn't it be fun to score with him?"

"Hang on," Marco said. "Don't go just blaming your sister."

"Oh, I blame you as well."

"It wasn't deliberate," Deborah said through tight lips. "It . . . happened."

"Bet it did. You make me sick. You take over my home, my business, my daughter, and now my lover. What was wrong, Deborah, didn't you have enough of your own things that you had to have mine as well?"

Marco grabbed Anne's arm. "That's enough! I know you're mad, but you've said enough."

Anne shook herself free and advanced on Deborah. "You've got it all now, haven't you? You've got my aunt eating out of your hand, my daughter's adoration, my business looking like it was yours not mine, and my man. Bitch!"

Her hand flew up of its own accord and smashed against one side of Deborah's face, hitting her so hard that she staggered and had to grab the door frame to stop herself from falling.

In one move Marco propelled Anne out of the way and grabbed Deborah, pulling her against him.

Anne sank into a chair, appalled at what she had done. Even with Marco's protective arm about Deborah, she could see the red mark of her hand on her sister's face.

"I shouldn't have done that," she muttered. "I was so mad I—"

Marco pointed his finger at her. "You've said enough, okay? I'm taking Deborah away from here."

Deborah pulled away from him. "No. I want to explain to Anne what happened."

"She doesn't want to listen."

"I'll listen," Anne said, a fine tremor running through her.

Deborah sat down in Beth's old rocking chair, across the room from Anne. She spoke hesitantly at first and then more quickly and confidently. "It was instant friendship at first. Laughing at the same things. Our interest in business. Our ambition to make things succeed. All these similarities made us hit it off right away, but then they also sparked something more."

"Nothing happened between us," Marco interpolated, "until—"

"Until Friday, the night of Beth's fall. That was my fault, too. I had a fight with her and left her alone."

"What was the fight about?" Anne asked.

"She started talking about my grandmother, about how she abused me. It was the first time I knew about Beth's involvement in getting Ryan to come and get me." Deborah was biting at her nails now, leaving ragged white spots where the polish had been. "She got me so upset I stormed out of the house. I went looking for Marco. There wasn't anyone else to go to, you see."

Marco moved behind the rocking chair, so that they confronted Anne as a pair, a couple.

"So you just . . ." Anne shrugged. ". . . sort of used him. Is that what you're saying?"

Deborah looked up at Marco and smiled. "No," she said softly. "I went to him because he was my friend and, I'm sorry to say, because I really care for him and I think he feels the same way."

Marco glanced warily at Anne and then gave Deborah a beaming smile. It was obvious that her words had surprised him.

"I want to stay here in Winnipeg and help him build up his business," Deborah continued. "But if you and he want to stay together, then I'll go back to England."

And what about Graham? Anne was about to ask, when it hit her like a cannonball in the stomach, taking her breath away.

"I am so very sorry," Deborah continued. "We never meant this to happen. If you and Marco decide to be together, I'll be on the next plane, out of the way. You need never see me again."

"Is that what you want?" Anne asked.

"Obviously, it isn't. My main concern was that this could mean the end of all we've managed to salvage from our shaky past. Much as I care about him, I don't think I could stay with Marco if it meant not ever seeing you again."

"What's it like having two sisters fighting over you?" Anne asked Marco, her voice edged with sarcasm.

"You don't really want me," Marco told her angrily. "I asked you before you left Canada, and you couldn't give me an answer then. I knew you didn't love me enough to get married, but you wouldn't say so because you didn't want to be alone."

Anne hated him for putting the truth so blatantly into words.

"I thought you'd change, start getting excited about my business," he continued, "but you never did. I could see you getting like my ex-wife about it," he said bitterly. "That's how it was with her. Between you and me it was the same thing, too. We just weren't right for each other."

"But you and Deborah are?"

"Just like you and Graham would be right for each other," Deborah suddenly said. "Had you thought about that, Anne? You two had real chemistry together. It really annoyed me. All that excitement about gardens and about Somerford, shutting me out."

Now it was Anne's turn to redden. "Don't be stupid. Graham and I are thousands of miles apart, literally."

"Come to think of it, how did you two get along after I left England?" Deborah's gaze was like a laser beam. "You had more than two weeks without me. Did you do anything other than garden together?" she asked pointedly.

"Nothing but develop our friendship," Anne said.

"There's friendship and friendship."

Anne felt her face grow even warmer. "Don't change the subject. We were talking about you and Marco."

"No more talk," Marco said. "It's time you gave me your answer, Anne. Do you want to stay with me or not?"

Anne glanced at Deborah. "Not now I don't."

"Be fair to Marco," Deborah said. "What were you going to tell him if you hadn't found out about us?"

Anne looked from her sister to Marco, and back again. Then she sighed. "You're right. I was going to say I didn't want to get married. Marco's right, too. I was afraid of being alone if he found someone else. And now it seems that he has. My own sister."

"I'm so sorry." Deborah got up and moved away, detaching herself from Marco.

Anne hesitated and then crossed the room. "Not as sorry as I am . . . about this," she said, touching Deborah's cheek. It still bore the fading imprint of her hand.

"Stop worrying about it. I deserved it." Deborah smiled. "Why don't you go and ring Graham, Anne?"

"Who's this Graham?" Marco asked, puzzled.

"He's Deborah's lover," Anne said.

"And why would you call Deborah's lover?"

Anne and Deborah exchanged glances. "I'll explain later," Deborah told Marco.

"You're the one should call him," Marco said to Deborah belligerently.

"Why?" Deborah asked.

"To tell him you aren't lovers anymore."

"My goodness, how deliciously possessive of you," Deborah said, laughing. "I suppose you're right. Tell you what, Anne. I have to speak to Daddy anyway, about all this stuff with Conrad. Then I'll speak to Graham. After that, it will be your turn."

"No, I think it's far too soon." Anne felt as if she was losing all semblance of control here.

"Nonsense. Strike while the iron is hot. You know how you'd love to live at Somerford. I can just see you and Graham in your old age happily pruning the roses together in the rose garden."

"Very funny," Anne said, but she couldn't help smiling at the thought.

"Just make sure he doesn't completely neglect his business, though, or you won't be able to afford Somerford."

"Don't you think you're rushing things a bit?" Anne protested. "I don't even live in England."

"That can be arranged. I'm going to ring Daddy." Deborah looked from Anne to Marco. "That should give you two a little time to talk." She picked up the portable telephone and went downstairs to the basement.

"You okay?" Marco asked Anne softly.

Anne shook her head. "I feel as if I've been caught in a hurricane. Wow!"

"She's like that, your sister."

"You can say that again." Anne hesitated. "Is this really what you want? You and Deborah have known each other such a short time. I feel like I've pushed you into something too soon. I should have kept my big mouth shut."

"No, no. This is right, what you did. I've been feeling so bad since—" Marco paused. "Since you got here. So has your sister." He touched Anne's arm. "So long as you're okay, that's what matters. We were wrong to do it this way, Deborah and me, but you . . ." He raised his hands in an eloquent gesture of futility. "It just wasn't working, was it?"

Anne shook her head, her eyes brimming with tears. "No."

"But I make a good brother-in-law, yes?" Marco grinned at her.

"For heaven's sake, slow down," Anne said, half laughing, half crying. "Give yourselves time to get to know each other."

"We will. Don't worry." His face suddenly grew very serious. "My kids aren't going to be screwed up again, I promise you."

"How does Deborah get on with them?"

"Good. Less like a mamma and more like a big kid with them, but that's okay."

Anne put a hand to his face. "I hope she treats you well. You deserve it."

"You, too, *cara*."

The tears were still close to the surface. "I wish—" Anne said.

Marco placed two fingers over her lips and shook his head. "It was not God's will. *This*—Deborah— is His will, I'm sure of it."

"I hope so, for both of you."

"And this man of Deborah's, this—"

"Graham." Anne felt her cheeks grow warm under his questioning look. "You've probably guessed. I like him very much. We are . . ." She sought for the exact way to describe Graham and then it came to her. "We are *simpatico*."

"Ah, yes. Like Deborah and me. That's good."

"Anne!" Deborah called from downstairs.

"I'd better go." Anne's heart was beating very fast. "I don't know what she's said to him."

Marco gave her a little push. "Go."

She went. Deborah had just reached the top of the stairs. She thrust the telephone into her hands. "Graham," she said succinctly, and then gave her a Cheshire cat grin. "I'll call Ryan back after you've finished. He said it's going to take a long time to tell me everything about Conrad. Oh, before I forget.

Ryan relayed a message from Conrad. Of course he thinks it's something to do with business. Apparently Conrad said to tell me that he'll be sending a copy of the certificate I wanted by Federal Express."

"Thank God," Anne breathed.

"Amen to that." Deborah tapped the phone. "Graham."

"Right," Anne took the phone into her bedroom and closed the door. For some crazy reason she looked into the mirror, checking her hair. Then she sat on the side of her bed.

"Hello?"

"Anne?" Graham's voice was quite clear, as if he were right there, by her side. The sound of it took her breath away.

"Are you okay?" she said after a moment.

"I'm not quite sure."

"What did Deborah tell you?"

"She told me that she's fallen for your Italian friend or lover or whatever he is, and that this man feels the same about her. Have I got it right?" Anne's heart sank. Graham didn't sound at all happy.

"Just about."

"And where does this leave you? It sounds to me as if she's being typically Deborah and not even considering other people's feelings."

"I don't think it's quite like that," Anne said, picking her words very carefully. "They were both pretty worried about how I'd feel."

"I should hope they would be." A long pause. "And how do you feel?"

"I'm afraid I lost my temper at first."

"I can imagine you would."

"Then I remembered that Marco and I hadn't been

getting on as well as we used to and . . ." Anne swallowed.

"And?"

"How about you?" Anne asked hastily, not wanting to talk about herself anymore. "Has it been a shock for you?"

"A shock? Yes, I suppose so. Not an entirely unpleasant one, though, I must admit. Like you, there have been times recently when Deborah and I have not been getting along."

Another long pause. *For heaven's sake, get to the point,* Anne wanted to shout down the phone.

"So, do I take it that Deborah's news has affected you in much the same way as it has me?" Graham said.

"That's the problem with communicating by phone, isn't it? I don't really know how you feel about it."

"You want to know how I feel? To be absolutely honest, I'm elated. I'm thrilled. But only if you are, too."

"Oh, Graham." Anne didn't know whether to laugh or cry.

"I'm missing you like hell."

"That's exactly how I feel, but I didn't want to be the first to say it."

"At least in London I knew I wouldn't be seeing you. But here, at Hammerton, every time I come into a room I expect to find you there. I'm in a state of perpetual disappointment."

"I wish you were here with me."

"Would you like me to fly over?"

"That sounds so tempting. But you couldn't stay and then we'd have to say good-bye all over again. I couldn't stand that. But thanks for the offer. It means a lot to me."

"If you change your mind you just have to ask. I should imagine you're reeling at the moment."

"You're right. I must admit I feel as if I've been sandbagged. So much has happened I don't know what to think. I feel I'm being rushed into things before I've had time to think it all through. Oh, God, that sounds awful," she added quickly. "I didn't mean it the way it came out."

"You feel you need more time and less pressure to be able to work everything out, is that right?"

Anne breathed a relieved sigh. "Yes, exactly right." She should have known that Graham would understand.

"There's no pressure being exerted from this end . . . other than a hope that when next spring comes you'll be here to see all the bulbs come into bloom at Somerford."

Anne swallowed the lump in her throat. "That sounds wonderful," she whispered down the phone.

"And I shall be needing someone to supervise the development of the gardens and house there. I can't keep taking so much time off from work. Would you be interested?"

"You bet I would." She suddenly came down to earth. "That would mean leaving Canada."

"Would that be difficult for you? Remember, Sandy won't be there."

Nor eventually would Beth. Neither said it, but both acknowledged it silently.

"Deborah will be, though. My sister and I will be parted all over again." Anne was thinking aloud.

"You'd be only a few hours' flight away."

"You're right." Besides, Anne doubted that she and her sister would ever be truly parted again, however great the physical distance between them.

"Anyway, if she and Marco stay together they won't want me around all the time."

"Quite true," Graham agreed.

At last Anne allowed herself to indulge in the possibility that this could really happen. "Oh, Graham, it sounds absolutely wonderful, but . . . you do realize I wouldn't be able to come for ages. There's Beth and the business . . . and so much else to see to."

"That's understood. Somerford has been waiting a long time for its renaissance. It won't hurt it—or me—to wait a little longer."

Her heartbeat quickened at the thought of Graham and Somerford waiting patiently for her at the end of what she knew was going to be a long, hard winter. "Are you sure?"

"I couldn't be more certain about anything." His voice seemed so close she felt she could reach out and touch him. "Then, my darling Anne, we will see what life has in store for us."

Later, when Marco had gone home, and Deborah had finished her long phone conversation with Ryan, the sisters sat in the living room, drinking a bottle of Marco's wine, discussing what had happened.

"It's been a crazy day." Anne said, shaking her head. "I really can't believe it all happened." She smiled. "Poor Marco. He must have wondered what hit him."

"Never mind Marco. What about me?" Deborah demanded, rubbing her cheek.

"Oh, Debbie, I am sorry about that."

"Forget it. I can see we two are quite alike, despite our seeming differences. You're far more fiery than I thought—"

"And you're more understanding. At heart we're very alike."

Deborah raised her eyebrows at her sister. "Particularly when it comes to men. Which is good, considering what's happened. Can you imagine how I'd be feeling now if you hadn't fallen for Graham?"

Anne poured more wine into Deborah's glass. "But are you sure you'll be happy here? I mean, after living in London, running an upscale business . . ."

"First of all, we've agreed that we're going to build up the garden center, make it successful." Deborah leaned forward, her face flushed with excitement. "At the same time I'm going to help Marco get going on his restaurant franchise. I have a few contacts in the States and Graham will help me out there, as well. He knows everyone in the hotel and restaurant industry."

"What happens if I go to England next year?" Anne asked.

"You mean *when* you go to England. There's no 'if' involved. Whatever happens, you're going to be with Graham next spring, even if it has to be just for a visit at first. I'll make sure Beth is comfortable and well looked after," Deborah said, putting Anne's unspoken concern into words.

"She comes first," Anne said.

"Of course she does. But, later on, you will settle in England and live comfortably and be able to see the world, as you so richly deserve to do. And I'll settle wherever Marco ends up, which could be Winnipeg . . . or anywhere." Deborah grinned. "But I'll bet you anything you like, sister mine, that Marco will become as successful and as wealthy as Graham. What would you like to bet on it?"

"Nothing," Anne said, laughing. "I believe you. Marco and you will be a pretty potent combination."

"Better believe it." Deborah picked up her glass, her expression suddenly very serious. "Here's to you, Anne. Without you none of this would have happened."

"Me? What did I do?"

"You never forgot us, Daddy and me. You kept us in your heart all these years. It was you who wrote that letter, you who came uninvited to visit us." Tears sparkled on Deborah's lashes as she held up her glass in a toast. "I drink to you, Anne. To my sister."

"And to mine." Anne raised her glass. "Here's to us, the Barry sisters."

Epilogue

SEPTEMBER

Ryan walked along the grassy path between the rows of graves. He hadn't been here since Janine's funeral, but Anne had told him exactly where the grave was. He could have guessed, anyway, which one it was. The white marble headstone was quite small, but the plot was a riot of color—golden marigolds, scarlet geraniums, and white petunias, the late bloomers of early fall. A lump came into Ryan's throat at the sight of them.

Janine had always loved flowers.

The prairie wind ruffled his hair as he read the writing on the stone. *Dearly loved wife of Ryan and mother of Anne and Deborah.* Beneath the line had been added, in smaller letters, *Sister of Beth.*

He stood for a long time staring down at the grave. Then, having looked around to make sure no one was nearby, he spoke. "Sorry it's taken me so long to get here, love. But that doesn't mean I haven't been thinking about you. It was just that I couldn't bear to come back. But I'm here in Winnipeg now, visiting the girls."

He smiled down. Then, feeling that the distance between them was too great, he rolled up the rain jacket he'd brought with him, and sat down on it, opposite the headstone.

"I know you're probably plugged into everything that's been going on in our lives, but let me tell you, just in case. I've lost a lot of money, but I'm going to be okay. Once I've sold Hammerton Towers and Debbie's sold her company, there'll be enough to help Debbie build up the garden center and to keep Sandy at Juilliard. Looks like Annie will be going to England next year and won't need much help. And Debbie will be staying on here, with Marco. So she's okay. Strange how it all worked out, isn't it? Debbie coming to Canada and Annie going to England. I told you I'd look after our girls, didn't I? When I make a promise I keep it."

Although there was no sound but the honking from a flock of geese flying in formation above him, he imagined he could hear Janine's laughter.

"Okay, okay. So it took me a while." Ryan shredded a piece of grass and sighed. "More than thirty years. But if I hadn't sent that money to Sandy all this would never have happened. So I did something good."

A sudden breeze ruffled the petals of the flowers.

"We all went to see my father today. He's living in the past most of the time, his mind back in Ireland, but he knew me and was really pleased to see Debbie. She gave Dad a big hug and thanked him for all he'd done for her when she was a kid. He looked a bit muddled by that, but then Debbie took out a picture of Annie and her that Beth had taken at a birthday party, and Dad knew then who she was." Ryan smiled at the memory. "You should have seen his face, Jan! He kept looking at Debbie and saying, 'Little Debbie. Who'd believe it?' "

A small clump of chickweed was growing by the foot of the stone. He leaned over to root it out with his fingers, smoothing the soil over when he'd finished.

"Beth's home now. Annie's looking after her with lots of help. There's a place in a hospice all lined up for when it's needed. But for now she prefers being home. So, as you can see, everything and everyone's being looked after."

Ryan put his hand on the headstone. "I miss you, sweetheart," he whispered. "I shall never stop missing you."

He closed his eyes for a moment, seeing her heart-shaped face.

"But life goes on. You know about Eileen. She came to Canada with me. We're going to get married, Eileen and me. I think we'll move to Ireland. We'd both like that. Eileen won't mind living in a smaller house. Said she'd prefer it. You know, it wasn't till I looked at this headstone that I realized Eileen's younger than you would be now if you'd lived. Five years younger. But to me, Jan, you'll always be twenty-four."

He leaned across and pressed his forehead against the grainy headstone. "Like I wrote in my song," he whispered, "you were the love of my life."

Supporting himself by leaning on the stone, he stood up. "So long, sweetheart." For a long moment he gazed at the flowers. Then he turned to walk briskly back to the car park near the entrance to the Garden of Rest, where Eileen was waiting for him.